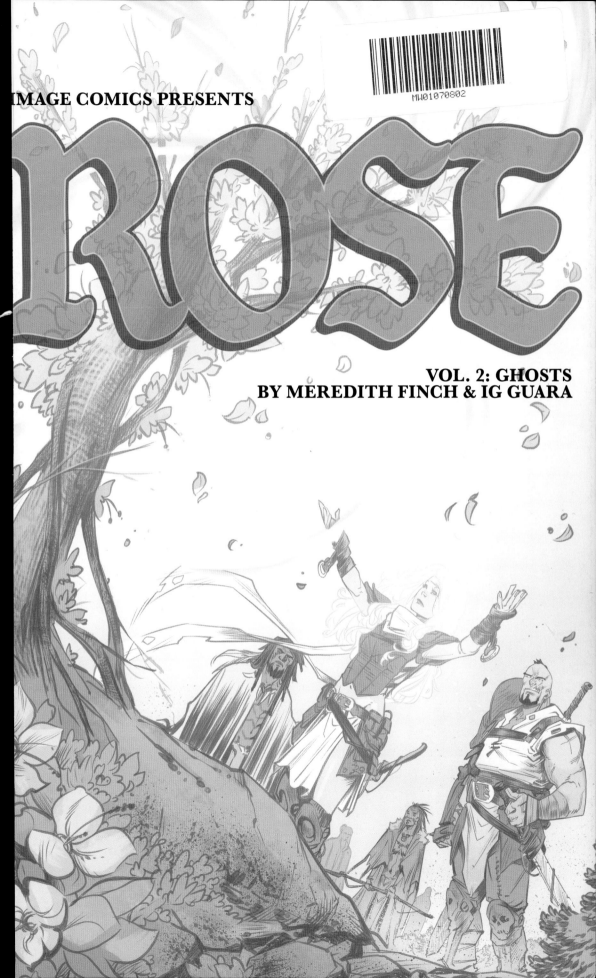

IMAGE COMICS PRESENTS

ROSE

VOL. 2: GHOSTS
BY MEREDITH FINCH & IG GUARA

IMAGE COMICS, INC.

Robert Kirkman: Chief Operating Officer
Erik Larsen: Chief Financial Officer
Todd McFarlane: President
Marc Silvestri: Chief Executive Officer
Jim Valentino: Vice President
Eric Stephenson: Publisher &
Chief Creative Officer
Corey Hart: Director of Sales
Jeff Boison: Director of Publishing Planning &
Book Trade Sales
Chris Ross: Director of Digital Sales
Jeff Stang: Director of Specialty Sales
Kat Salazar: Director of PR & Marketing
Drew Gill: Art Director
Heather Doornink: Production Director
Nicole Lapalme: Controller
IMAGECOMICS.COM

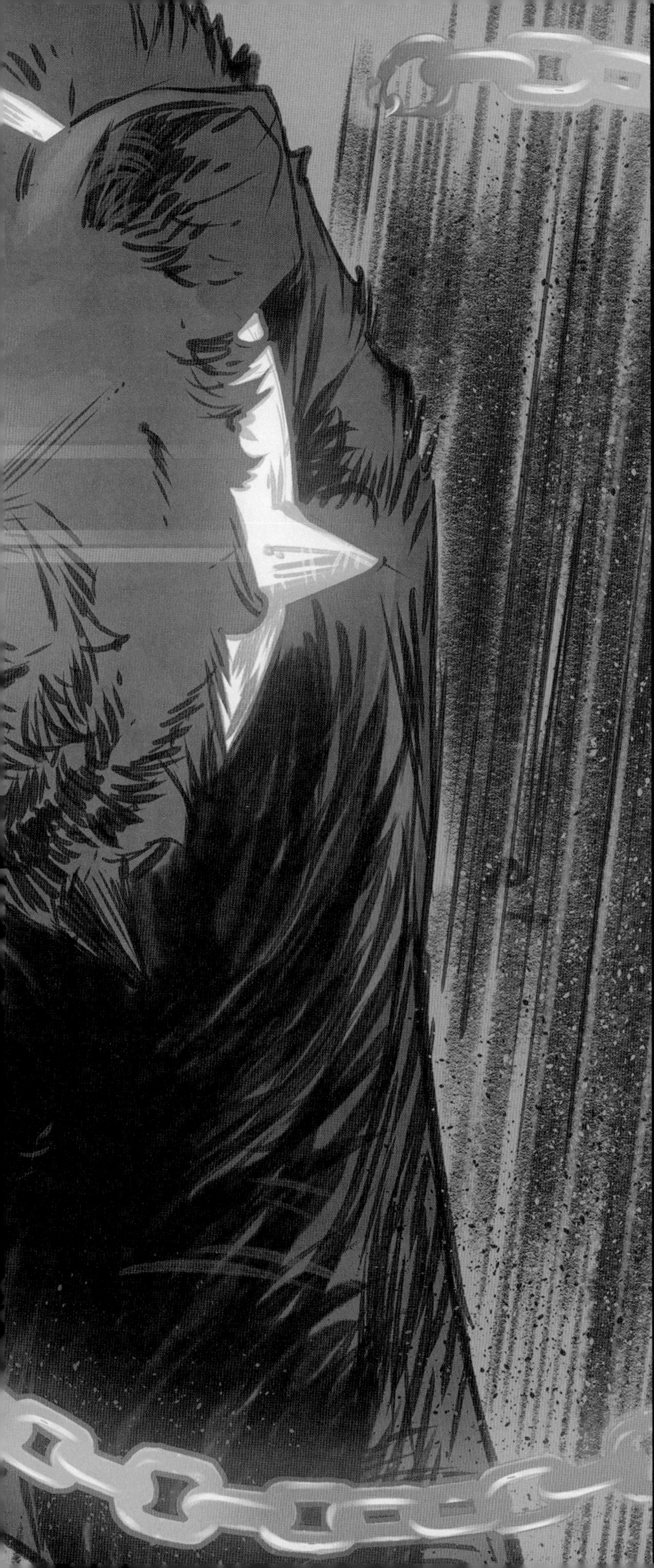

written by
MEREDITH FINCH

pencils & inks by
IG GUARA

colors by
TRIONA FARRELL

letters by
CARDINAL RAE

collection cover by
IG GUARA &
TRIONA FARRELL

collection design by
CAREY HALL

ROSE created by
MEREDITH FINCH

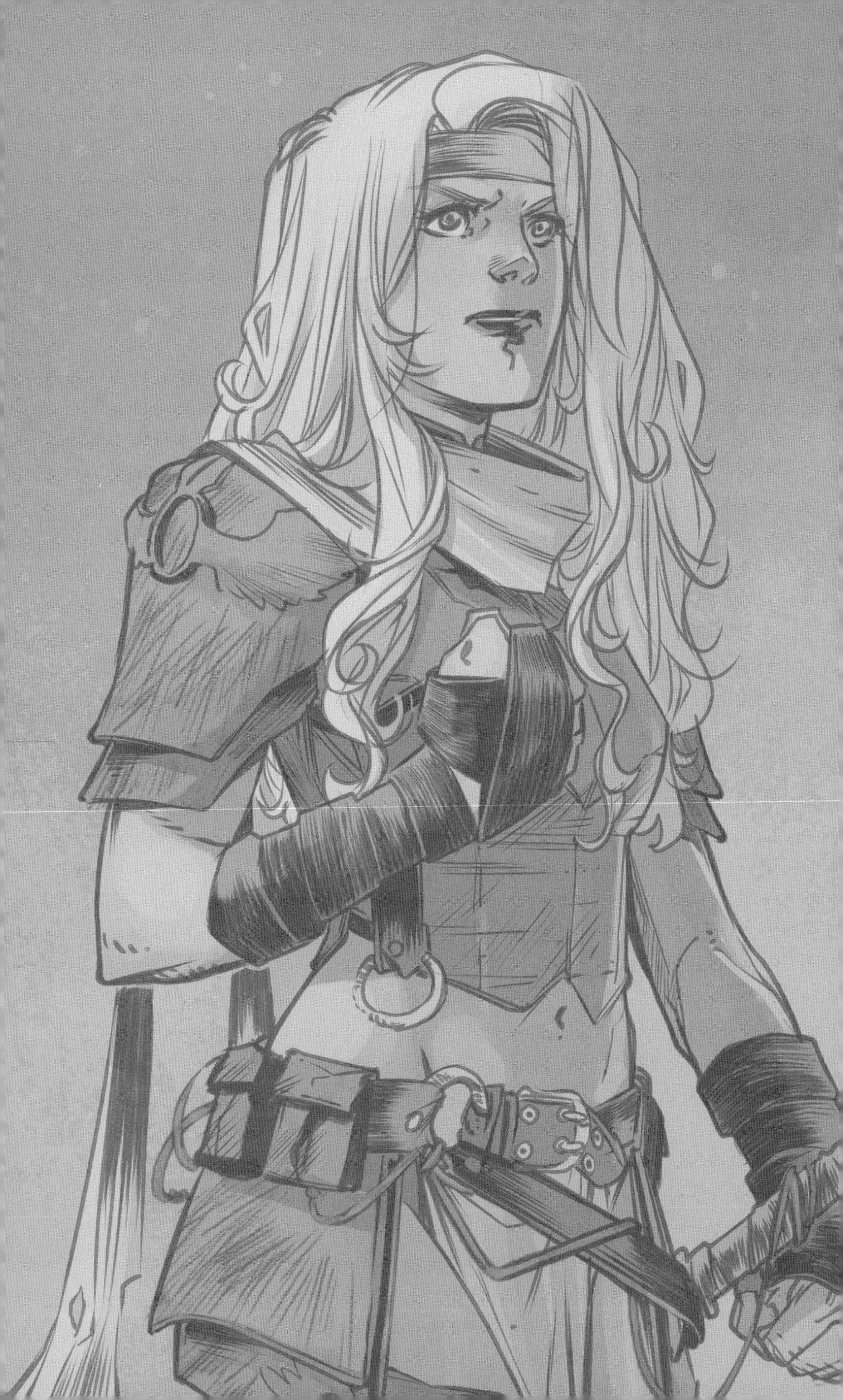

SEVEN

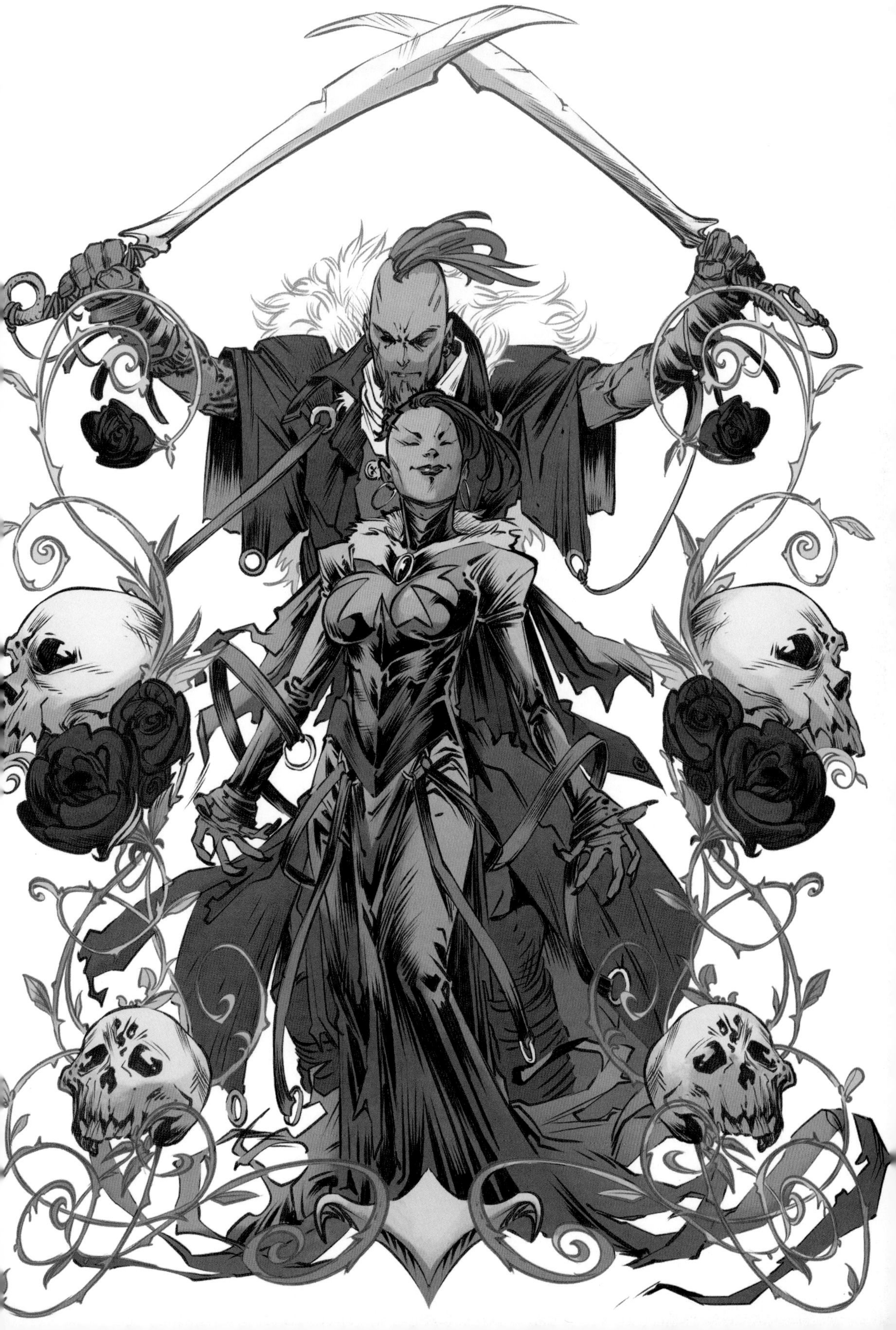

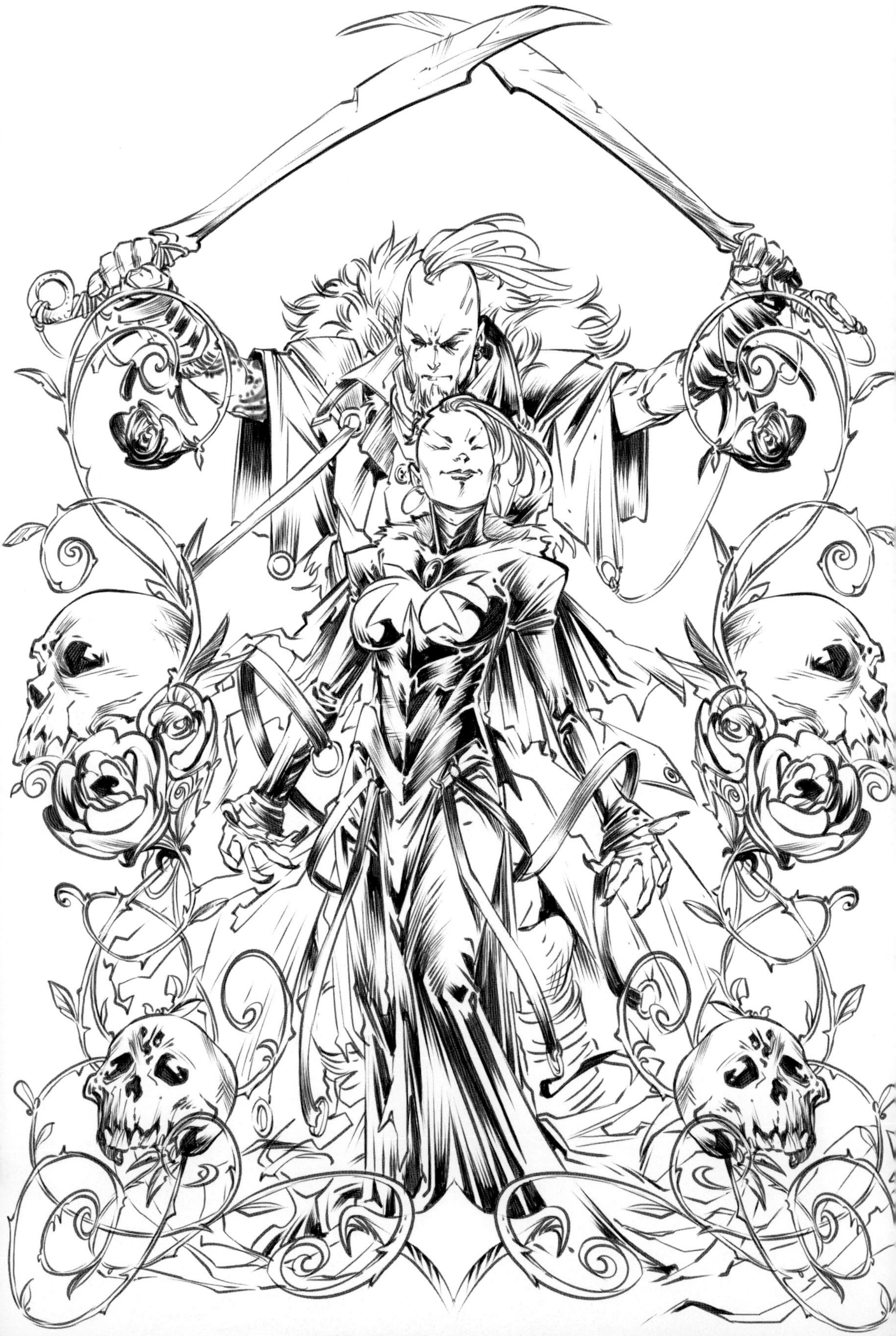

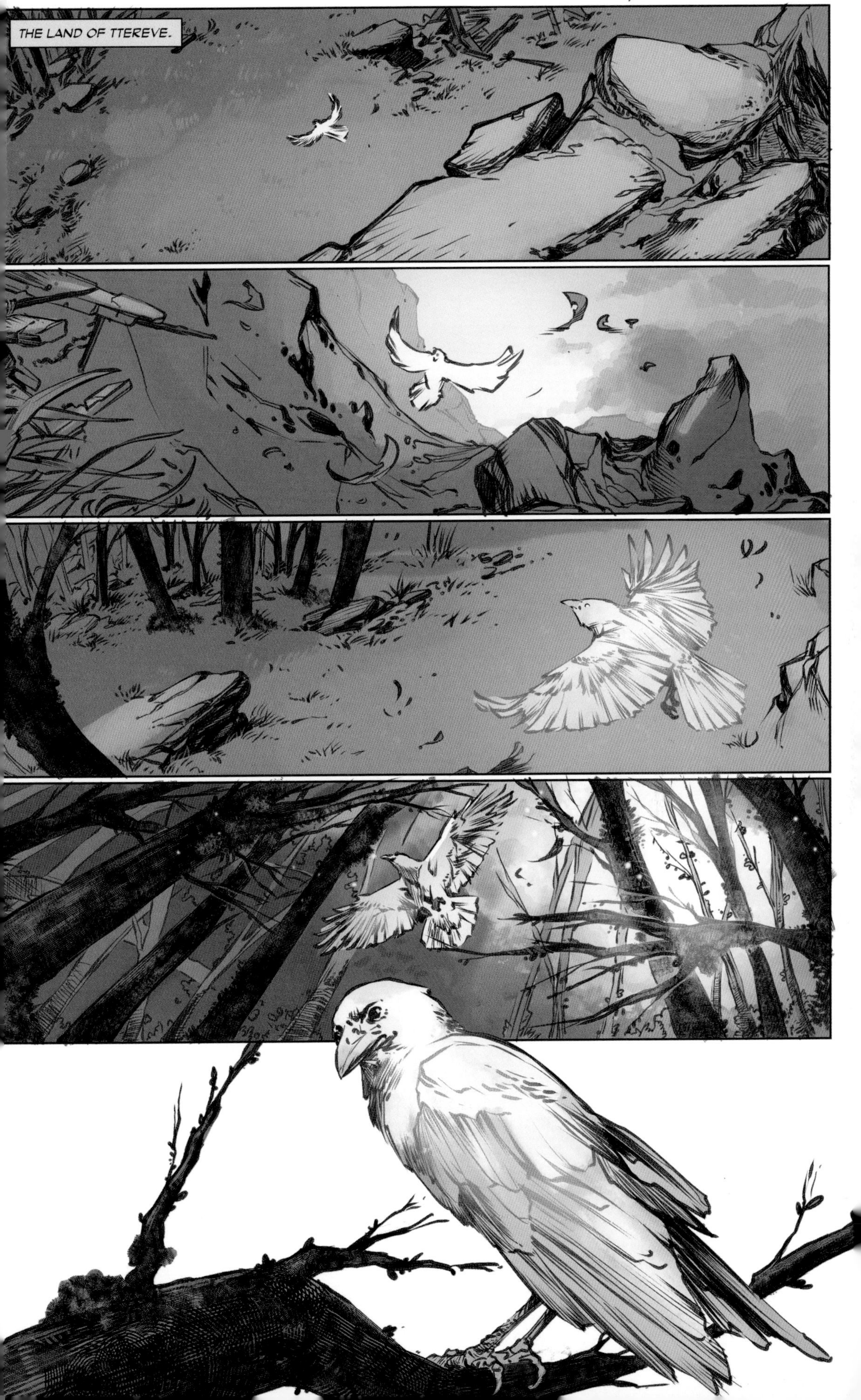
THE LAND OF TTEREVE.

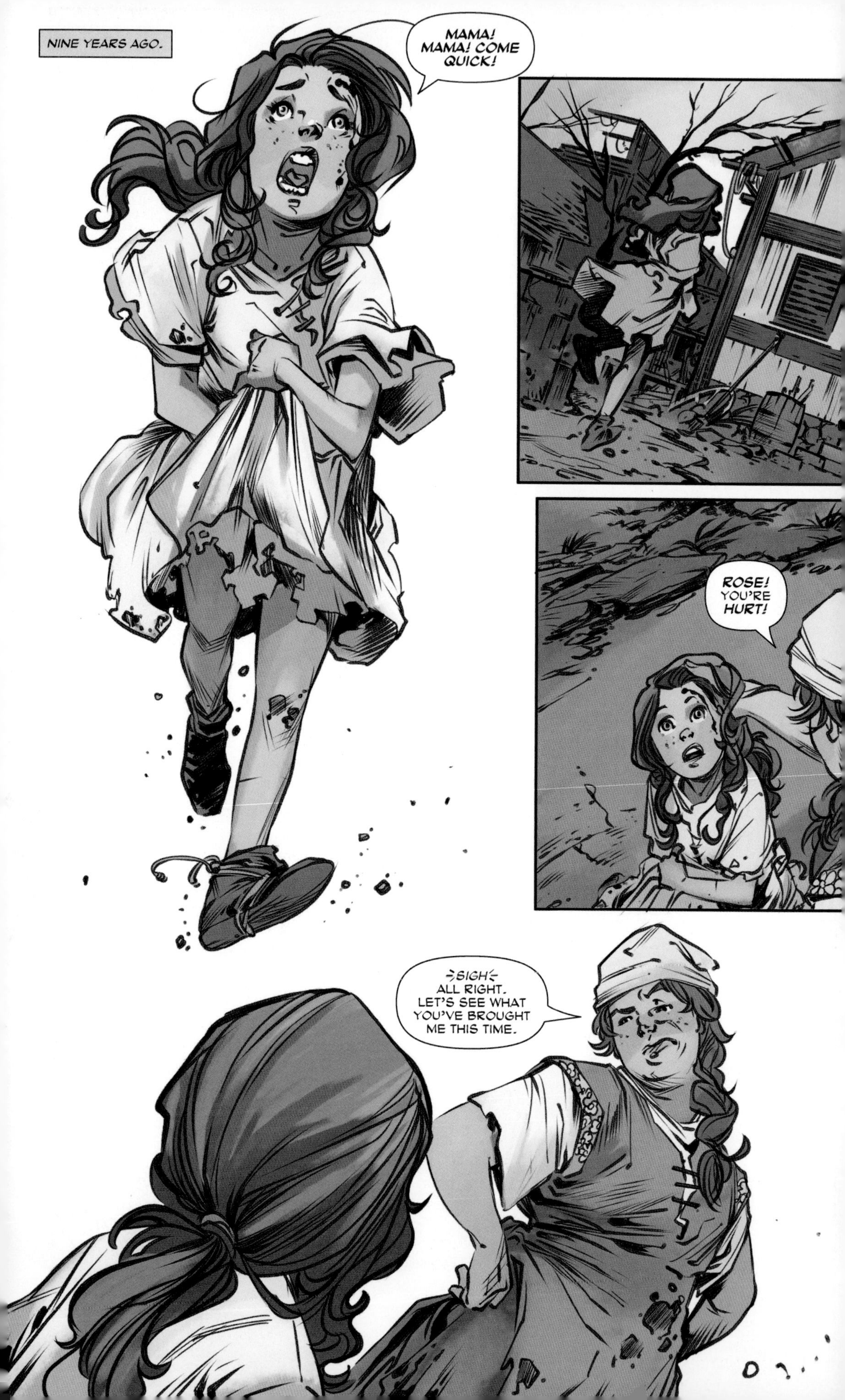
NINE YEARS AGO.
MAMA! MAMA! COME QUICK!
ROSE! YOU'RE HURT!
⇒SIGH⇐ ALL RIGHT. LET'S SEE WHAT YOU'VE BROUGHT ME THIS TIME.

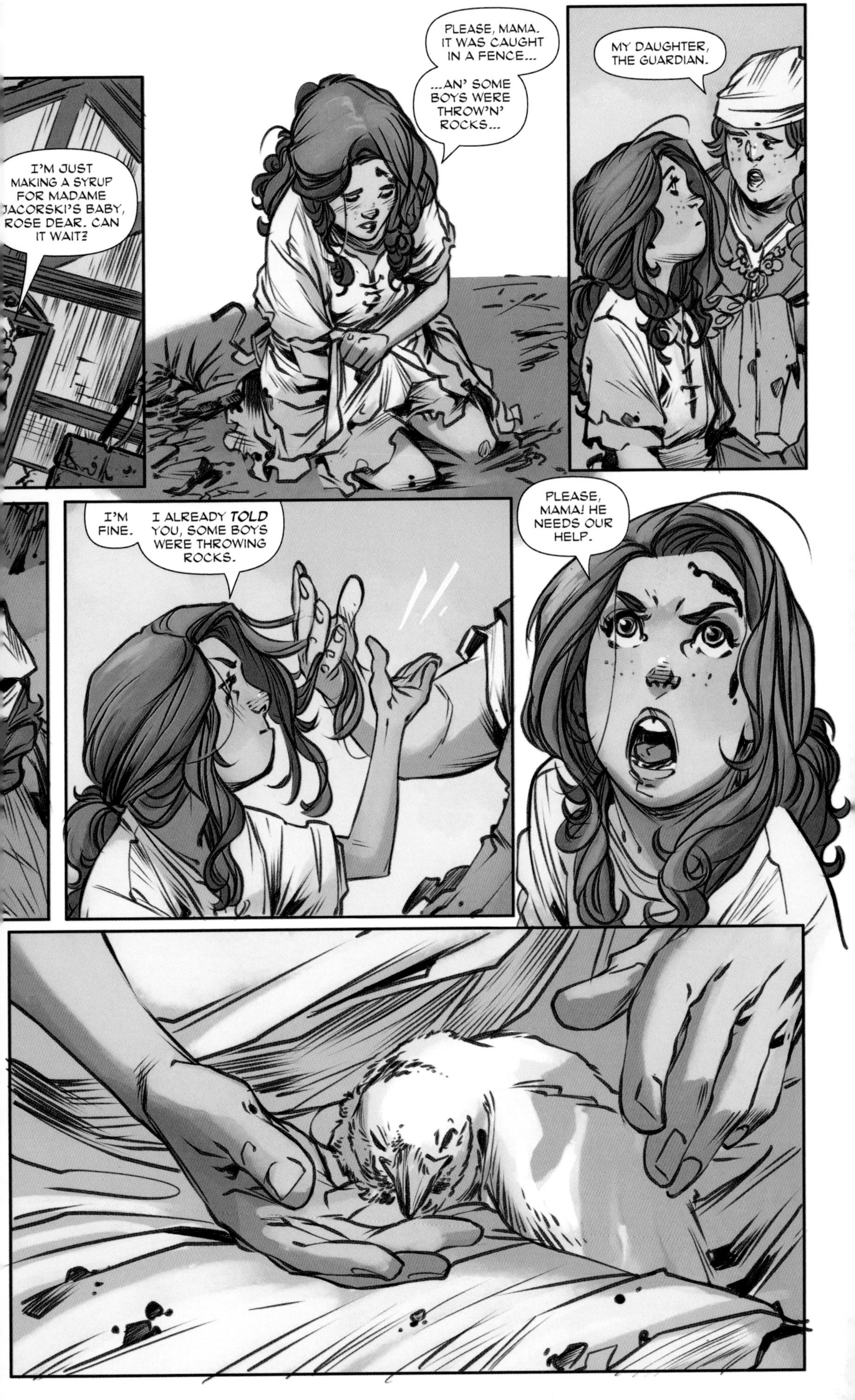
I'M JUST MAKING A SYRUP FOR MADAME JACORSKI'S BABY, ROSE DEAR. CAN IT WAIT?
PLEASE, MAMA. IT WAS CAUGHT IN A FENCE...
...AN' SOME BOYS WERE THROW'N' ROCKS...
MY DAUGHTER, THE GUARDIAN.
I'M FINE.
I ALREADY *TOLD* YOU, SOME BOYS WERE THROWING ROCKS.
PLEASE, MAMA! HE NEEDS OUR HELP.

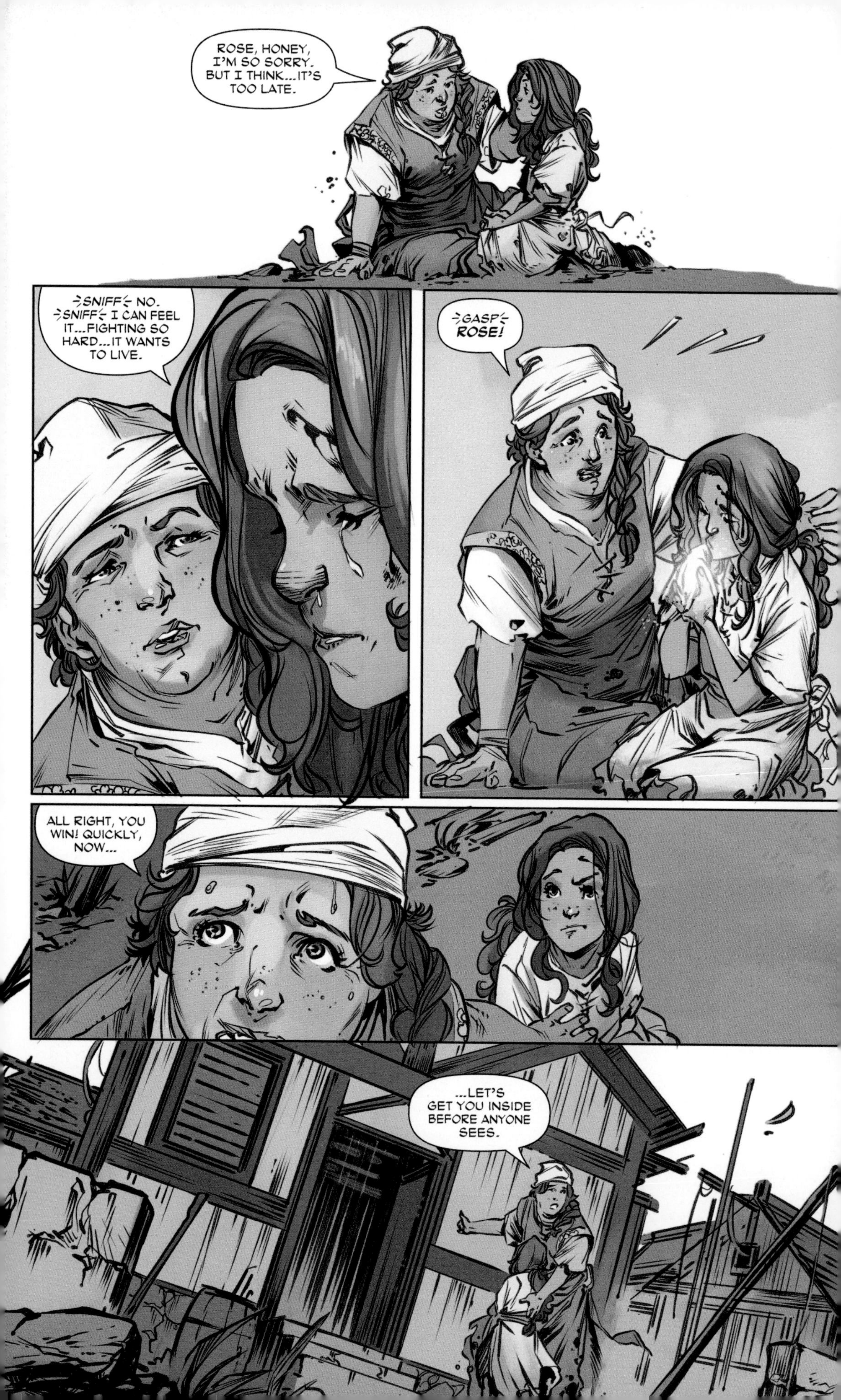
ROSE, HONEY, I'M SO SORRY. BUT I THINK...IT'S TOO LATE.
SNIFF NO. SNIFF I CAN FEEL IT...FIGHTING SO HARD...IT WANTS TO LIVE.
GASP ROSE!
ALL RIGHT, YOU WIN! QUICKLY, NOW...
...LET'S GET YOU INSIDE BEFORE ANYONE SEES.

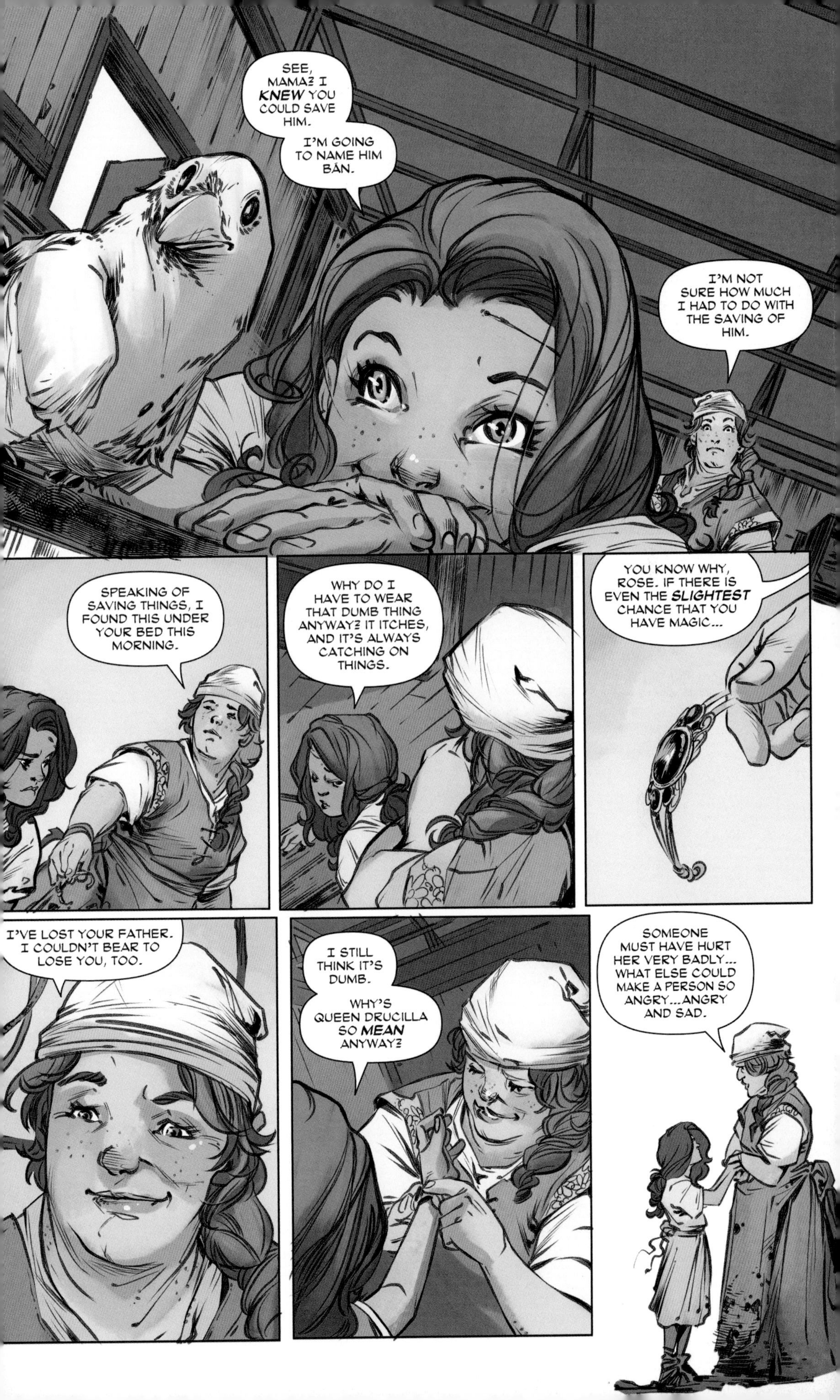
SEE, MAMA? I KNEW YOU COULD SAVE HIM.
I'M GOING TO NAME HIM BÁN.
I'M NOT SURE HOW MUCH I HAD TO DO WITH THE SAVING OF HIM.
SPEAKING OF SAVING THINGS, I FOUND THIS UNDER YOUR BED THIS MORNING.
WHY DO I HAVE TO WEAR THAT DUMB THING ANYWAY? IT ITCHES, AND IT'S ALWAYS CATCHING ON THINGS.
YOU KNOW WHY, ROSE. IF THERE IS EVEN THE SLIGHTEST CHANCE THAT YOU HAVE MAGIC...
I'VE LOST YOUR FATHER. I COULDN'T BEAR TO LOSE YOU, TOO.
I STILL THINK IT'S DUMB.
WHY'S QUEEN DRUCILLA SO MEAN ANYWAY?
SOMEONE MUST HAVE HURT HER VERY BADLY... WHAT ELSE COULD MAKE A PERSON SO ANGRY...ANGRY AND SAD.

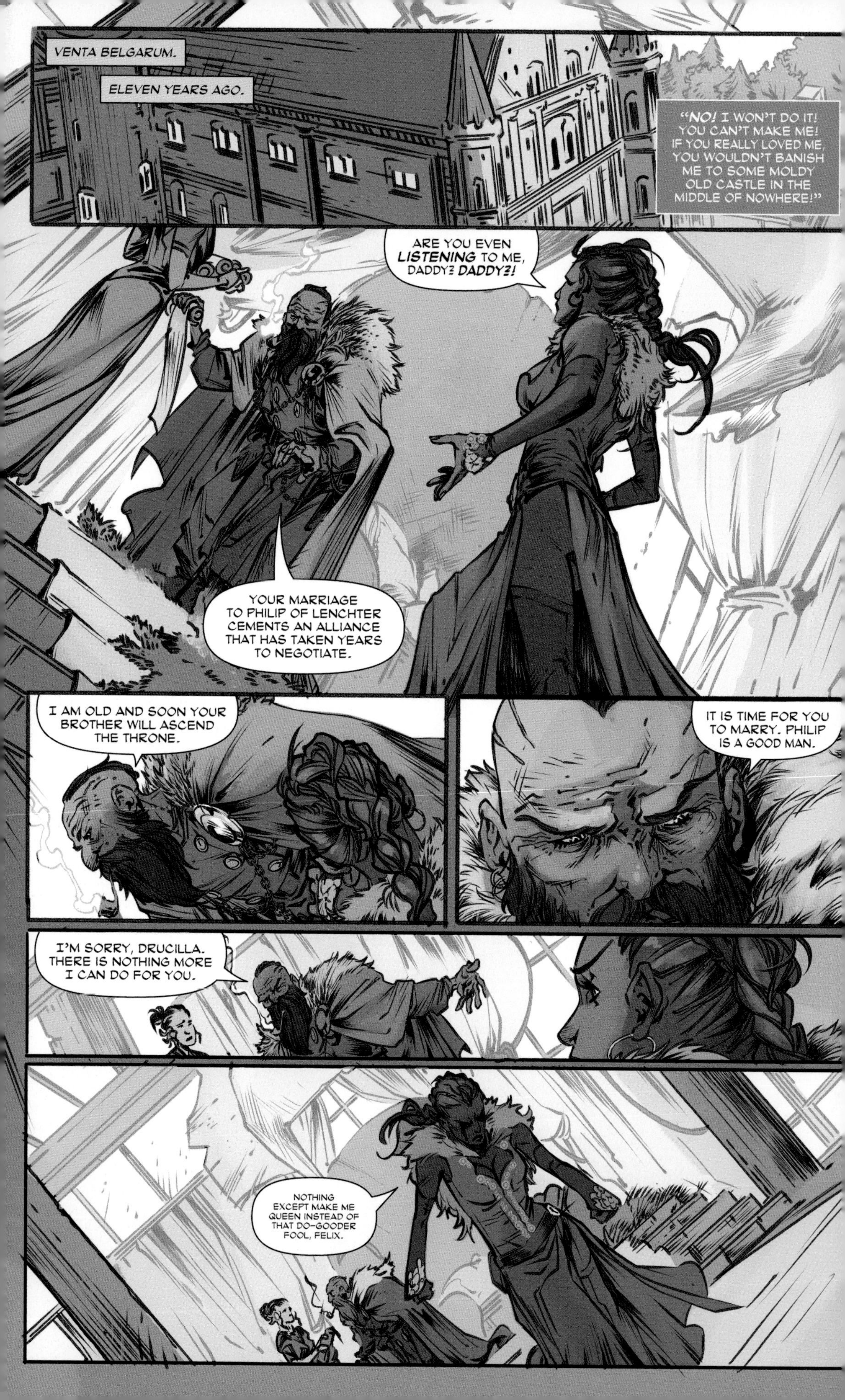

VENTA BELGARUM.
ELEVEN YEARS AGO.
"NO! I WON'T DO IT! YOU CAN'T MAKE ME! IF YOU REALLY LOVED ME, YOU WOULDN'T BANISH ME TO SOME MOLDY OLD CASTLE IN THE MIDDLE OF NOWHERE!"
ARE YOU EVEN LISTENING TO ME, DADDY? DADDY?!
YOUR MARRIAGE TO PHILIP OF LENCHTER CEMENTS AN ALLIANCE THAT HAS TAKEN YEARS TO NEGOTIATE.
I AM OLD AND SOON YOUR BROTHER WILL ASCEND THE THRONE.
IT IS TIME FOR YOU TO MARRY. PHILIP IS A GOOD MAN.
I'M SORRY, DRUCILLA. THERE IS NOTHING MORE I CAN DO FOR YOU.
NOTHING EXCEPT MAKE ME QUEEN INSTEAD OF THAT DO-GOODER FOOL, FELIX.

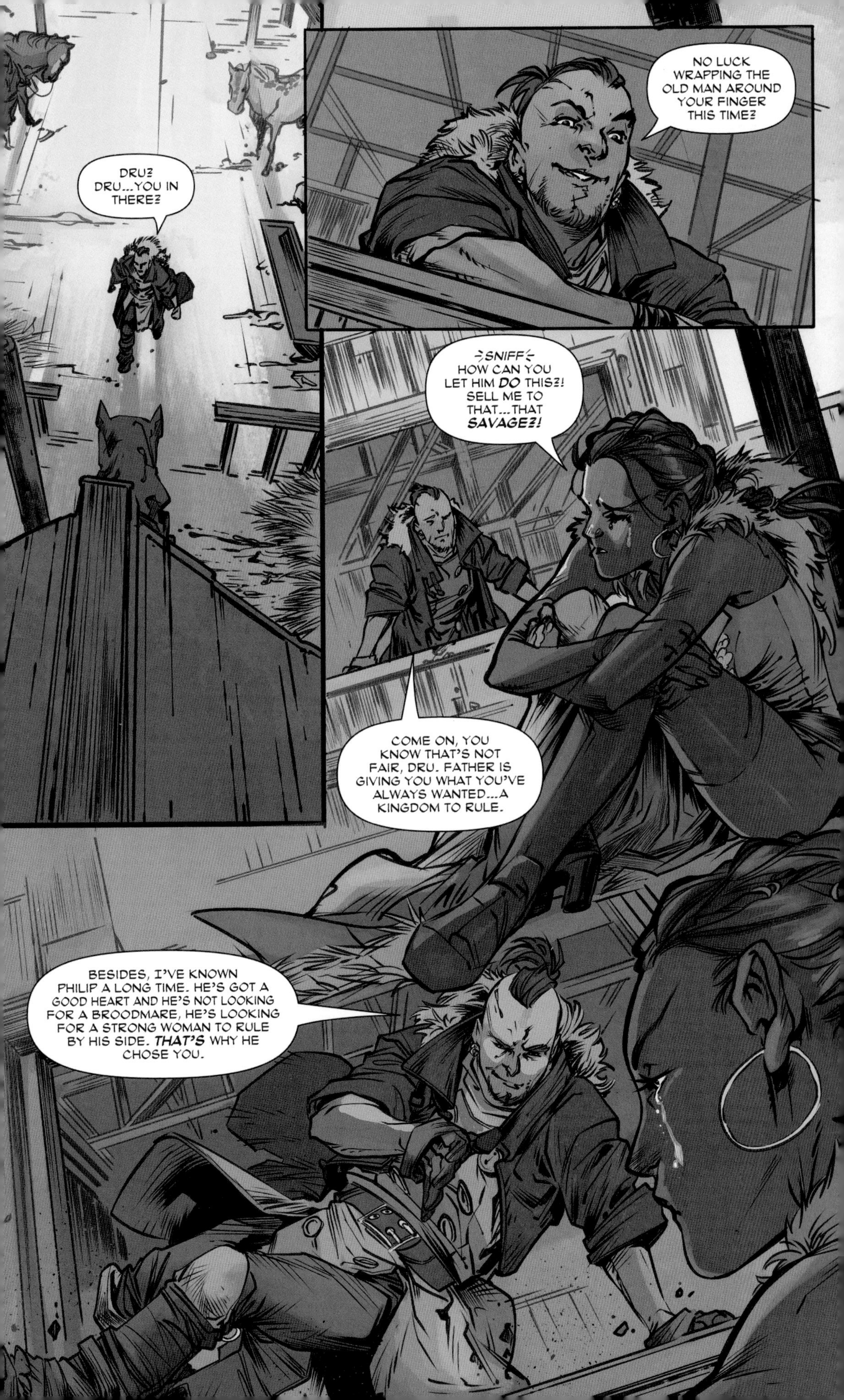
DRU? DRU...YOU IN THERE?
NO LUCK WRAPPING THE OLD MAN AROUND YOUR FINGER THIS TIME?
SNIFF
HOW CAN YOU LET HIM *DO* THIS?! SELL ME TO THAT...THAT ***SAVAGE?!***
COME ON, YOU KNOW THAT'S NOT FAIR, DRU. FATHER IS GIVING YOU WHAT YOU'VE ALWAYS WANTED...A KINGDOM TO RULE.
BESIDES, I'VE KNOWN PHILIP A LONG TIME. HE'S GOT A GOOD HEART AND HE'S NOT LOOKING FOR A BROODMARE, HE'S LOOKING FOR A STRONG WOMAN TO RULE BY HIS SIDE. ***THAT'S*** WHY HE CHOSE YOU.

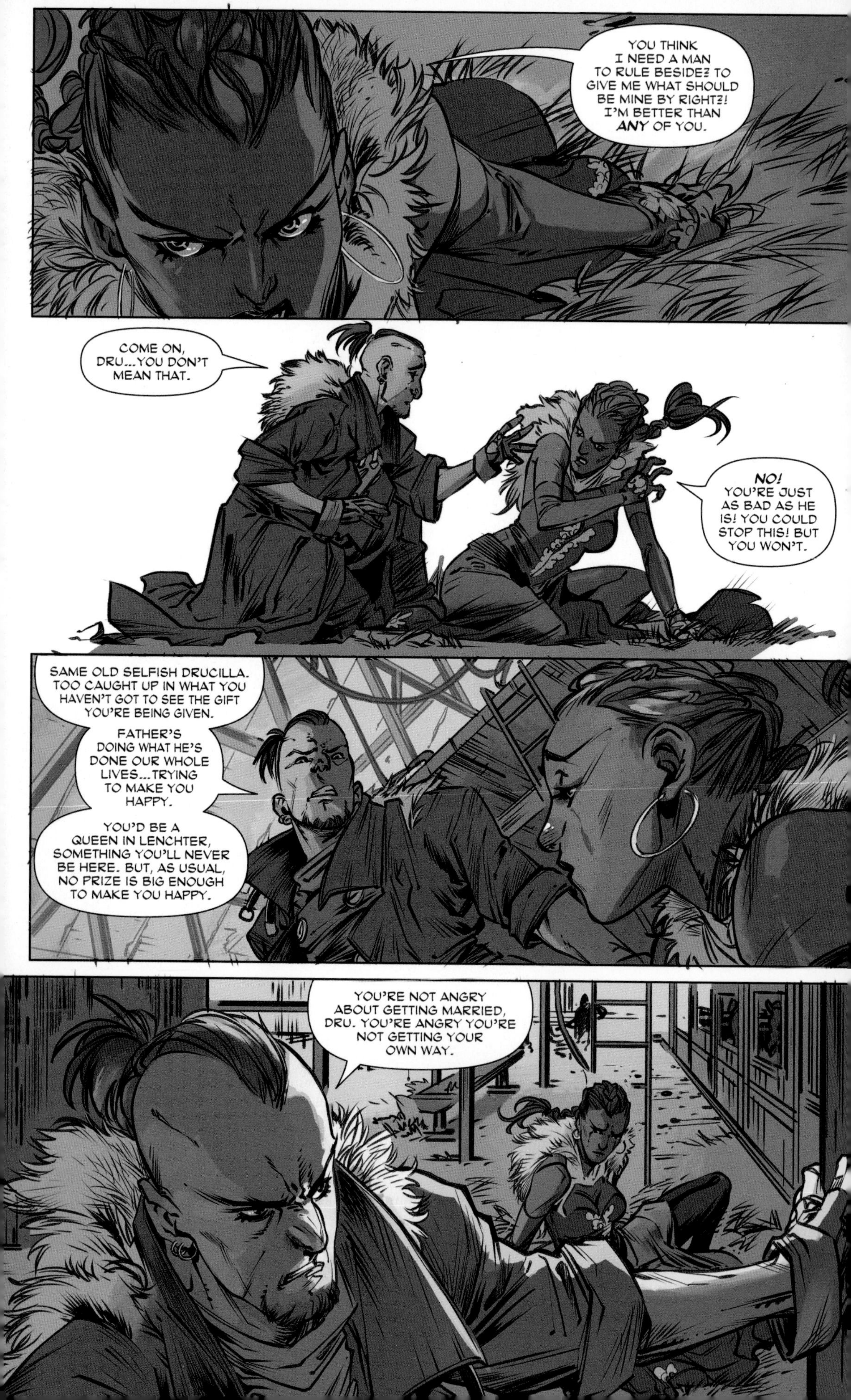

YOU THINK I NEED A MAN TO RULE BESIDE? TO GIVE ME WHAT SHOULD BE MINE BY RIGHT?! I'M BETTER THAN ANY OF YOU.
COME ON, DRU...YOU DON'T MEAN THAT.
NO! YOU'RE JUST AS BAD AS HE IS! YOU COULD STOP THIS! BUT YOU WON'T.
SAME OLD SELFISH DRUCILLA. TOO CAUGHT UP IN WHAT YOU HAVEN'T GOT TO SEE THE GIFT YOU'RE BEING GIVEN.
FATHER'S DOING WHAT HE'S DONE OUR WHOLE LIVES...TRYING TO MAKE YOU HAPPY.
YOU'D BE A QUEEN IN LENCHTER, SOMETHING YOU'LL NEVER BE HERE. BUT, AS USUAL, NO PRIZE IS BIG ENOUGH TO MAKE YOU HAPPY.
YOU'RE NOT ANGRY ABOUT GETTING MARRIED, DRU. YOU'RE ANGRY YOU'RE NOT GETTING YOUR OWN WAY.

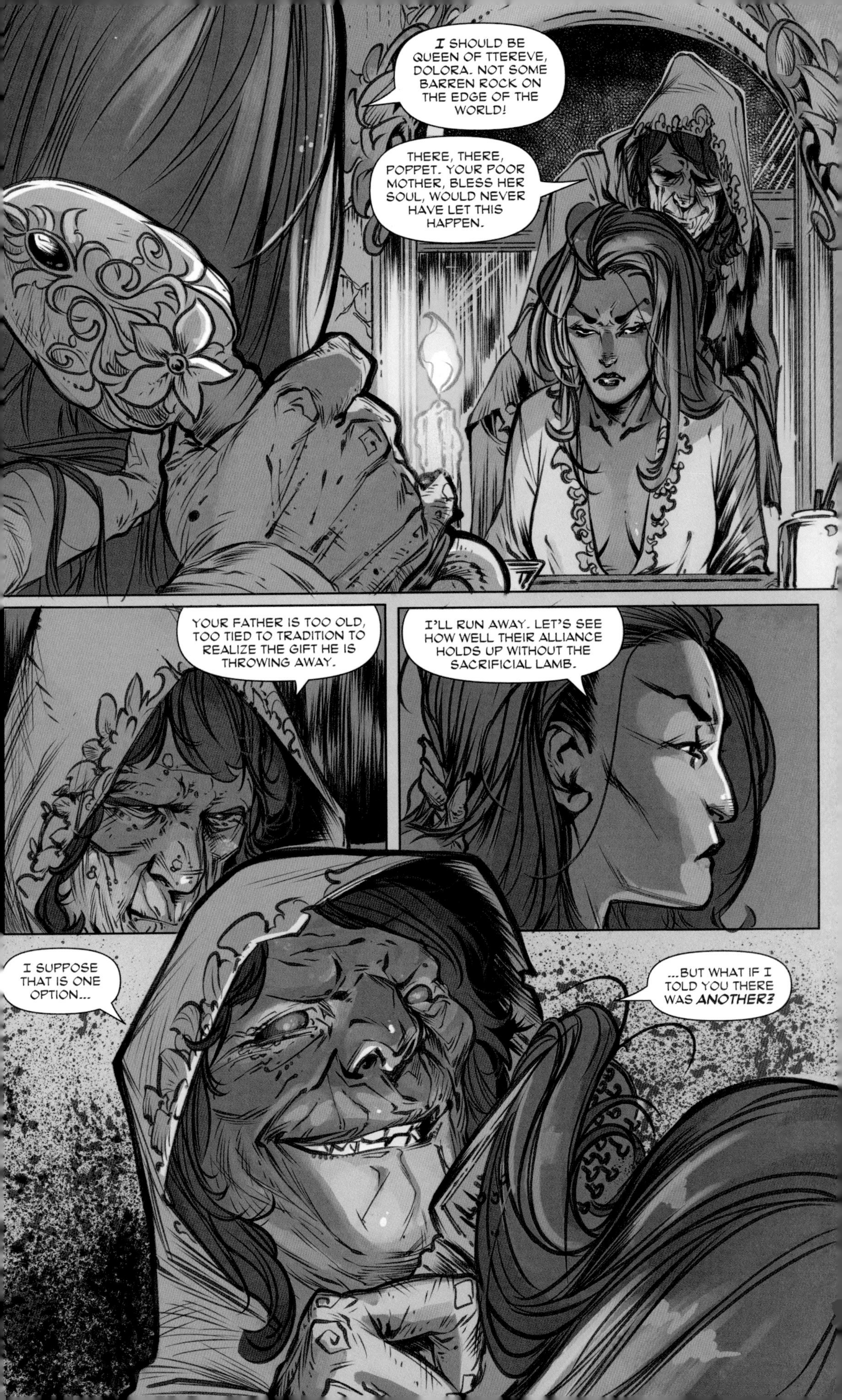
I SHOULD BE QUEEN OF TTEREVE, DOLORA. NOT SOME BARREN ROCK ON THE EDGE OF THE WORLD!
THERE, THERE, POPPET. YOUR POOR MOTHER, BLESS HER SOUL, WOULD NEVER HAVE LET THIS HAPPEN.
YOUR FATHER IS TOO OLD, TOO TIED TO TRADITION TO REALIZE THE GIFT HE IS THROWING AWAY.
I'LL RUN AWAY. LET'S SEE HOW WELL THEIR ALLIANCE HOLDS UP WITHOUT THE SACRIFICIAL LAMB.
I SUPPOSE THAT IS ONE OPTION...
...BUT WHAT IF I TOLD YOU THERE WAS ANOTHER?

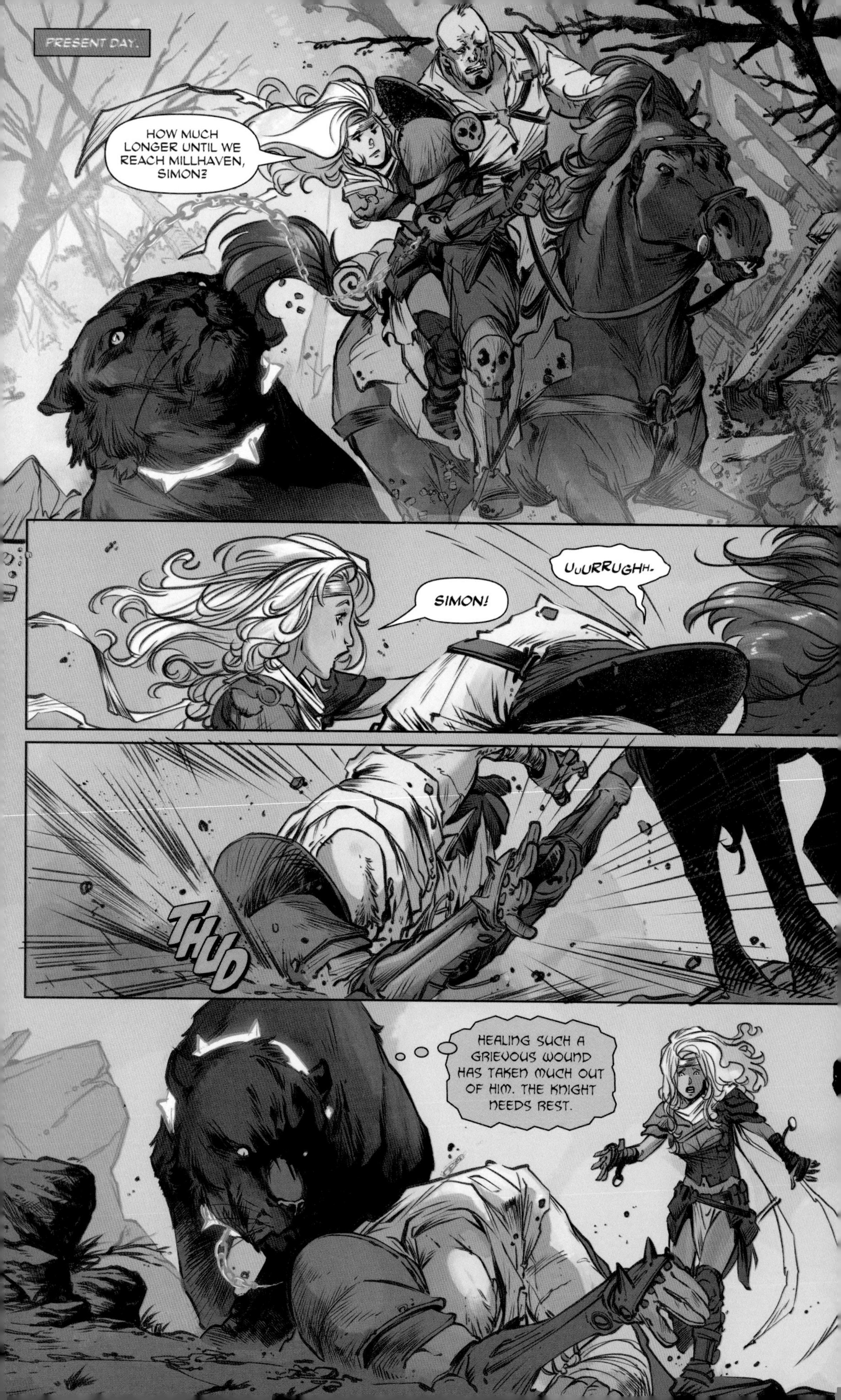
PRESENT DAY.
HOW MUCH LONGER UNTIL WE REACH MILLHAVEN, SIMON?
SIMON!
UUURRUGHH.
THUD
HEALING SUCH A GRIEVOUS WOUND HAS TAKEN MUCH OUT OF HIM. THE KNIGHT NEEDS REST.

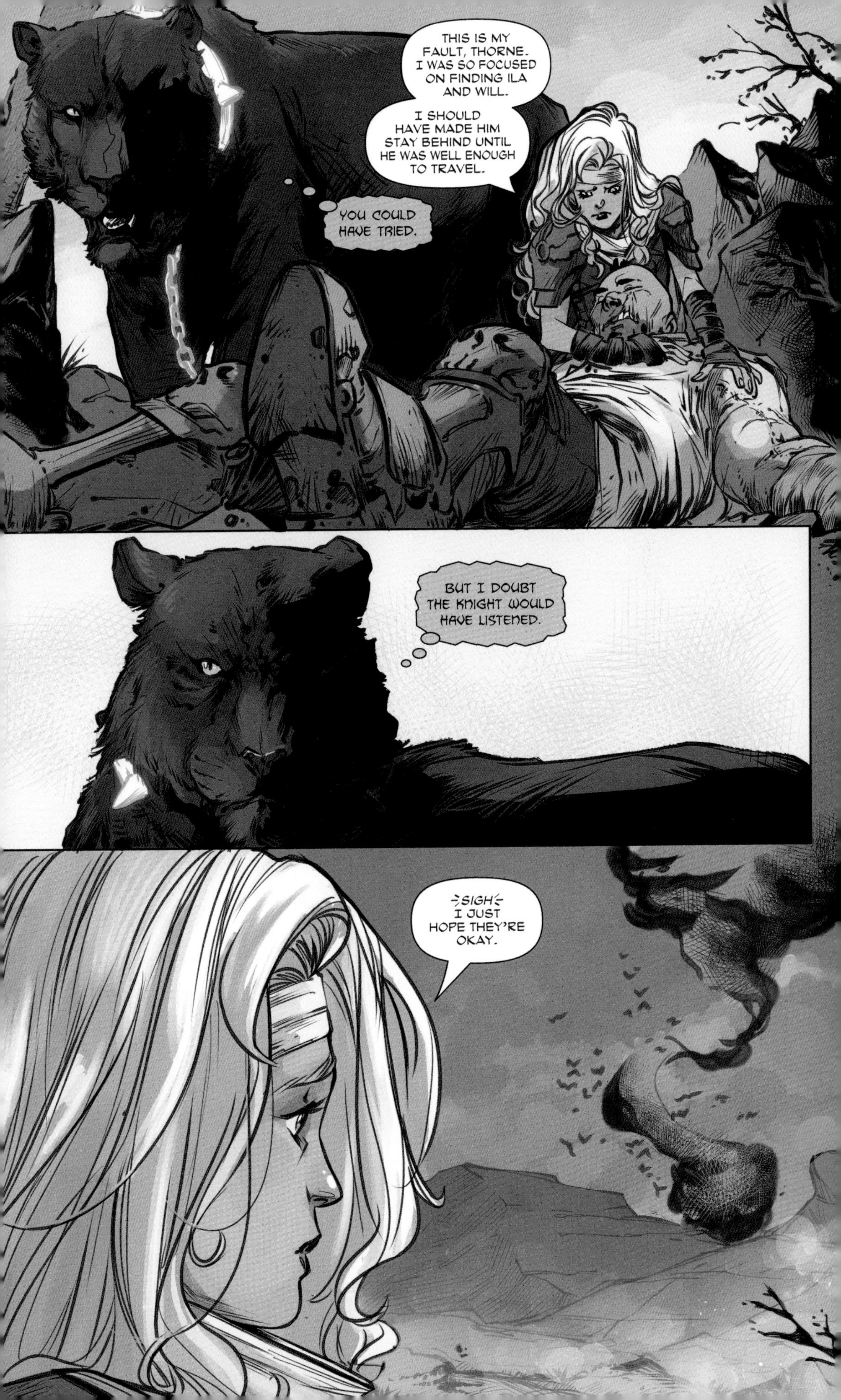
THIS IS MY FAULT, THORNE. I WAS SO FOCUSED ON FINDING ILA AND WILL.
I SHOULD HAVE MADE HIM STAY BEHIND UNTIL HE WAS WELL ENOUGH TO TRAVEL.
YOU COULD HAVE TRIED.
BUT I DOUBT THE KNIGHT WOULD HAVE LISTENED.
SIGH
I JUST HOPE THEY'RE OKAY.

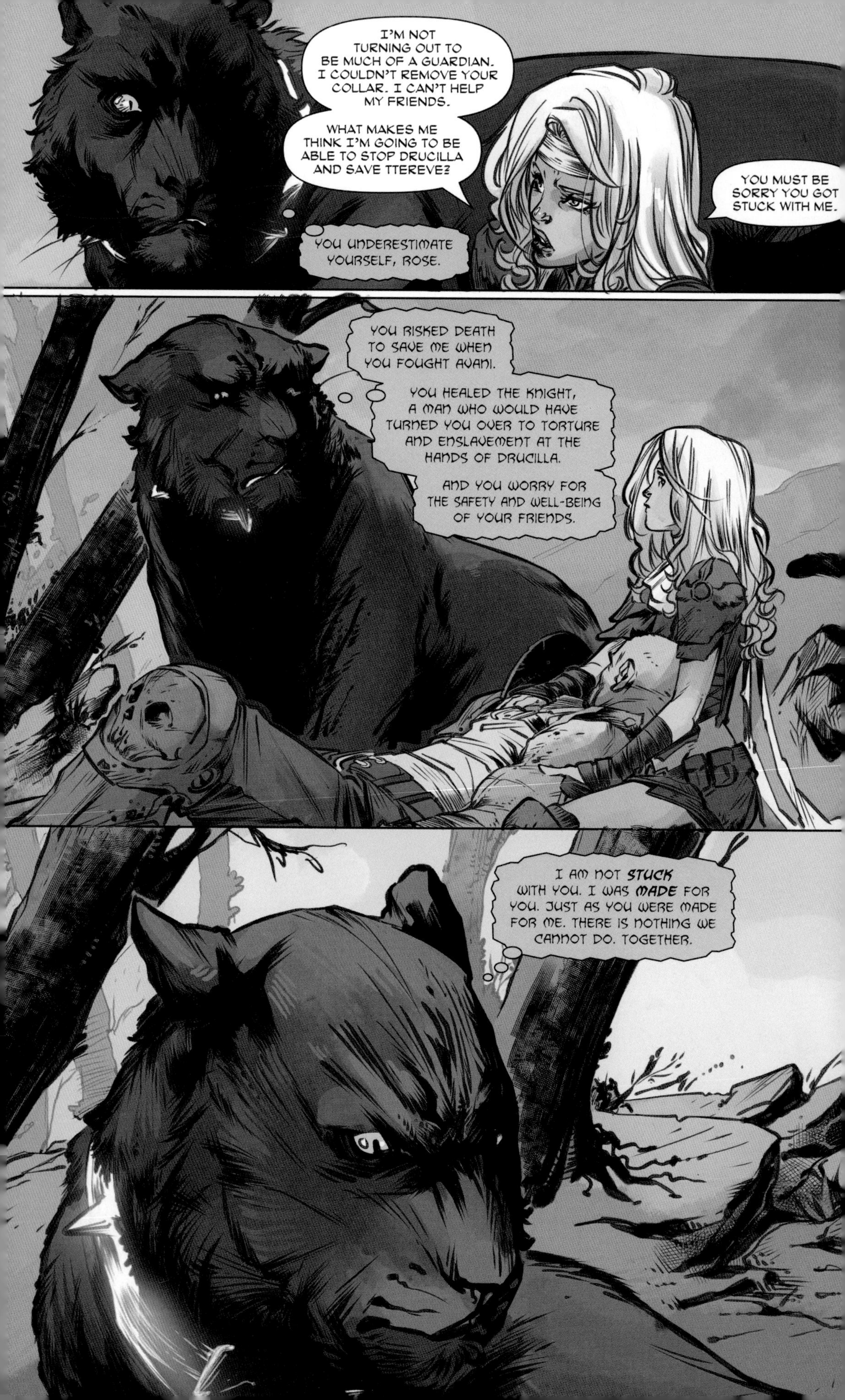
I'M NOT TURNING OUT TO BE MUCH OF A GUARDIAN. I COULDN'T REMOVE YOUR COLLAR. I CAN'T HELP MY FRIENDS.
WHAT MAKES ME THINK I'M GOING TO BE ABLE TO STOP DRUCILLA AND SAVE TTEREVE?
YOU MUST BE SORRY YOU GOT STUCK WITH ME.
YOU UNDERESTIMATE YOURSELF, ROSE.
YOU RISKED DEATH TO SAVE ME WHEN YOU FOUGHT AVANI.
YOU HEALED THE KNIGHT, A MAN WHO WOULD HAVE TURNED YOU OVER TO TORTURE AND ENSLAVEMENT AT THE HANDS OF DRUCILLA.
AND YOU WORRY FOR THE SAFETY AND WELL-BEING OF YOUR FRIENDS.
I AM NOT STUCK WITH YOU. I WAS MADE FOR YOU. JUST AS YOU WERE MADE FOR ME. THERE IS NOTHING WE CANNOT DO. TOGETHER.

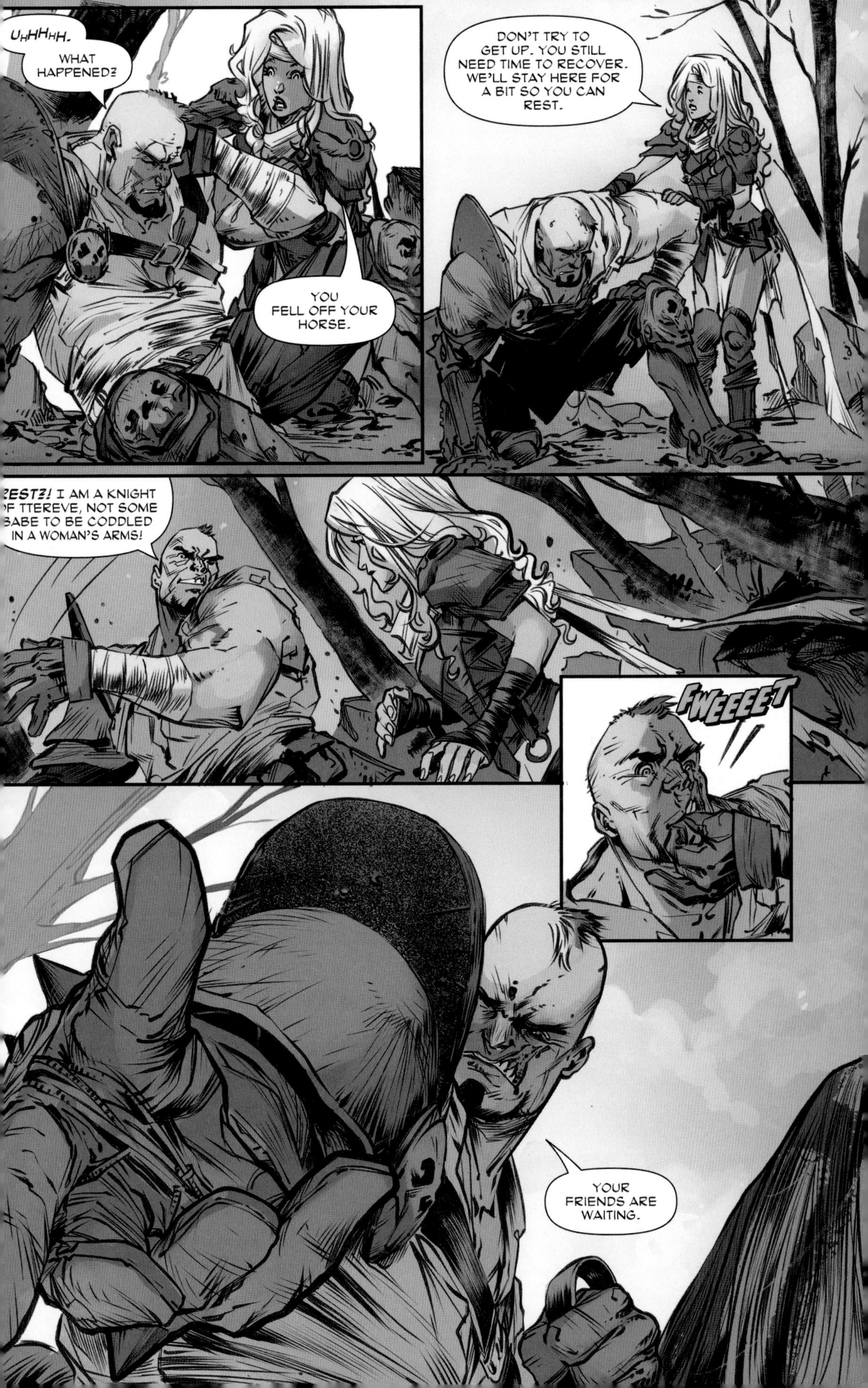

UHHHHH.
WHAT HAPPENED?
YOU FELL OFF YOUR HORSE.
DON'T TRY TO GET UP. YOU STILL NEED TIME TO RECOVER. WE'LL STAY HERE FOR A BIT SO YOU CAN REST.
REST?! I AM A KNIGHT OF TTEREVE, NOT SOME BABE TO BE CODDLED IN A WOMAN'S ARMS!
FWEEEEET
YOUR FRIENDS ARE WAITING.

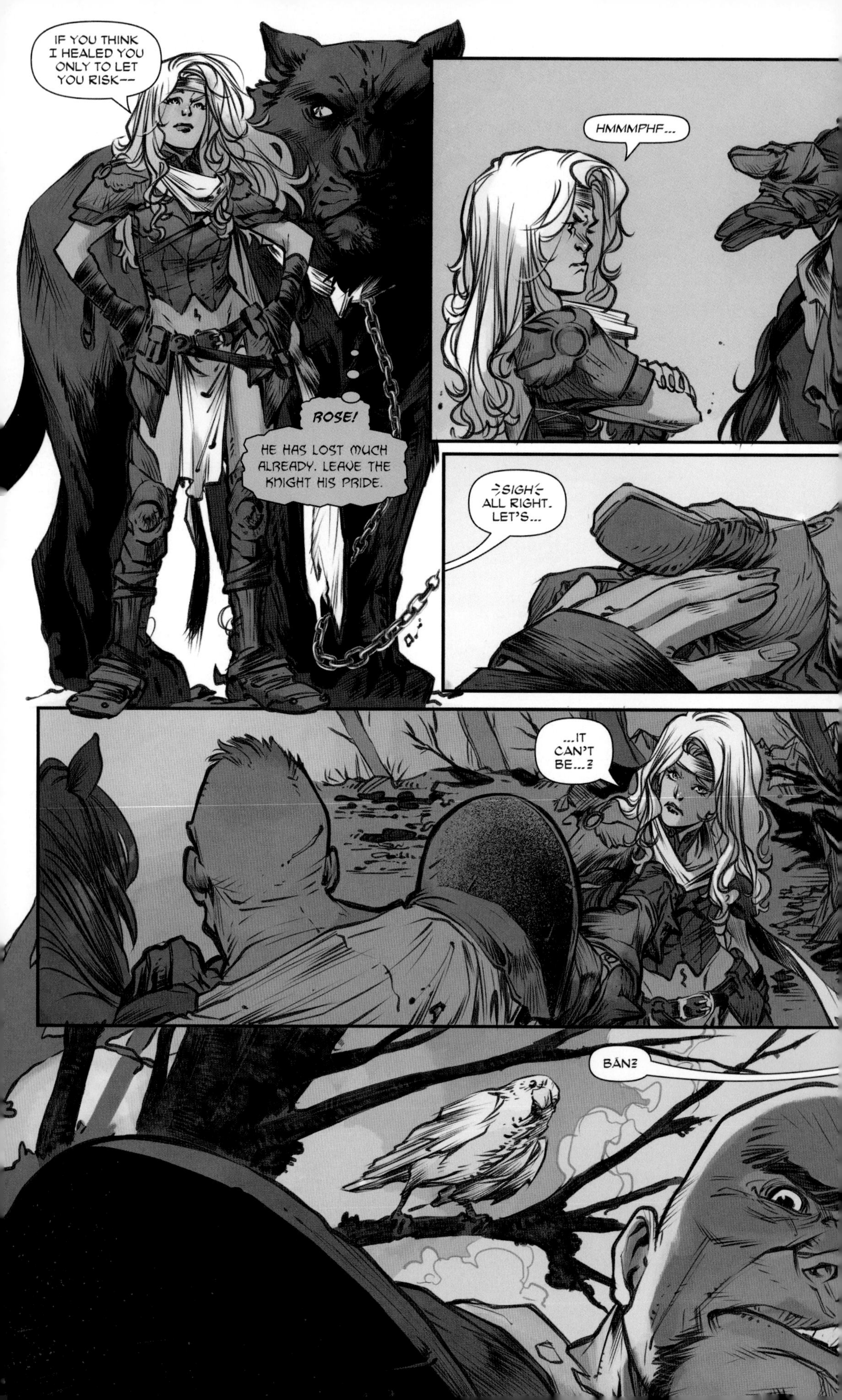
IF YOU THINK I HEALED YOU ONLY TO LET YOU RISK--
ROSE!
HE HAS LOST MUCH ALREADY. LEAVE THE KNIGHT HIS PRIDE.
HMMMPHF...
SIGH
ALL RIGHT. LET'S...
...IT CAN'T BE...?
BÄN?

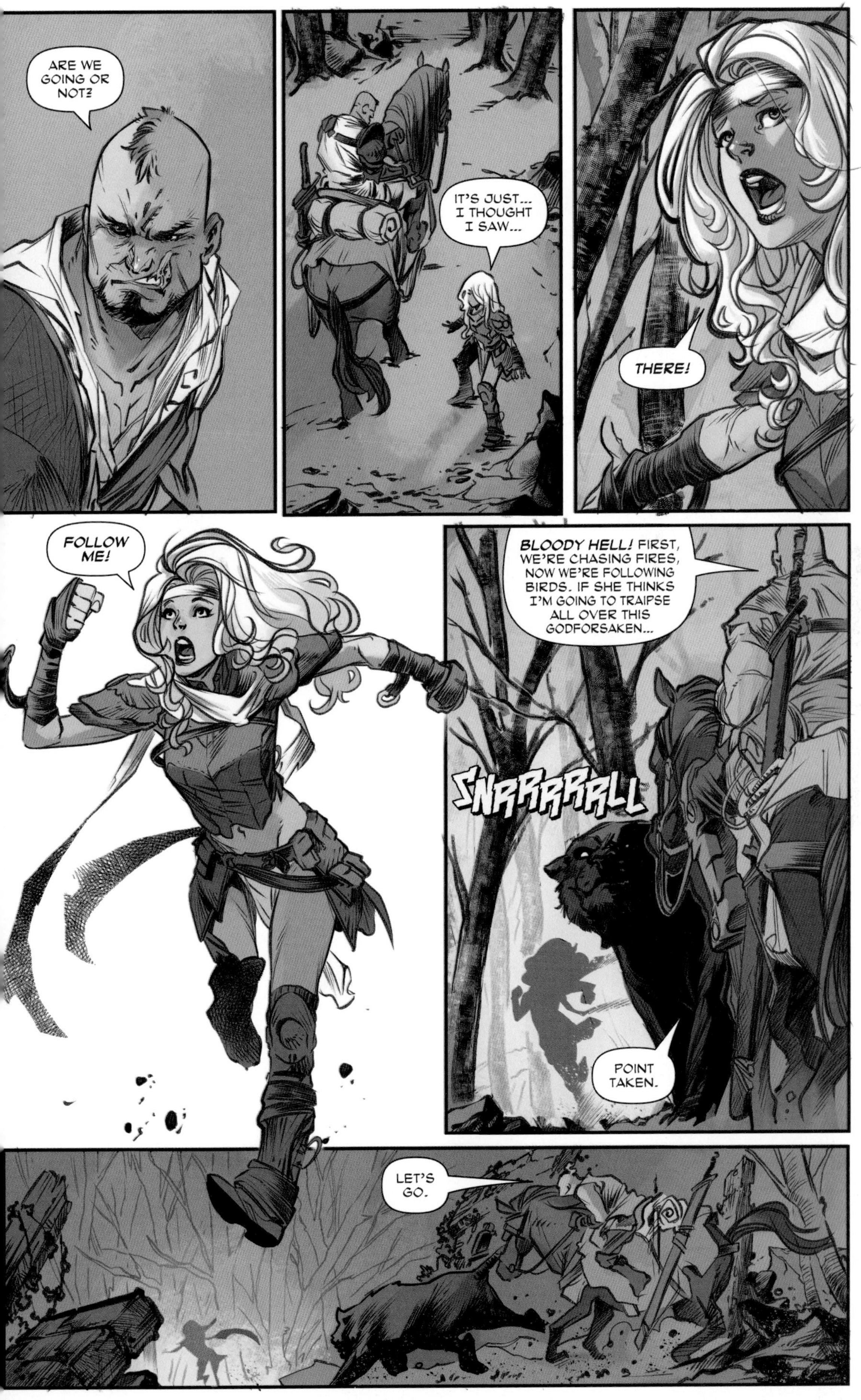
ARE WE GOING OR NOT?
IT'S JUST... I THOUGHT I SAW...
THERE!
FOLLOW ME!
BLOODY HELL! FIRST, WE'RE CHASING FIRES, NOW WE'RE FOLLOWING BIRDS. IF SHE THINKS I'M GOING TO TRAIPSE ALL OVER THIS GODFORSAKEN...
SNRRRRRLL
POINT TAKEN.
LET'S GO.

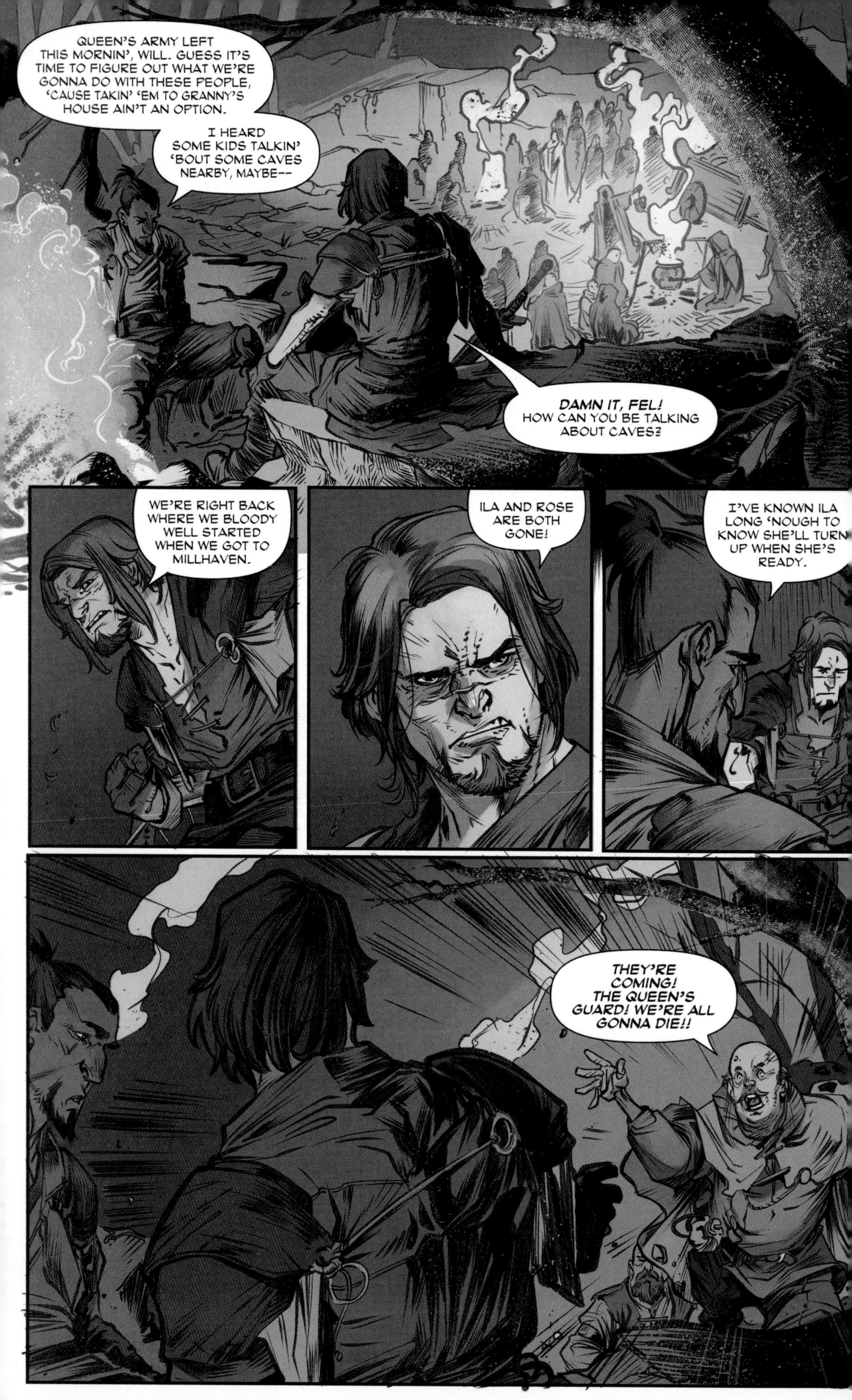
QUEEN'S ARMY LEFT THIS MORNIN', WILL. GUESS IT'S TIME TO FIGURE OUT WHAT WE'RE GONNA DO WITH THESE PEOPLE, 'CAUSE TAKIN' 'EM TO GRANNY'S HOUSE AIN'T AN OPTION.
I HEARD SOME KIDS TALKIN' 'BOUT SOME CAVES NEARBY, MAYBE--
DAMN IT, FEL! HOW CAN YOU BE TALKING ABOUT CAVES?
WE'RE RIGHT BACK WHERE WE BLOODY WELL STARTED WHEN WE GOT TO MILLHAVEN.
ILA AND ROSE ARE BOTH GONE!
I'VE KNOWN ILA LONG 'NOUGH TO KNOW SHE'LL TURN UP WHEN SHE'S READY.
THEY'RE COMING! THE QUEEN'S GUARD! WE'RE ALL GONNA DIE!!

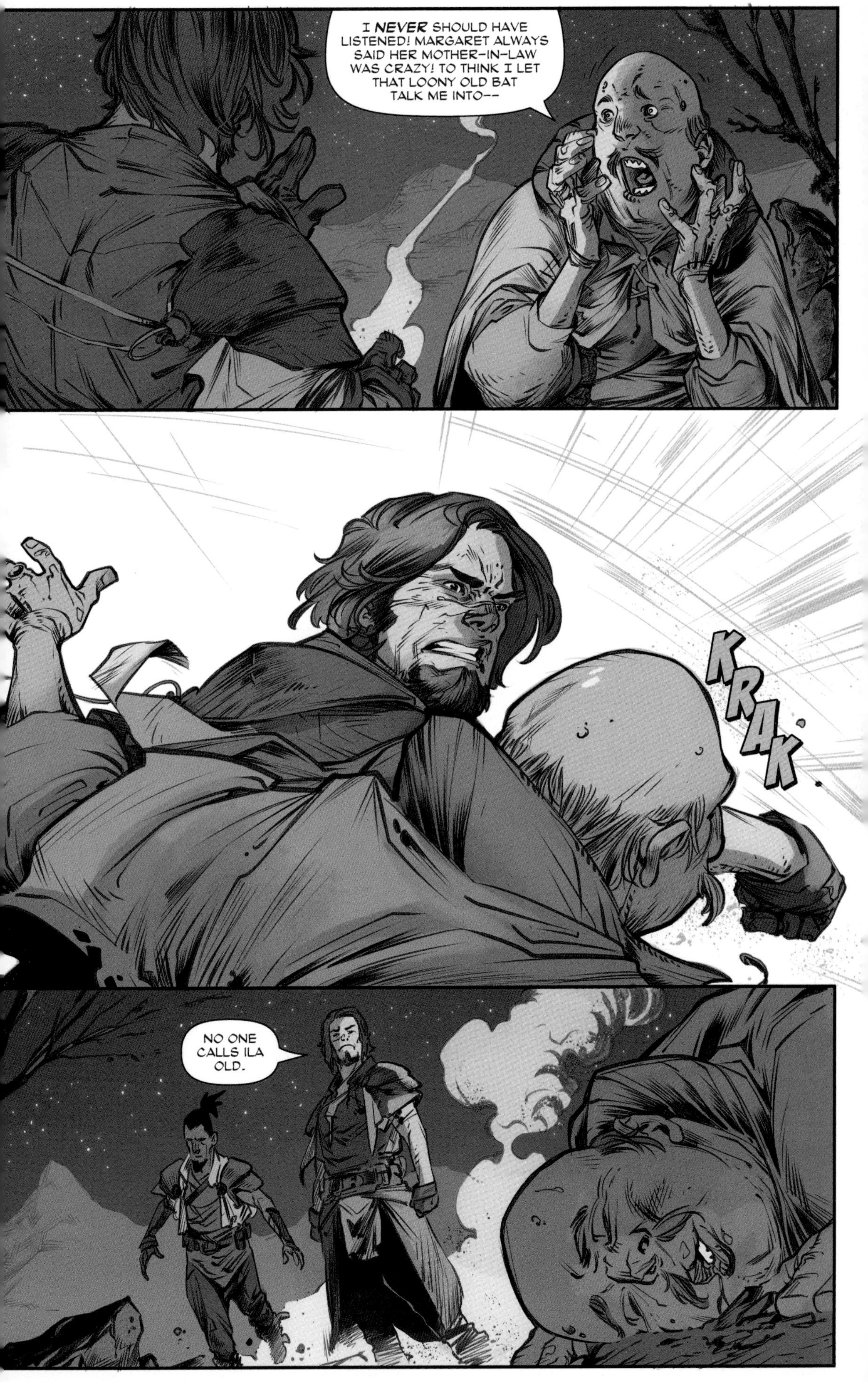
I NEVER SHOULD HAVE LISTENED! MARGARET ALWAYS SAID HER MOTHER-IN-LAW WAS CRAZY! TO THINK I LET THAT LOONY OLD BAT TALK ME INTO--
KRAK
NO ONE CALLS ILA OLD.

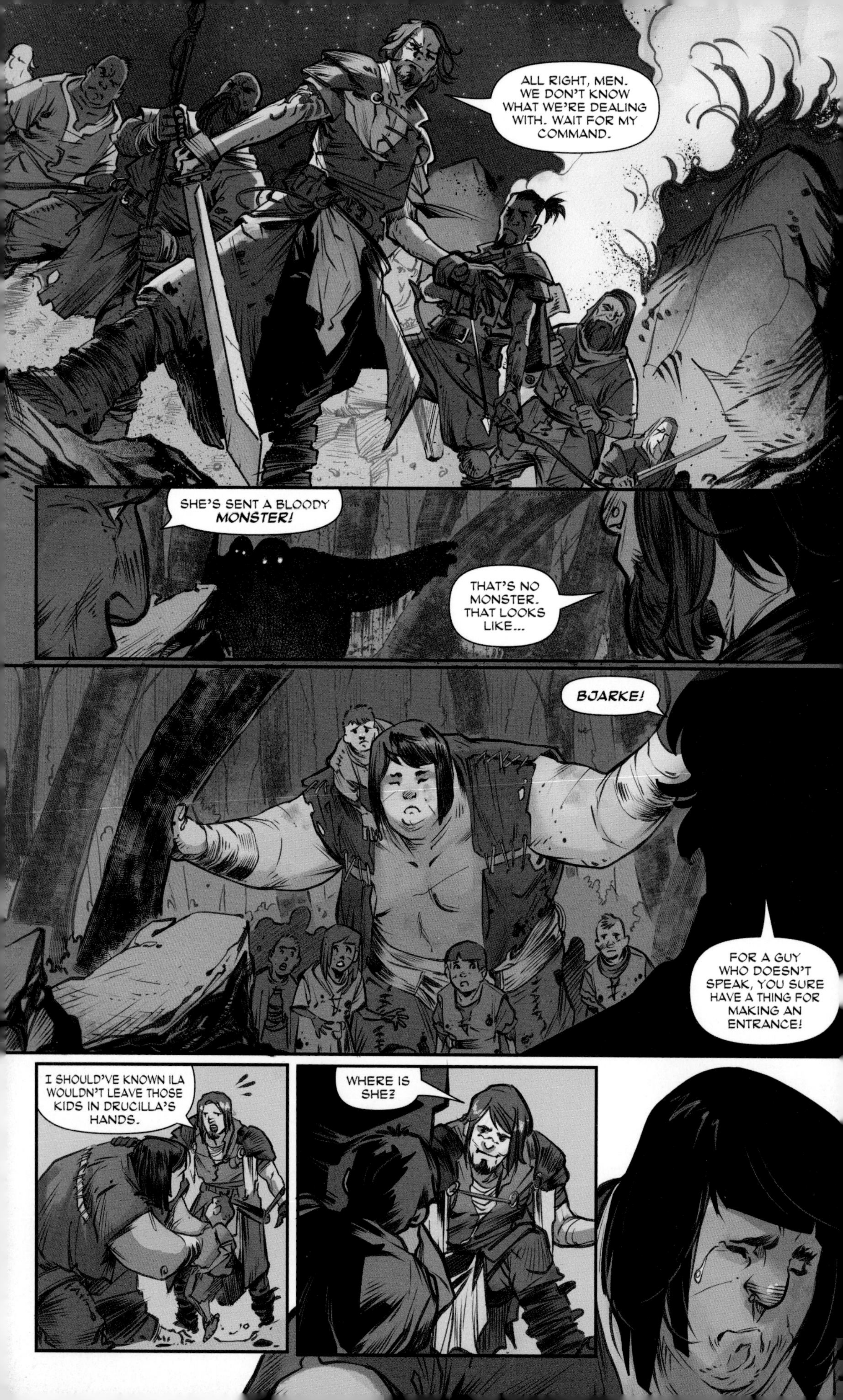
ALL RIGHT, MEN. WE DON'T KNOW WHAT WE'RE DEALING WITH. WAIT FOR MY COMMAND.
SHE'S SENT A BLOODY ***MONSTER!***
THAT'S NO MONSTER. THAT LOOKS LIKE...
BJARKE!
FOR A GUY WHO DOESN'T SPEAK, YOU SURE HAVE A THING FOR MAKING AN ENTRANCE!
I SHOULD'VE KNOWN ILA WOULDN'T LEAVE THOSE KIDS IN DRUCILLA'S HANDS.
WHERE IS SHE?

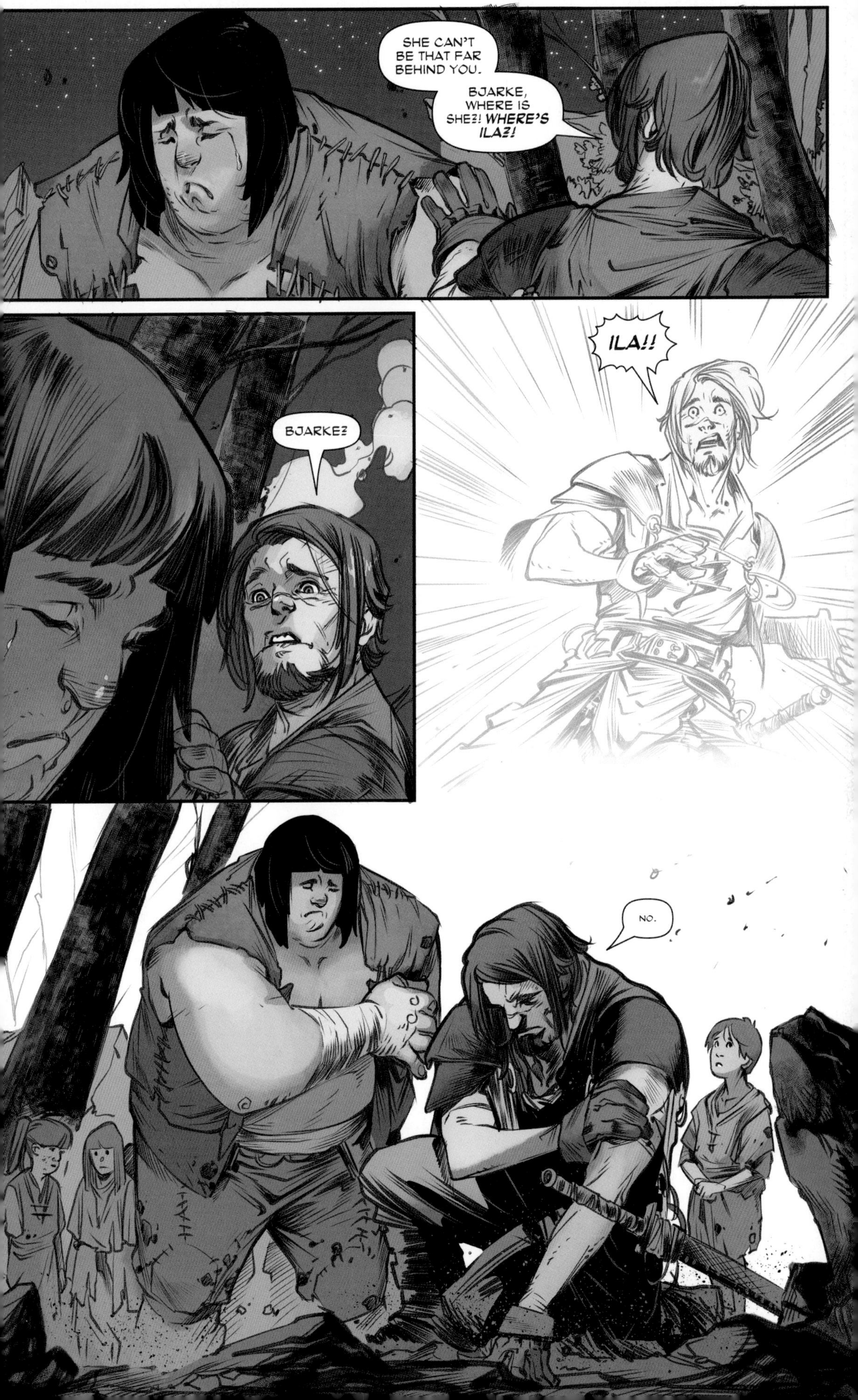
SHE CAN'T BE THAT FAR BEHIND YOU.
BJARKE, WHERE IS SHE?! WHERE'S ILA?!
BJARKE?
ILA!!
NO.

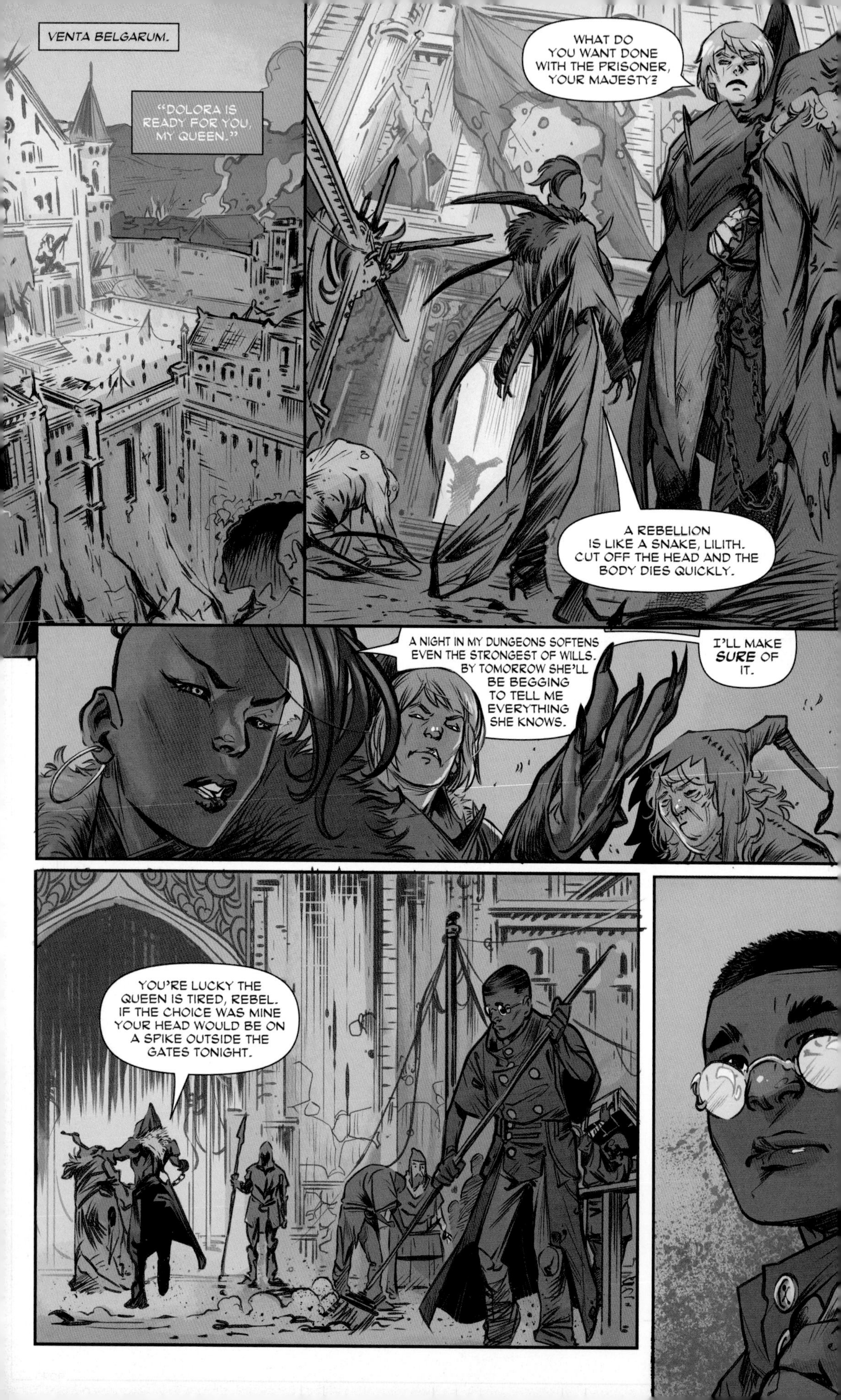
VENTA BELGARUM.
"DOLORA IS READY FOR YOU, MY QUEEN."
WHAT DO YOU WANT DONE WITH THE PRISONER, YOUR MAJESTY?
A REBELLION IS LIKE A SNAKE, LILITH. CUT OFF THE HEAD AND THE BODY DIES QUICKLY.
A NIGHT IN MY DUNGEONS SOFTENS EVEN THE STRONGEST OF WILLS. BY TOMORROW SHE'LL BE BEGGING TO TELL ME EVERYTHING SHE KNOWS.
I'LL MAKE SURE OF IT.
YOU'RE LUCKY THE QUEEN IS TIRED, REBEL. IF THE CHOICE WAS MINE YOUR HEAD WOULD BE ON A SPIKE OUTSIDE THE GATES TONIGHT.

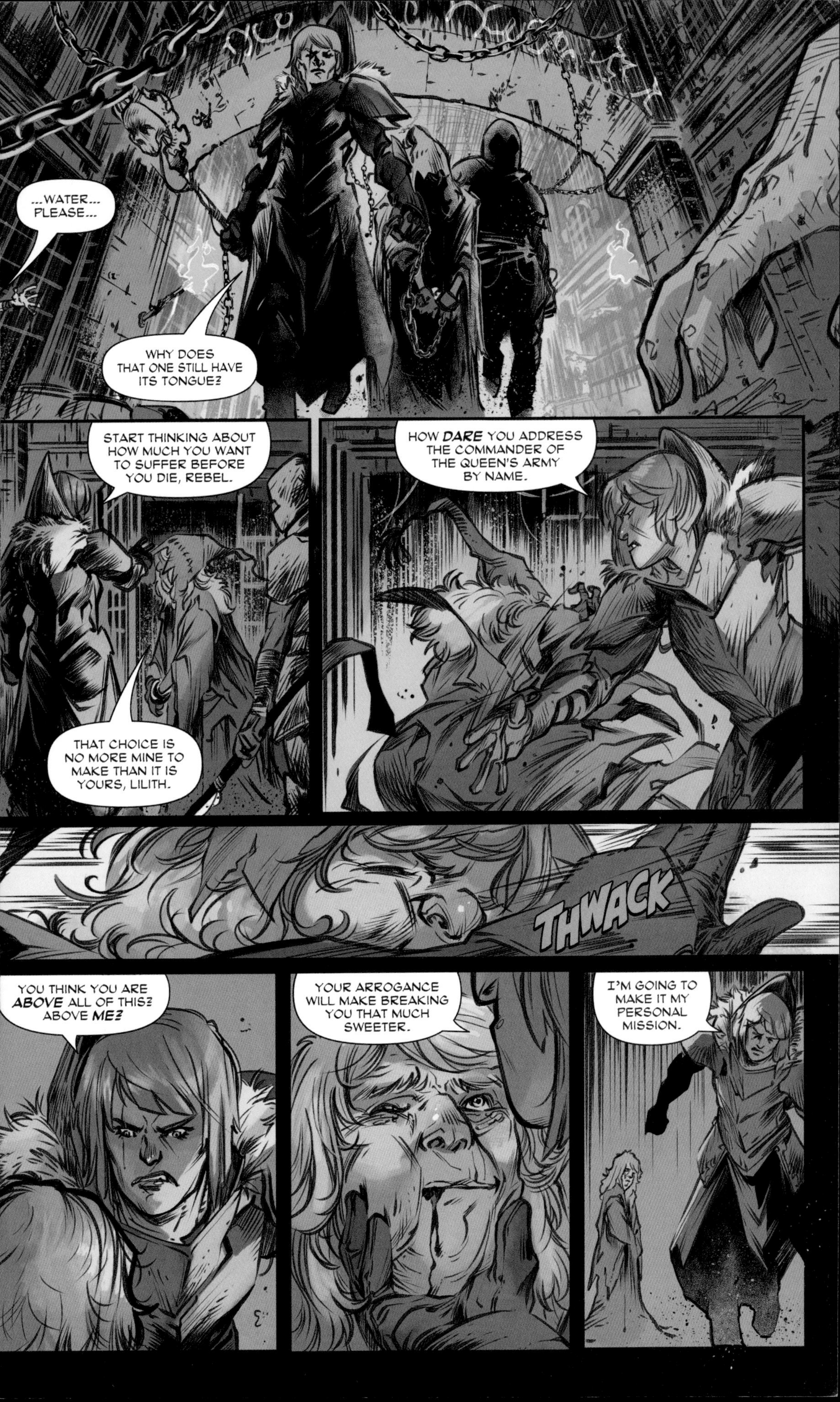
...WATER... PLEASE...
WHY DOES THAT ONE STILL HAVE ITS TONGUE?
START THINKING ABOUT HOW MUCH YOU WANT TO SUFFER BEFORE YOU DIE, REBEL.
THAT CHOICE IS NO MORE MINE TO MAKE THAN IT IS YOURS, LILITH.
HOW DARE YOU ADDRESS THE COMMANDER OF THE QUEEN'S ARMY BY NAME.
THWACK
YOU THINK YOU ARE ABOVE ALL OF THIS? ABOVE ME?
YOUR ARROGANCE WILL MAKE BREAKING YOU THAT MUCH SWEETER.
I'M GOING TO MAKE IT MY PERSONAL MISSION.

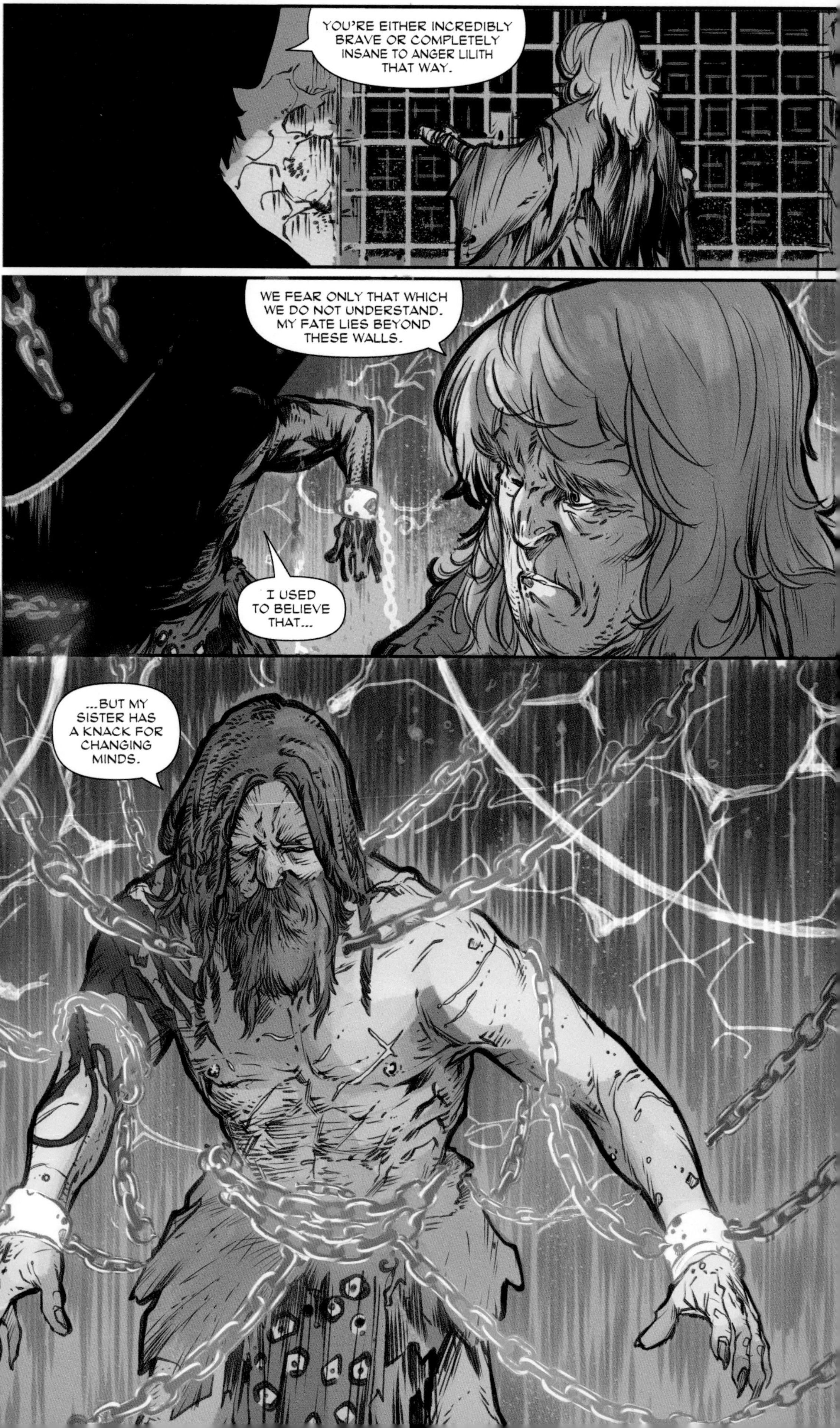
YOU'RE EITHER INCREDIBLY BRAVE OR COMPLETELY INSANE TO ANGER LILITH THAT WAY.
WE FEAR ONLY THAT WHICH WE DO NOT UNDERSTAND. MY FATE LIES BEYOND THESE WALLS.
I USED TO BELIEVE THAT...
...BUT MY SISTER HAS A KNACK FOR CHANGING MINDS.

EIGHT

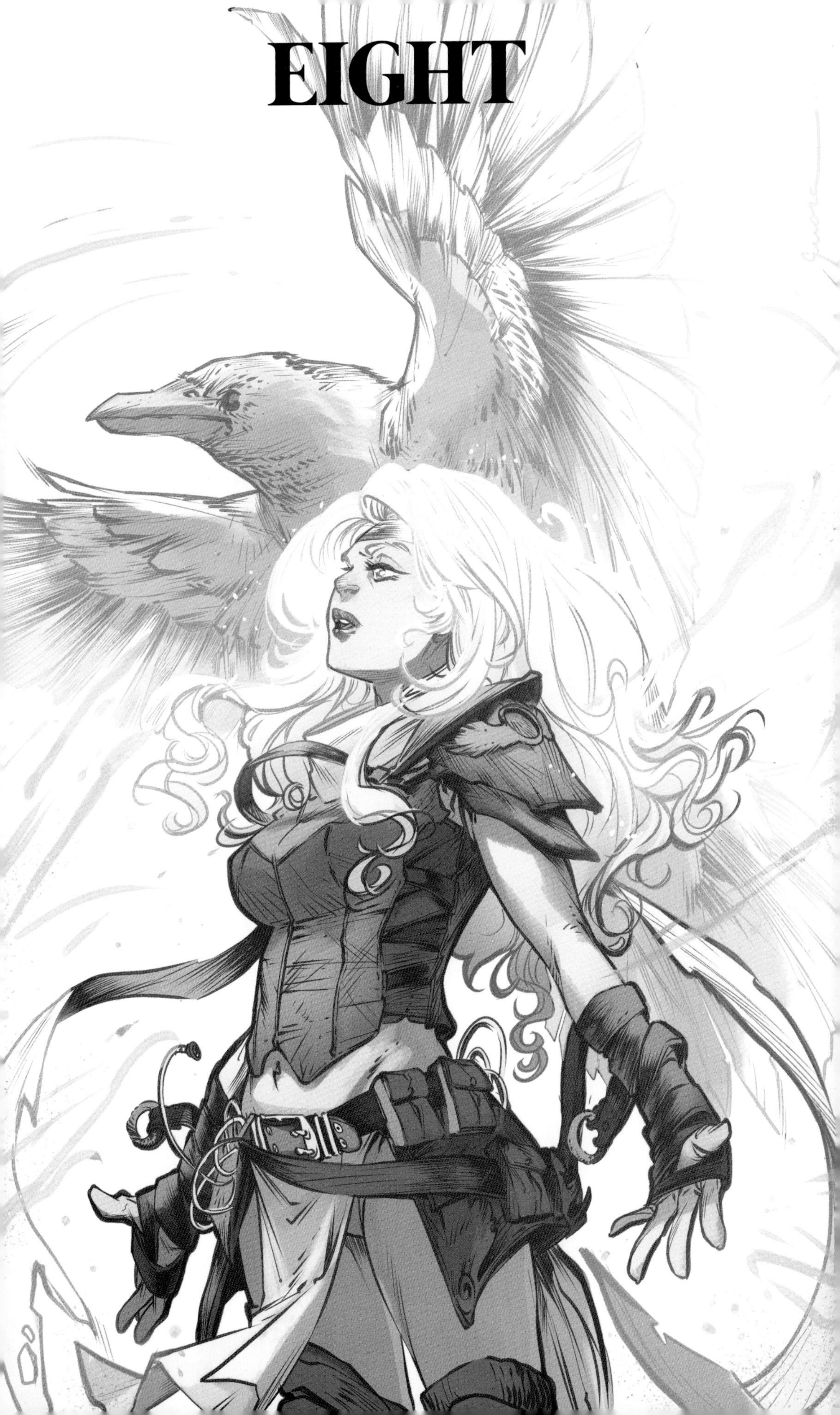

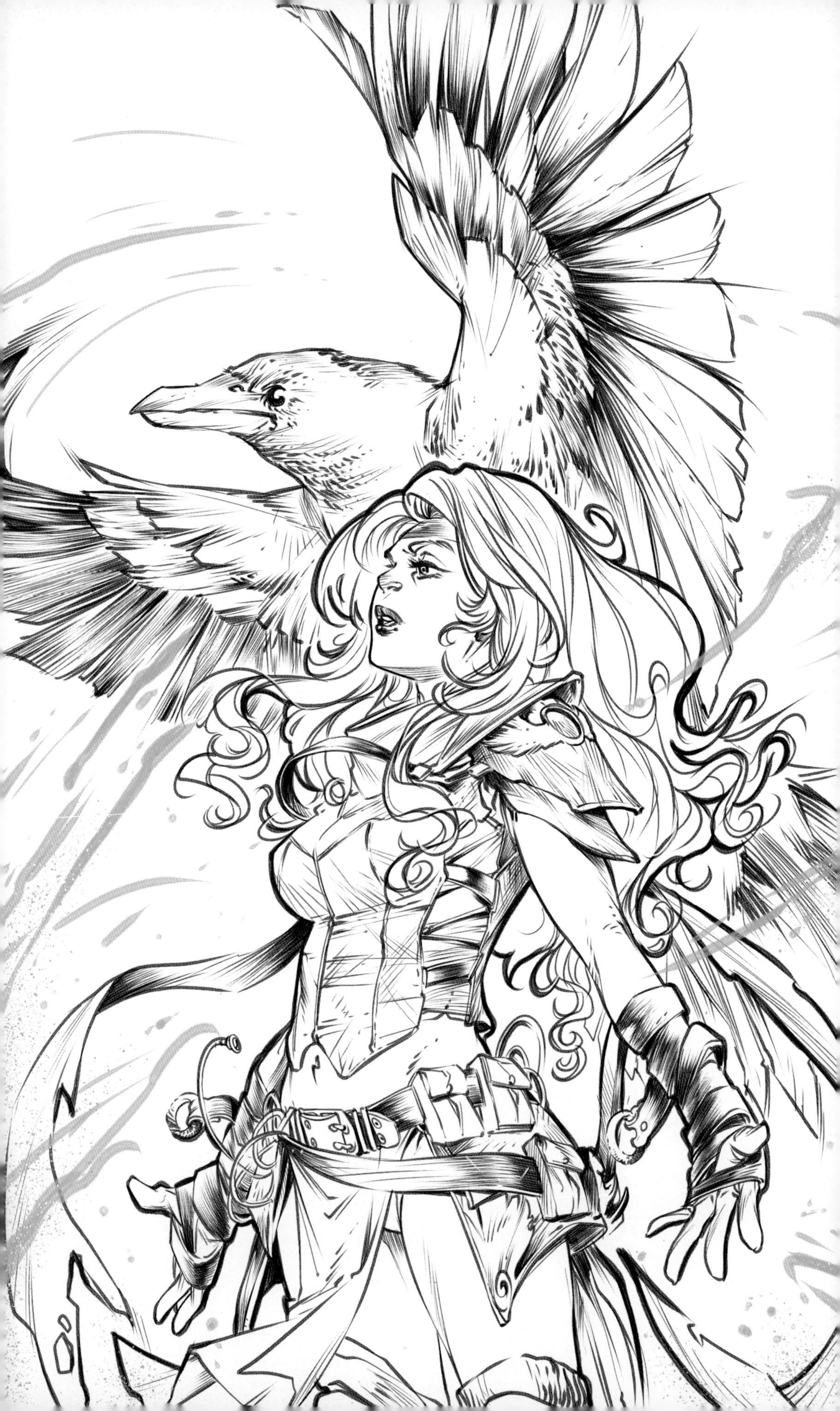

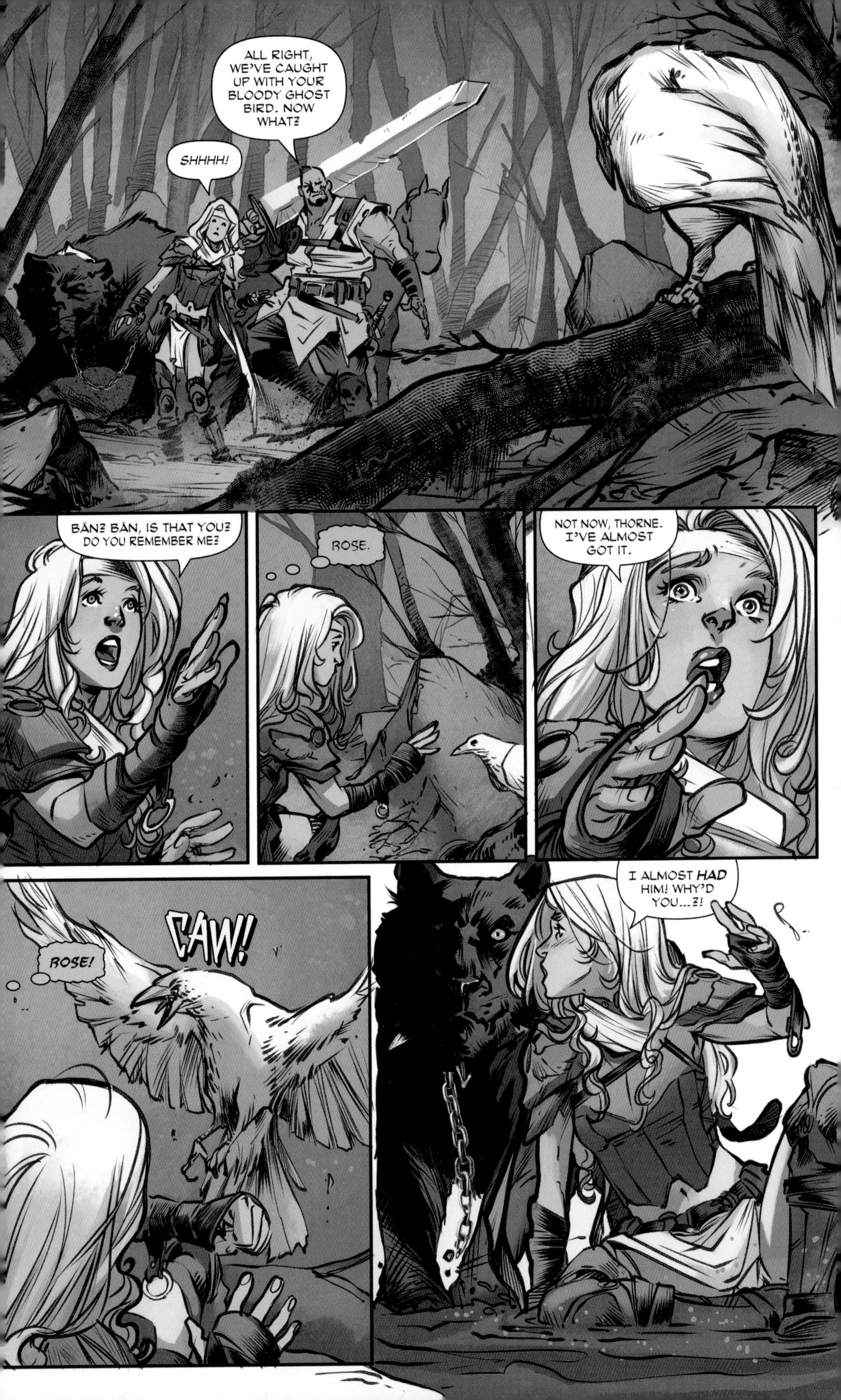

ALL RIGHT, WE'VE CAUGHT UP WITH YOUR BLOODY GHOST BIRD. NOW WHAT?
SHHHH!
BÁN? BÁN, IS THAT YOU? DO YOU REMEMBER ME?
ROSE.
NOT NOW, THORNE. I'VE ALMOST GOT IT.
CAW!
ROSE!
I ALMOST HAD HIM! WHY'D YOU...?!

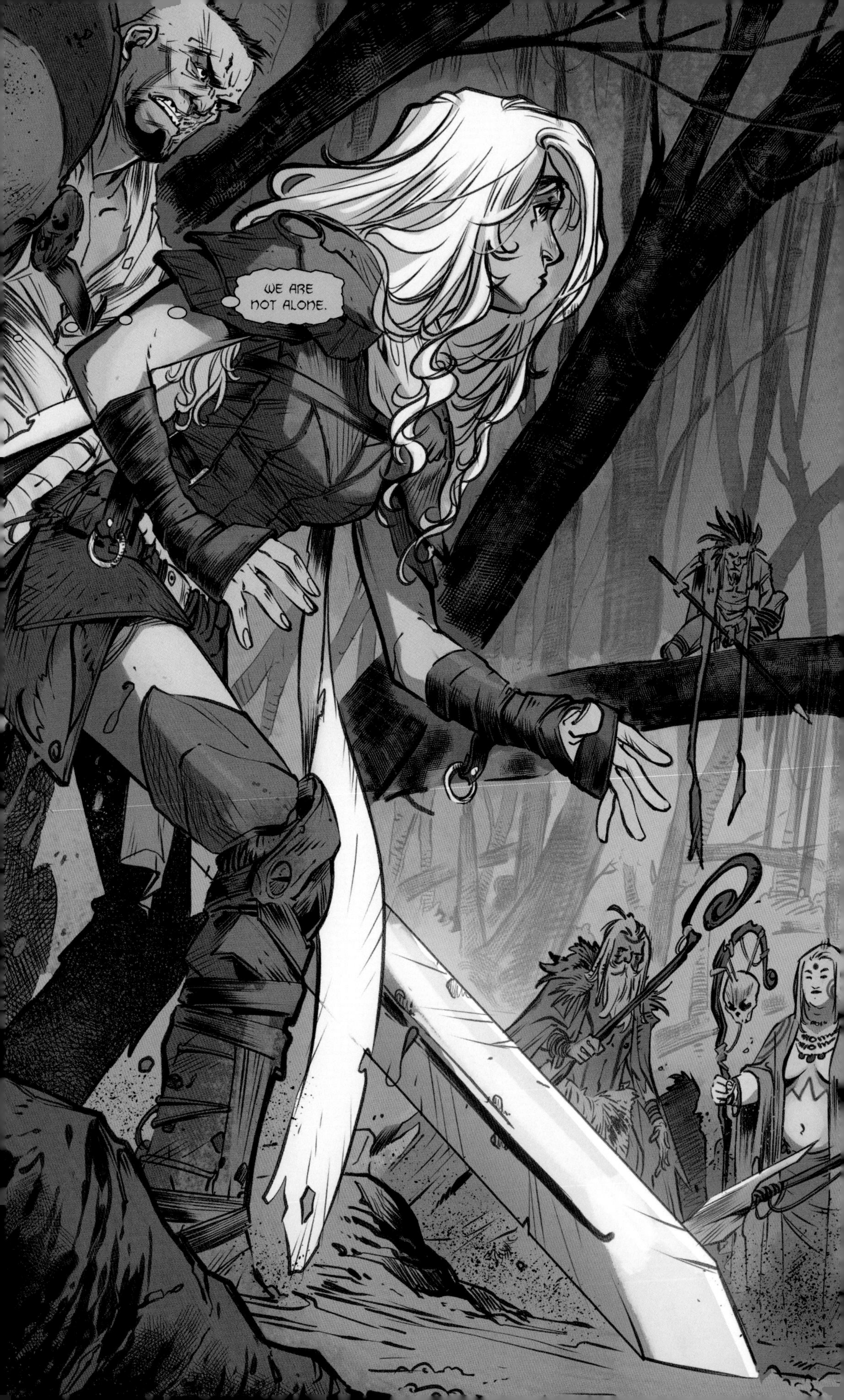
WE ARE NOT ALONE.

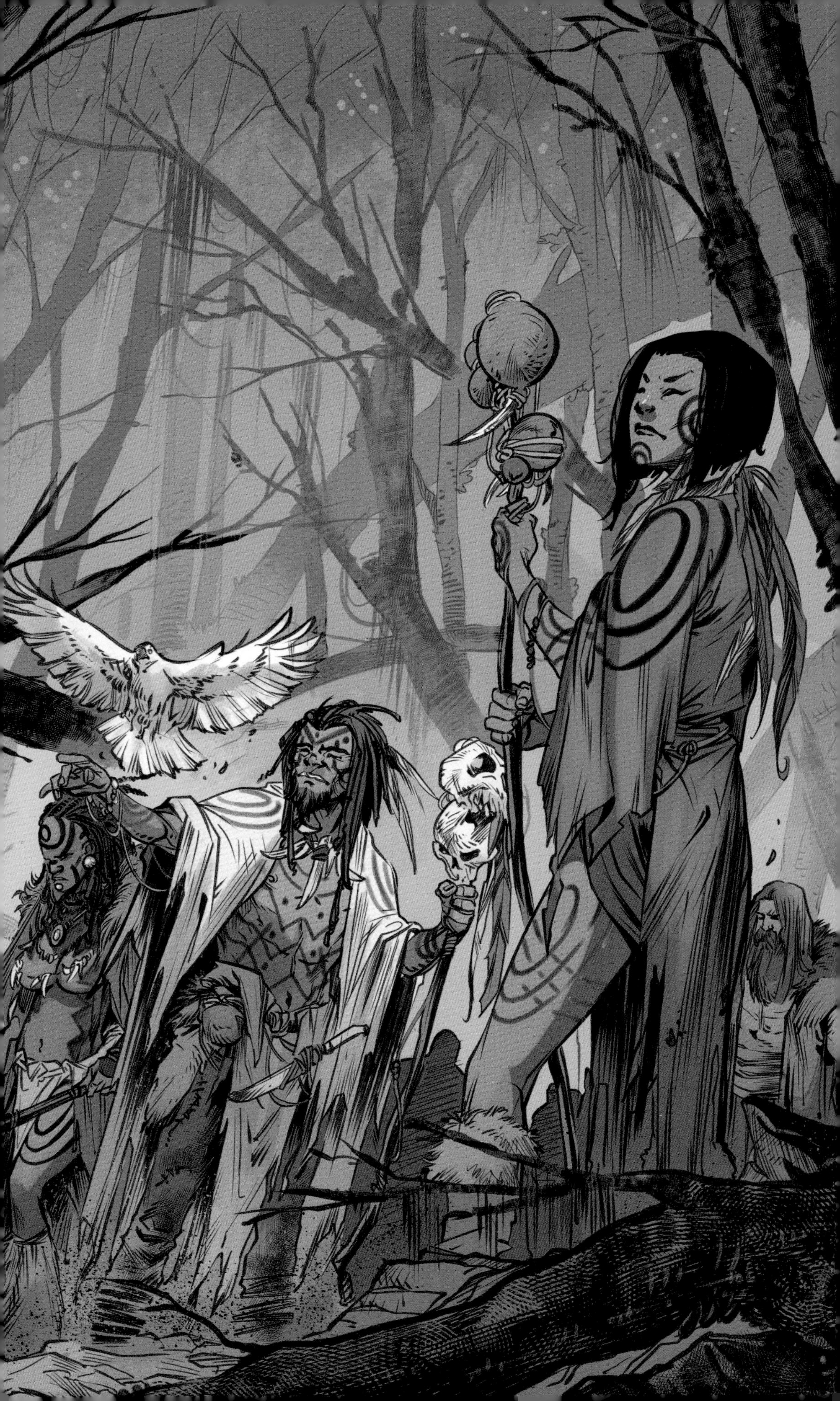

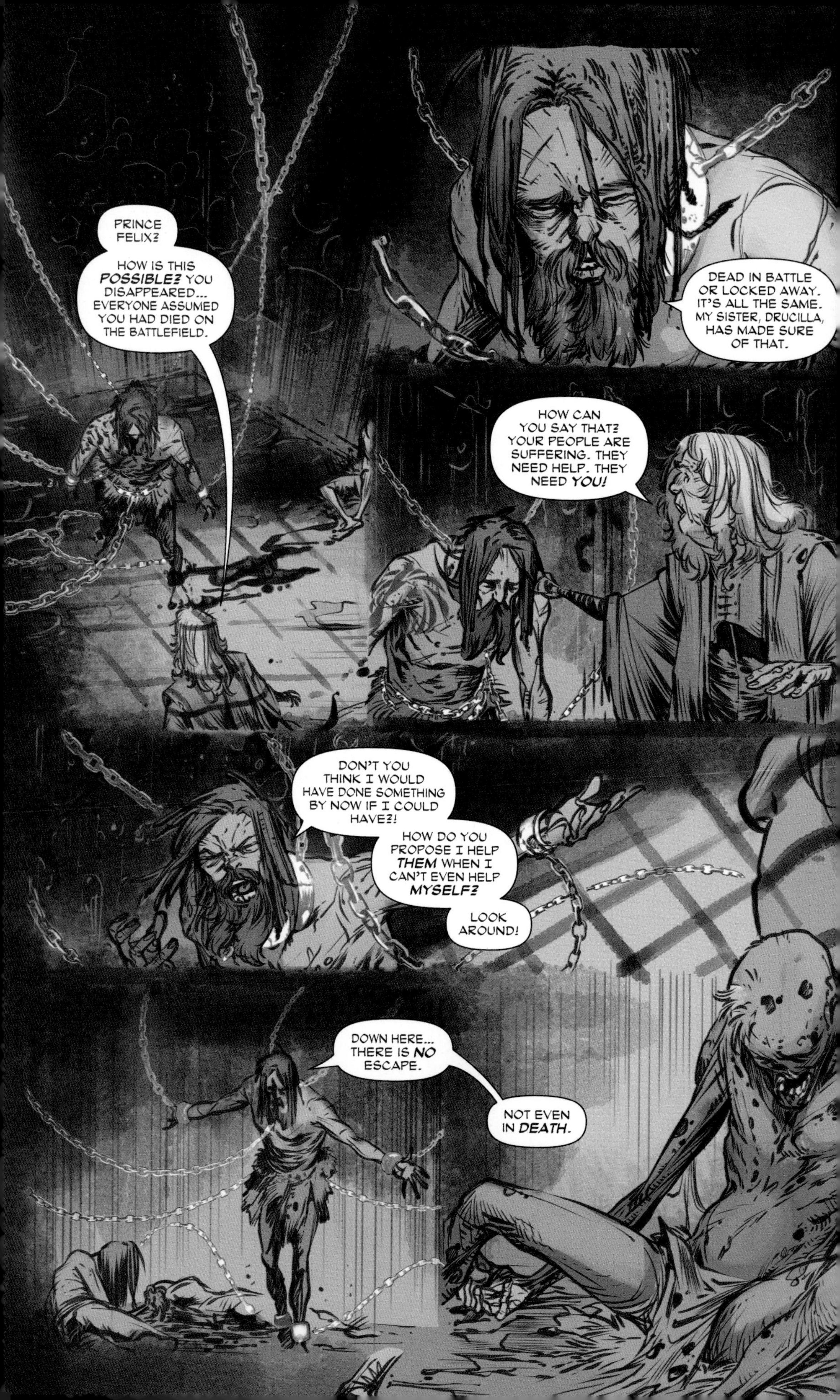
PRINCE FELIX?
HOW IS THIS POSSIBLE? YOU DISAPPEARED... EVERYONE ASSUMED YOU HAD DIED ON THE BATTLEFIELD.
DEAD IN BATTLE OR LOCKED AWAY. IT'S ALL THE SAME. MY SISTER, DRUCILLA, HAS MADE SURE OF THAT.
HOW CAN YOU SAY THAT? YOUR PEOPLE ARE SUFFERING. THEY NEED HELP. THEY NEED YOU!
DON'T YOU THINK I WOULD HAVE DONE SOMETHING BY NOW IF I COULD HAVE?!
HOW DO YOU PROPOSE I HELP THEM WHEN I CAN'T EVEN HELP MYSELF?
LOOK AROUND!
DOWN HERE... THERE IS NO ESCAPE.
NOT EVEN IN DEATH.

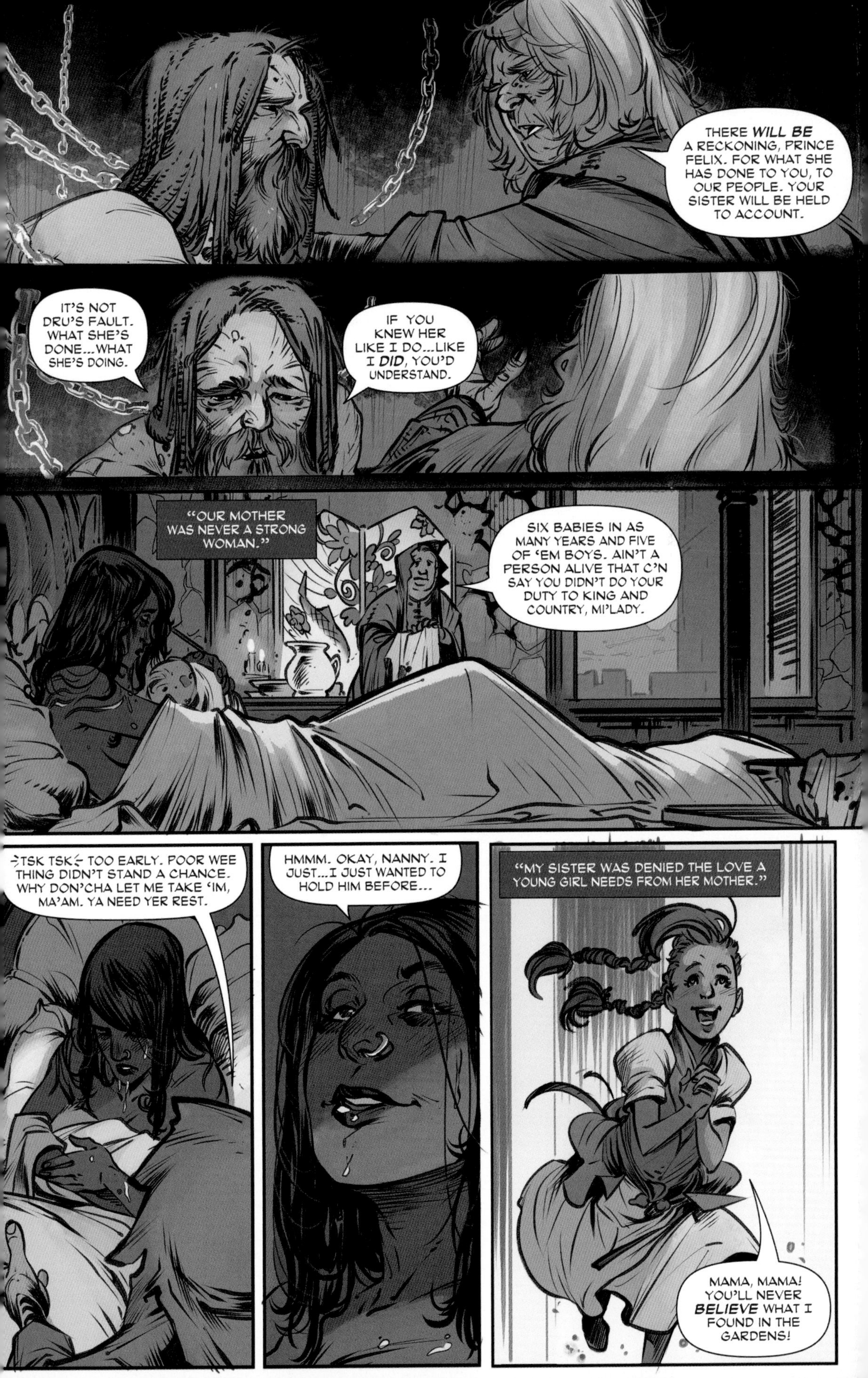
THERE WILL BE A RECKONING, PRINCE FELIX. FOR WHAT SHE HAS DONE TO YOU, TO OUR PEOPLE. YOUR SISTER WILL BE HELD TO ACCOUNT.
IT'S NOT DRU'S FAULT. WHAT SHE'S DONE...WHAT SHE'S DOING.
IF YOU KNEW HER LIKE I DO...LIKE I DID, YOU'D UNDERSTAND.
"OUR MOTHER WAS NEVER A STRONG WOMAN."
SIX BABIES IN AS MANY YEARS AND FIVE OF 'EM BOYS. AIN'T A PERSON ALIVE THAT C'N SAY YOU DIDN'T DO YOUR DUTY TO KING AND COUNTRY, MI'LADY.
=TSK TSK= TOO EARLY. POOR WEE THING DIDN'T STAND A CHANCE. WHY DON'CHA LET ME TAKE 'IM, MA'AM. YA NEED YER REST.
HMMM. OKAY, NANNY. I JUST...I JUST WANTED TO HOLD HIM BEFORE...
"MY SISTER WAS DENIED THE LOVE A YOUNG GIRL NEEDS FROM HER MOTHER."
MAMA, MAMA! YOU'LL NEVER BELIEVE WHAT I FOUND IN THE GARDENS!

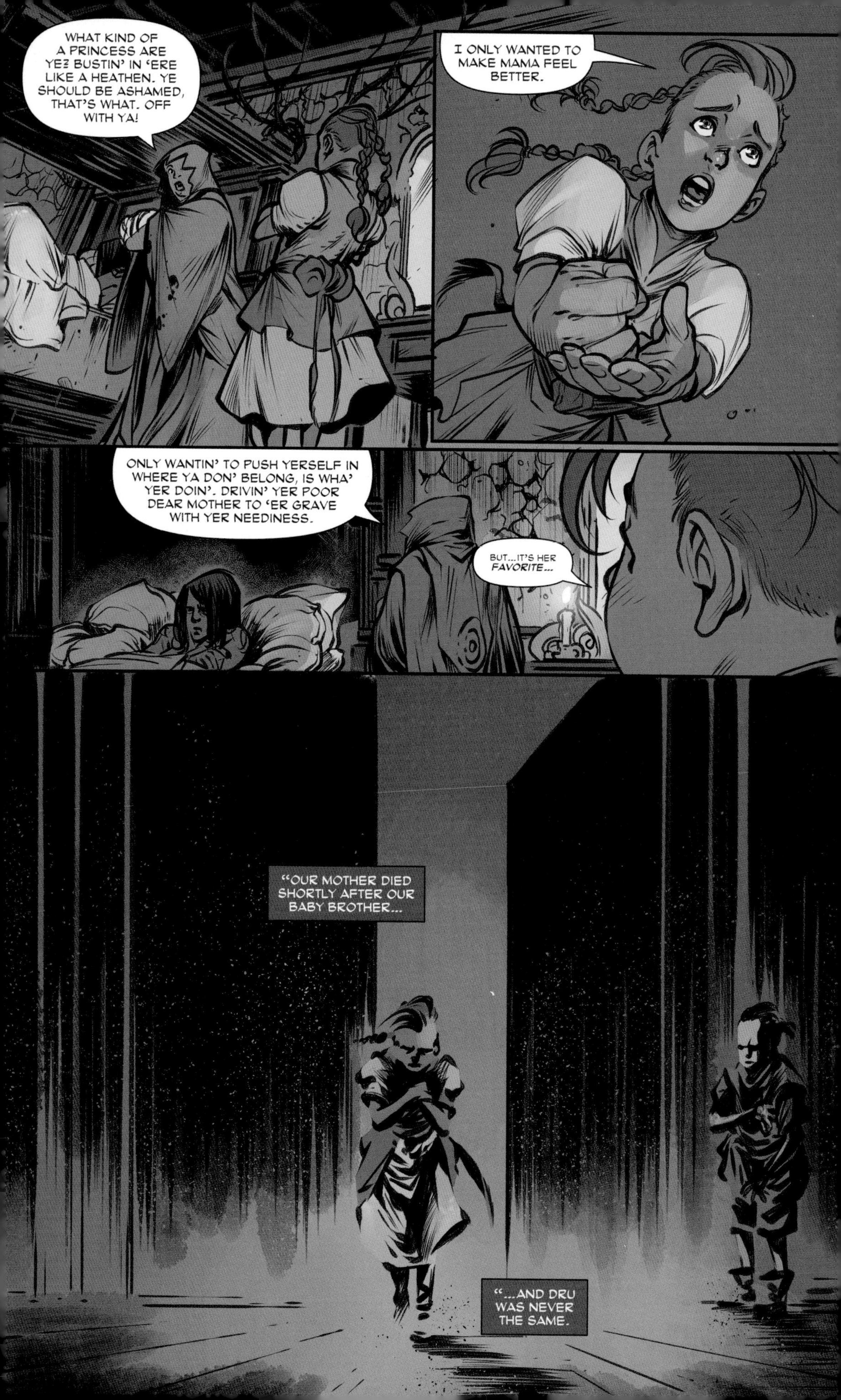
WHAT KIND OF A PRINCESS ARE YE? BUSTIN' IN 'ERE LIKE A HEATHEN. YE SHOULD BE ASHAMED, THAT'S WHAT. OFF WITH YA!
I ONLY WANTED TO MAKE MAMA FEEL BETTER.
ONLY WANTIN' TO PUSH YERSELF IN WHERE YA DON' BELONG, IS WHA' YER DOIN'. DRIVIN' YER POOR DEAR MOTHER TO 'ER GRAVE WITH YER NEEDINESS.
BUT...IT'S HER *FAVORITE...*
"OUR MOTHER DIED SHORTLY AFTER OUR BABY BROTHER...
"...AND DRU WAS NEVER THE SAME.

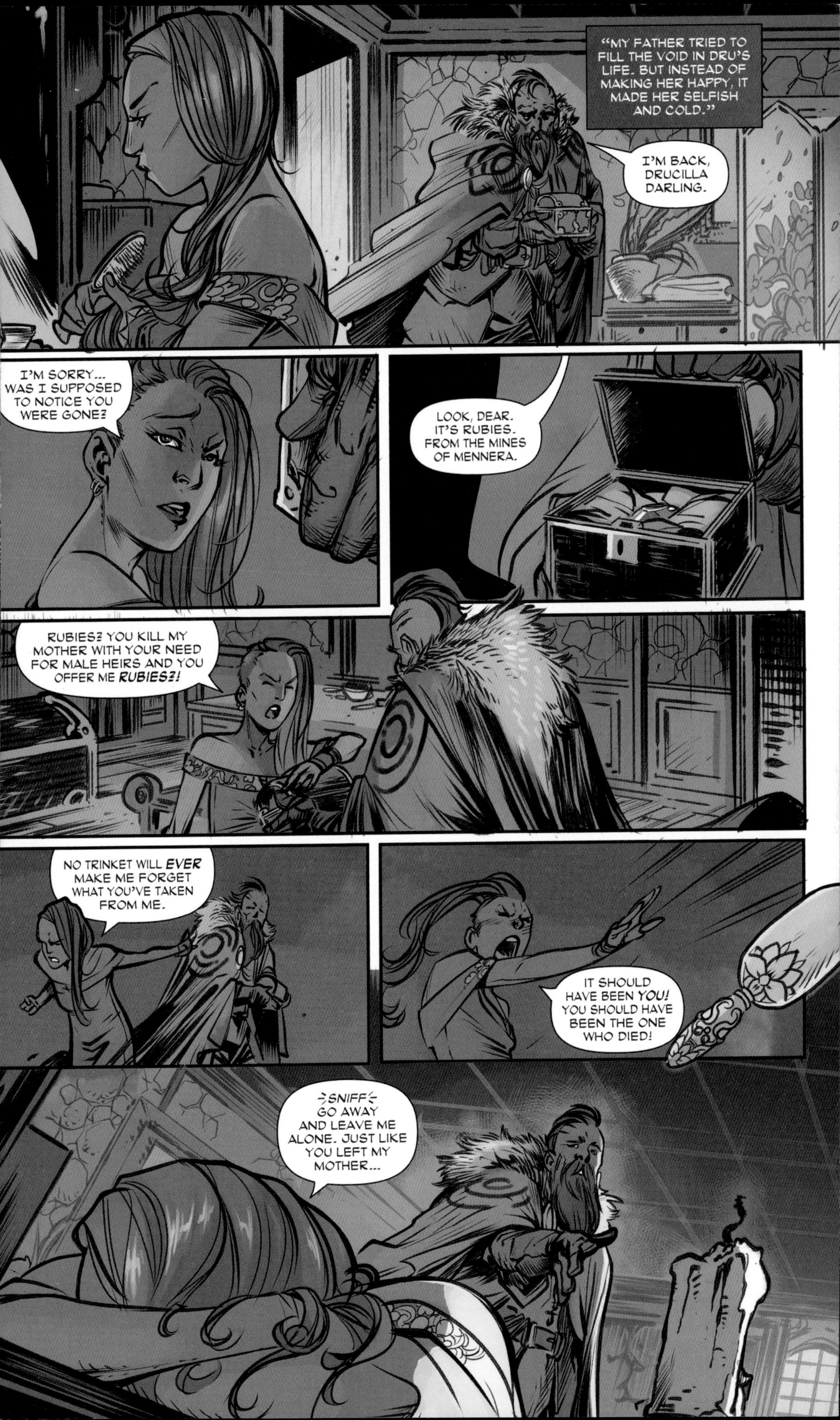
"MY FATHER TRIED TO FILL THE VOID IN DRU'S LIFE. BUT INSTEAD OF MAKING HER HAPPY, IT MADE HER SELFISH AND COLD."
I'M BACK, DRUCILLA DARLING.
I'M SORRY... WAS I SUPPOSED TO NOTICE YOU WERE GONE?
LOOK, DEAR. IT'S RUBIES. FROM THE MINES OF MENNERA.
RUBIES? YOU KILL MY MOTHER WITH YOUR NEED FOR MALE HEIRS AND YOU OFFER ME *RUBIES?!*
NO TRINKET WILL *EVER* MAKE ME FORGET WHAT YOU'VE TAKEN FROM ME.
IT SHOULD HAVE BEEN *YOU!* YOU SHOULD HAVE BEEN THE ONE WHO DIED!
SNIFF GO AWAY AND LEAVE ME ALONE. JUST LIKE YOU LEFT MY MOTHER...

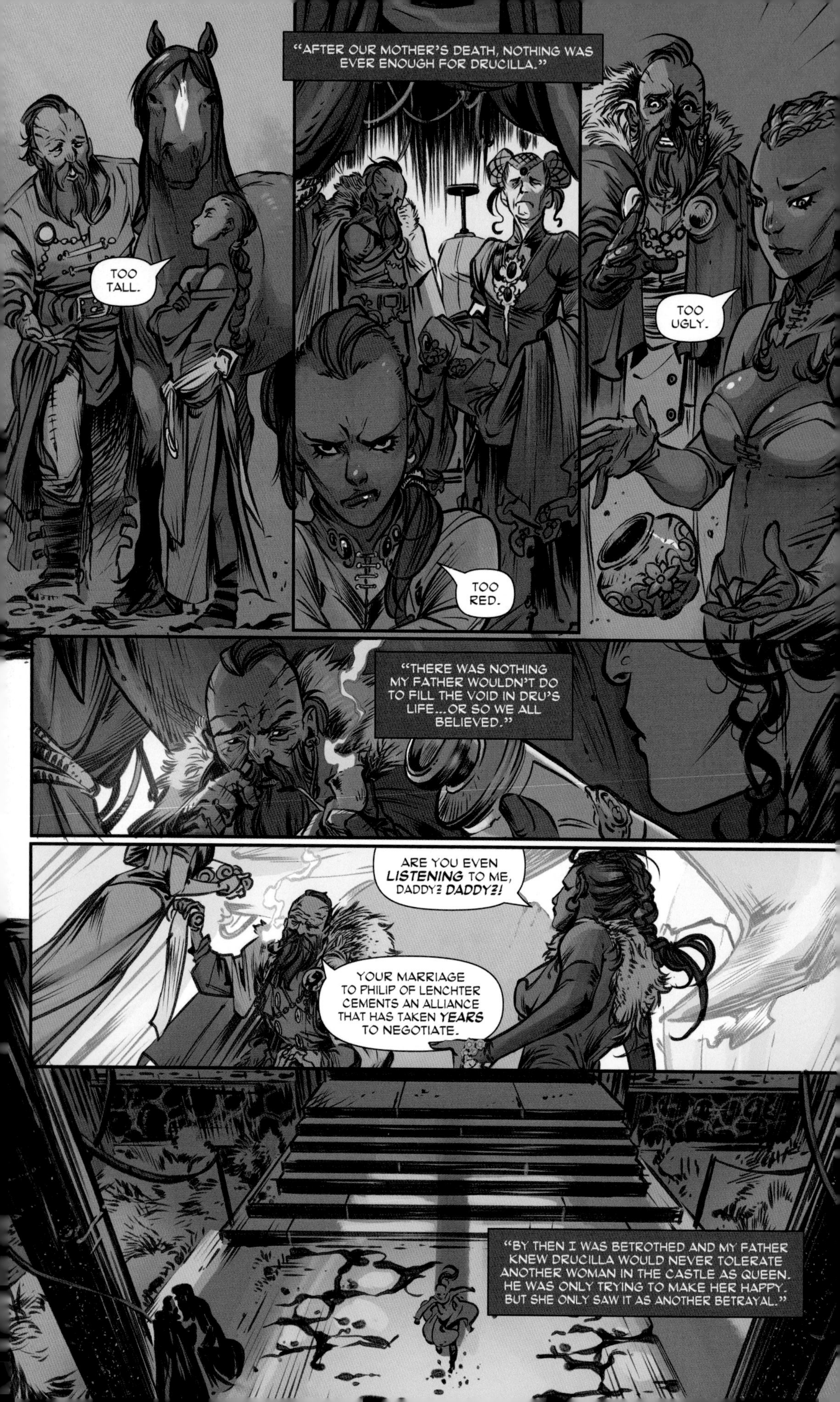
"AFTER OUR MOTHER'S DEATH, NOTHING WAS EVER ENOUGH FOR DRUCILLA."
TOO TALL.
TOO RED.
TOO UGLY.
"THERE WAS NOTHING MY FATHER WOULDN'T DO TO FILL THE VOID IN DRU'S LIFE...OR SO WE ALL BELIEVED."
ARE YOU EVEN LISTENING TO ME, DADDY? DADDY?!
YOUR MARRIAGE TO PHILIP OF LENCHTER CEMENTS AN ALLIANCE THAT HAS TAKEN YEARS TO NEGOTIATE.
"BY THEN I WAS BETROTHED AND MY FATHER KNEW DRUCILLA WOULD NEVER TOLERATE ANOTHER WOMAN IN THE CASTLE AS QUEEN. HE WAS ONLY TRYING TO MAKE HER HAPPY. BUT SHE ONLY SAW IT AS ANOTHER BETRAYAL."

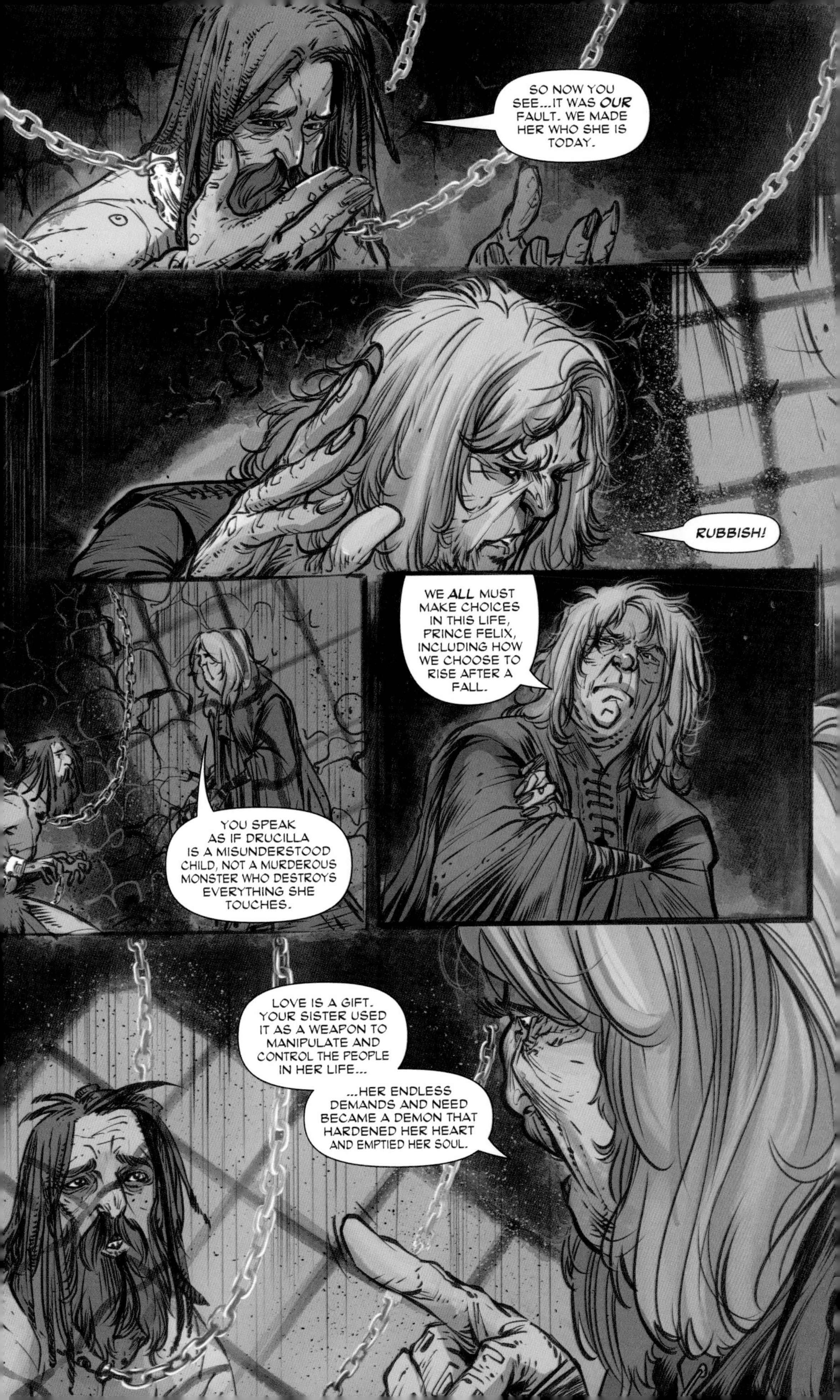
SO NOW YOU SEE...IT WAS OUR FAULT. WE MADE HER WHO SHE IS TODAY.
RUBBISH!
WE ALL MUST MAKE CHOICES IN THIS LIFE, PRINCE FELIX, INCLUDING HOW WE CHOOSE TO RISE AFTER A FALL.
YOU SPEAK AS IF DRUCILLA IS A MISUNDERSTOOD CHILD, NOT A MURDEROUS MONSTER WHO DESTROYS EVERYTHING SHE TOUCHES.
LOVE IS A GIFT. YOUR SISTER USED IT AS A WEAPON TO MANIPULATE AND CONTROL THE PEOPLE IN HER LIFE...
...HER ENDLESS DEMANDS AND NEED BECAME A DEMON THAT HARDENED HER HEART AND EMPTIED HER SOUL.

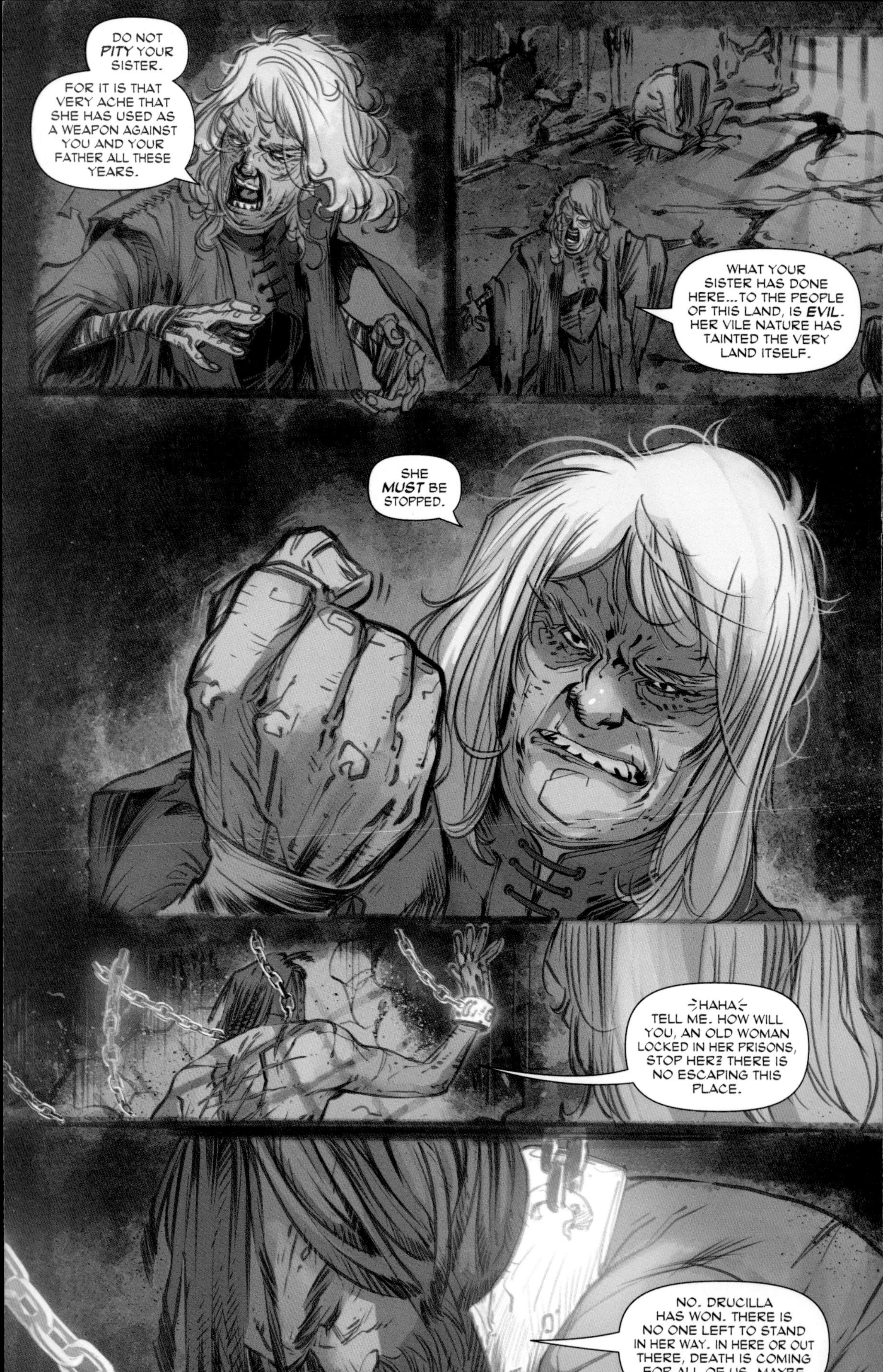

DO NOT PITY YOUR SISTER.
FOR IT IS THAT VERY ACHE THAT SHE HAS USED AS A WEAPON AGAINST YOU AND YOUR FATHER ALL THESE YEARS.
WHAT YOUR SISTER HAS DONE HERE...TO THE PEOPLE OF THIS LAND, IS EVIL. HER VILE NATURE HAS TAINTED THE VERY LAND ITSELF.
SHE MUST BE STOPPED.
HAHA
TELL ME. HOW WILL YOU, AN OLD WOMAN LOCKED IN HER PRISONS, STOP HER? THERE IS NO ESCAPING THIS PLACE.
NO. DRUCILLA HAS WON. THERE IS NO ONE LEFT TO STAND IN HER WAY. IN HERE OR OUT THERE, DEATH IS COMING FOR ALL OF US. MAYBE WE DESERVE IT.

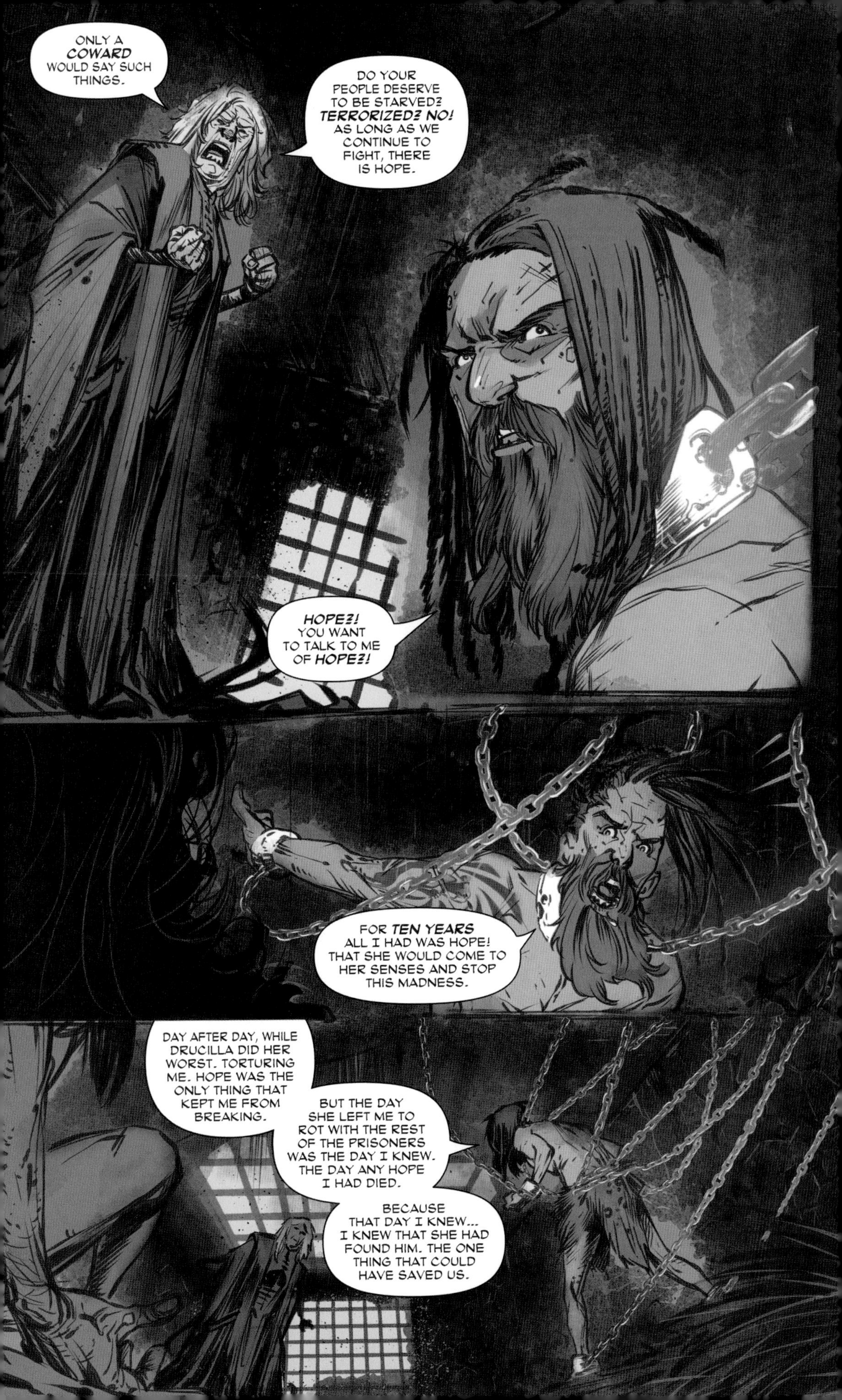
ONLY A COWARD WOULD SAY SUCH THINGS.
DO YOUR PEOPLE DESERVE TO BE STARVED? TERRORIZED? NO! AS LONG AS WE CONTINUE TO FIGHT, THERE IS HOPE.
HOPE?! YOU WANT TO TALK TO ME OF HOPE?!
FOR TEN YEARS ALL I HAD WAS HOPE! THAT SHE WOULD COME TO HER SENSES AND STOP THIS MADNESS.
DAY AFTER DAY, WHILE DRUCILLA DID HER WORST. TORTURING ME. HOPE WAS THE ONLY THING THAT KEPT ME FROM BREAKING.
BUT THE DAY SHE LEFT ME TO ROT WITH THE REST OF THE PRISONERS WAS THE DAY I KNEW. THE DAY ANY HOPE I HAD DIED.
BECAUSE THAT DAY I KNEW... I KNEW THAT SHE HAD FOUND HIM. THE ONE THING THAT COULD HAVE SAVED US.

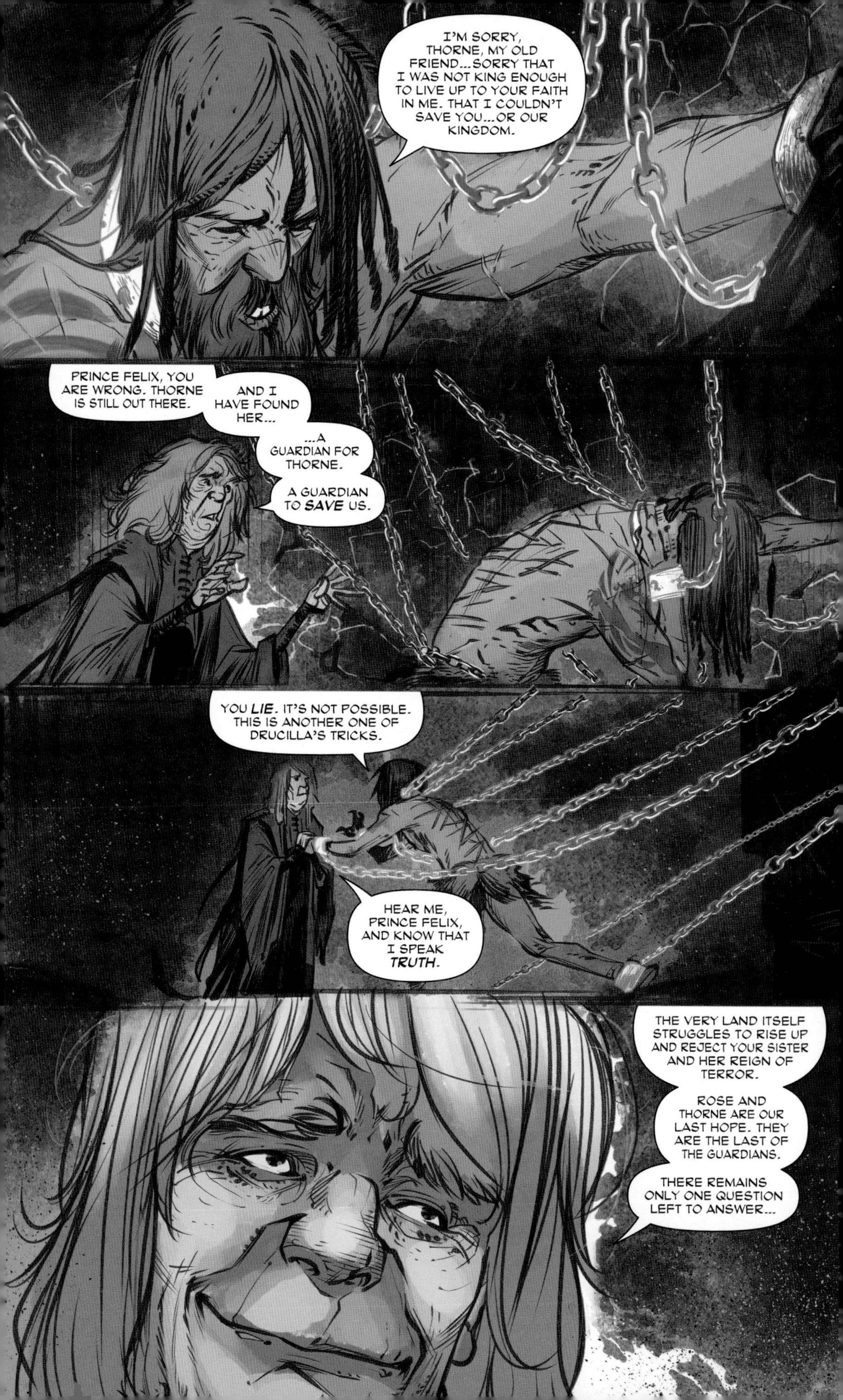
I'M SORRY, THORNE, MY OLD FRIEND... SORRY THAT I WAS NOT KING ENOUGH TO LIVE UP TO YOUR FAITH IN ME. THAT I COULDN'T SAVE YOU...OR OUR KINGDOM.
PRINCE FELIX, YOU ARE WRONG. THORNE IS STILL OUT THERE.
AND I HAVE FOUND HER...
...A GUARDIAN FOR THORNE.
A GUARDIAN TO *SAVE* US.
YOU *LIE*. IT'S NOT POSSIBLE. THIS IS ANOTHER ONE OF DRUCILLA'S TRICKS.
HEAR ME, PRINCE FELIX, AND KNOW THAT I SPEAK *TRUTH*.
THE VERY LAND ITSELF STRUGGLES TO RISE UP AND REJECT YOUR SISTER AND HER REIGN OF TERROR.
ROSE AND THORNE ARE OUR LAST HOPE. THEY ARE THE LAST OF THE GUARDIANS.
THERE REMAINS ONLY ONE QUESTION LEFT TO ANSWER...

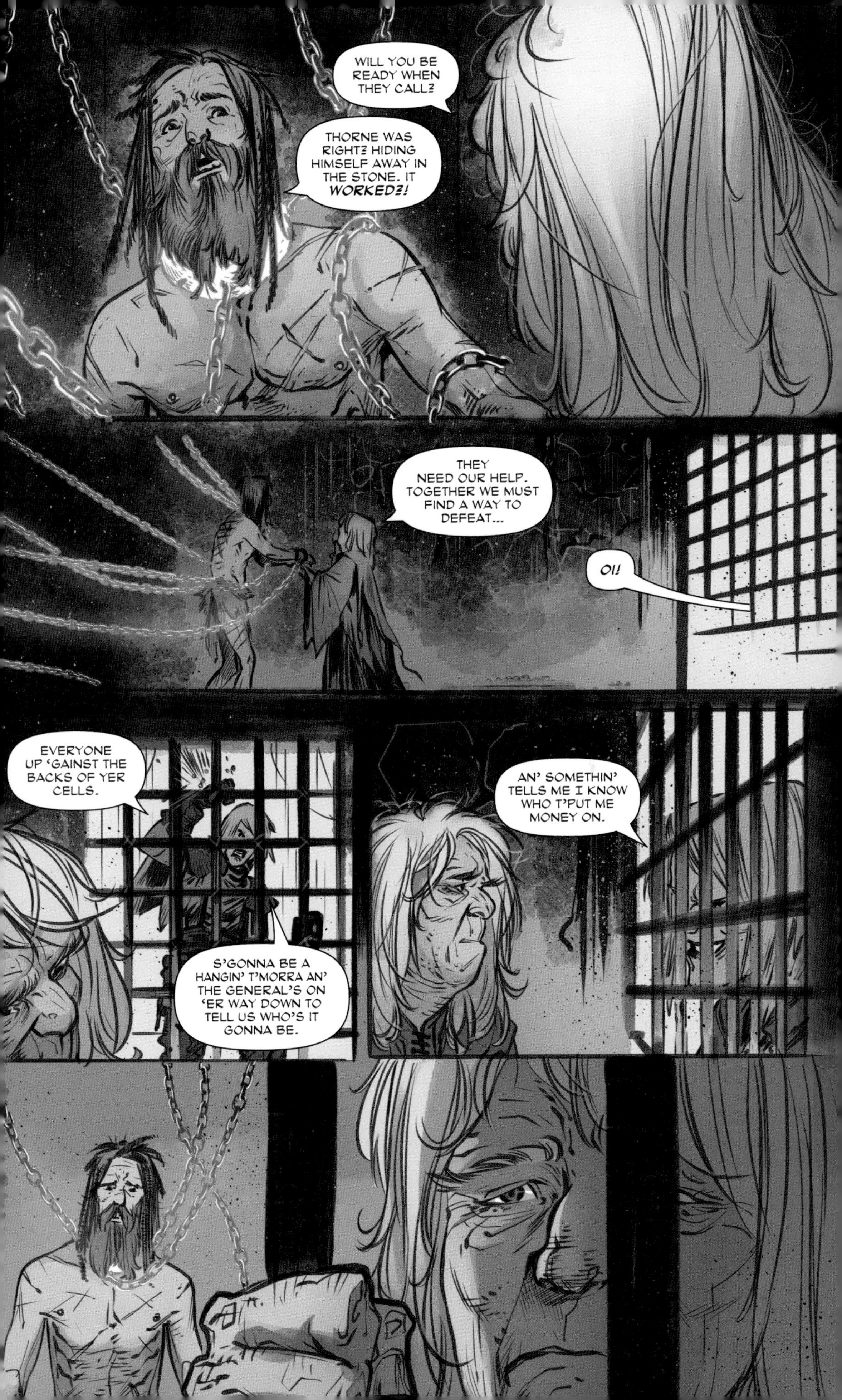
WILL YOU BE READY WHEN THEY CALL?
THORNE WAS RIGHT? HIDING HIMSELF AWAY IN THE STONE. IT *WORKED?!*
THEY NEED OUR HELP. TOGETHER WE MUST FIND A WAY TO DEFEAT...
OI!
EVERYONE UP 'GAINST THE BACKS OF YER CELLS.
S'GONNA BE A HANGIN' T'MORRA AN' THE GENERAL'S ON 'ER WAY DOWN TO TELL US WHO'S IT GONNA BE.
AN' SOMETHIN' TELLS ME I KNOW WHO T'PUT ME MONEY ON.

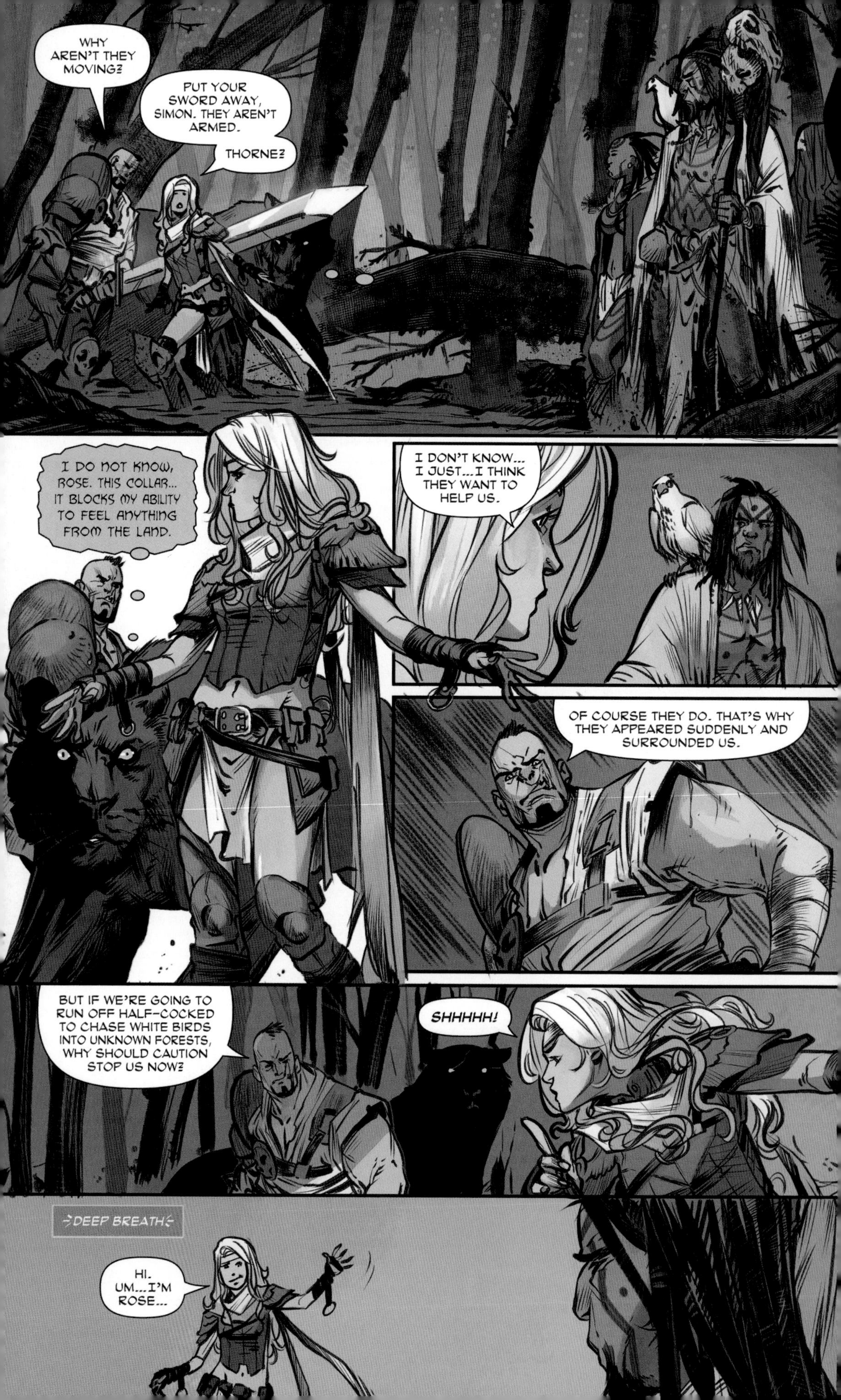
WHY AREN'T THEY MOVING?
PUT YOUR SWORD AWAY, SIMON. THEY AREN'T ARMED.
THORNE?
I DO NOT KNOW, ROSE. THIS COLLAR... IT BLOCKS MY ABILITY TO FEEL ANYTHING FROM THE LAND.
I DON'T KNOW... I JUST...I THINK THEY WANT TO HELP US.
OF COURSE THEY DO. THAT'S WHY THEY APPEARED SUDDENLY AND SURROUNDED US.
BUT IF WE'RE GOING TO RUN OFF HALF-COCKED TO CHASE WHITE BIRDS INTO UNKNOWN FORESTS, WHY SHOULD CAUTION STOP US NOW?
SHHHHH!
DEEP BREATH
HI. UM...I'M ROSE...

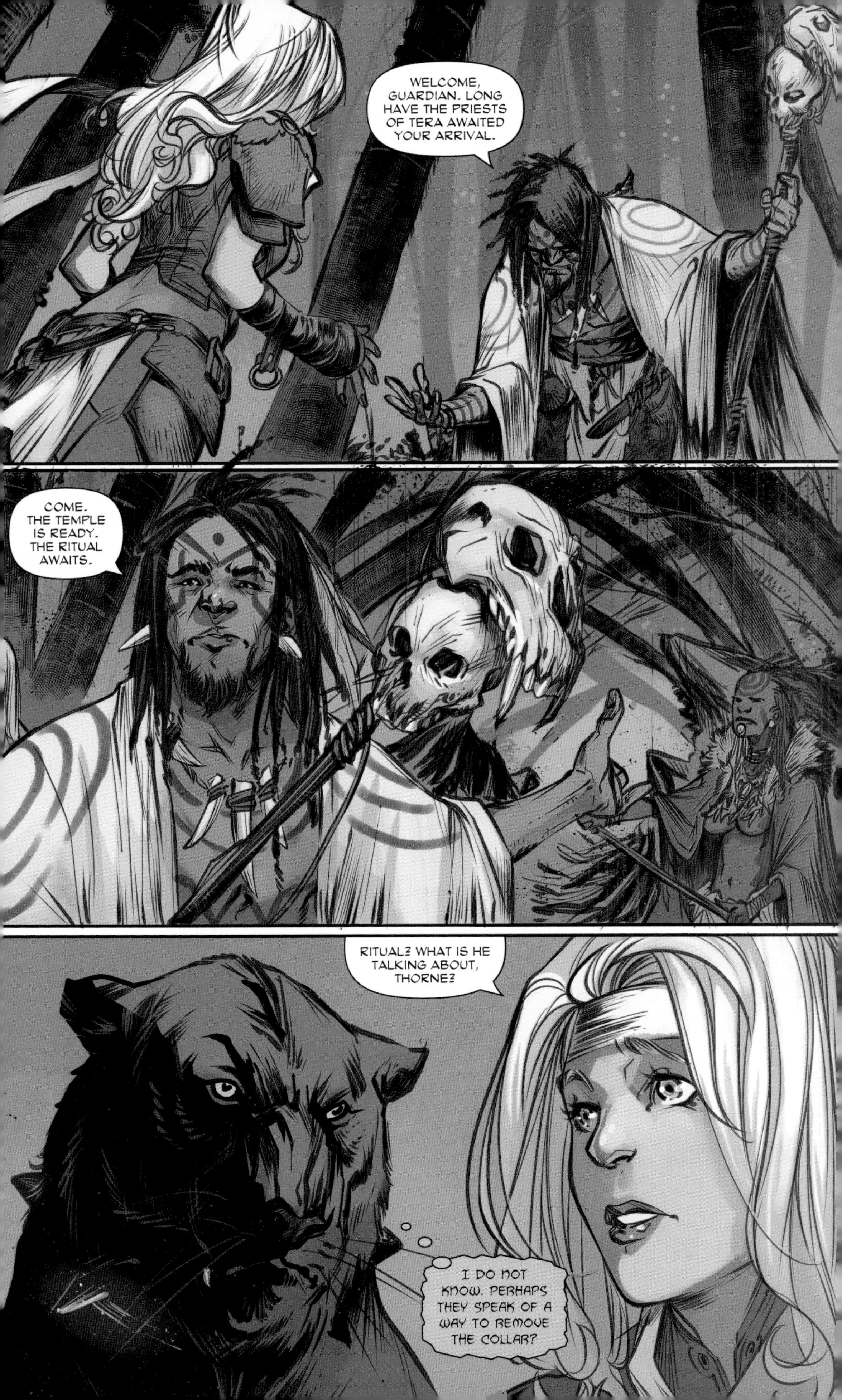
WELCOME, GUARDIAN. LONG HAVE THE PRIESTS OF TERA AWAITED YOUR ARRIVAL.
COME. THE TEMPLE IS READY. THE RITUAL AWAITS.
RITUAL? WHAT IS HE TALKING ABOUT, THORNE?
I DO NOT KNOW. PERHAPS THEY SPEAK OF A WAY TO REMOVE THE COLLAR?

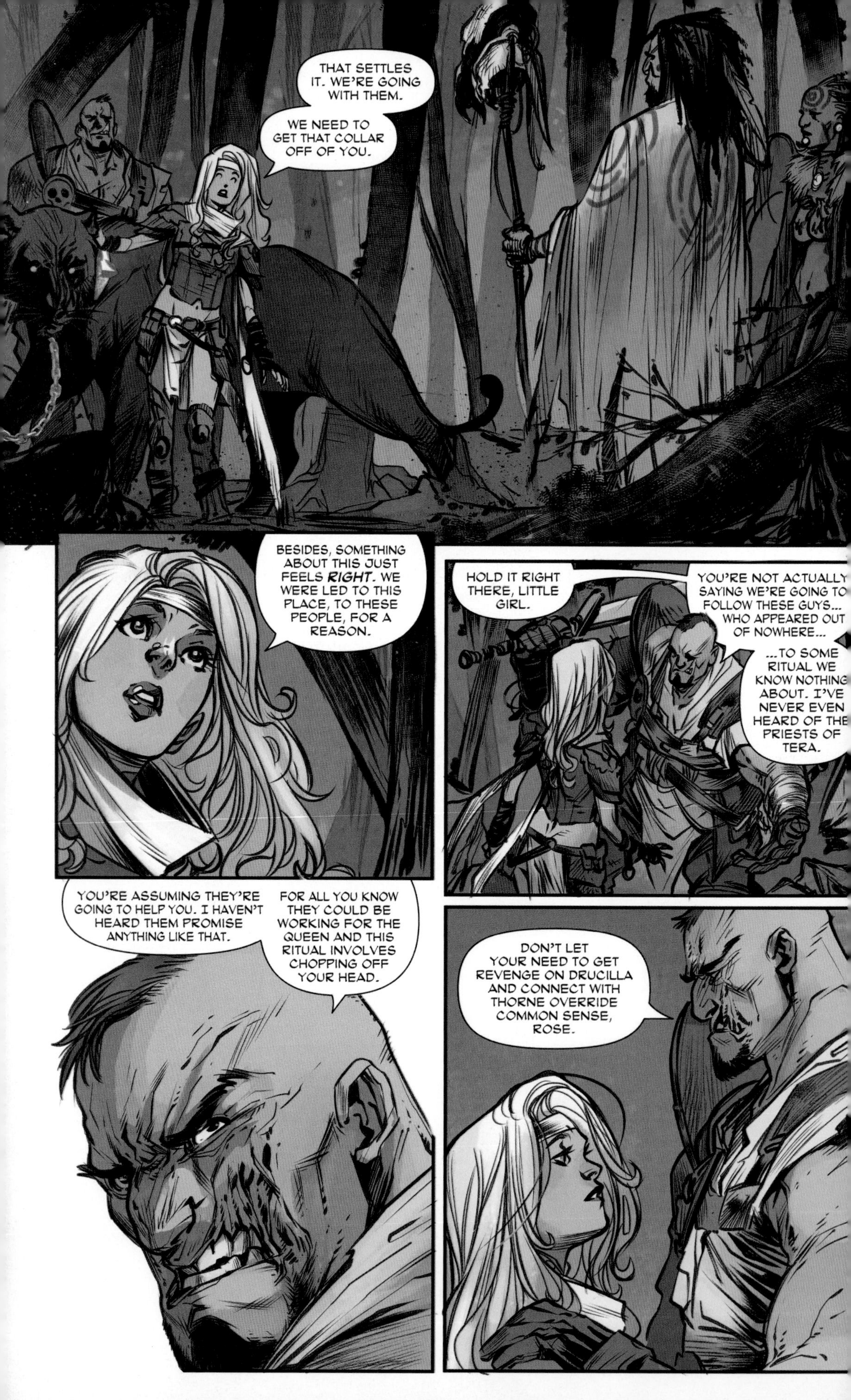

THAT SETTLES IT. WE'RE GOING WITH THEM.
WE NEED TO GET THAT COLLAR OFF OF YOU.
BESIDES, SOMETHING ABOUT THIS JUST FEELS ***RIGHT***. WE WERE LED TO THIS PLACE, TO THESE PEOPLE, FOR A REASON.
HOLD IT RIGHT THERE, LITTLE GIRL.
YOU'RE NOT ACTUALLY SAYING WE'RE GOING TO FOLLOW THESE GUYS... WHO APPEARED OUT OF NOWHERE...
...TO SOME RITUAL WE KNOW NOTHING ABOUT. I'VE NEVER EVEN HEARD OF THE PRIESTS OF TERA.
YOU'RE ASSUMING THEY'RE GOING TO HELP YOU. I HAVEN'T HEARD THEM PROMISE ANYTHING LIKE THAT.
FOR ALL YOU KNOW THEY COULD BE WORKING FOR THE QUEEN AND THIS RITUAL INVOLVES CHOPPING OFF YOUR HEAD.
DON'T LET YOUR NEED TO GET REVENGE ON DRUCILLA AND CONNECT WITH THORNE OVERRIDE COMMON SENSE, ROSE.

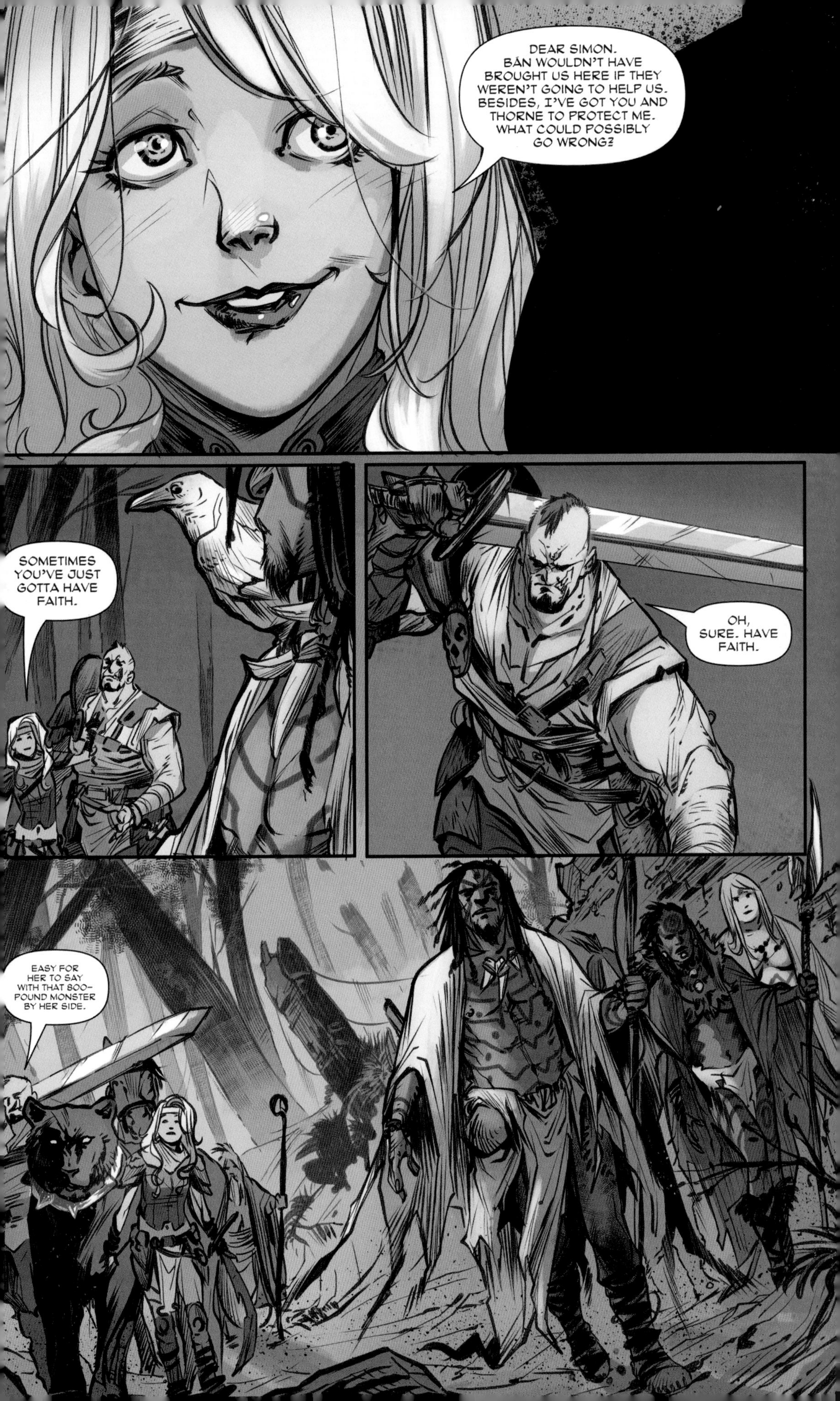
DEAR SIMON. BÁN WOULDN'T HAVE BROUGHT US HERE IF THEY WEREN'T GOING TO HELP US. BESIDES, I'VE GOT YOU AND THORNE TO PROTECT ME. WHAT COULD POSSIBLY GO WRONG?
SOMETIMES YOU'VE JUST GOTTA HAVE FAITH.
OH, SURE. HAVE FAITH.
EASY FOR HER TO SAY WITH THAT 800-POUND MONSTER BY HER SIDE.

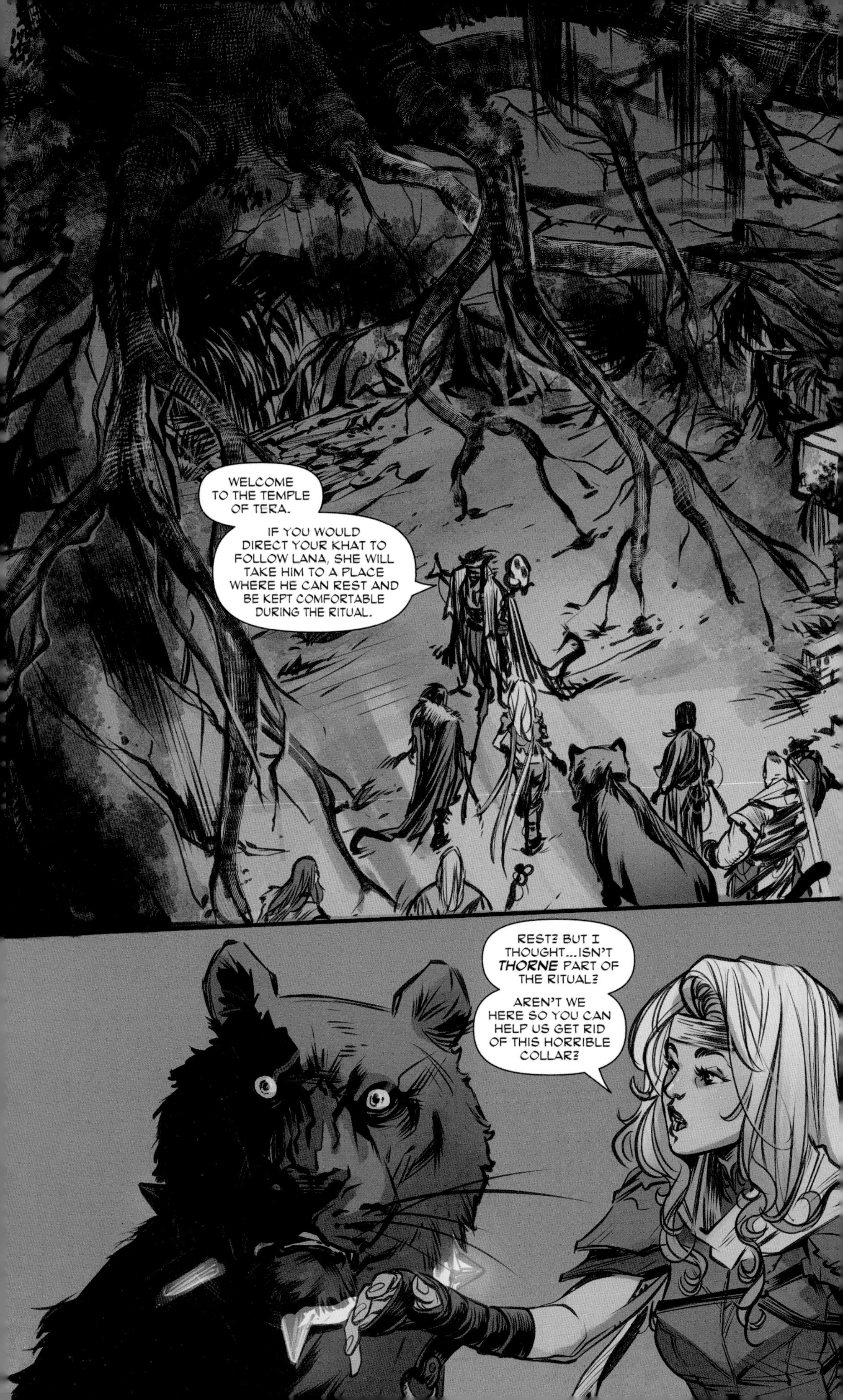
WELCOME TO THE TEMPLE OF TERA.
IF YOU WOULD DIRECT YOUR KHAT TO FOLLOW LANA, SHE WILL TAKE HIM TO A PLACE WHERE HE CAN REST AND BE KEPT COMFORTABLE DURING THE RITUAL.
REST? BUT I THOUGHT...ISN'T *THORNE* PART OF THE RITUAL?
AREN'T WE HERE SO YOU CAN HELP US GET RID OF THIS HORRIBLE COLLAR?

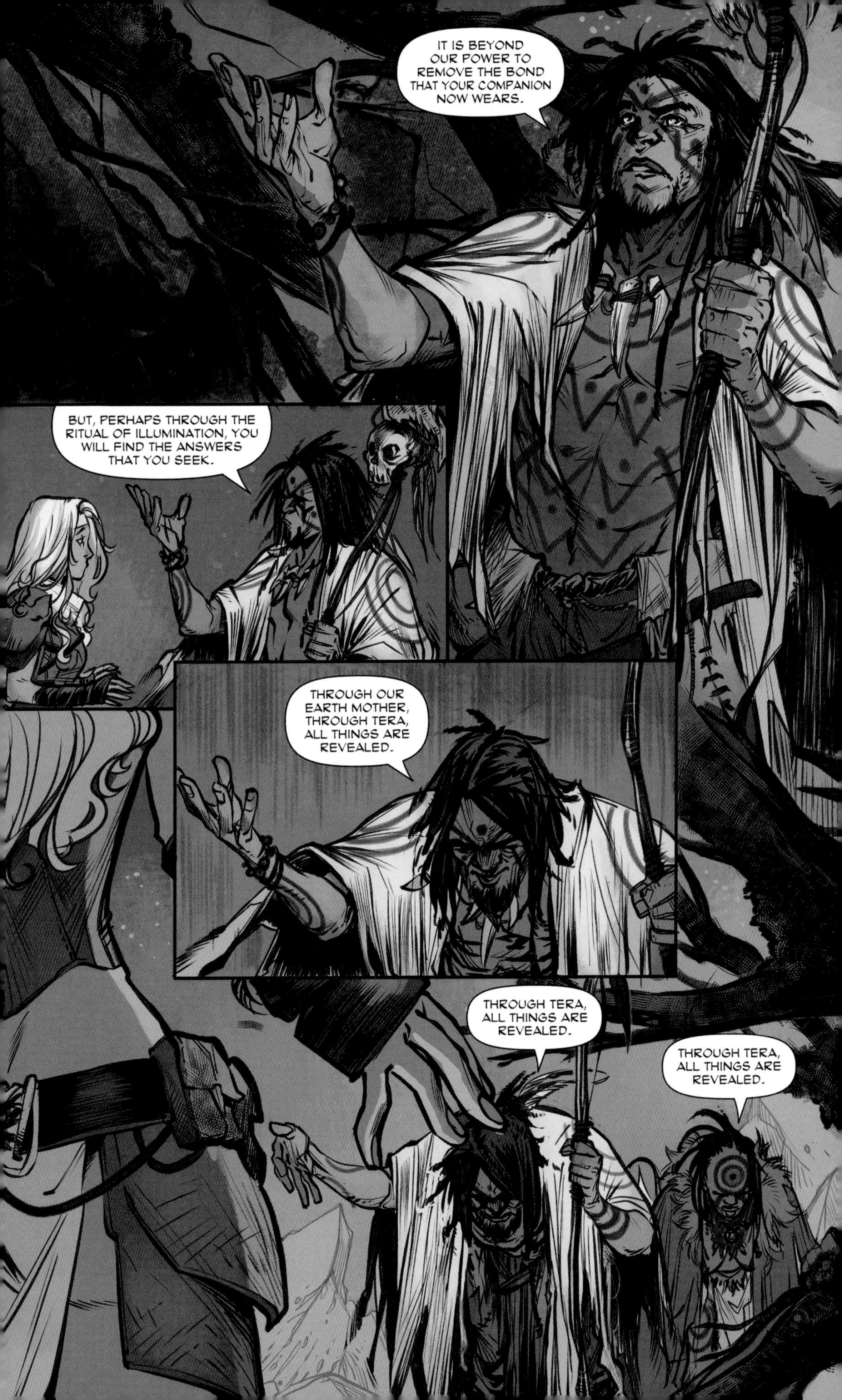
IT IS BEYOND OUR POWER TO REMOVE THE BOND THAT YOUR COMPANION NOW WEARS.
BUT, PERHAPS THROUGH THE RITUAL OF ILLUMINATION, YOU WILL FIND THE ANSWERS THAT YOU SEEK.
THROUGH OUR EARTH MOTHER, THROUGH TERA, ALL THINGS ARE REVEALED.
THROUGH TERA, ALL THINGS ARE REVEALED.
THROUGH TERA, ALL THINGS ARE REVEALED.

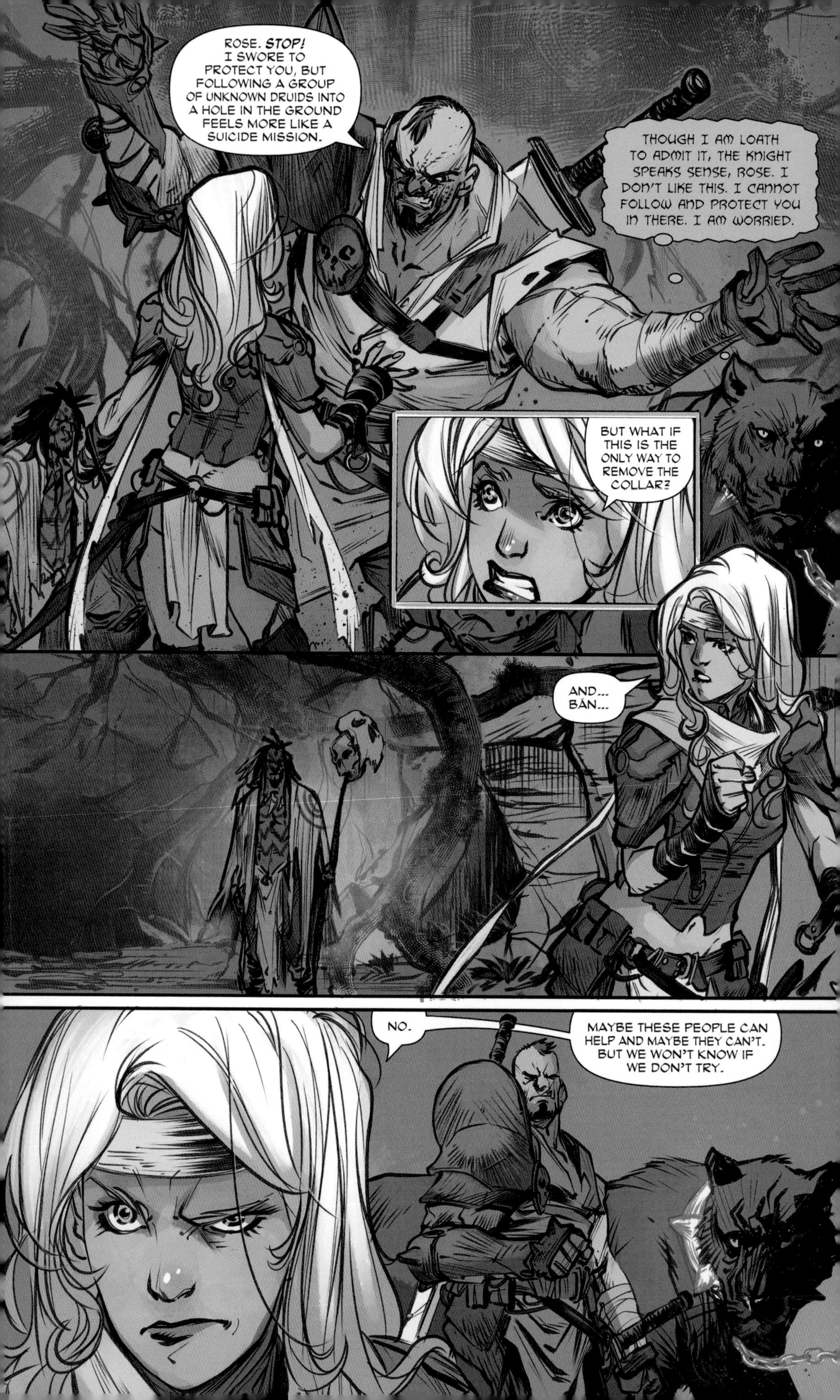
ROSE. STOP! I SWORE TO PROTECT YOU, BUT FOLLOWING A GROUP OF UNKNOWN DRUIDS INTO A HOLE IN THE GROUND FEELS MORE LIKE A SUICIDE MISSION.
THOUGH I AM LOATH TO ADMIT IT, THE KNIGHT SPEAKS SENSE, ROSE. I DON'T LIKE THIS. I CANNOT FOLLOW AND PROTECT YOU IN THERE. I AM WORRIED.
BUT WHAT IF THIS IS THE ONLY WAY TO REMOVE THE COLLAR?
AND... BÁN...
NO.
MAYBE THESE PEOPLE CAN HELP AND MAYBE THEY CAN'T. BUT WE WON'T KNOW IF WE DON'T TRY.

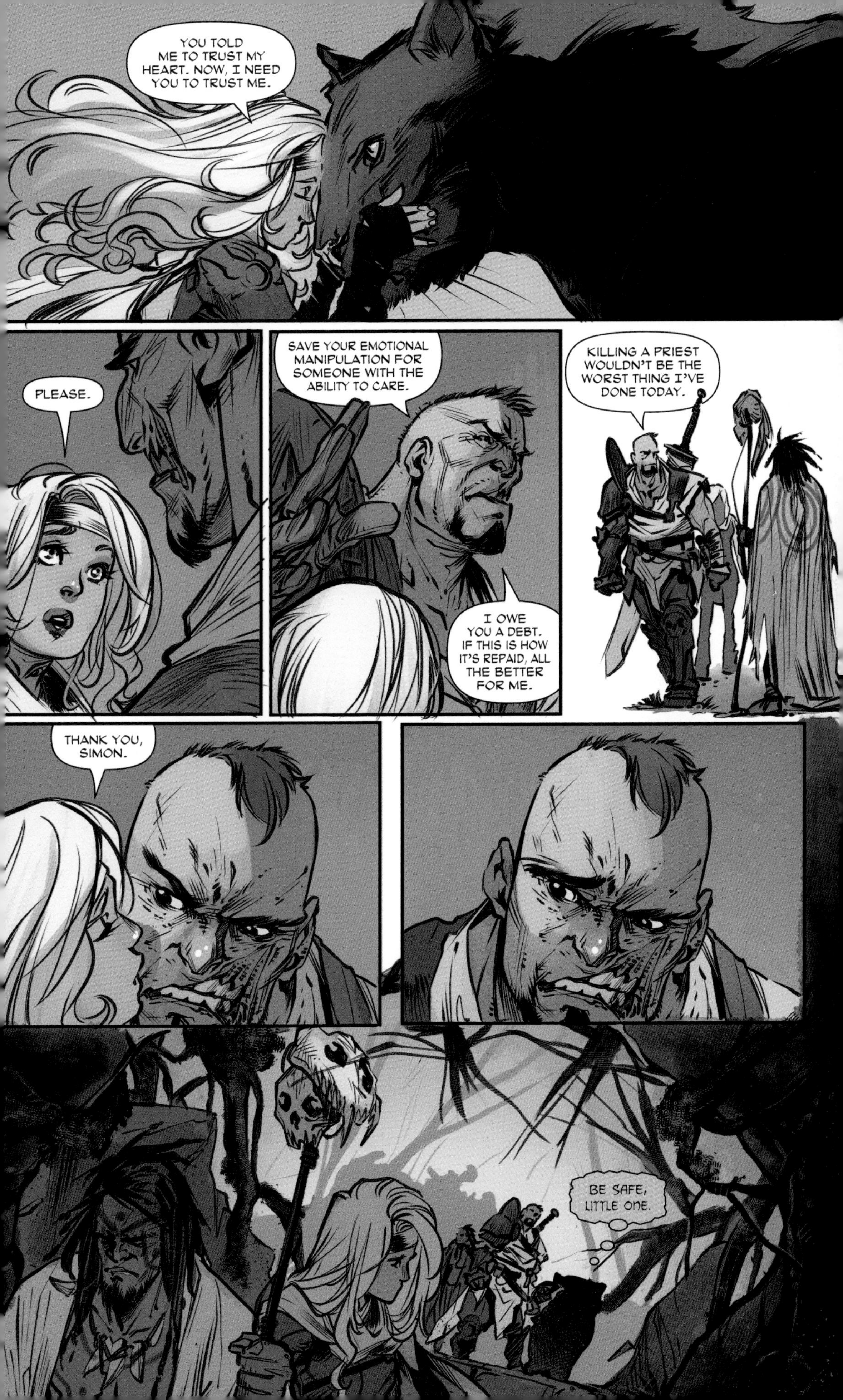
YOU TOLD ME TO TRUST MY HEART. NOW, I NEED YOU TO TRUST ME.
PLEASE.
SAVE YOUR EMOTIONAL MANIPULATION FOR SOMEONE WITH THE ABILITY TO CARE.
I OWE YOU A DEBT. IF THIS IS HOW IT'S REPAID, ALL THE BETTER FOR ME.
KILLING A PRIEST WOULDN'T BE THE WORST THING I'VE DONE TODAY.
THANK YOU, SIMON.
BE SAFE, LITTLE ONE.

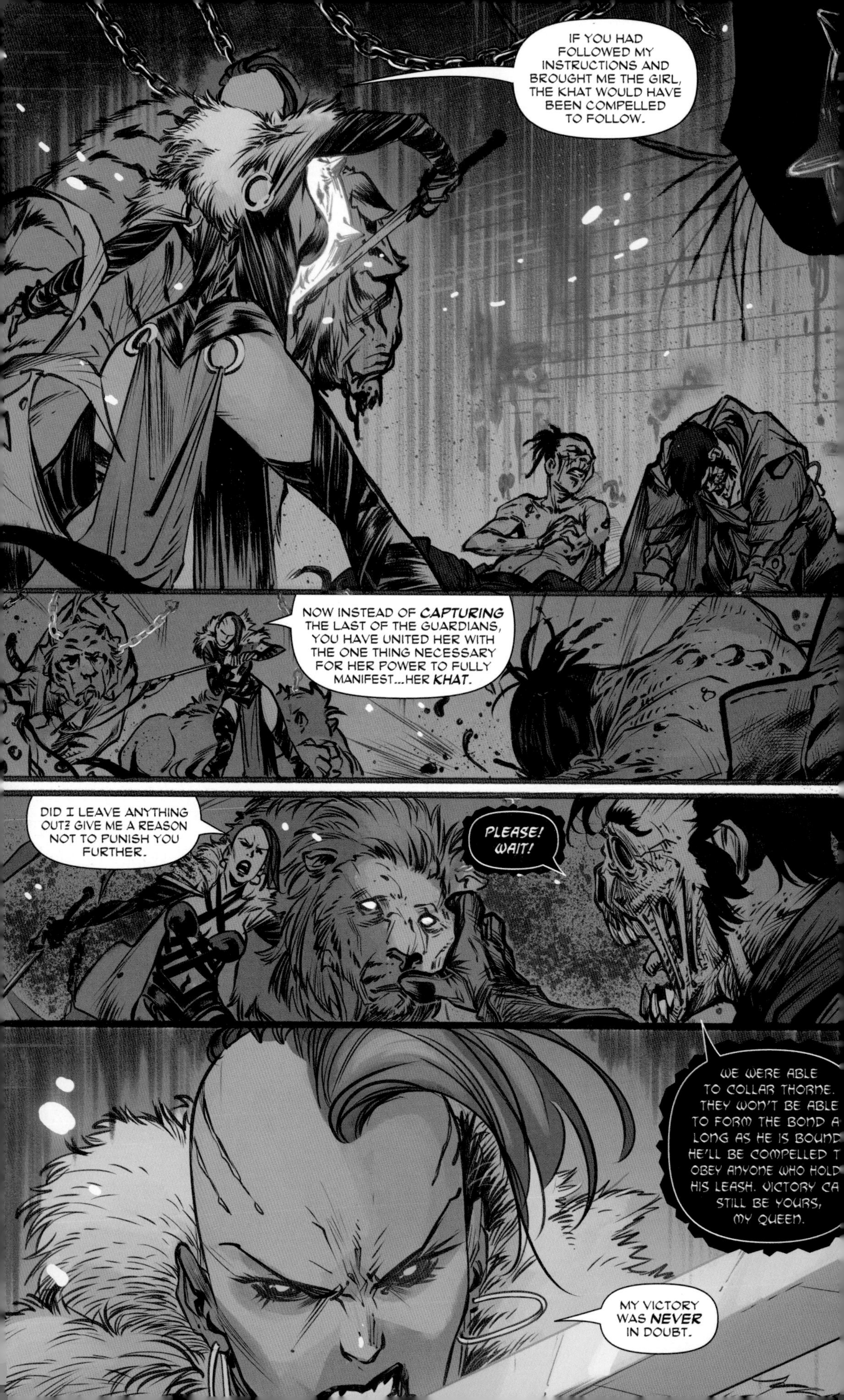

IF YOU HAD FOLLOWED MY INSTRUCTIONS AND BROUGHT ME THE GIRL, THE KHAT WOULD HAVE BEEN COMPELLED TO FOLLOW.
NOW INSTEAD OF CAPTURING THE LAST OF THE GUARDIANS, YOU HAVE UNITED HER WITH THE ONE THING NECESSARY FOR HER POWER TO FULLY MANIFEST...HER KHAT.
DID I LEAVE ANYTHING OUT? GIVE ME A REASON NOT TO PUNISH YOU FURTHER.
PLEASE! WAIT!
WE WERE ABLE TO COLLAR THORNE. THEY WON'T BE ABLE TO FORM THE BOND A LONG AS HE IS BOUND HE'LL BE COMPELLED T OBEY ANYONE WHO HOLD HIS LEASH. VICTORY CA STILL BE YOURS, MY QUEEN.
MY VICTORY WAS NEVER IN DOUBT.

NINE

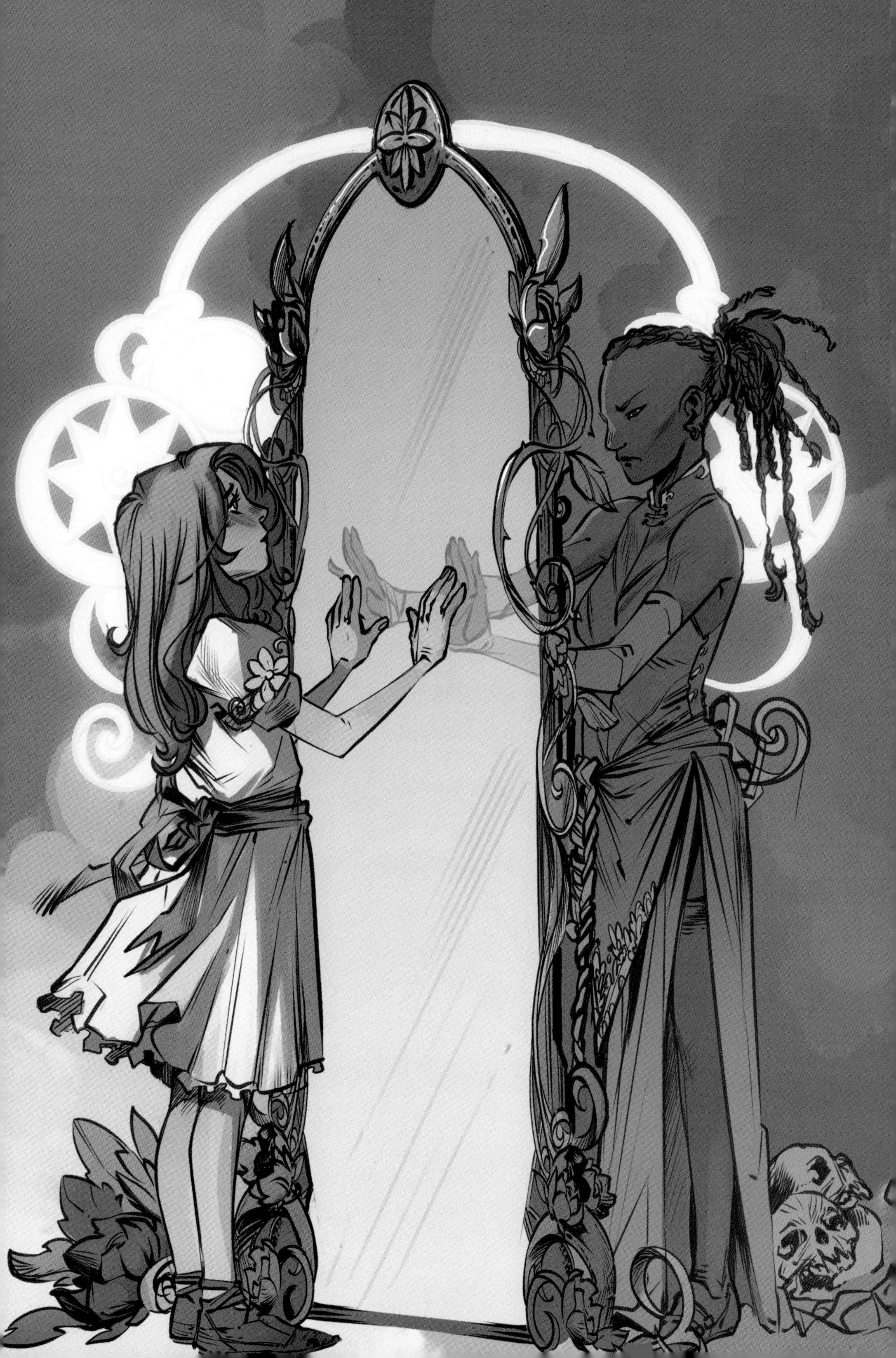

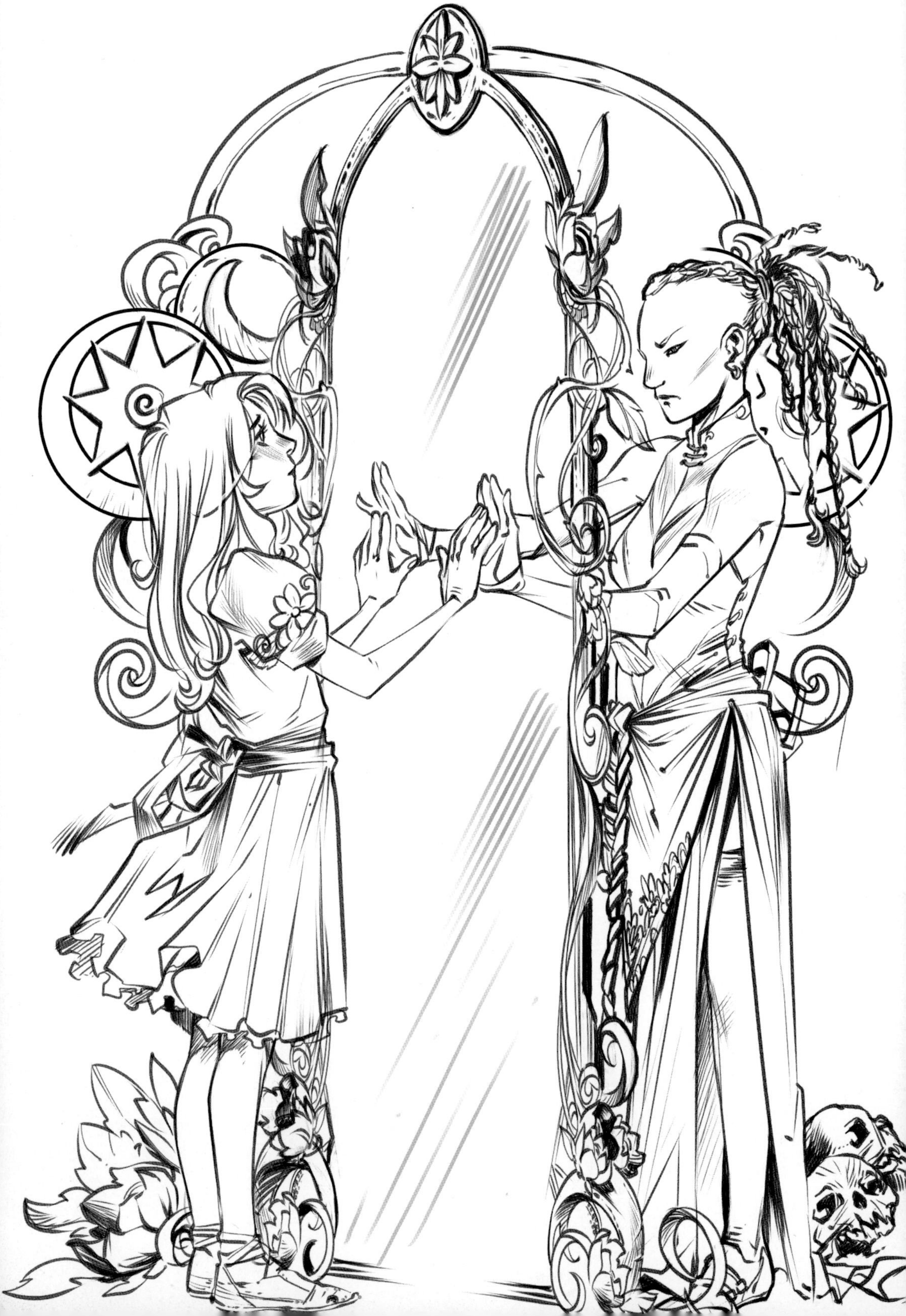

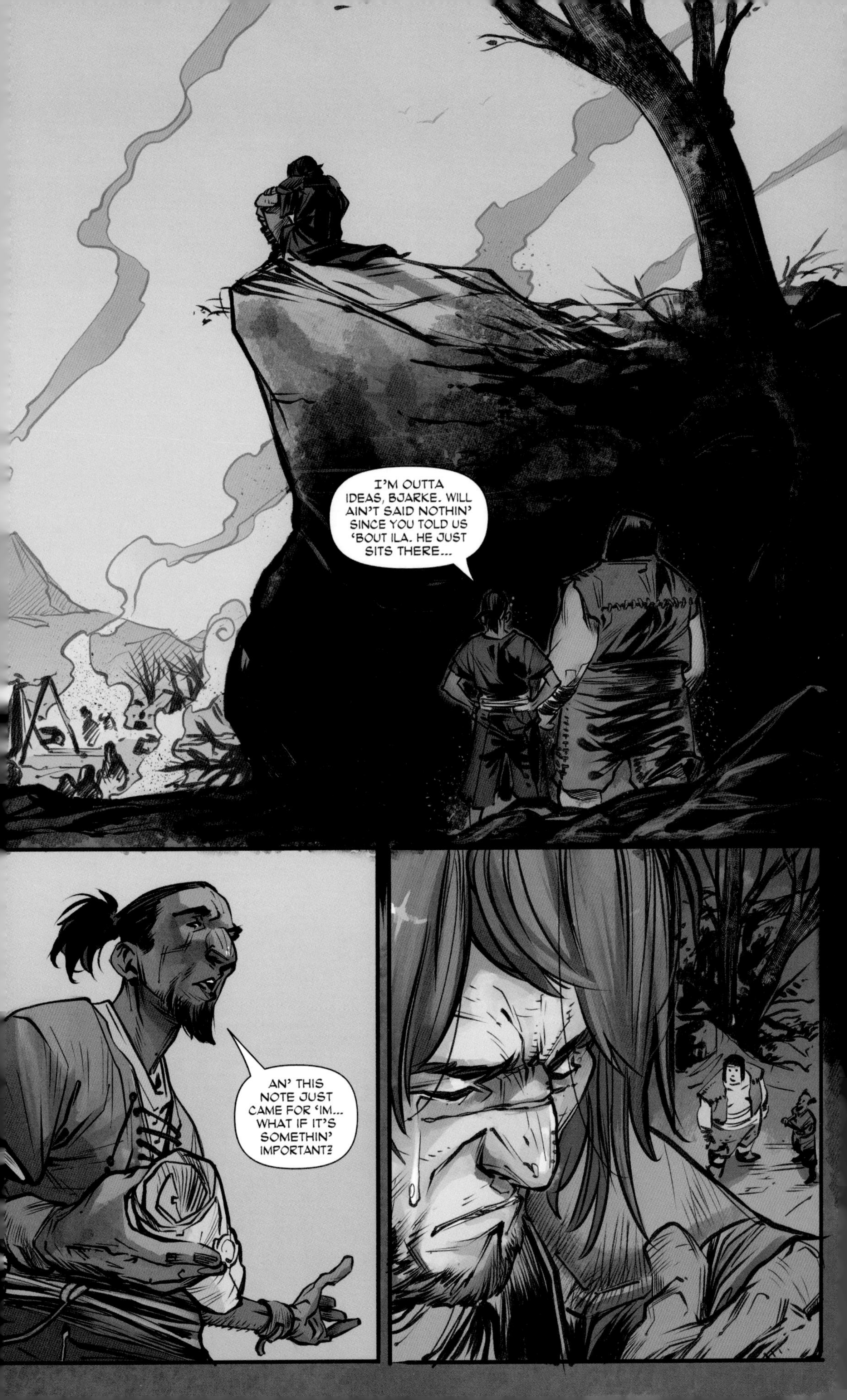
I'M OUTTA IDEAS, BJARKE. WILL AIN'T SAID NOTHIN' SINCE YOU TOLD US 'BOUT ILA. HE JUST SITS THERE...
AN' THIS NOTE JUST CAME FOR 'IM... WHAT IF IT'S SOMETHIN' IMPORTANT?

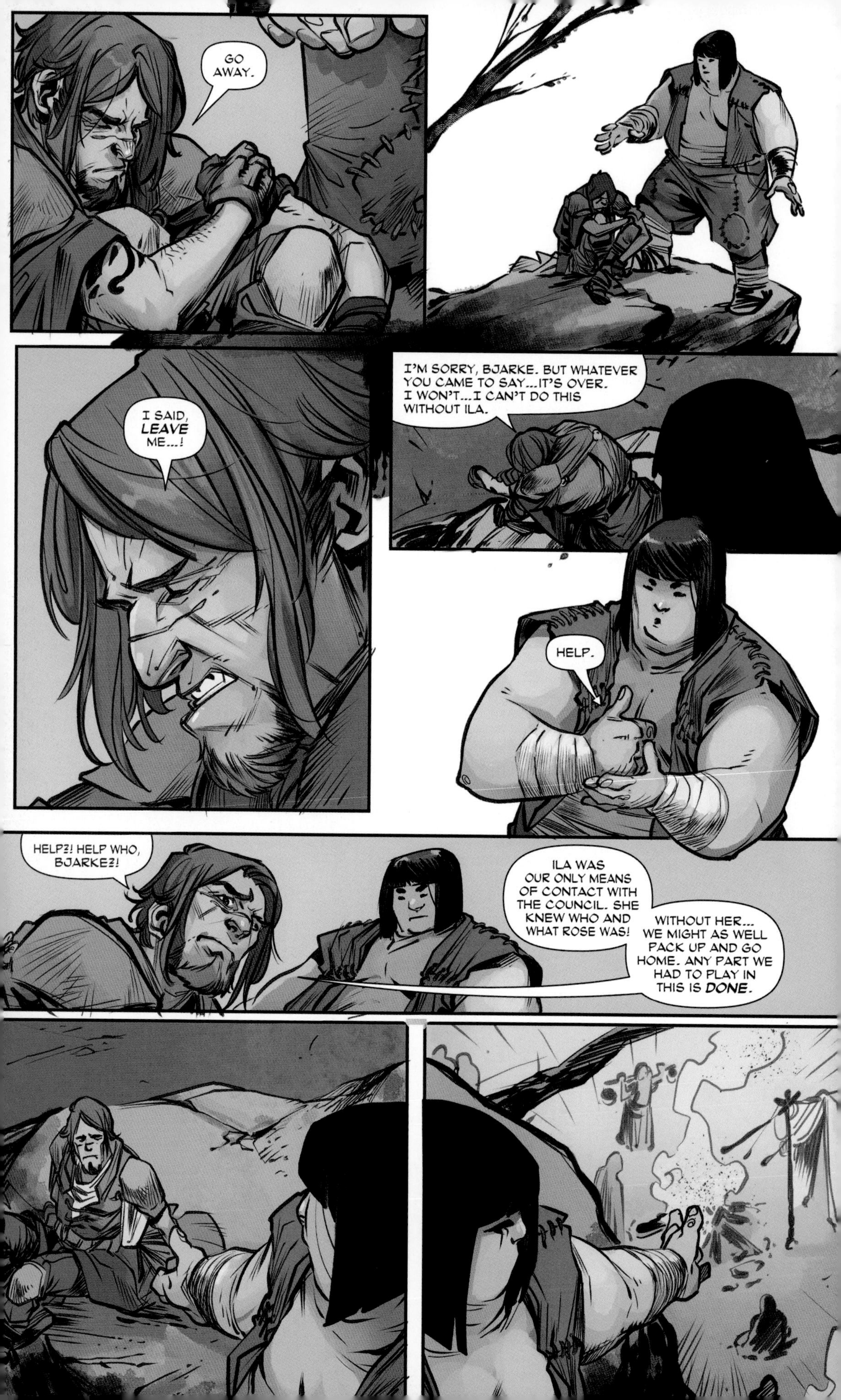
GO AWAY.
I SAID, LEAVE ME...!
I'M SORRY, BJARKE. BUT WHATEVER YOU CAME TO SAY...IT'S OVER. I WON'T...I CAN'T DO THIS WITHOUT ILA.
HELP.
HELP?! HELP WHO, BJARKE?!
ILA WAS OUR ONLY MEANS OF CONTACT WITH THE COUNCIL. SHE KNEW WHO AND WHAT ROSE WAS!
WITHOUT HER... WE MIGHT AS WELL PACK UP AND GO HOME. ANY PART WE HAD TO PLAY IN THIS IS DONE.

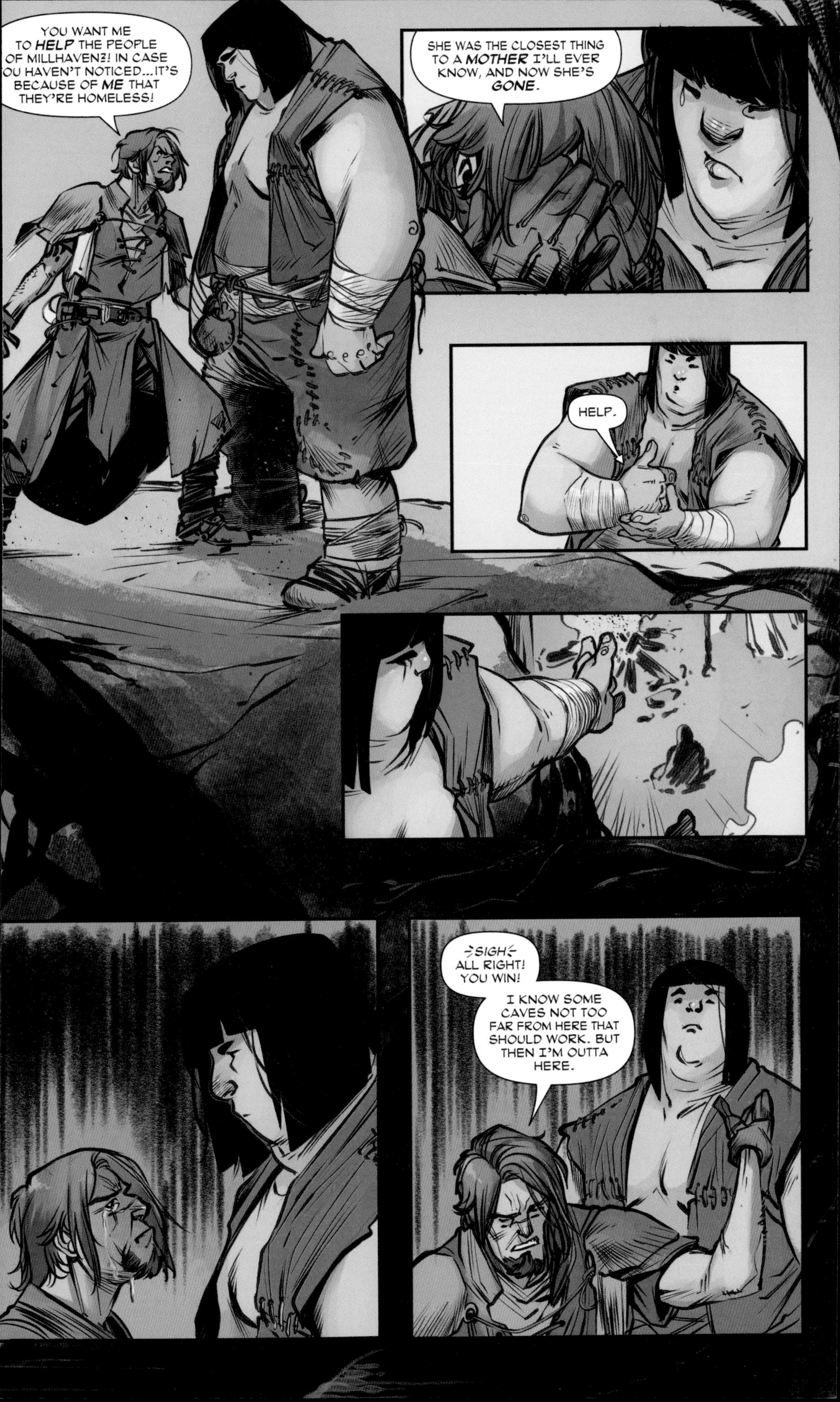
YOU WANT ME TO HELP THE PEOPLE OF MILLHAVEN?! IN CASE YOU HAVEN'T NOTICED...IT'S BECAUSE OF ME THAT THEY'RE HOMELESS!
SHE WAS THE CLOSEST THING TO A MOTHER I'LL EVER KNOW, AND NOW SHE'S GONE.
HELP.
SIGH
ALL RIGHT! YOU WIN!
I KNOW SOME CAVES NOT TOO FAR FROM HERE THAT SHOULD WORK. BUT THEN I'M OUTTA HERE.

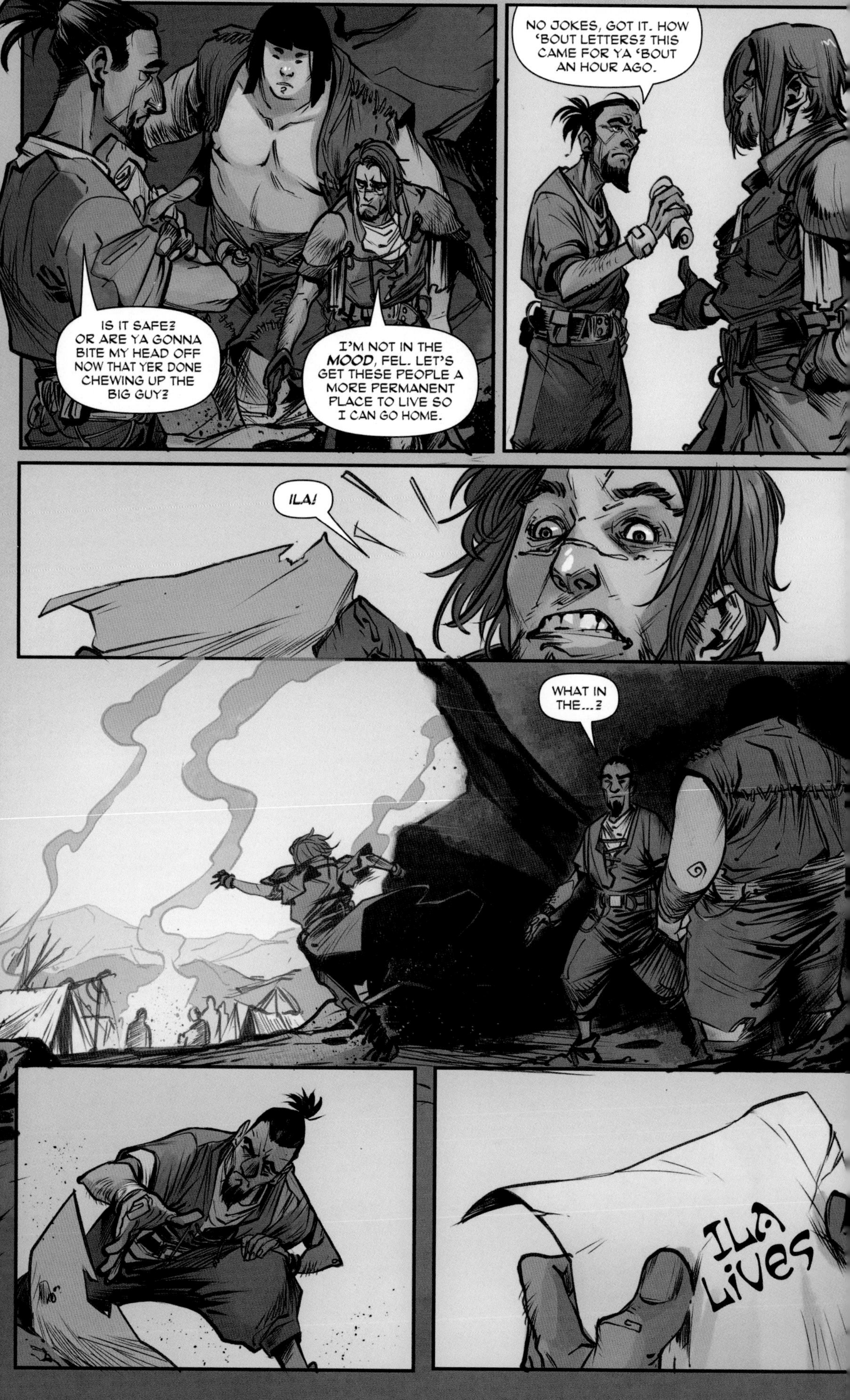
IS IT SAFE? OR ARE YA GONNA BITE MY HEAD OFF NOW THAT YER DONE CHEWING UP THE BIG GUY?
I'M NOT IN THE *MOOD*, FEL. LET'S GET THESE PEOPLE A MORE PERMANENT PLACE TO LIVE SO I CAN GO HOME.
NO JOKES, GOT IT. HOW 'BOUT LETTERS? THIS CAME FOR YA 'BOUT AN HOUR AGO.
ILA!
WHAT IN THE...?
ILA LIVES

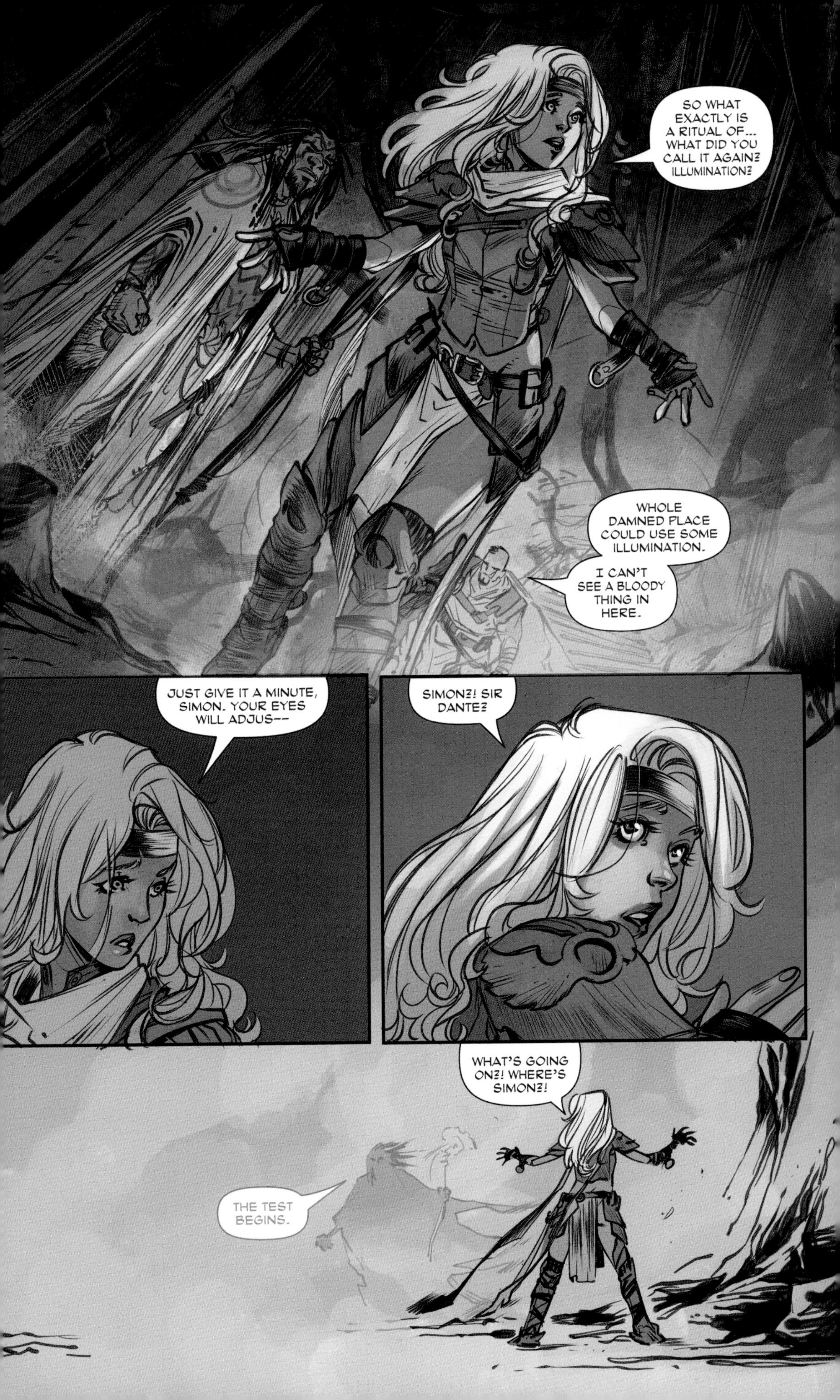
SO WHAT EXACTLY IS A RITUAL OF... WHAT DID YOU CALL IT AGAIN? ILLUMINATION?
WHOLE DAMNED PLACE COULD USE SOME ILLUMINATION.
I CAN'T SEE A BLOODY THING IN HERE.
JUST GIVE IT A MINUTE, SIMON. YOUR EYES WILL ADJUS--
SIMON?! SIR DANTE?
WHAT'S GOING ON?! WHERE'S SIMON?!
THE TEST BEGINS.

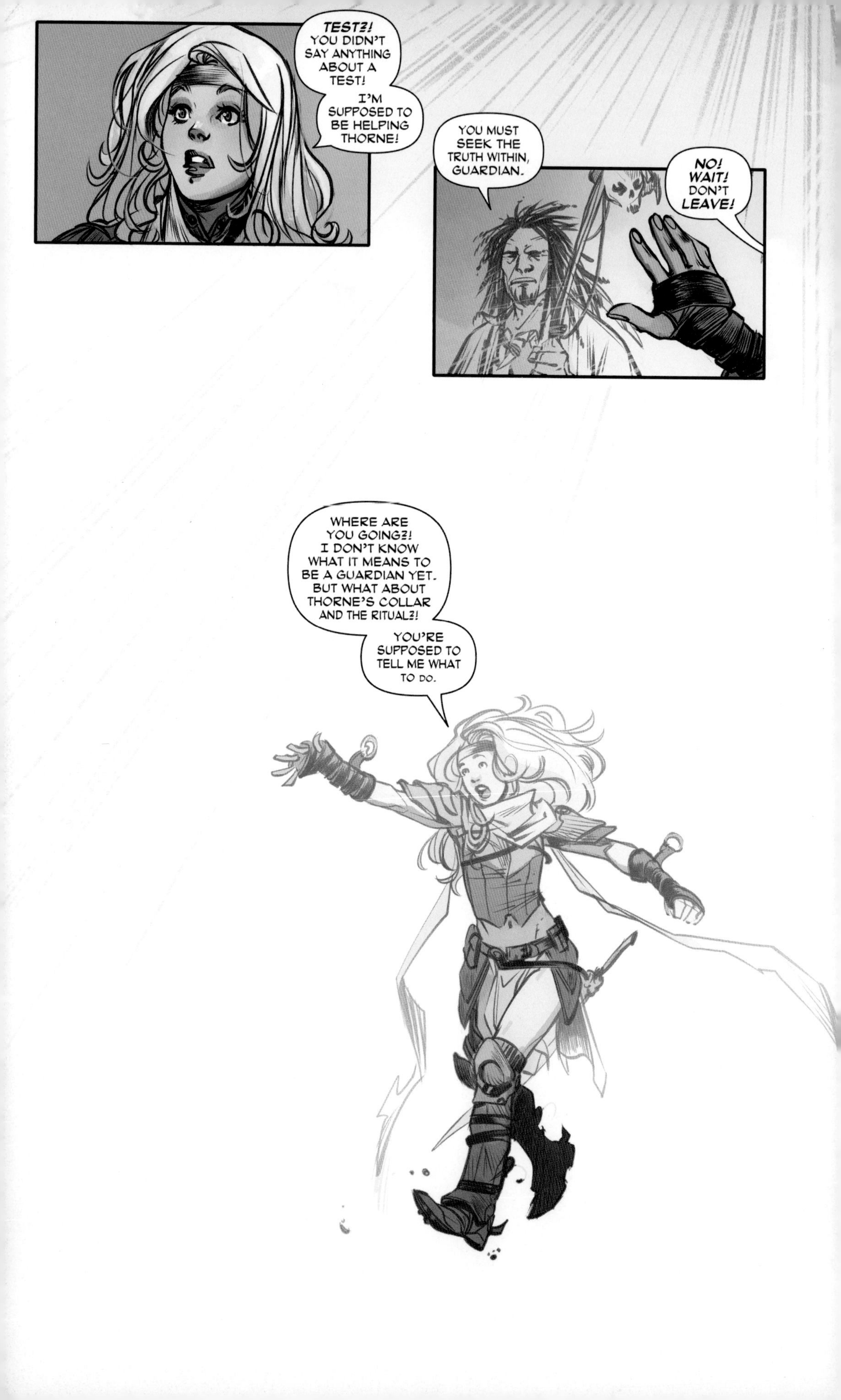

TEST?! YOU DIDN'T SAY ANYTHING ABOUT A TEST!
I'M SUPPOSED TO BE HELPING THORNE!
YOU MUST SEEK THE TRUTH WITHIN, GUARDIAN.
NO! WAIT! DON'T LEAVE!
WHERE ARE YOU GOING?! I DON'T KNOW WHAT IT MEANS TO BE A GUARDIAN YET. BUT WHAT ABOUT THORNE'S COLLAR AND THE RITUAL?!
YOU'RE SUPPOSED TO TELL ME WHAT TO DO.

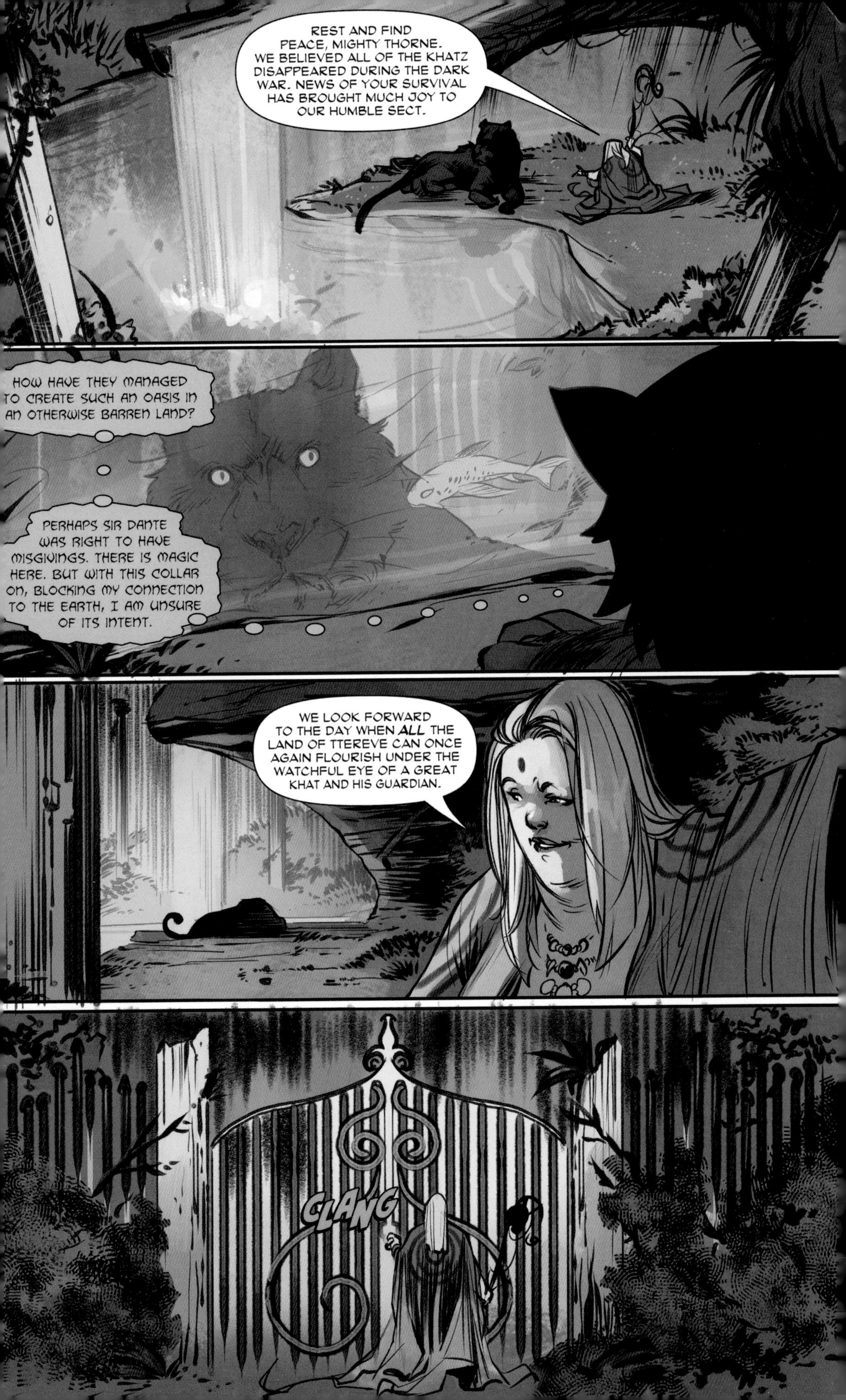
REST AND FIND PEACE, MIGHTY THORNE. WE BELIEVED ALL OF THE KHATZ DISAPPEARED DURING THE DARK WAR. NEWS OF YOUR SURVIVAL HAS BROUGHT MUCH JOY TO OUR HUMBLE SECT.
HOW HAVE THEY MANAGED TO CREATE SUCH AN OASIS IN AN OTHERWISE BARREN LAND?
PERHAPS SIR DANTE WAS RIGHT TO HAVE MISGIVINGS. THERE IS MAGIC HERE. BUT WITH THIS COLLAR ON, BLOCKING MY CONNECTION TO THE EARTH, I AM UNSURE OF ITS INTENT.
WE LOOK FORWARD TO THE DAY WHEN ALL THE LAND OF TTEREVE CAN ONCE AGAIN FLOURISH UNDER THE WATCHFUL EYE OF A GREAT KHAT AND HIS GUARDIAN.
CLANG

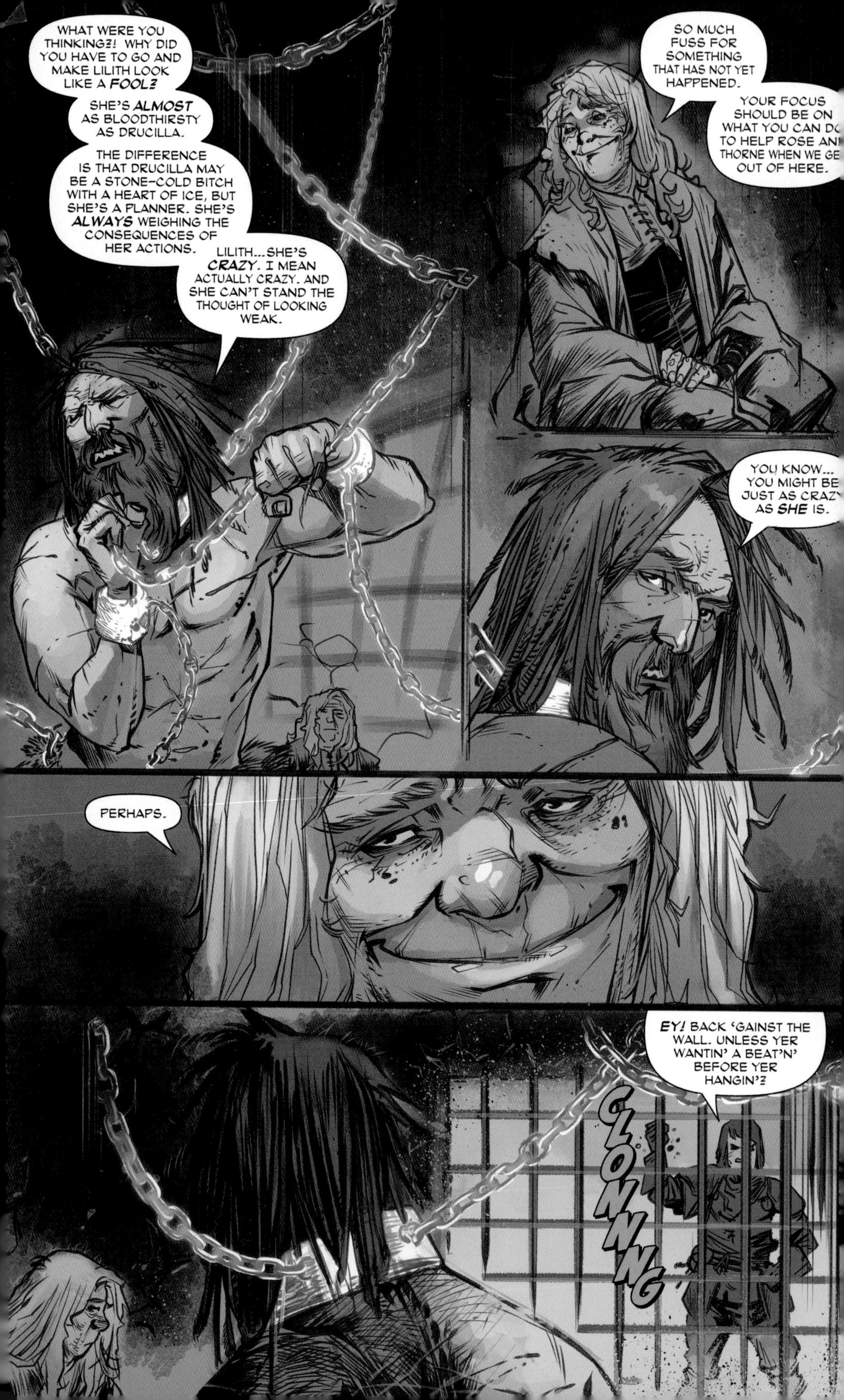
WHAT WERE YOU THINKING?! WHY DID YOU HAVE TO GO AND MAKE LILITH LOOK LIKE A FOOL?
SHE'S ALMOST AS BLOODTHIRSTY AS DRUCILLA.
THE DIFFERENCE IS THAT DRUCILLA MAY BE A STONE-COLD BITCH WITH A HEART OF ICE, BUT SHE'S A PLANNER. SHE'S ALWAYS WEIGHING THE CONSEQUENCES OF HER ACTIONS.
LILITH...SHE'S CRAZY. I MEAN ACTUALLY CRAZY. AND SHE CAN'T STAND THE THOUGHT OF LOOKING WEAK.
SO MUCH FUSS FOR SOMETHING THAT HAS NOT YET HAPPENED.
YOUR FOCUS SHOULD BE ON WHAT YOU CAN DO TO HELP ROSE AND THORNE WHEN WE GET OUT OF HERE.
YOU KNOW... YOU MIGHT BE JUST AS CRAZY AS SHE IS.
PERHAPS.
EY! BACK 'GAINST THE WALL. UNLESS YER WANTIN' A BEAT'N' BEFORE YER HANGIN'?
CLONNNG

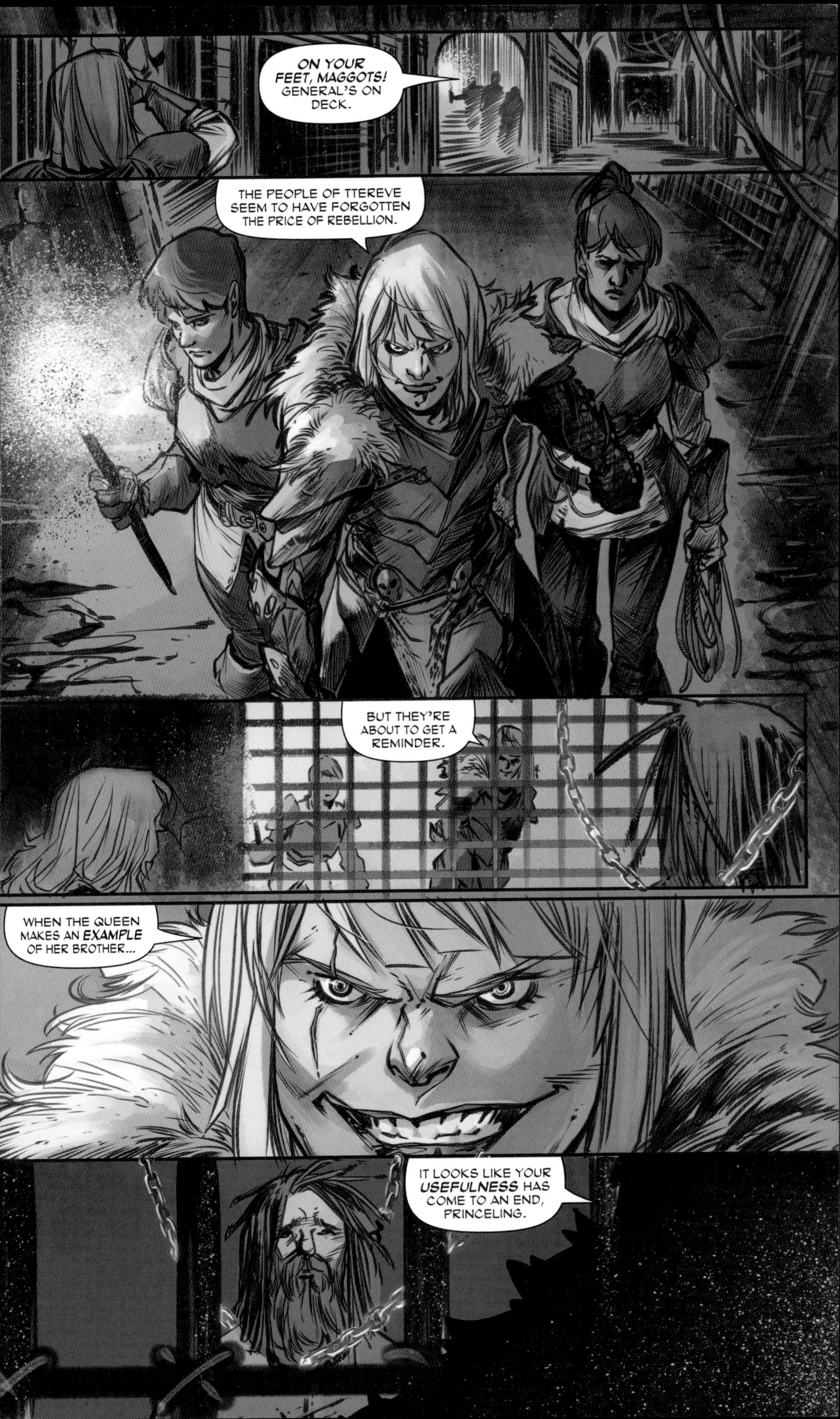
ON YOUR FEET, MAGGOTS! GENERAL'S ON DECK.
THE PEOPLE OF TTEREVE SEEM TO HAVE FORGOTTEN THE PRICE OF REBELLION.
BUT THEY'RE ABOUT TO GET A REMINDER.
WHEN THE QUEEN MAKES AN EXAMPLE OF HER BROTHER...
IT LOOKS LIKE YOUR USEFULNESS HAS COME TO AN END, PRINCELING.

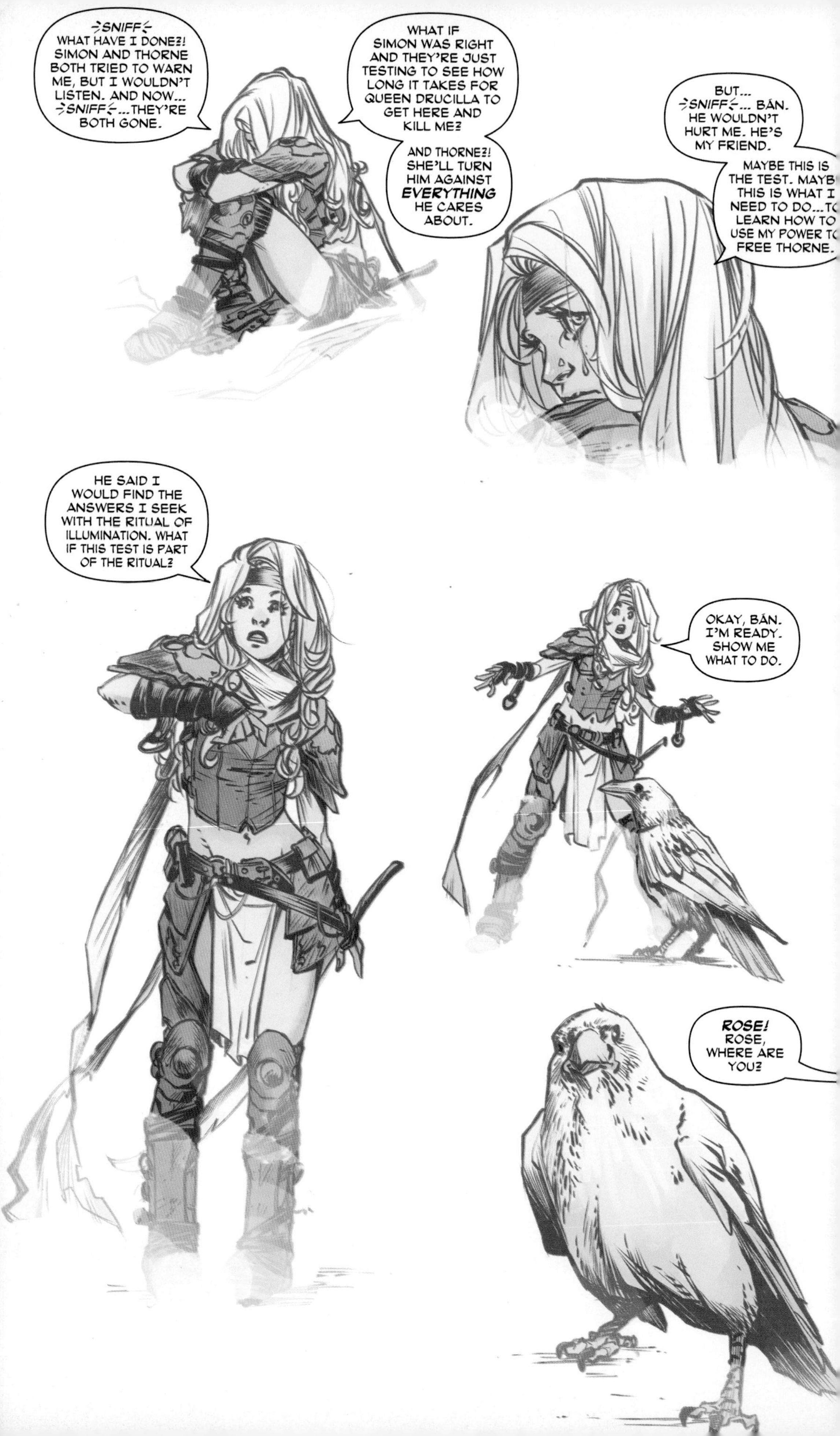

⇒SNIFF⇐ WHAT HAVE I DONE?! SIMON AND THORNE BOTH TRIED TO WARN ME, BUT I WOULDN'T LISTEN. AND NOW... ⇒SNIFF⇐...THEY'RE BOTH GONE.
WHAT IF SIMON WAS RIGHT AND THEY'RE JUST TESTING TO SEE HOW LONG IT TAKES FOR QUEEN DRUCILLA TO GET HERE AND KILL ME?
AND THORNE?! SHE'LL TURN HIM AGAINST *EVERYTHING* HE CARES ABOUT.
BUT... ⇒SNIFF⇐... BÁN. HE WOULDN'T HURT ME. HE'S MY FRIEND.
MAYBE THIS IS THE TEST. MAYB THIS IS WHAT I NEED TO DO...T LEARN HOW TO USE MY POWER T FREE THORNE.
HE SAID I WOULD FIND THE ANSWERS I SEEK WITH THE RITUAL OF ILLUMINATION. WHAT IF THIS TEST IS PART OF THE RITUAL?
OKAY, BÁN. I'M READY. SHOW ME WHAT TO DO.
ROSE! ROSE, WHERE ARE YOU?

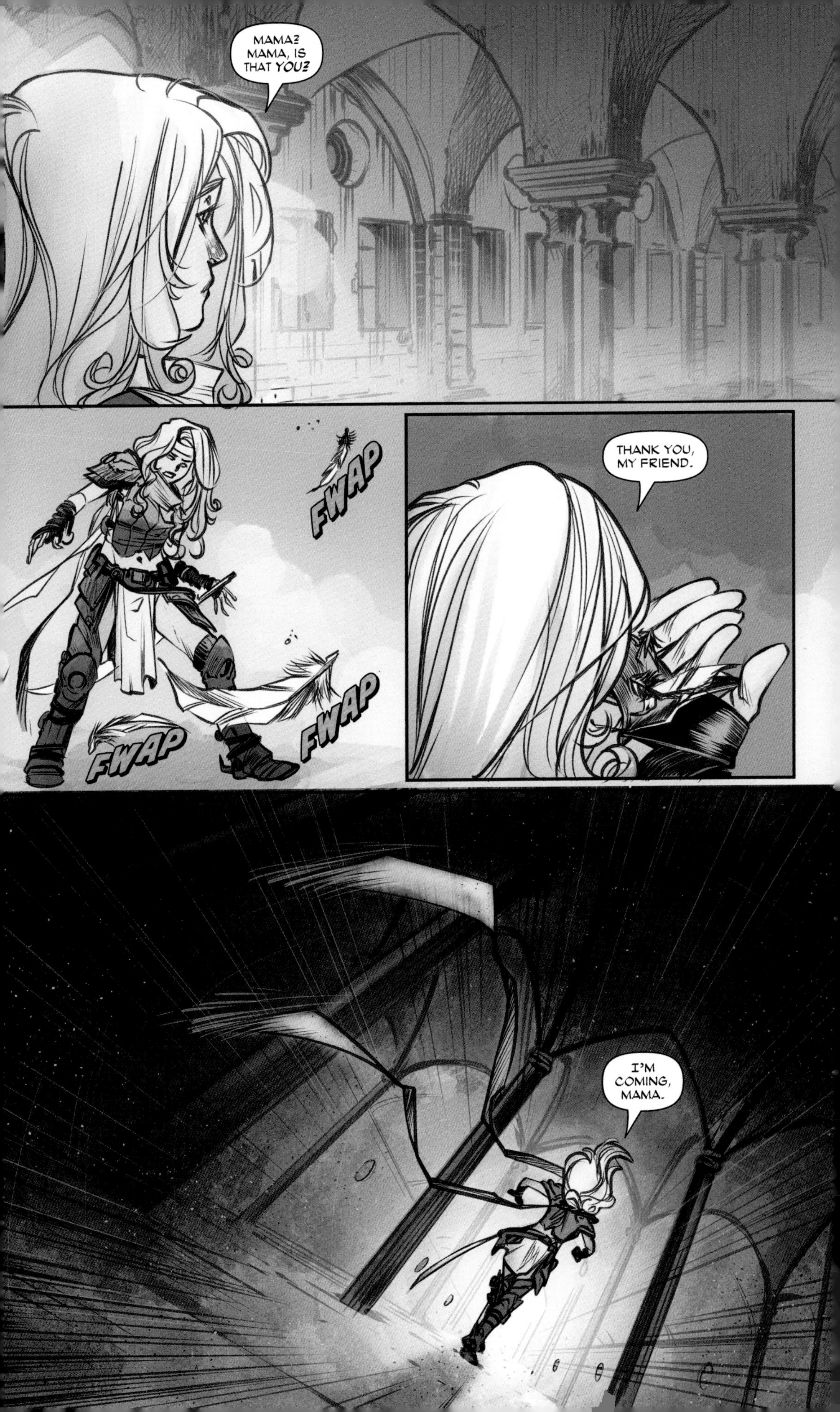
MAMA? MAMA, IS THAT YOU?
FWAP
FWAP
FWAP
THANK YOU, MY FRIEND.
I'M COMING, MAMA.

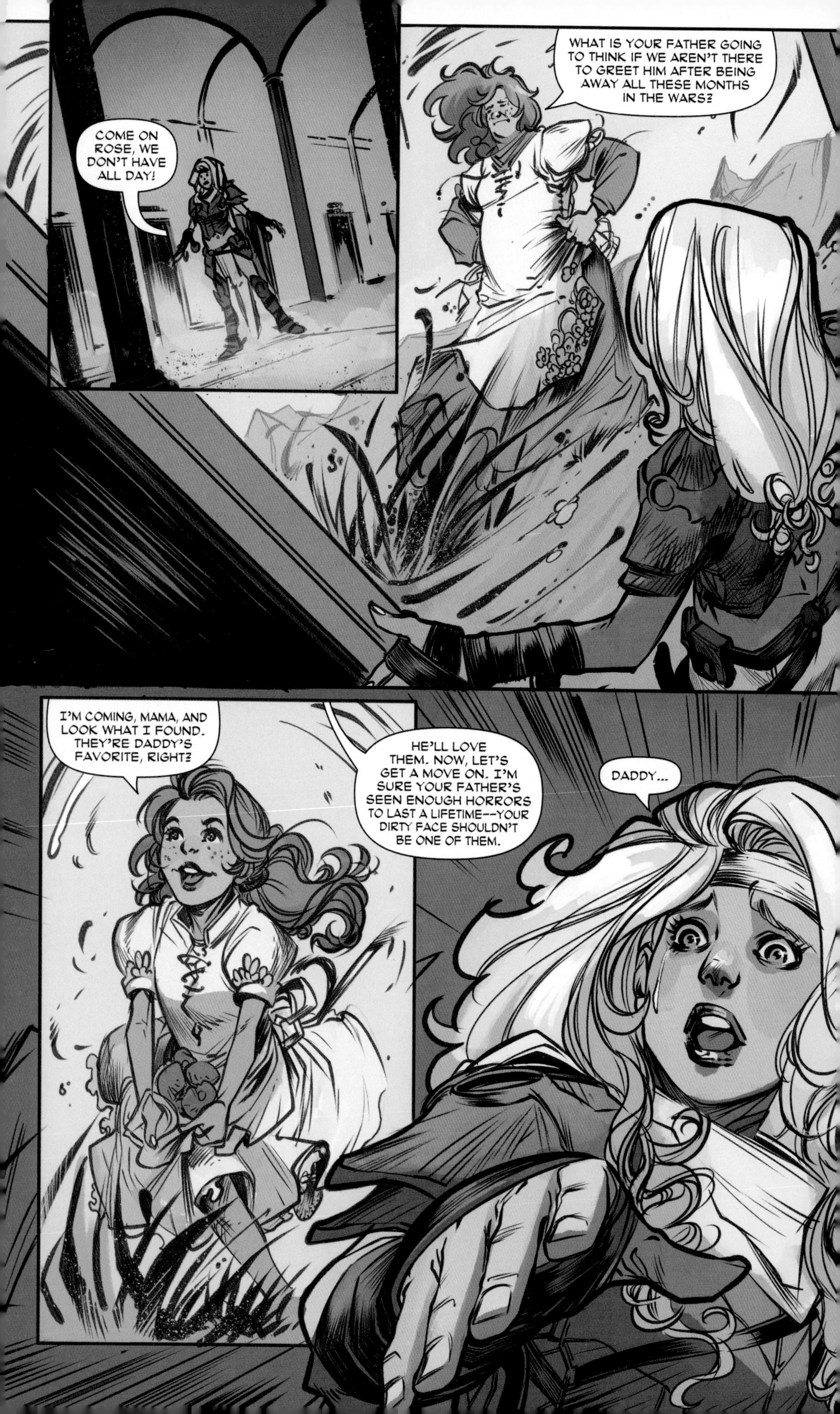
COME ON ROSE, WE DON'T HAVE ALL DAY!
WHAT IS YOUR FATHER GOING TO THINK IF WE AREN'T THERE TO GREET HIM AFTER BEING AWAY ALL THESE MONTHS IN THE WARS?
I'M COMING, MAMA, AND LOOK WHAT I FOUND. THEY'RE DADDY'S FAVORITE, RIGHT?
HE'LL LOVE THEM. NOW, LET'S GET A MOVE ON. I'M SURE YOUR FATHER'S SEEN ENOUGH HORRORS TO LAST A LIFETIME--YOUR DIRTY FACE SHOULDN'T BE ONE OF THEM.
DADDY...

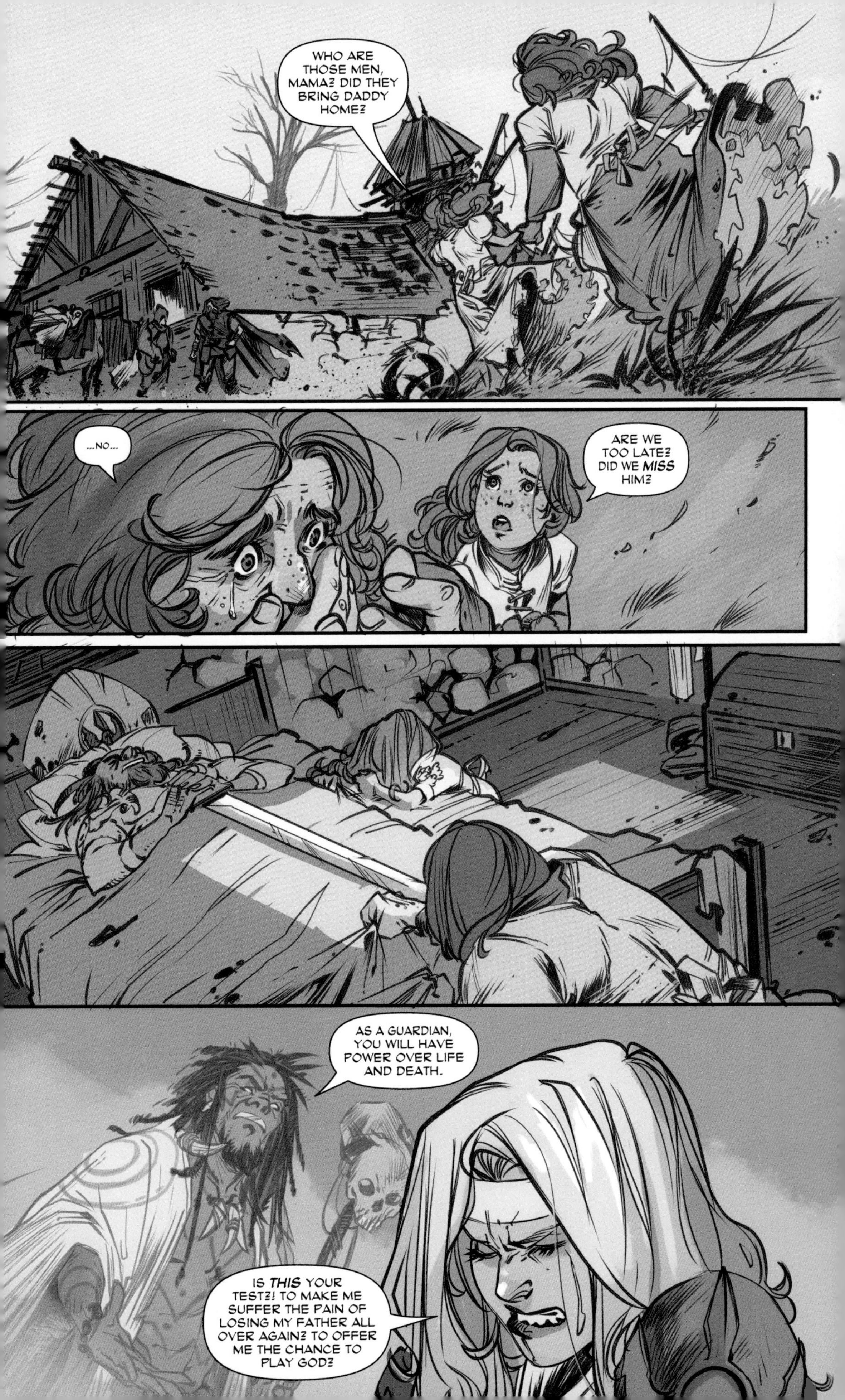
WHO ARE THOSE MEN, MAMA? DID THEY BRING DADDY HOME?
...NO...
ARE WE TOO LATE? DID WE *MISS* HIM?
AS A GUARDIAN, YOU WILL HAVE POWER OVER LIFE AND DEATH.
IS *THIS* YOUR TEST?! TO MAKE ME SUFFER THE PAIN OF LOSING MY FATHER ALL OVER AGAIN? TO OFFER ME THE CHANCE TO PLAY GOD?

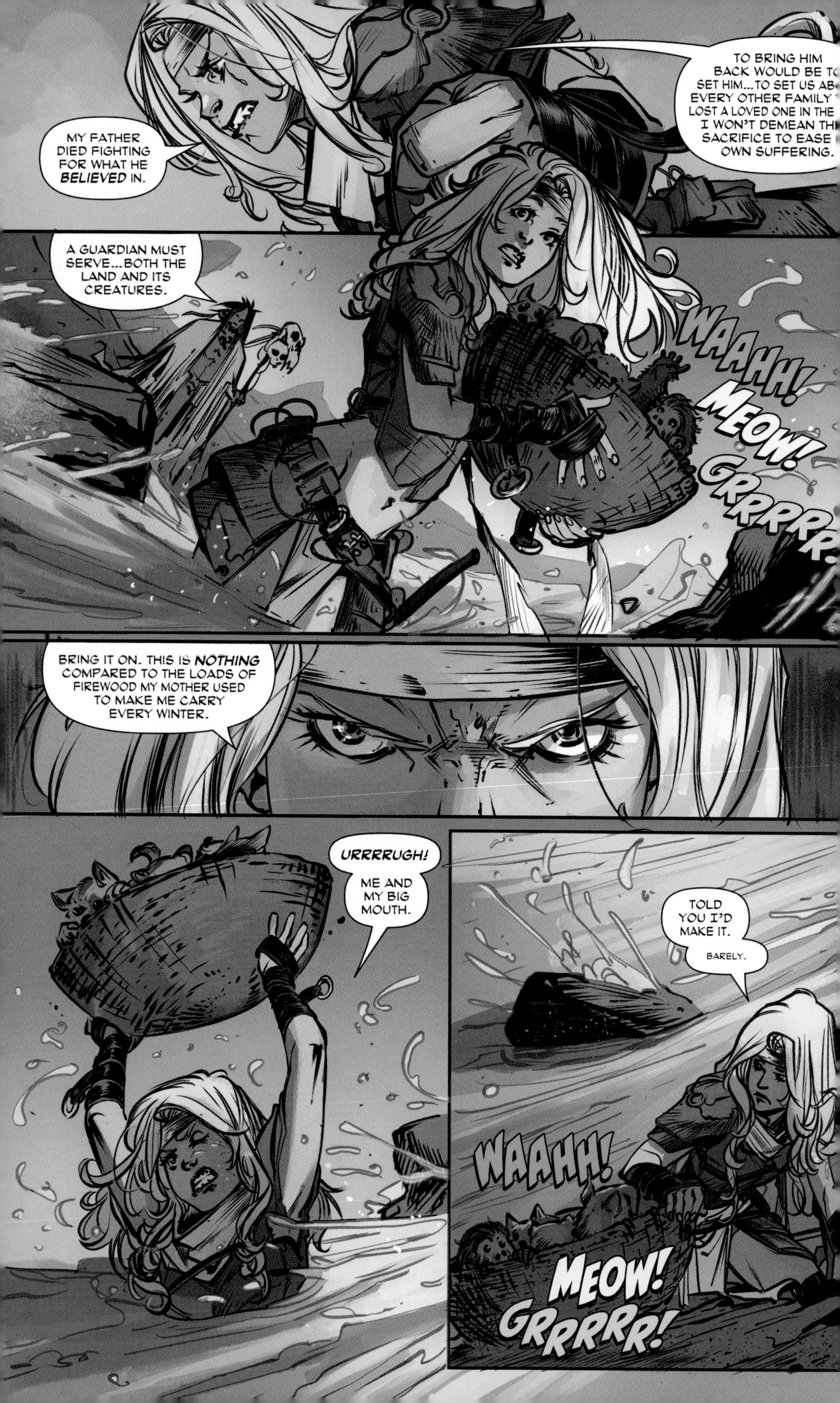
MY FATHER DIED FIGHTING FOR WHAT HE *BELIEVED* IN.
TO BRING HIM BACK WOULD BE T SET HIM...TO SET US AB EVERY OTHER FAMILY LOST A LOVED ONE IN THE I WON'T DEMEAN TH SACRIFICE TO EASE OWN SUFFERING.
A GUARDIAN MUST SERVE...BOTH THE LAND AND ITS CREATURES.
WAAHH!
MEOW!
GRRRRR.
BRING IT ON. THIS IS *NOTHING* COMPARED TO THE LOADS OF FIREWOOD MY MOTHER USED TO MAKE ME CARRY EVERY WINTER.
URRRRUGH!
ME AND MY BIG MOUTH.
TOLD YOU I'D MAKE IT.
BARELY.
WAAHH!
MEOW!
GRRRRR!

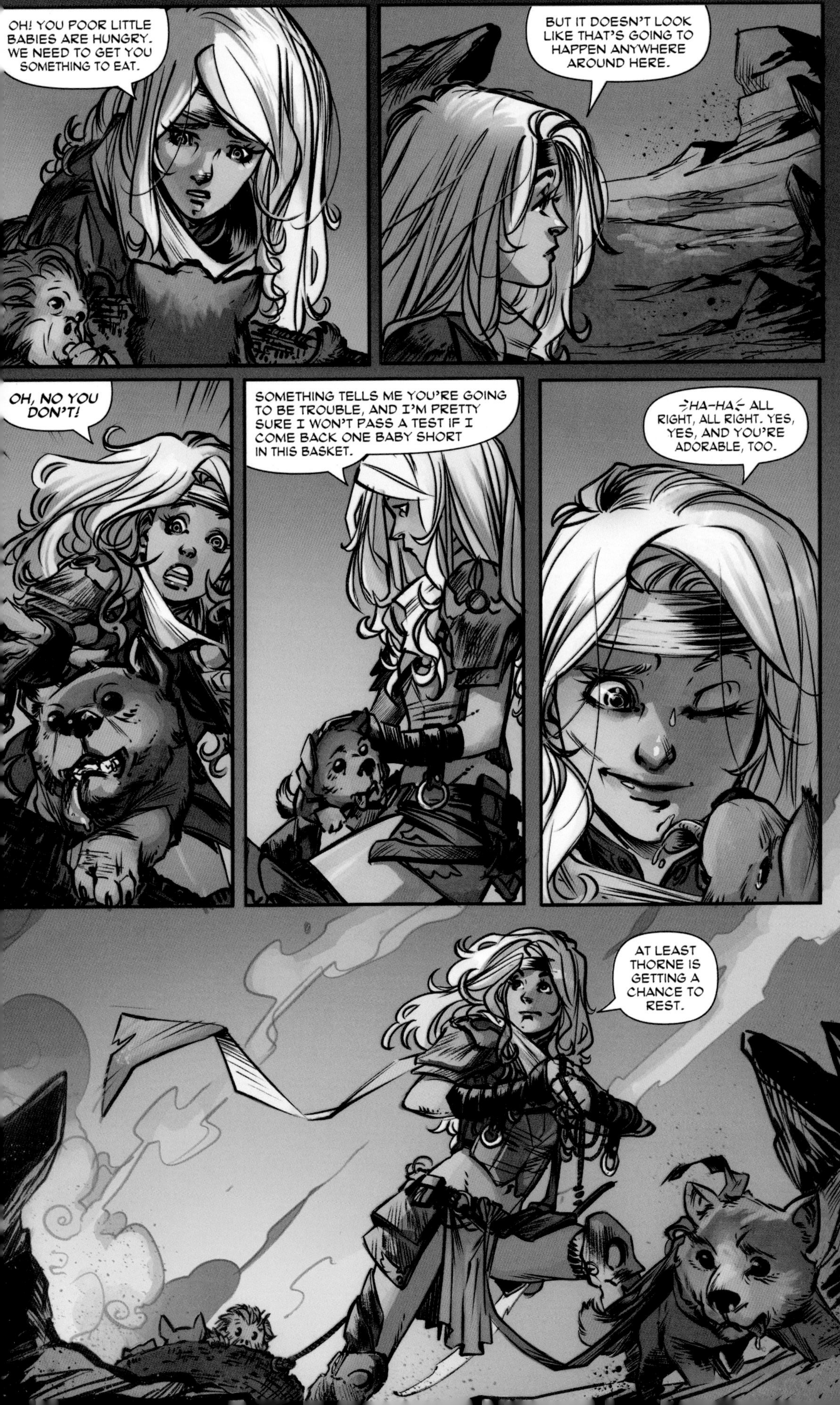

OH! YOU POOR LITTLE BABIES ARE HUNGRY. WE NEED TO GET YOU SOMETHING TO EAT.
BUT IT DOESN'T LOOK LIKE THAT'S GOING TO HAPPEN ANYWHERE AROUND HERE.
OH, NO YOU DON'T!
SOMETHING TELLS ME YOU'RE GOING TO BE TROUBLE, AND I'M PRETTY SURE I WON'T PASS A TEST IF I COME BACK ONE BABY SHORT IN THIS BASKET.
-HA-HA- ALL RIGHT, ALL RIGHT. YES, YES, AND YOU'RE ADORABLE, TOO.
AT LEAST THORNE IS GETTING A CHANCE TO REST.

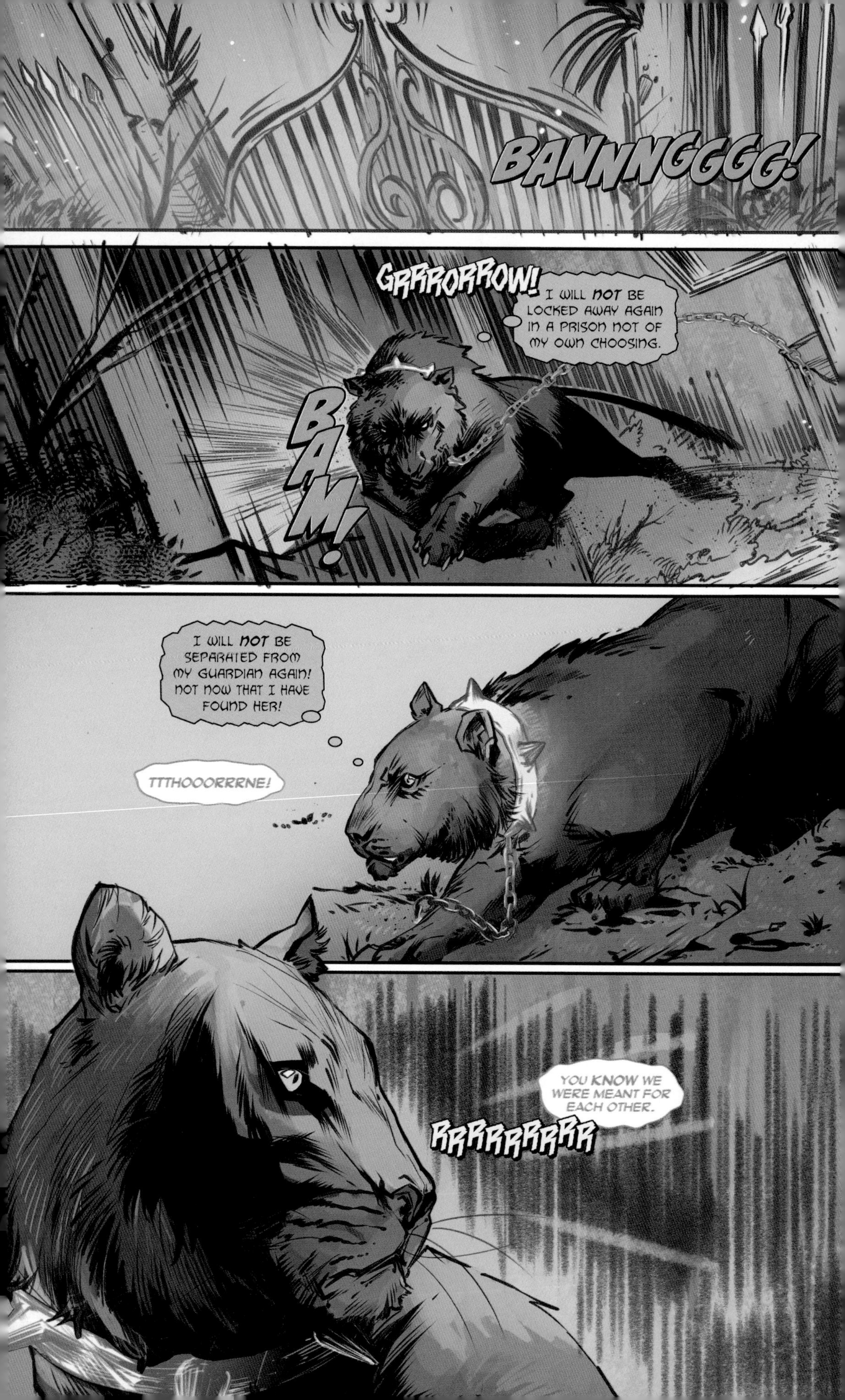
BANNNGGGG!
GRRRORROW!
I WILL *NOT* BE LOCKED AWAY AGAIN IN A PRISON NOT OF MY OWN CHOOSING.
BAM!
I WILL *NOT* BE SEPARATED FROM MY GUARDIAN AGAIN! NOT NOW THAT I HAVE FOUND HER!
TTTHOOORRRNE!
RRRRRRRRR
YOU **KNOW** WE WERE MEANT FOR EACH OTHER.

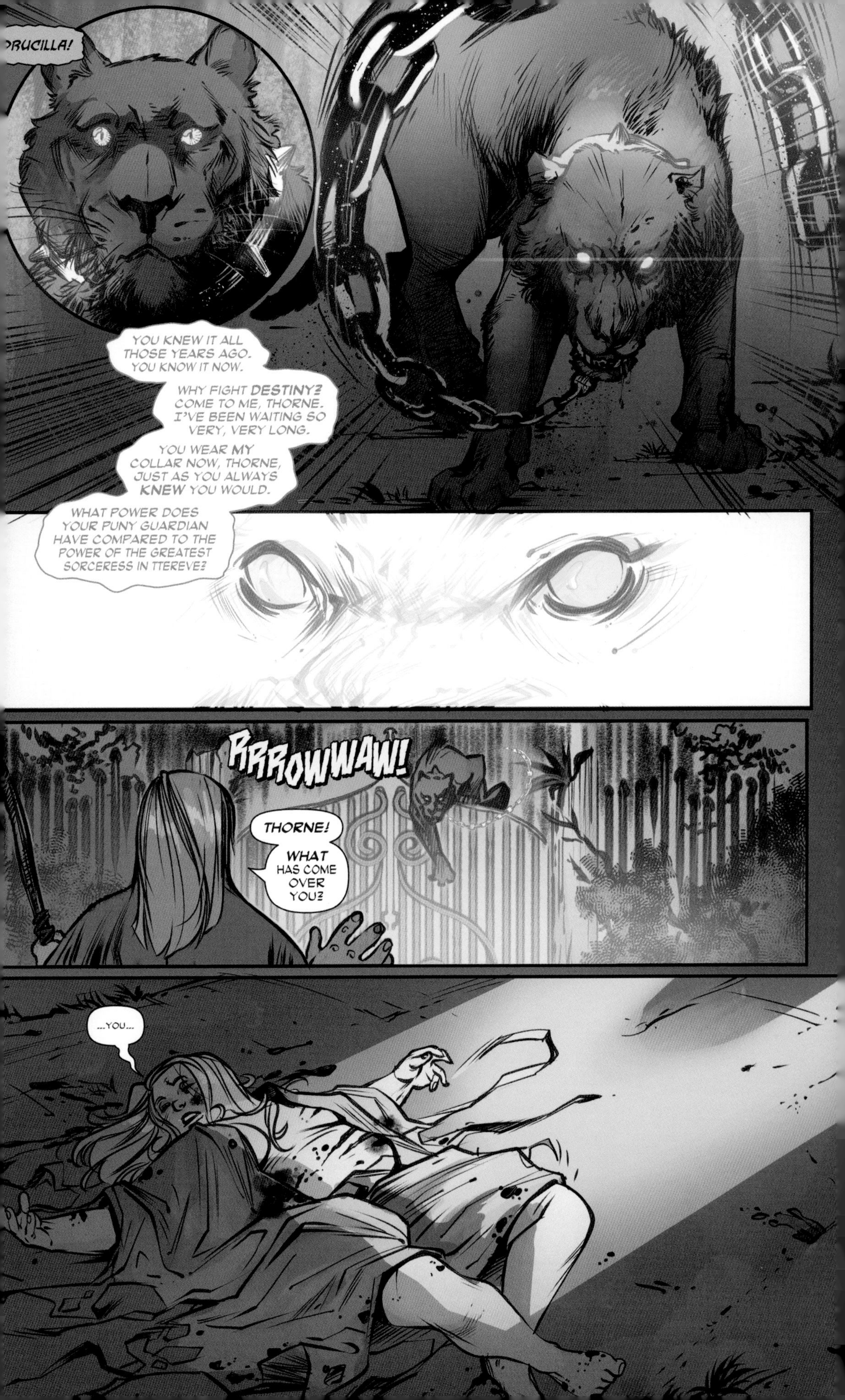

DRUCILLA!
YOU KNEW IT ALL THOSE YEARS AGO. YOU KNOW IT NOW.
WHY FIGHT DESTINY? COME TO ME, THORNE. I'VE BEEN WAITING SO VERY, VERY LONG.
YOU WEAR MY COLLAR NOW, THORNE, JUST AS YOU ALWAYS KNEW YOU WOULD.
WHAT POWER DOES YOUR PUNY GUARDIAN HAVE COMPARED TO THE POWER OF THE GREATEST SORCERESS IN TTEREVE?
RRROWWAW!
THORNE!
WHAT HAS COME OVER YOU?
...YOU...

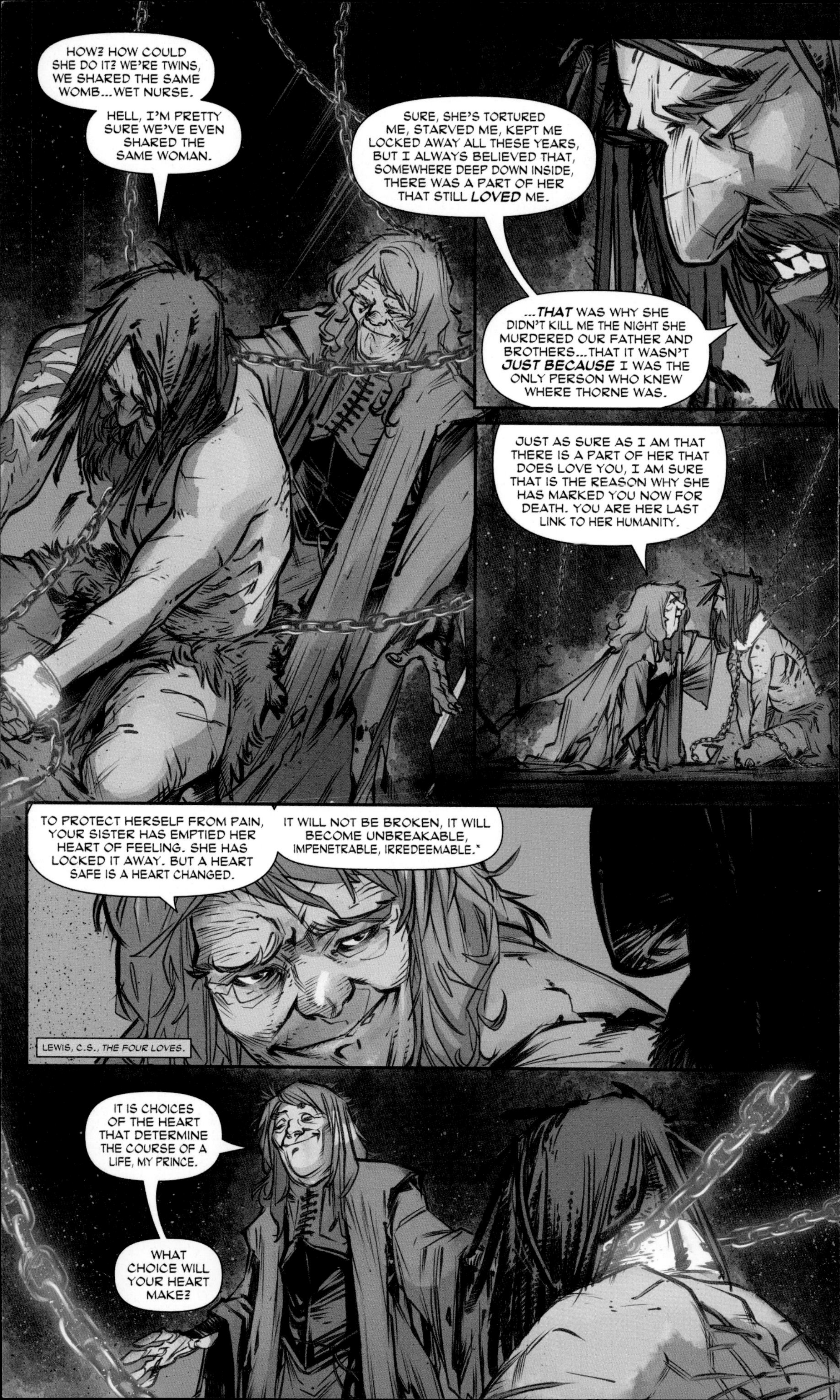
HOW? HOW COULD SHE DO IT? WE'RE TWINS, WE SHARED THE SAME WOMB...WET NURSE.
HELL, I'M PRETTY SURE WE'VE EVEN SHARED THE SAME WOMAN.
SURE, SHE'S TORTURED ME, STARVED ME, KEPT ME LOCKED AWAY ALL THESE YEARS, BUT I ALWAYS BELIEVED THAT, SOMEWHERE DEEP DOWN INSIDE, THERE WAS A PART OF HER THAT STILL *LOVED* ME.
...*THAT* WAS WHY SHE DIDN'T KILL ME THE NIGHT SHE MURDERED OUR FATHER AND BROTHERS...THAT IT WASN'T *JUST BECAUSE* I WAS THE ONLY PERSON WHO KNEW WHERE THORNE WAS.
JUST AS SURE AS I AM THAT THERE IS A PART OF HER THAT DOES LOVE YOU, I AM SURE THAT IS THE REASON WHY SHE HAS MARKED YOU NOW FOR DEATH. YOU ARE HER LAST LINK TO HER HUMANITY.
TO PROTECT HERSELF FROM PAIN, YOUR SISTER HAS EMPTIED HER HEART OF FEELING. SHE HAS LOCKED IT AWAY. BUT A HEART SAFE IS A HEART CHANGED.
IT WILL NOT BE BROKEN, IT WILL BECOME UNBREAKABLE, IMPENETRABLE, IRREDEEMABLE.*
LEWIS, C.S., *THE FOUR LOVES*.
IT IS CHOICES OF THE HEART THAT DETERMINE THE COURSE OF A LIFE, MY PRINCE.
WHAT CHOICE WILL YOUR HEART MAKE?

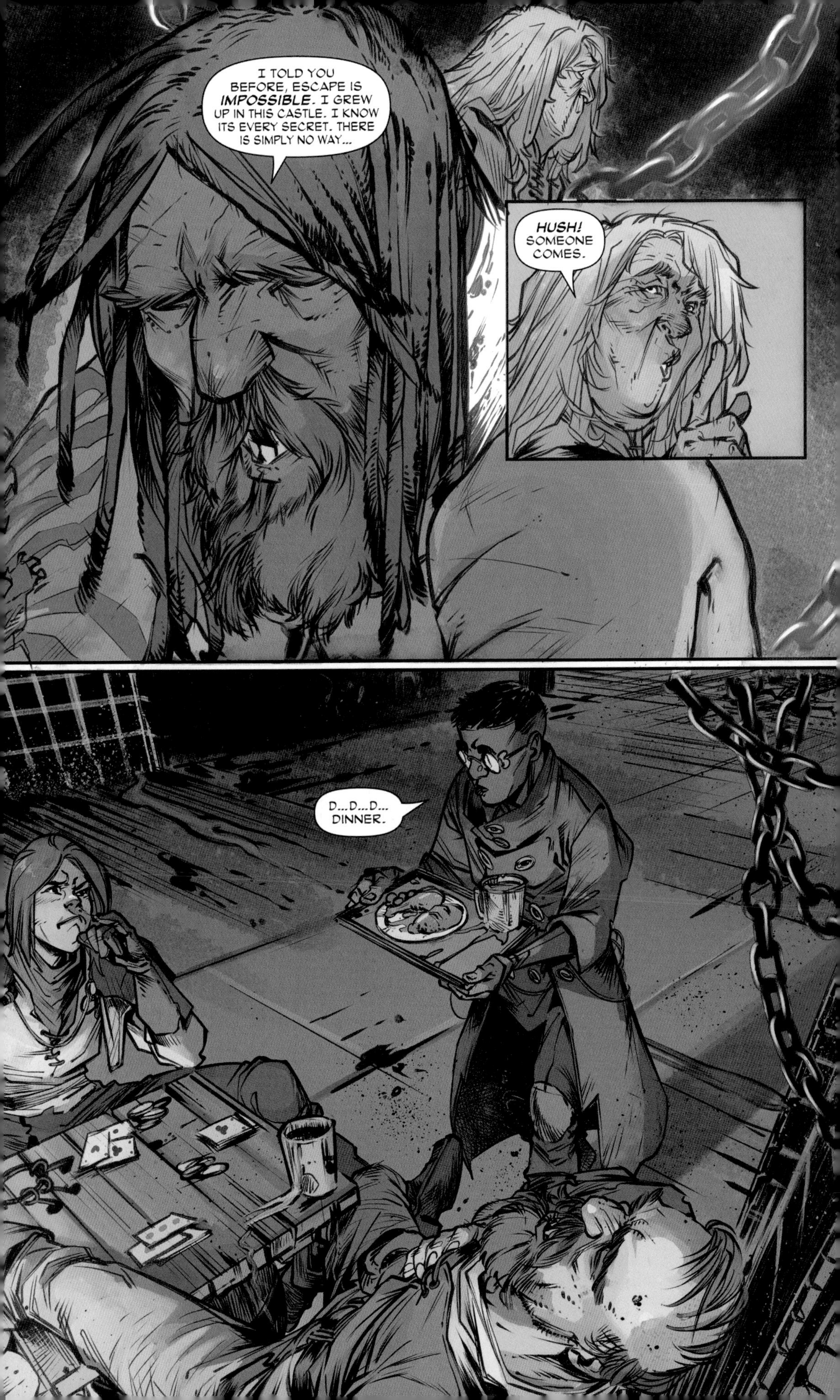
I TOLD YOU BEFORE, ESCAPE IS *IMPOSSIBLE.* I GREW UP IN THIS CASTLE. I KNOW ITS EVERY SECRET. THERE IS SIMPLY NO WAY...
HUSH! SOMEONE COMES.
D...D...D... DINNER.

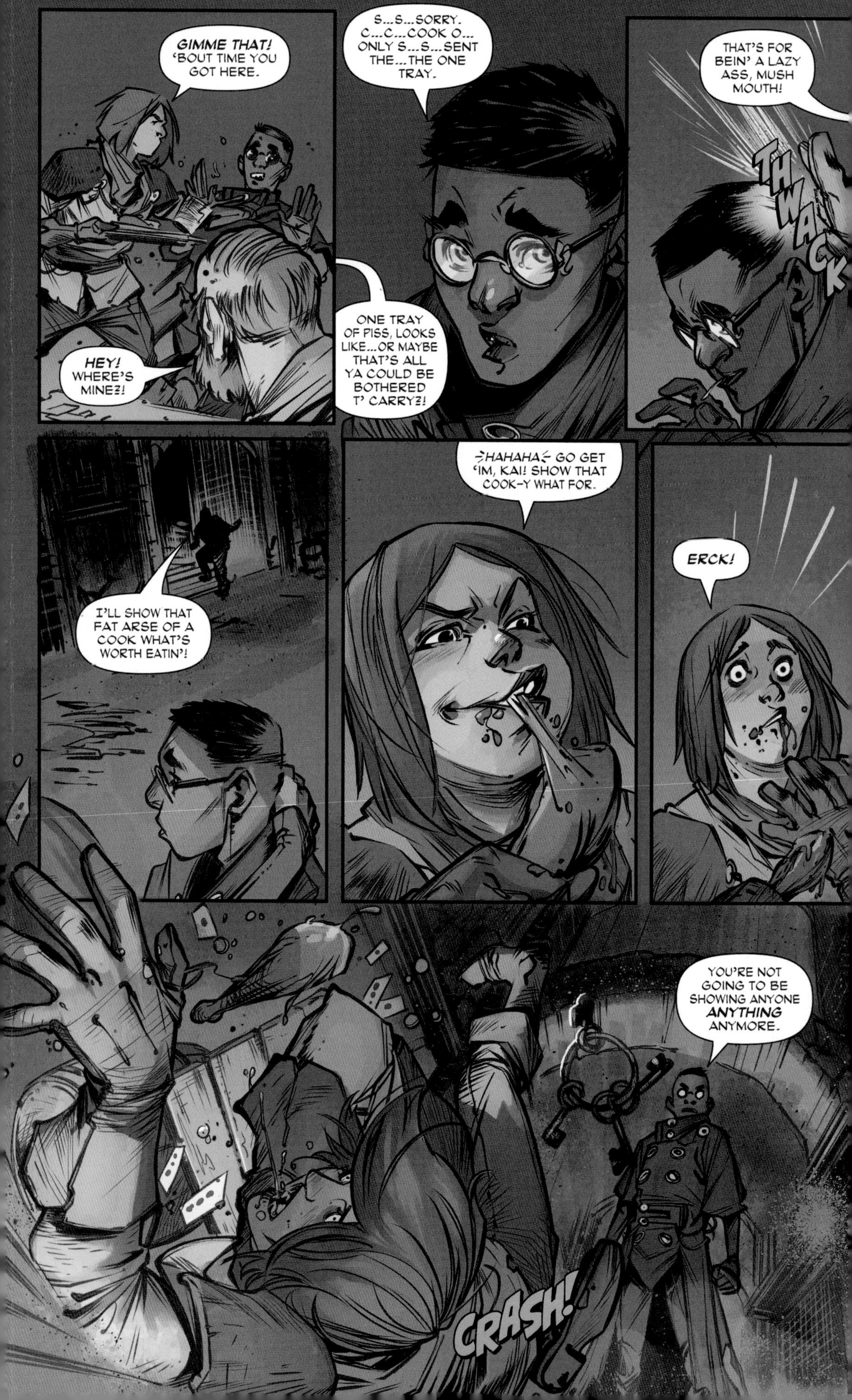
GIMME THAT! 'BOUT TIME YOU GOT HERE.
HEY! WHERE'S MINE?!
S...S...SORRY. C...C...COOK O... ONLY S...S...SENT THE...THE ONE TRAY.
ONE TRAY OF PISS, LOOKS LIKE...OR MAYBE THAT'S ALL YA COULD BE BOTHERED T' CARRY?!
THAT'S FOR BEIN' A LAZY ASS, MUSH MOUTH!
THWACK
I'LL SHOW THAT FAT ARSE OF A COOK WHAT'S WORTH EATIN'!
HAHAHA GO GET 'IM, KAI! SHOW THAT COOK-Y WHAT FOR.
ERCK!
YOU'RE NOT GOING TO BE SHOWING ANYONE ANYTHING ANYMORE.
CRASH!

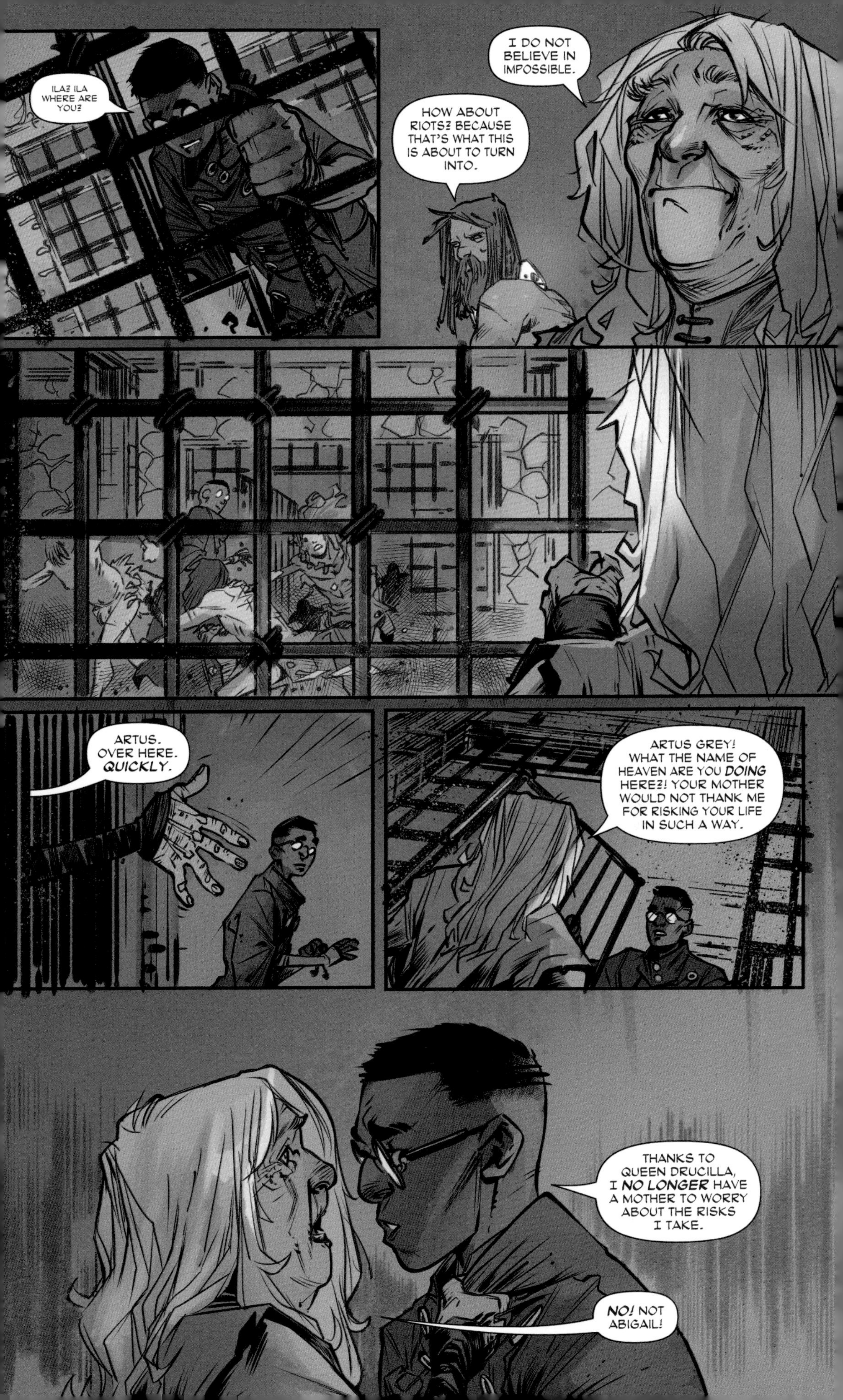
ILA? ILA WHERE ARE YOU?
I DO NOT BELIEVE IN IMPOSSIBLE.
HOW ABOUT RIOTS? BECAUSE THAT'S WHAT THIS IS ABOUT TO TURN INTO.
ARTUS. OVER HERE. *QUICKLY*.
ARTUS GREY! WHAT THE NAME OF HEAVEN ARE YOU *DOING* HERE?! YOUR MOTHER WOULD NOT THANK ME FOR RISKING YOUR LIFE IN SUCH A WAY.
THANKS TO QUEEN DRUCILLA, I *NO LONGER* HAVE A MOTHER TO WORRY ABOUT THE RISKS I TAKE.
NO! NOT ABIGAIL!

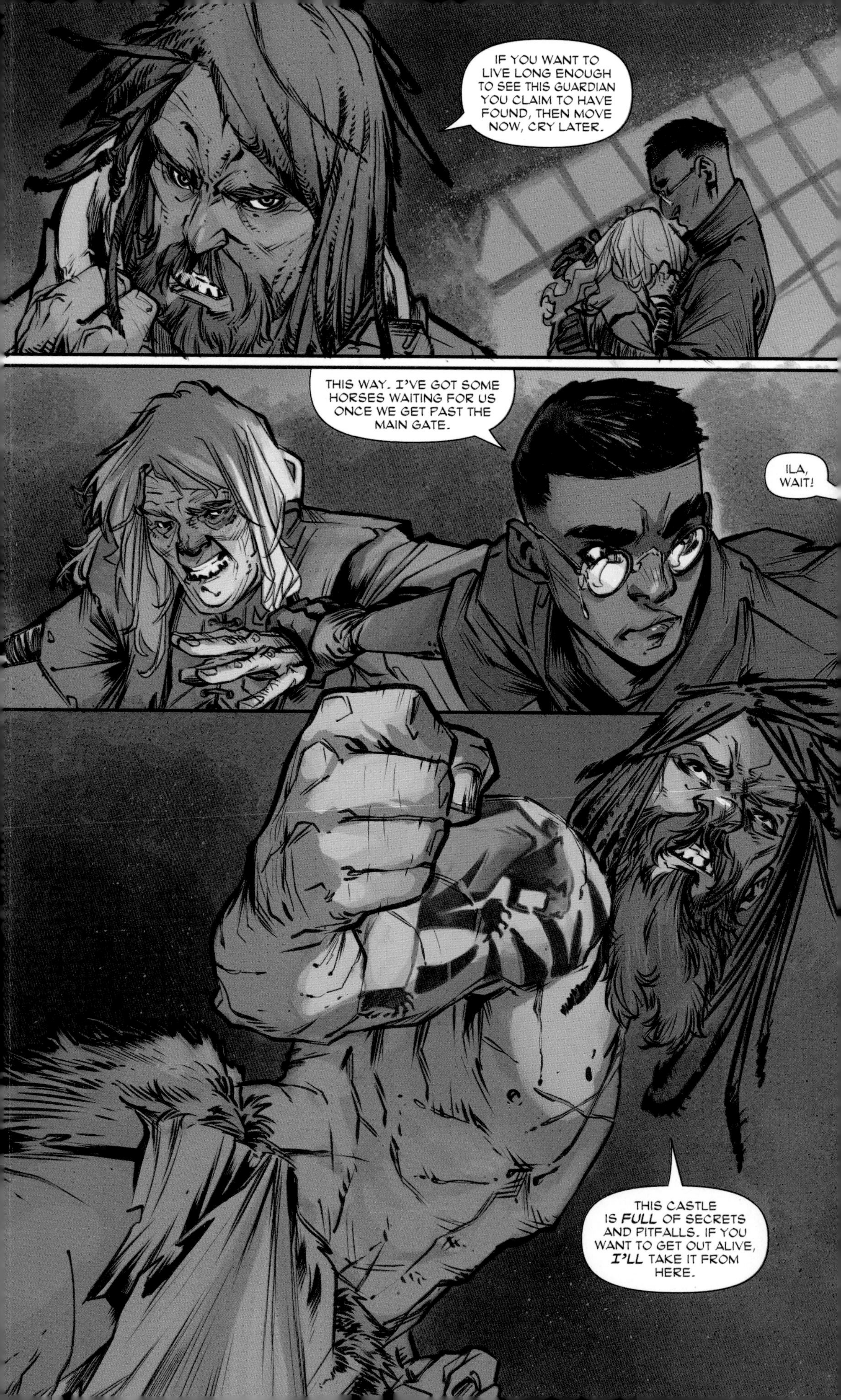
IF YOU WANT TO LIVE LONG ENOUGH TO SEE THIS GUARDIAN YOU CLAIM TO HAVE FOUND, THEN MOVE NOW, CRY LATER.
THIS WAY. I'VE GOT SOME HORSES WAITING FOR US ONCE WE GET PAST THE MAIN GATE.
ILA, WAIT!
THIS CASTLE IS *FULL* OF SECRETS AND PITFALLS. IF YOU WANT TO GET OUT ALIVE, *I'LL* TAKE IT FROM HERE.

TEN

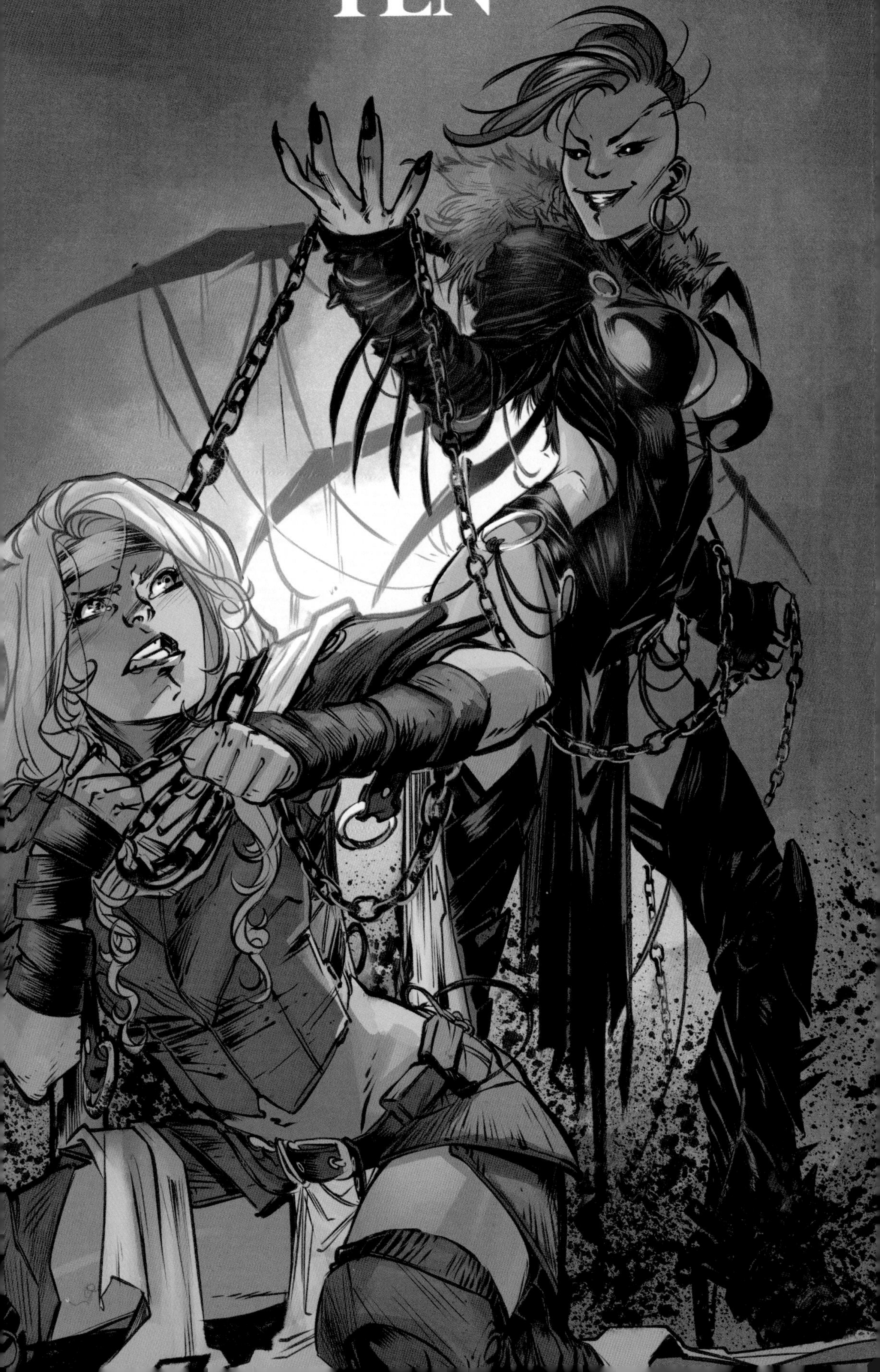

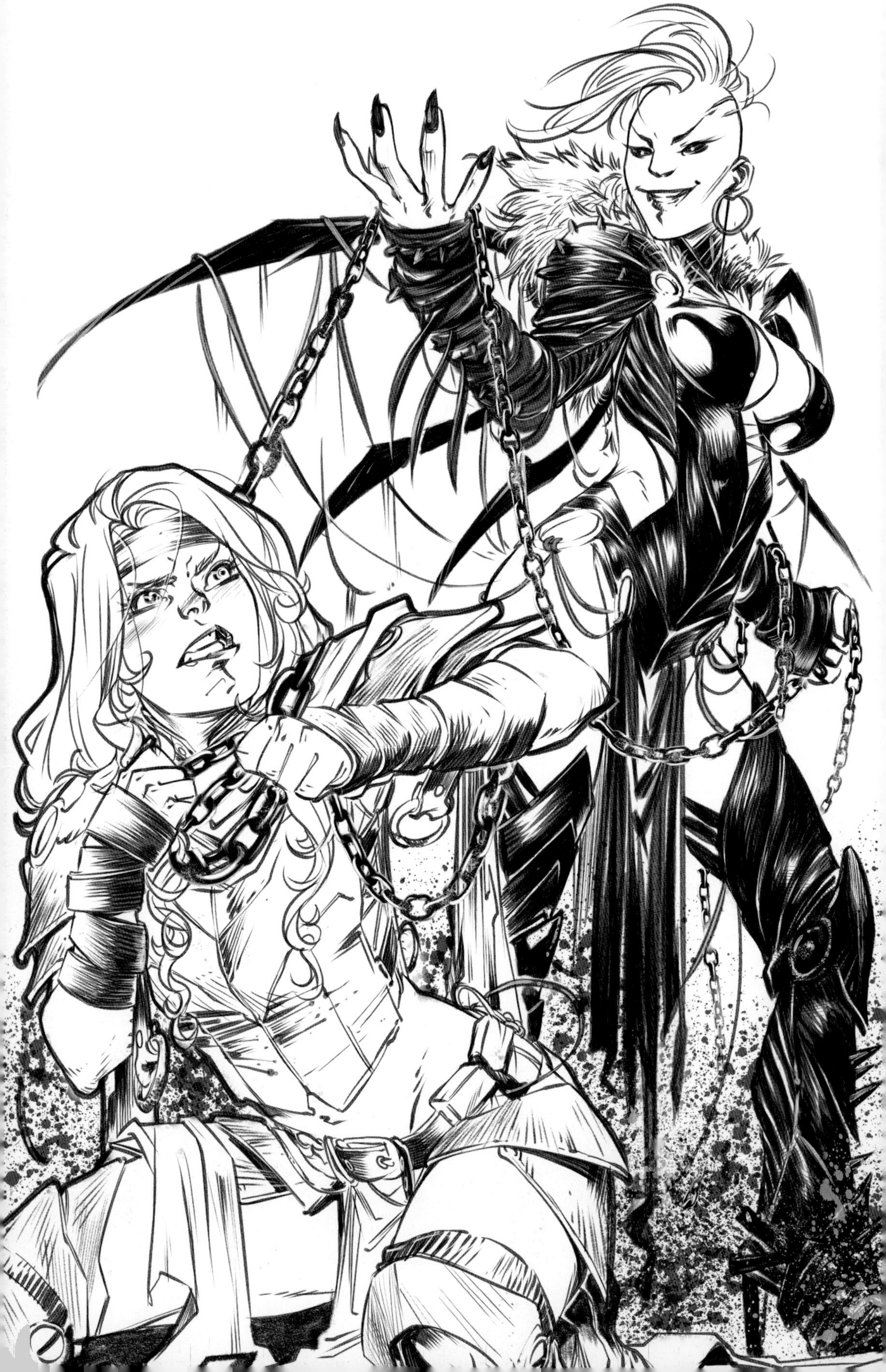

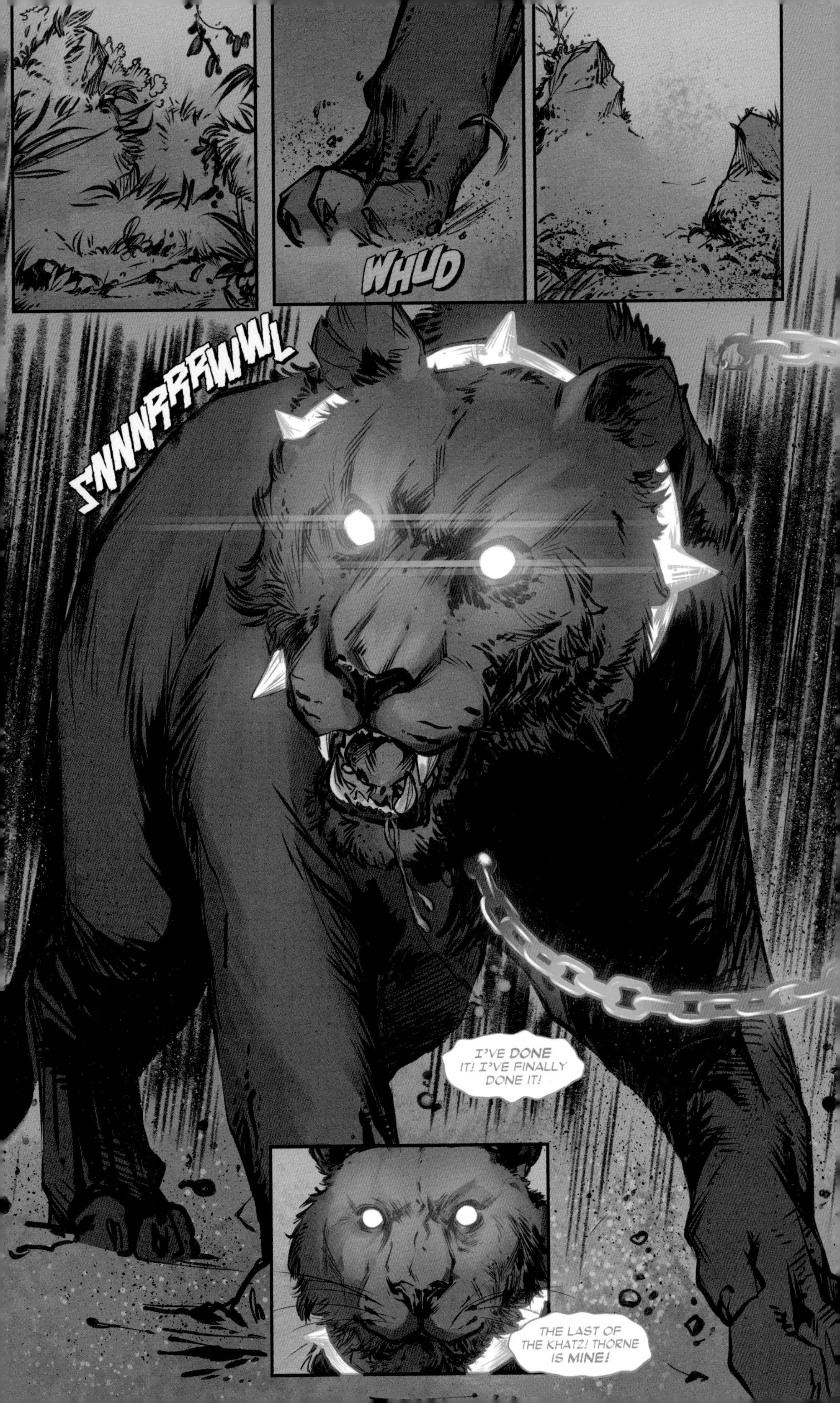

WHUD
SNNNRRRWWL
I'VE DONE IT! I'VE FINALLY DONE IT!
THE LAST OF THE KHATZ! THORNE IS MINE!

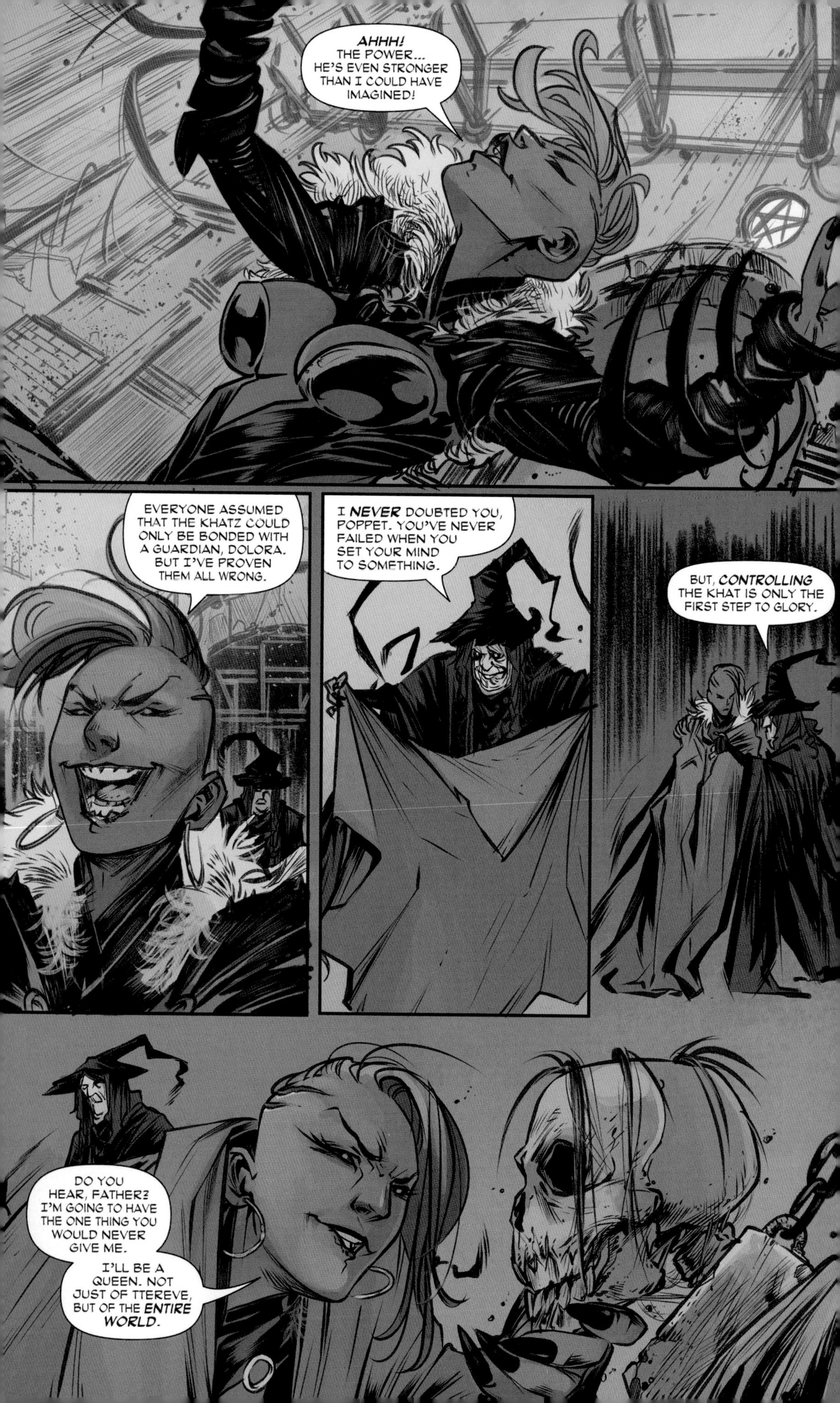
AHHH! THE POWER... HE'S EVEN STRONGER THAN I COULD HAVE IMAGINED!
EVERYONE ASSUMED THAT THE KHATZ COULD ONLY BE BONDED WITH A GUARDIAN, DOLORA. BUT I'VE PROVEN THEM ALL WRONG.
I NEVER DOUBTED YOU, POPPET. YOU'VE NEVER FAILED WHEN YOU SET YOUR MIND TO SOMETHING.
BUT, CONTROLLING THE KHAT IS ONLY THE FIRST STEP TO GLORY.
DO YOU HEAR, FATHER? I'M GOING TO HAVE THE ONE THING YOU WOULD NEVER GIVE ME.
I'LL BE A QUEEN. NOT JUST OF TTEREVE, BUT OF THE ENTIRE WORLD.

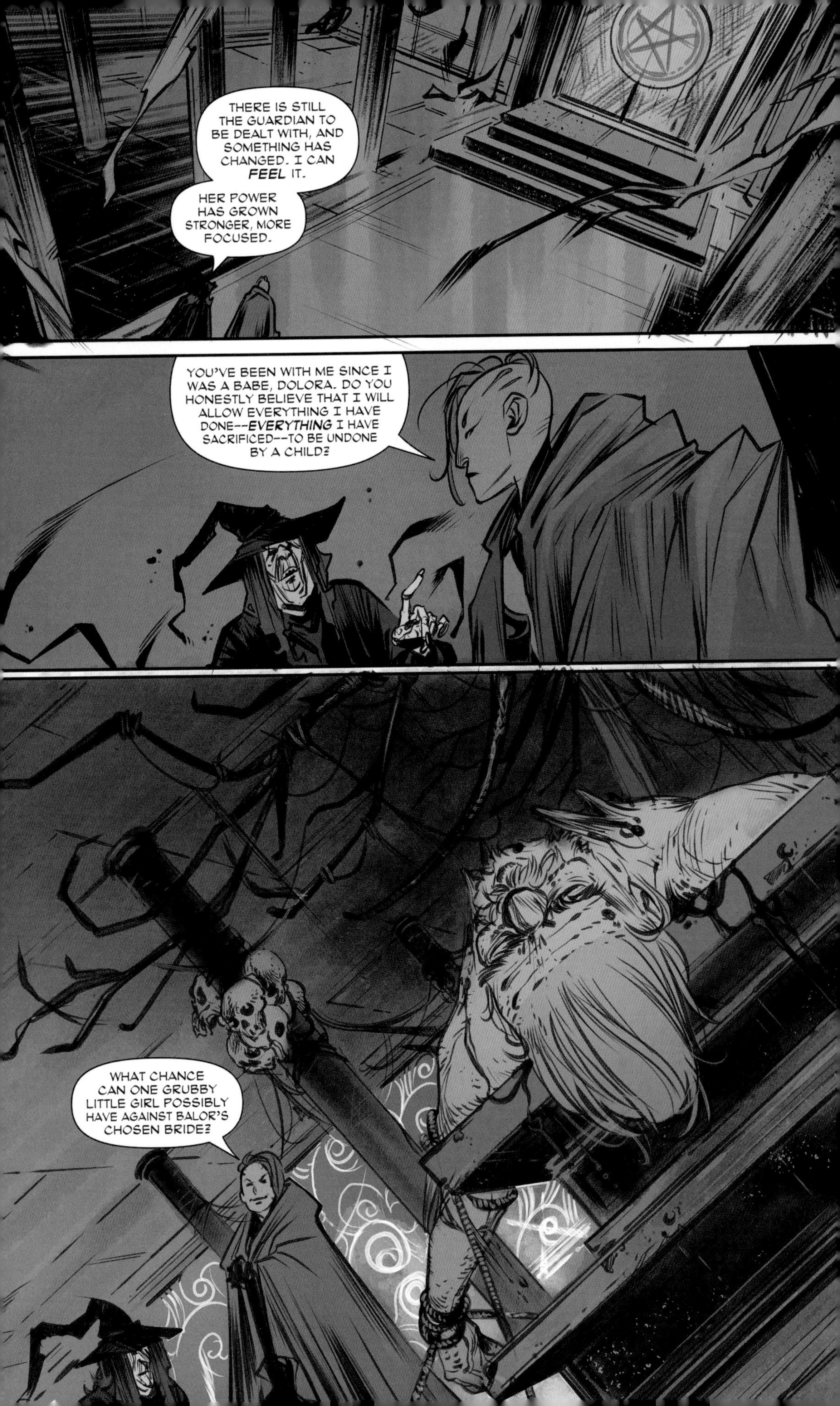
THERE IS STILL THE GUARDIAN TO BE DEALT WITH, AND SOMETHING HAS CHANGED. I CAN *FEEL* IT.
HER POWER HAS GROWN STRONGER, MORE FOCUSED.
YOU'VE BEEN WITH ME SINCE I WAS A BABE, DOLORA. DO YOU HONESTLY BELIEVE THAT I WILL ALLOW EVERYTHING I HAVE DONE--*EVERYTHING* I HAVE SACRIFICED--TO BE UNDONE BY A CHILD?
WHAT CHANCE CAN ONE GRUBBY LITTLE GIRL POSSIBLY HAVE AGAINST BALOR'S CHOSEN BRIDE?

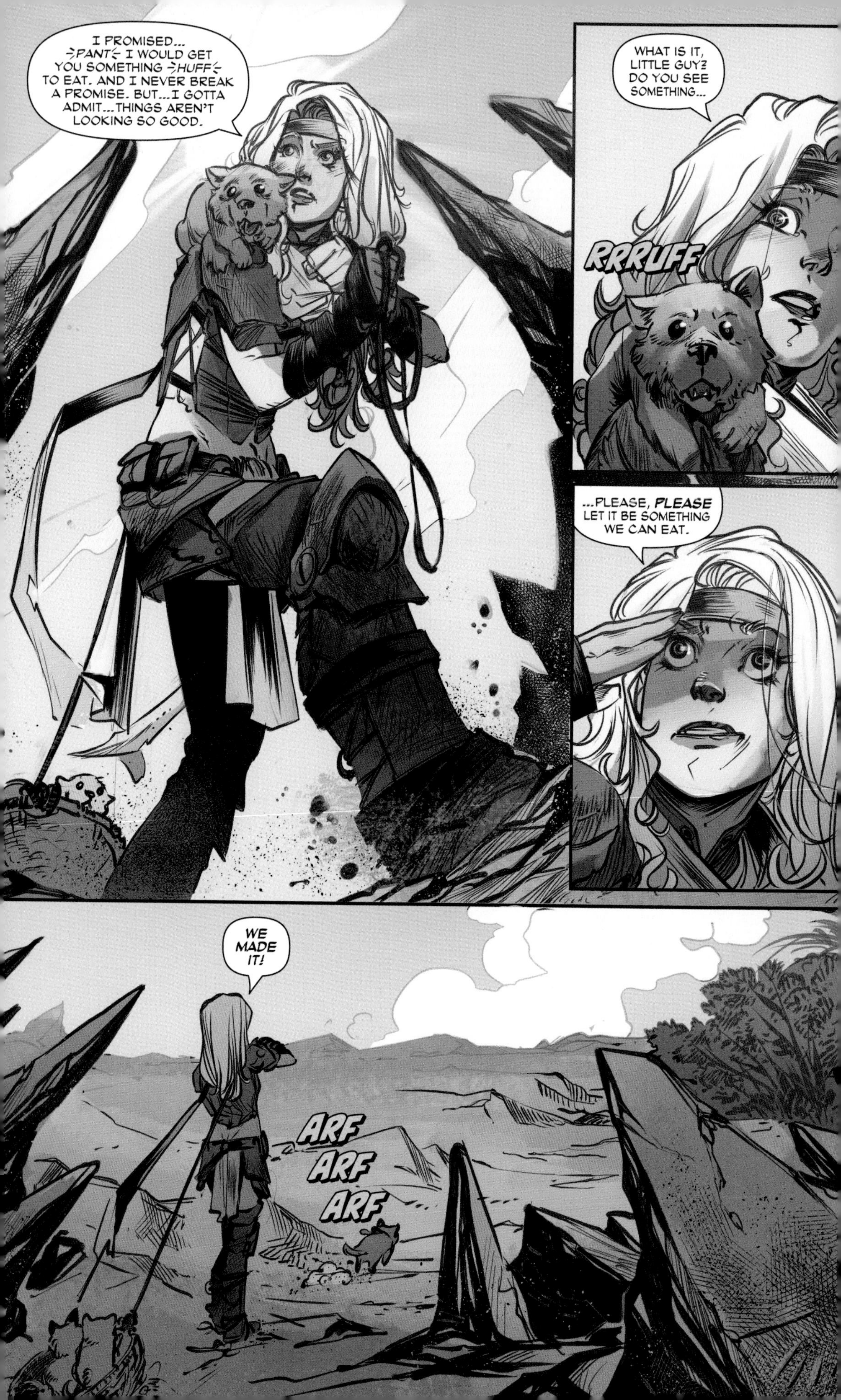

I PROMISED... ⇒PANT⇐ I WOULD GET YOU SOMETHING ⇒HUFF⇐ TO EAT. AND I NEVER BREAK A PROMISE. BUT...I GOTTA ADMIT...THINGS AREN'T LOOKING SO GOOD.
WHAT IS IT, LITTLE GUY? DO YOU SEE SOMETHING...
RRRUFF
...PLEASE, *PLEASE* LET IT BE SOMETHING WE CAN EAT.
WE MADE IT!
ARF
ARF
ARF

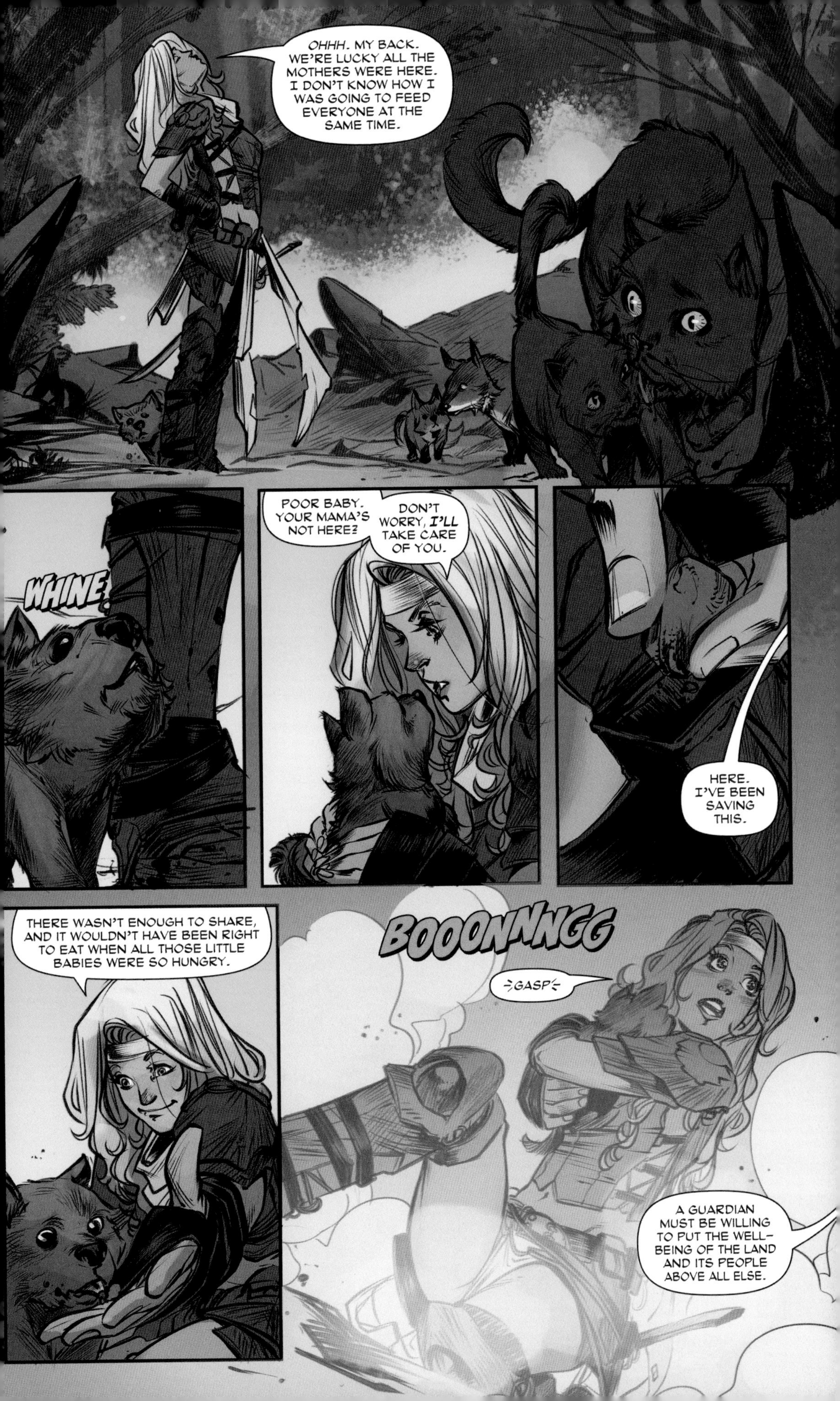
OHHH. MY BACK. WE'RE LUCKY ALL THE MOTHERS WERE HERE. I DON'T KNOW HOW I WAS GOING TO FEED EVERYONE AT THE SAME TIME.
WHINE
POOR BABY. YOUR MAMA'S NOT HERE?
DON'T WORRY, I'LL TAKE CARE OF YOU.
HERE. I'VE BEEN SAVING THIS.
THERE WASN'T ENOUGH TO SHARE, AND IT WOULDN'T HAVE BEEN RIGHT TO EAT WHEN ALL THOSE LITTLE BABIES WERE SO HUNGRY.
BOOONNNGG
GASP
A GUARDIAN MUST BE WILLING TO PUT THE WELL-BEING OF THE LAND AND ITS PEOPLE ABOVE ALL ELSE.

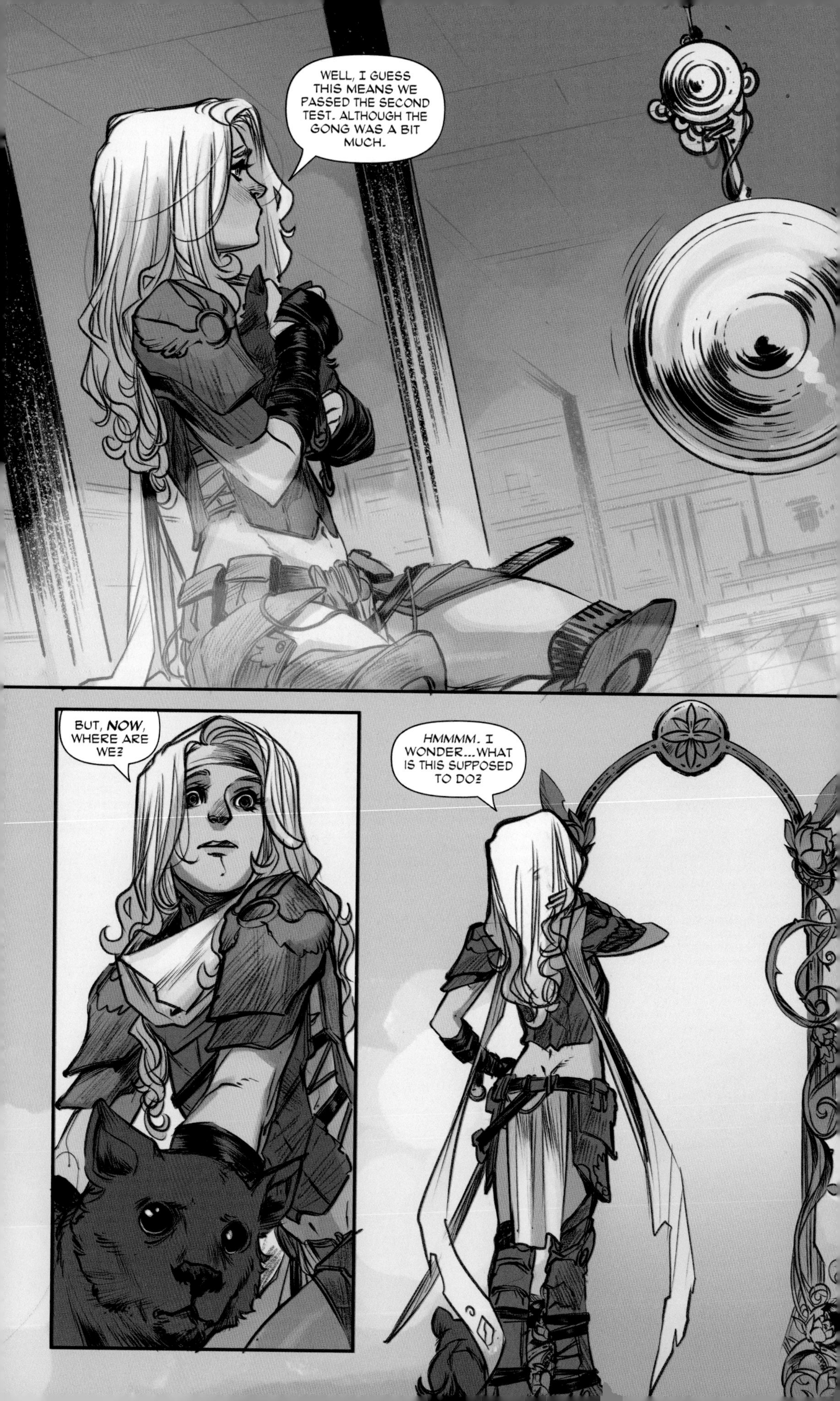

WELL, I GUESS THIS MEANS WE PASSED THE SECOND TEST. ALTHOUGH THE GONG WAS A BIT MUCH.
BUT, NOW, WHERE ARE WE?
HMMMM. I WONDER...WHAT IS THIS SUPPOSED TO DO?

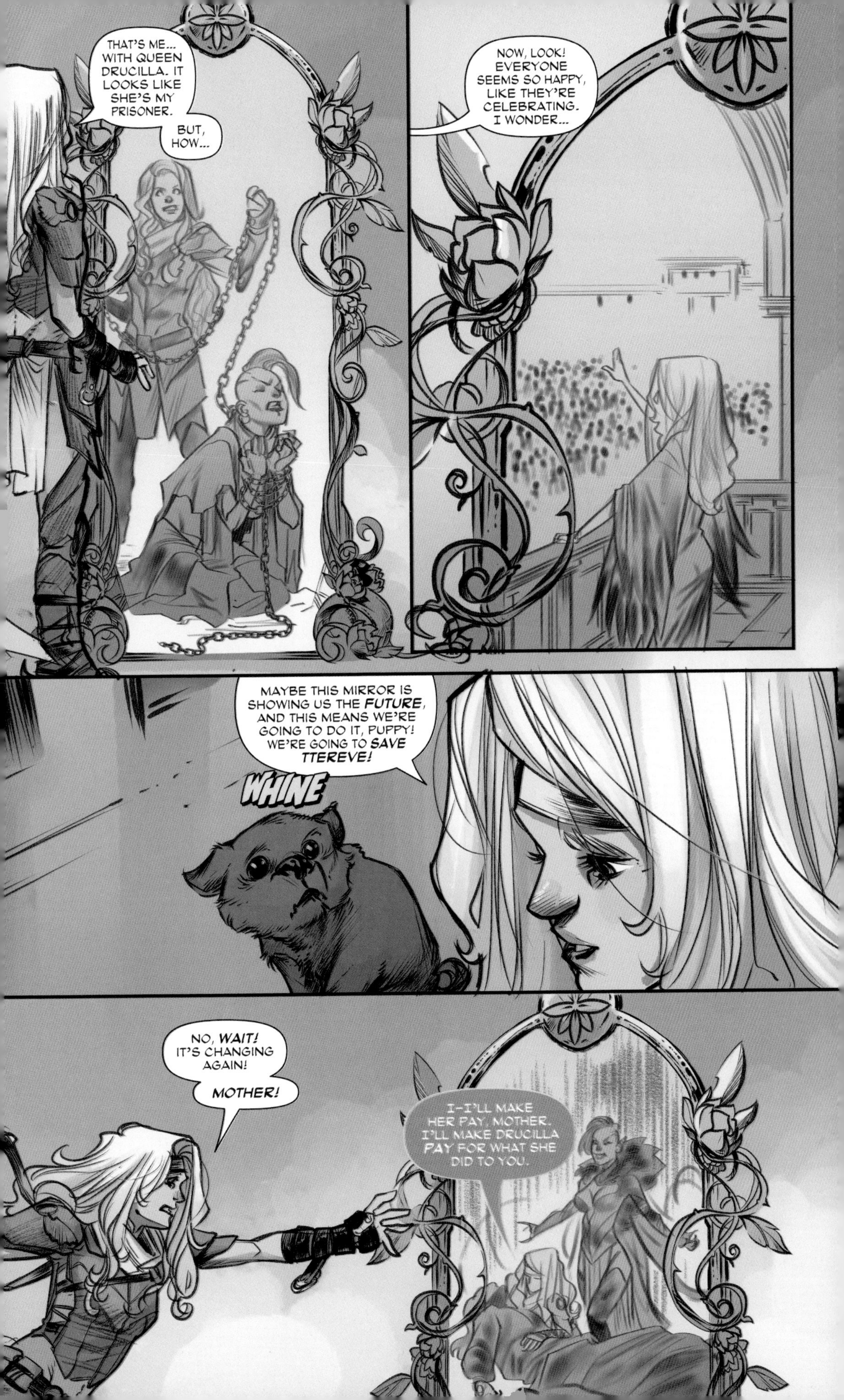
THAT'S ME... WITH QUEEN DRUCILLA. IT LOOKS LIKE SHE'S MY PRISONER.
BUT, HOW...
NOW, LOOK! EVERYONE SEEMS SO HAPPY, LIKE THEY'RE CELEBRATING. I WONDER...
MAYBE THIS MIRROR IS SHOWING US THE FUTURE, AND THIS MEANS WE'RE GOING TO DO IT, PUPPY! WE'RE GOING TO SAVE TTEREVE!
WHINE
NO, WAIT! IT'S CHANGING AGAIN!
MOTHER!
I-I'LL MAKE HER PAY, MOTHER. I'LL MAKE DRUCILLA PAY FOR WHAT SHE DID TO YOU.

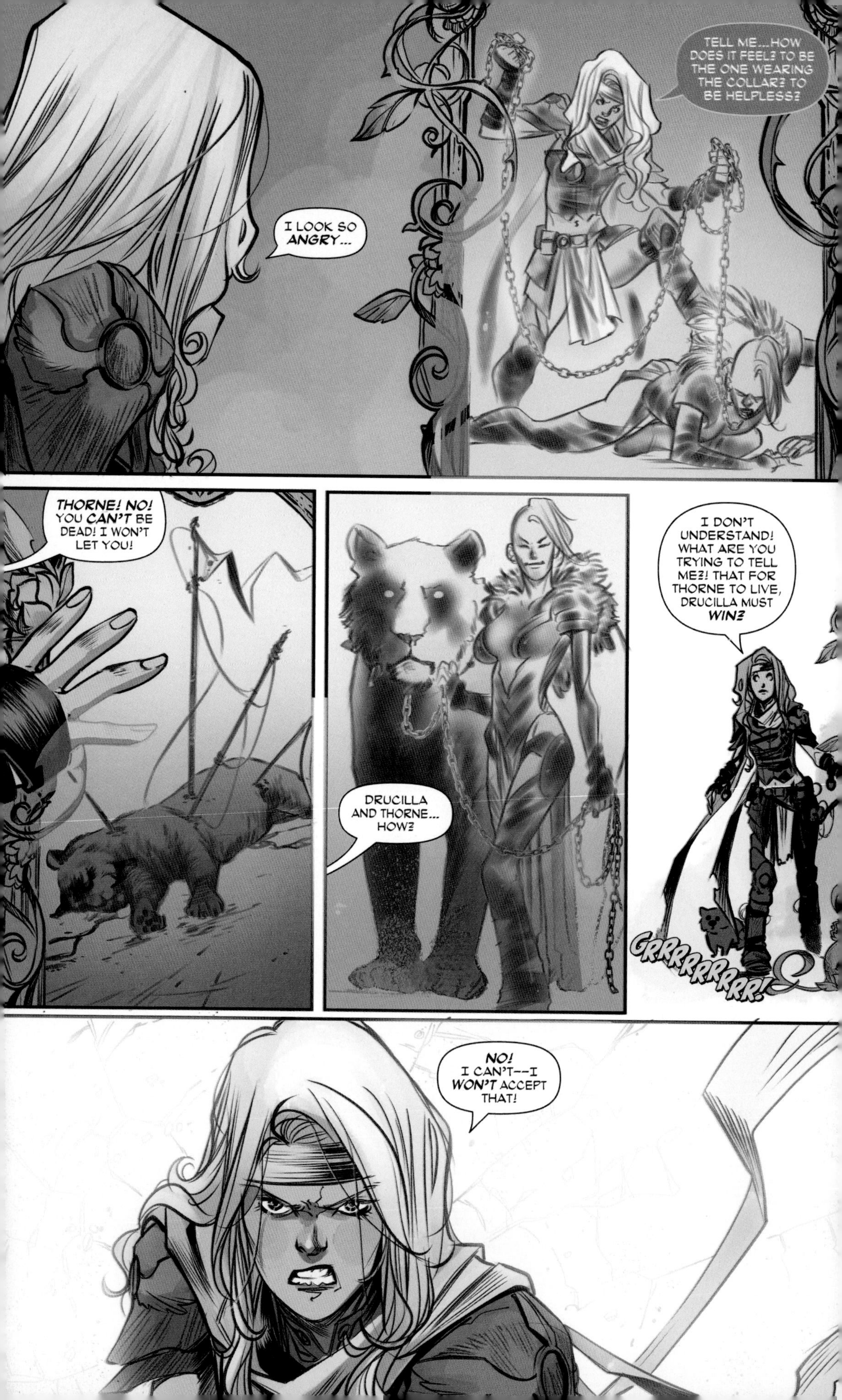
I LOOK SO ANGRY...
TELL ME...HOW DOES IT FEEL? TO BE THE ONE WEARING THE COLLAR? TO BE HELPLESS?
THORNE! NO! YOU CAN'T BE DEAD! I WON'T LET YOU!
DRUCILLA AND THORNE... HOW?
I DON'T UNDERSTAND! WHAT ARE YOU TRYING TO TELL ME?! THAT FOR THORNE TO LIVE, DRUCILLA MUST WIN?
GRRRRRRRRR!
NO! I CAN'T--I WON'T ACCEPT THAT!

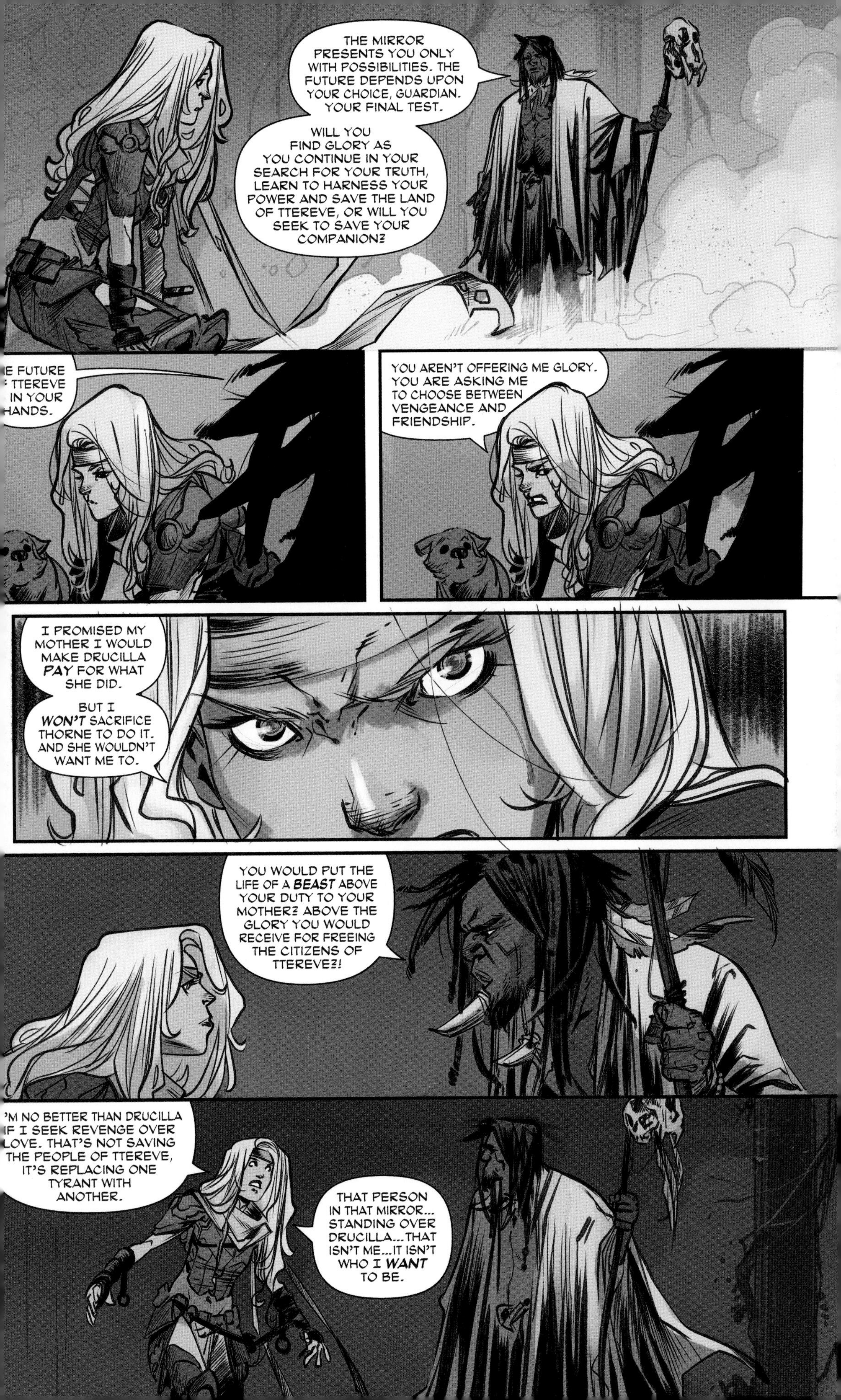
THE MIRROR PRESENTS YOU ONLY WITH POSSIBILITIES. THE FUTURE DEPENDS UPON YOUR CHOICE, GUARDIAN. YOUR FINAL TEST.
WILL YOU FIND GLORY AS YOU CONTINUE IN YOUR SEARCH FOR YOUR TRUTH, LEARN TO HARNESS YOUR POWER AND SAVE THE LAND OF TTEREVE, OR WILL YOU SEEK TO SAVE YOUR COMPANION?
E FUTURE F TTEREVE IN YOUR HANDS.
YOU AREN'T OFFERING ME GLORY. YOU ARE ASKING ME TO CHOOSE BETWEEN VENGEANCE AND FRIENDSHIP.
I PROMISED MY MOTHER I WOULD MAKE DRUCILLA PAY FOR WHAT SHE DID.
BUT I WON'T SACRIFICE THORNE TO DO IT. AND SHE WOULDN'T WANT ME TO.
YOU WOULD PUT THE LIFE OF A BEAST ABOVE YOUR DUTY TO YOUR MOTHER? ABOVE THE GLORY YOU WOULD RECEIVE FOR FREEING THE CITIZENS OF TTEREVE?!
'M NO BETTER THAN DRUCILLA IF I SEEK REVENGE OVER LOVE. THAT'S NOT SAVING THE PEOPLE OF TTEREVE, IT'S REPLACING ONE TYRANT WITH ANOTHER.
THAT PERSON IN THAT MIRROR... STANDING OVER DRUCILLA...THAT ISN'T ME...IT ISN'T WHO I WANT TO BE.

MAYBE I'LL END UP A PRISONER, BUT THORNE WILL BE ALIVE, AND WHERE THERE IS LIFE, THERE IS *HOPE.*

A DAY WILL COME IN THE BATTLE AHEAD WHERE YOU MAY HAVE CAUSE TO LOSE HOPE, TO LOSE FAITH IN WHO AND WHAT YOU ARE.

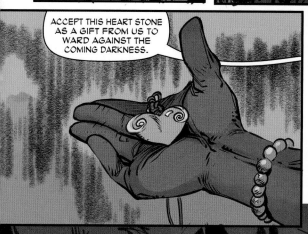

ACCEPT THIS HEART STONE AS A GIFT FROM US TO WARD AGAINST THE COMING DARKNESS.

LIKE YOU, ITS *TRUE* POWER COMES FROM WITHIN.

GOOD OR BAD, IT WILL REFLECT BACK THE ESSENCE OF THE POWER THAT LIES WITHIN THE WEARER.

NOW. LET US SEE IF WE CAN FREE YOUR KHAT FROM HIS CHAINS AND MAKE YOU A PROPER GUARDIAN.

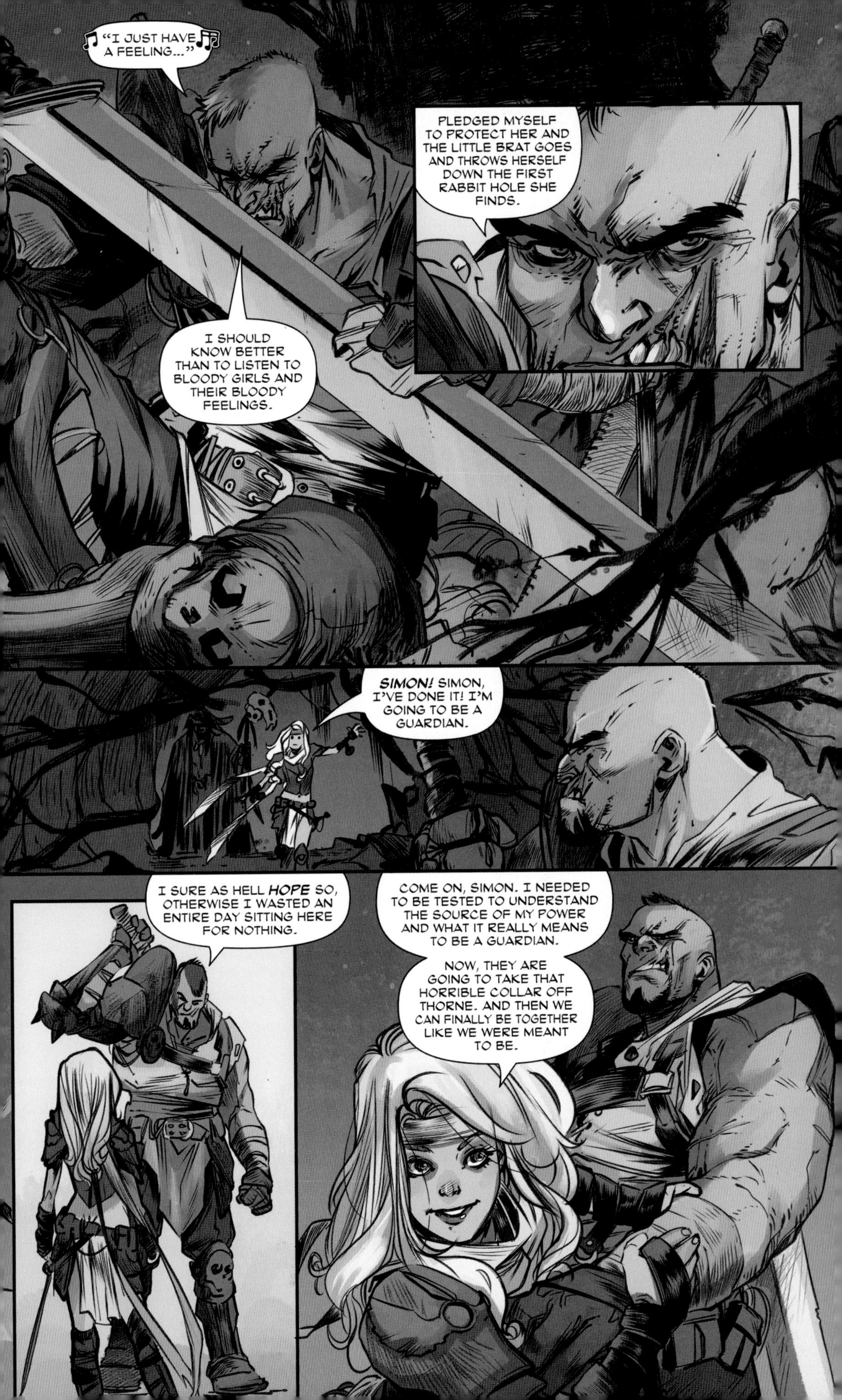

♫ "I JUST HAVE A FEELING..." ♫
PLEDGED MYSELF TO PROTECT HER AND THE LITTLE BRAT GOES AND THROWS HERSELF DOWN THE FIRST RABBIT HOLE SHE FINDS.
I SHOULD KNOW BETTER THAN TO LISTEN TO BLOODY GIRLS AND THEIR BLOODY FEELINGS.
SIMON! SIMON, I'VE DONE IT! I'M GOING TO BE A GUARDIAN.
I SURE AS HELL HOPE SO, OTHERWISE I WASTED AN ENTIRE DAY SITTING HERE FOR NOTHING.
COME ON, SIMON. I NEEDED TO BE TESTED TO UNDERSTAND THE SOURCE OF MY POWER AND WHAT IT REALLY MEANS TO BE A GUARDIAN.
NOW, THEY ARE GOING TO TAKE THAT HORRIBLE COLLAR OFF THORNE. AND THEN WE CAN FINALLY BE TOGETHER LIKE WE WERE MEANT TO BE.

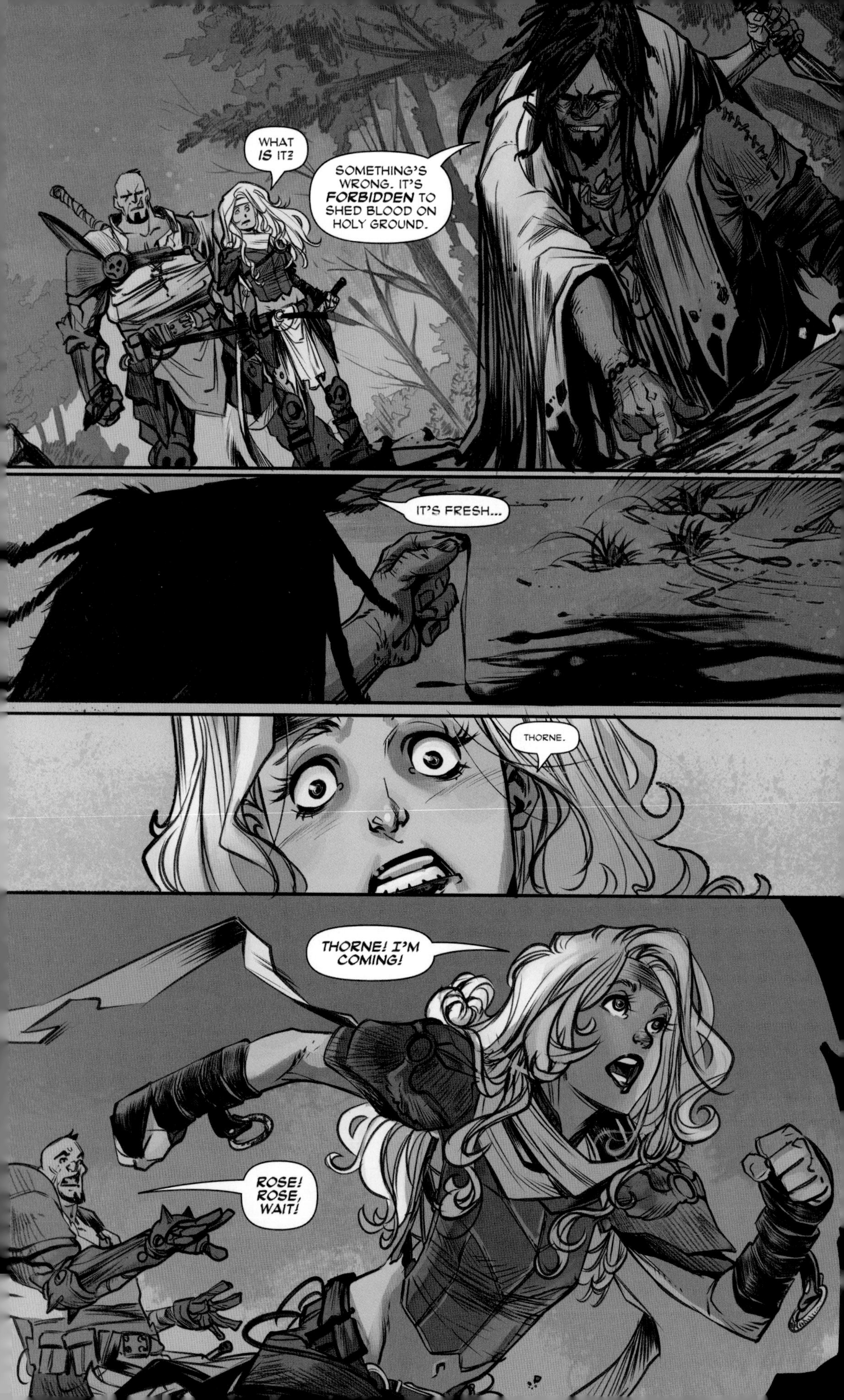
WHAT IS IT?
SOMETHING'S WRONG. IT'S FORBIDDEN TO SHED BLOOD ON HOLY GROUND.
IT'S FRESH...
THORNE.
THORNE! I'M COMING!
ROSE! ROSE, WAIT!

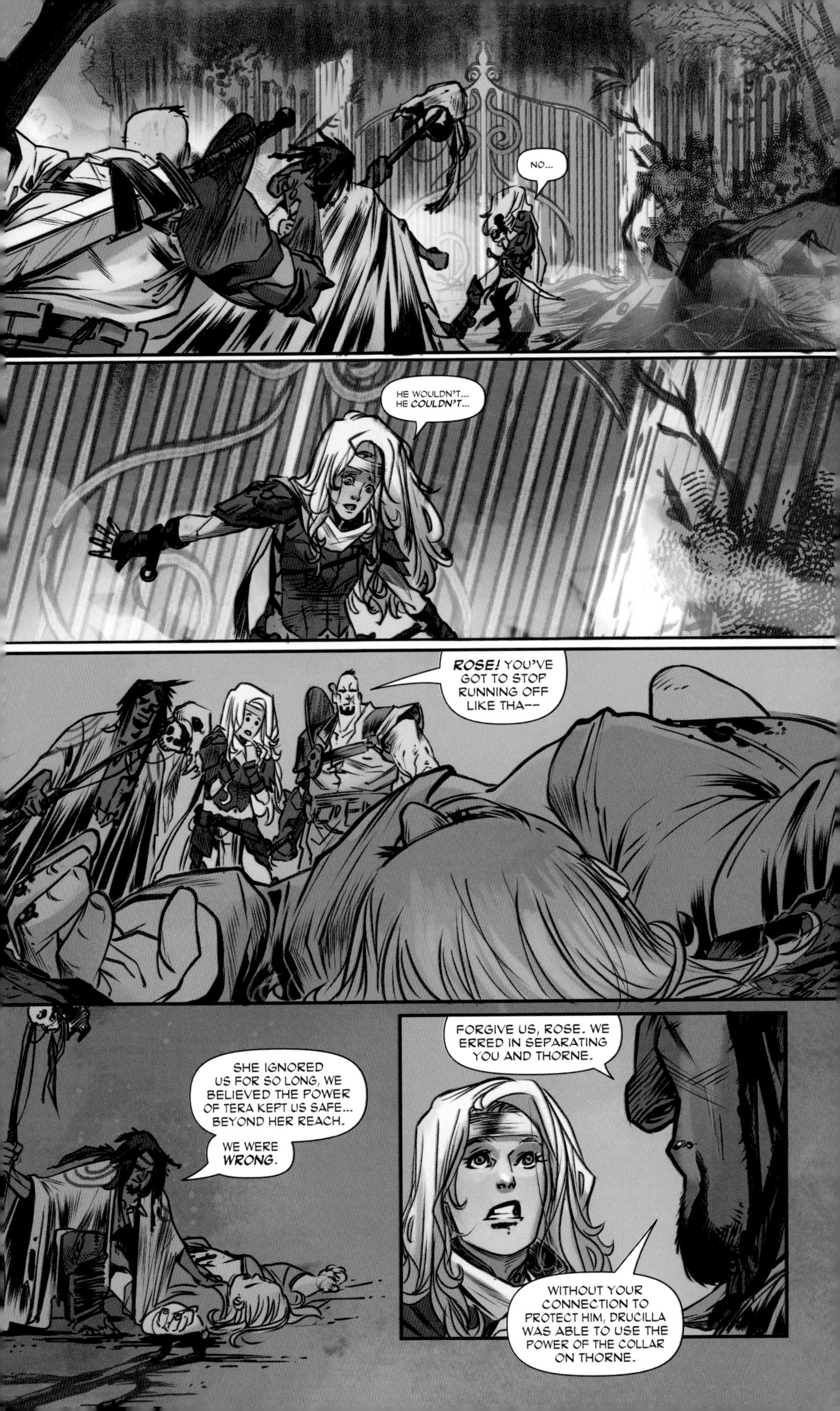
NO...
HE WOULDN'T... HE COULDN'T...
ROSE! YOU'VE GOT TO STOP RUNNING OFF LIKE THA--
SHE IGNORED US FOR SO LONG, WE BELIEVED THE POWER OF TERA KEPT US SAFE... BEYOND HER REACH.
WE WERE WRONG.
FORGIVE US, ROSE. WE ERRED IN SEPARATING YOU AND THORNE.
WITHOUT YOUR CONNECTION TO PROTECT HIM, DRUCILLA WAS ABLE TO USE THE POWER OF THE COLLAR ON THORNE.

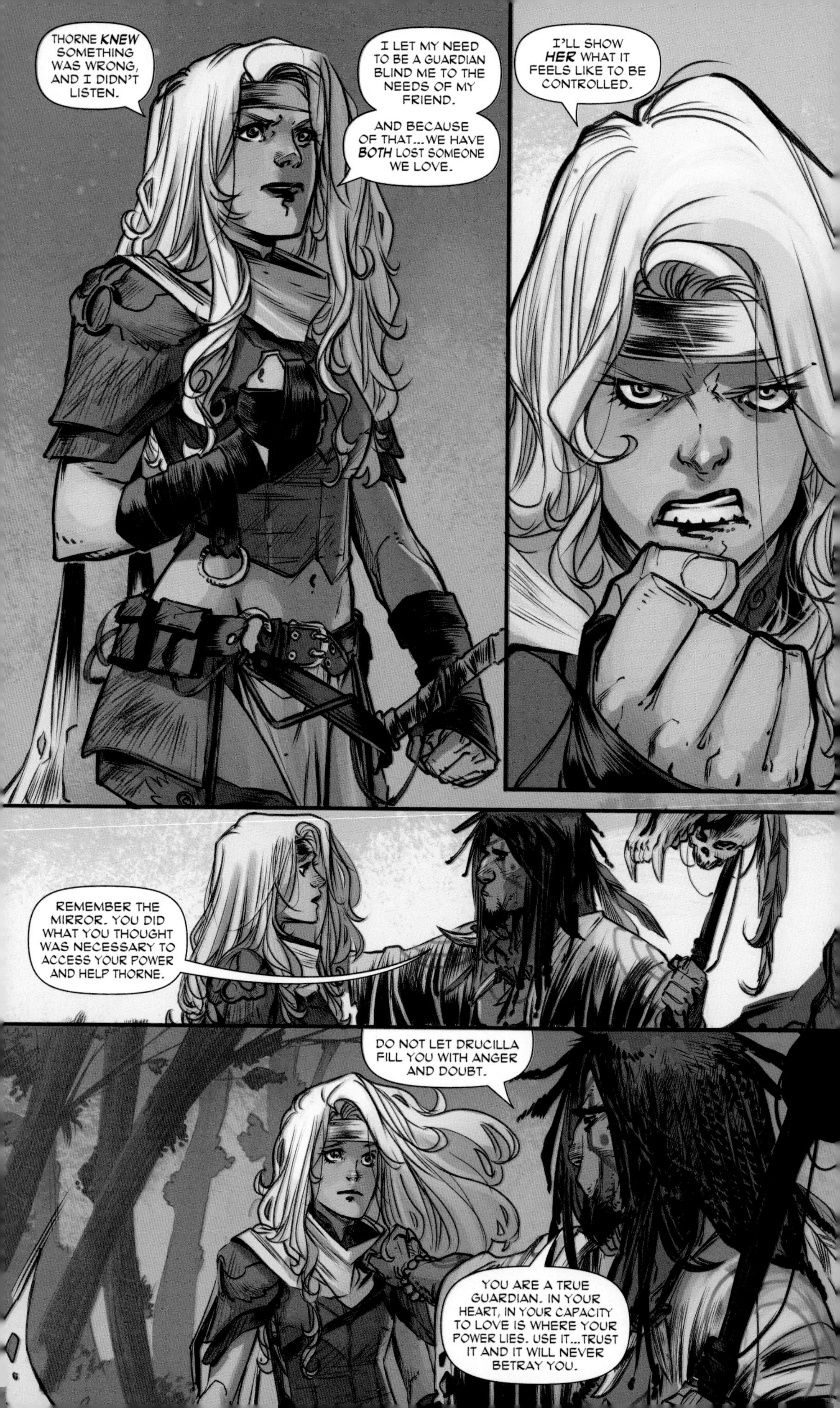
THORNE KNEW SOMETHING WAS WRONG, AND I DIDN'T LISTEN.
I LET MY NEED TO BE A GUARDIAN BLIND ME TO THE NEEDS OF MY FRIEND.
AND BECAUSE OF THAT...WE HAVE BOTH LOST SOMEONE WE LOVE.
I'LL SHOW HER WHAT IT FEELS LIKE TO BE CONTROLLED.
REMEMBER THE MIRROR. YOU DID WHAT YOU THOUGHT WAS NECESSARY TO ACCESS YOUR POWER AND HELP THORNE.
DO NOT LET DRUCILLA FILL YOU WITH ANGER AND DOUBT.
YOU ARE A TRUE GUARDIAN. IN YOUR HEART, IN YOUR CAPACITY TO LOVE IS WHERE YOUR POWER LIES. USE IT...TRUST IT AND IT WILL NEVER BETRAY YOU.

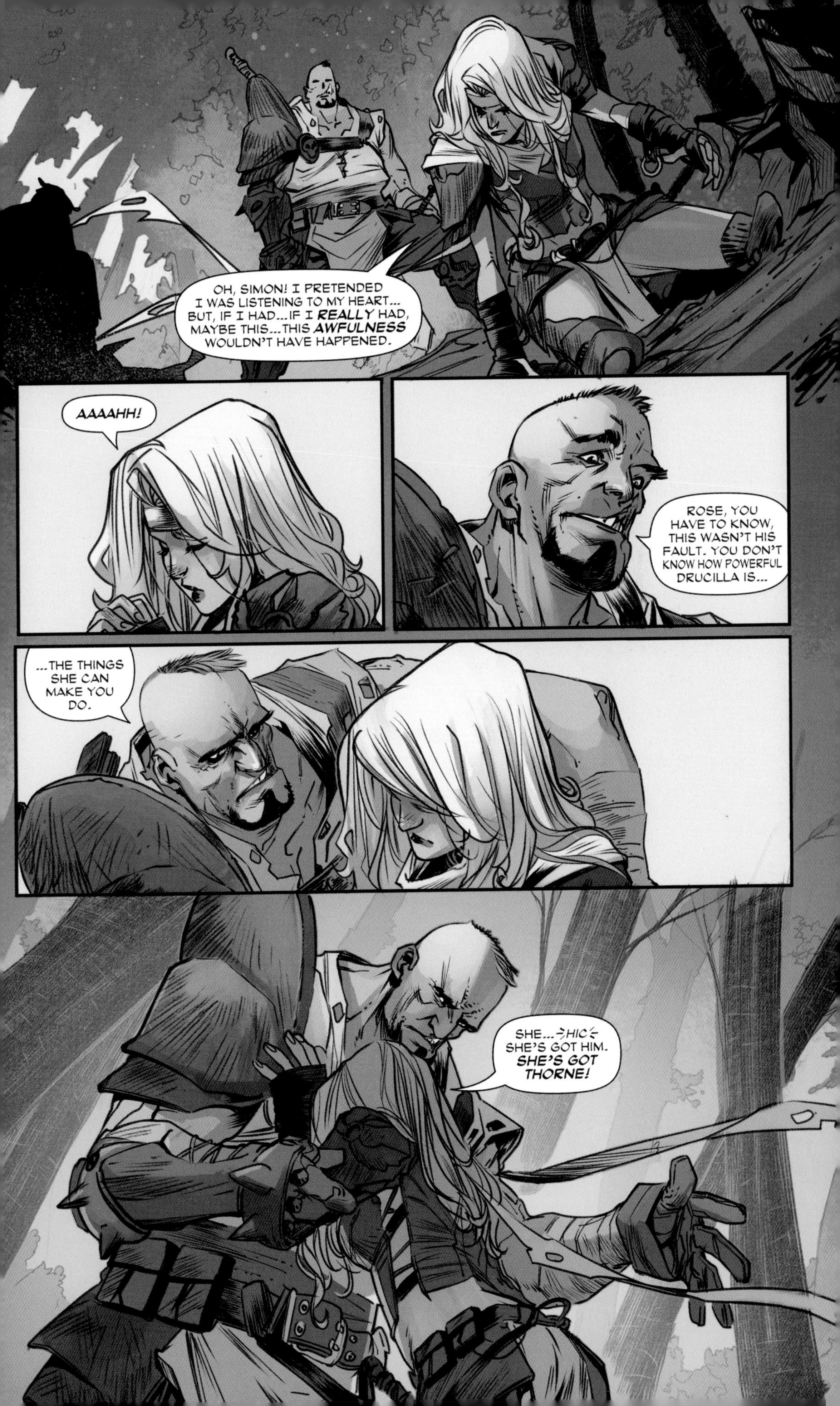
OH, SIMON! I PRETENDED I WAS LISTENING TO MY HEART... BUT, IF I HAD...IF I REALLY HAD, MAYBE THIS...THIS AWFULNESS WOULDN'T HAVE HAPPENED.
AAAAHH!
ROSE, YOU HAVE TO KNOW, THIS WASN'T HIS FAULT. YOU DON'T KNOW HOW POWERFUL DRUCILLA IS...
...THE THINGS SHE CAN MAKE YOU DO.
SHE... HIC SHE'S GOT HIM. SHE'S GOT THORNE!

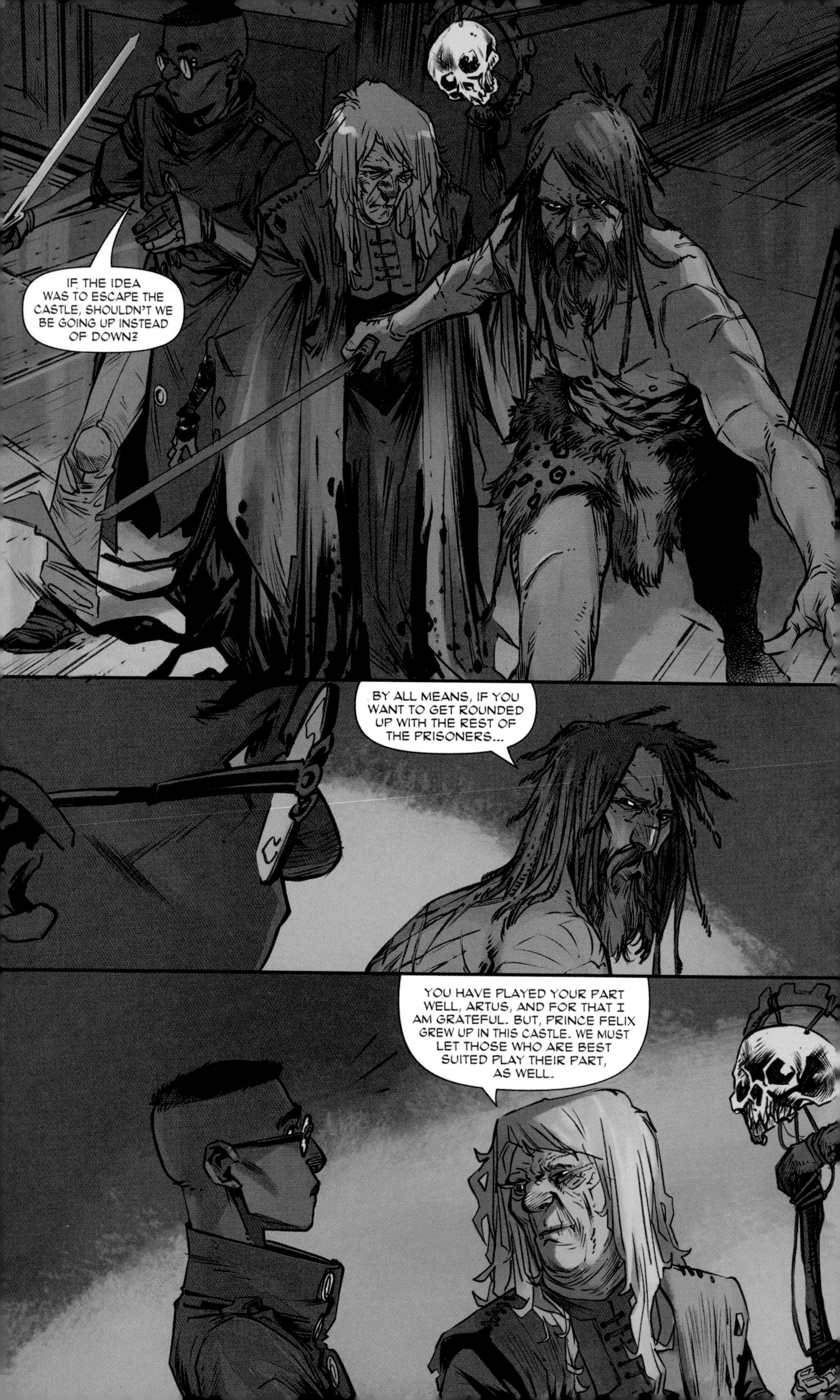
IF THE IDEA WAS TO ESCAPE THE CASTLE, SHOULDN'T WE BE GOING UP INSTEAD OF DOWN?
BY ALL MEANS, IF YOU WANT TO GET ROUNDED UP WITH THE REST OF THE PRISONERS...
YOU HAVE PLAYED YOUR PART WELL, ARTUS, AND FOR THAT I AM GRATEFUL. BUT, PRINCE FELIX GREW UP IN THIS CASTLE. WE MUST LET THOSE WHO ARE BEST SUITED PLAY THEIR PART, AS WELL.

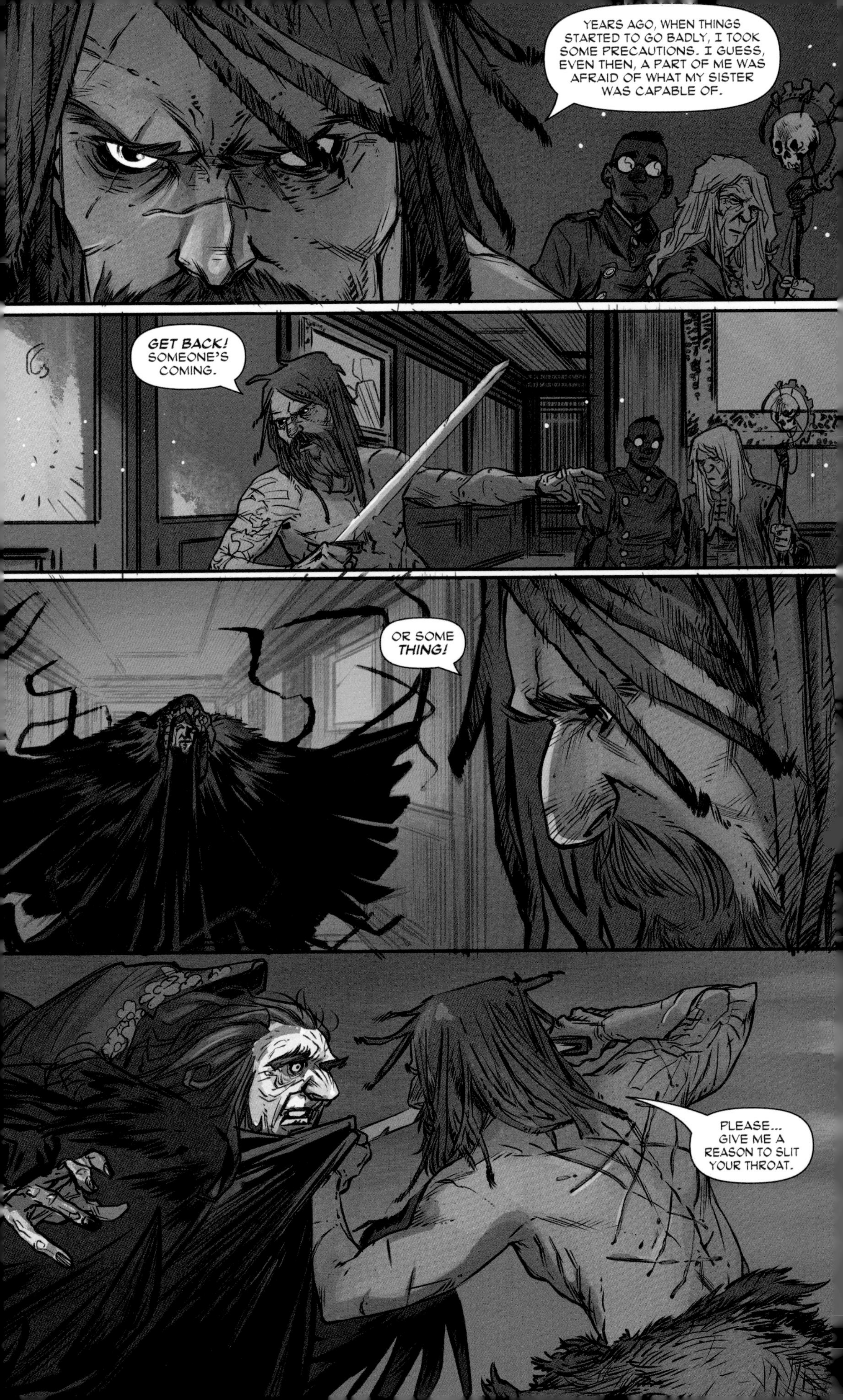
YEARS AGO, WHEN THINGS STARTED TO GO BADLY, I TOOK SOME PRECAUTIONS. I GUESS, EVEN THEN, A PART OF ME WAS AFRAID OF WHAT MY SISTER WAS CAPABLE OF.
GET BACK! SOMEONE'S COMING.
OR SOME *THING!*
PLEASE... GIVE ME A REASON TO SLIT YOUR THROAT.

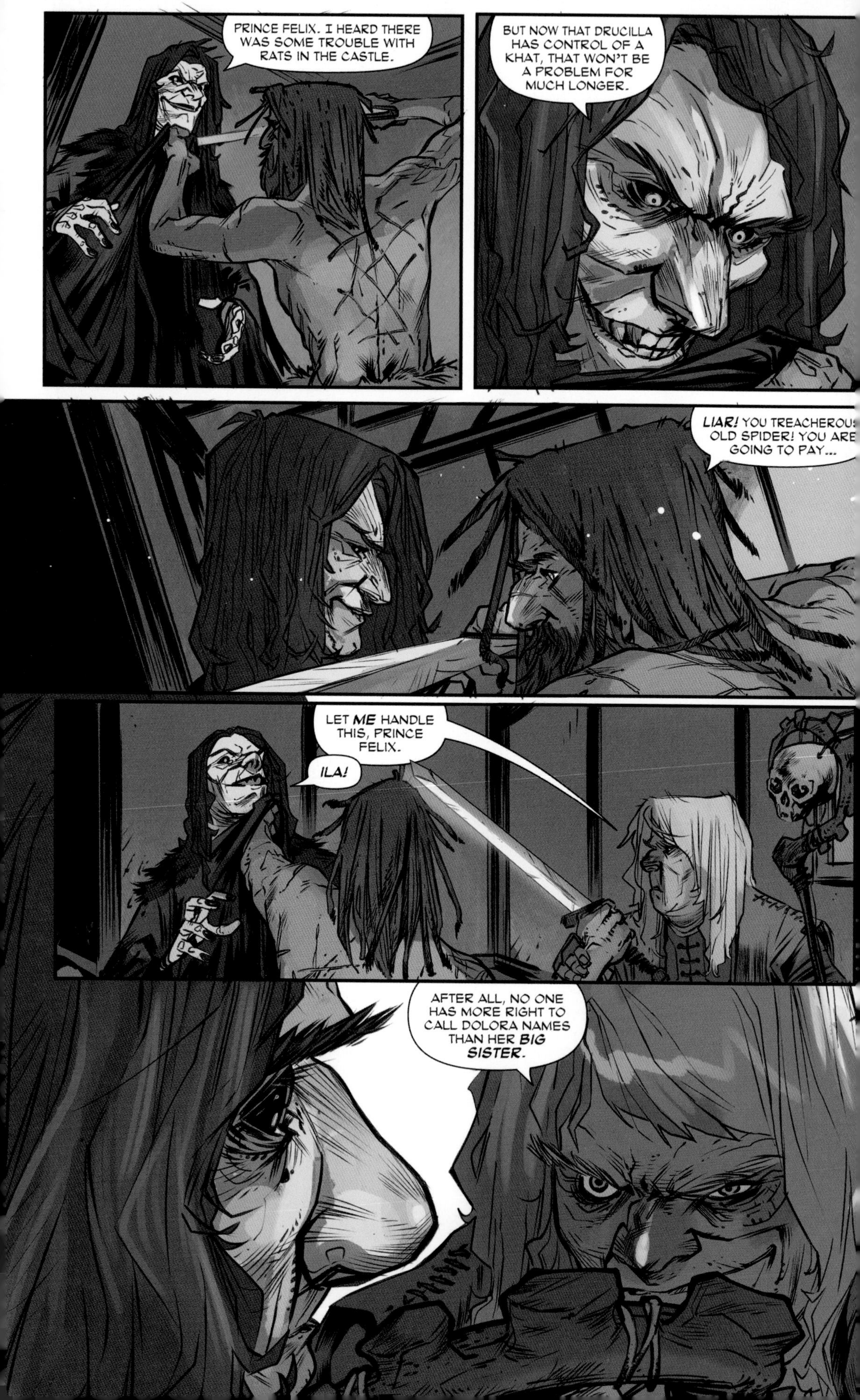
PRINCE FELIX. I HEARD THERE WAS SOME TROUBLE WITH RATS IN THE CASTLE.
BUT NOW THAT DRUCILLA HAS CONTROL OF A KHAT, THAT WON'T BE A PROBLEM FOR MUCH LONGER.
LIAR! YOU TREACHEROUS OLD SPIDER! YOU ARE GOING TO PAY...
LET ME HANDLE THIS, PRINCE FELIX.
ILA!
AFTER ALL, NO ONE HAS MORE RIGHT TO CALL DOLORA NAMES THAN HER BIG SISTER.

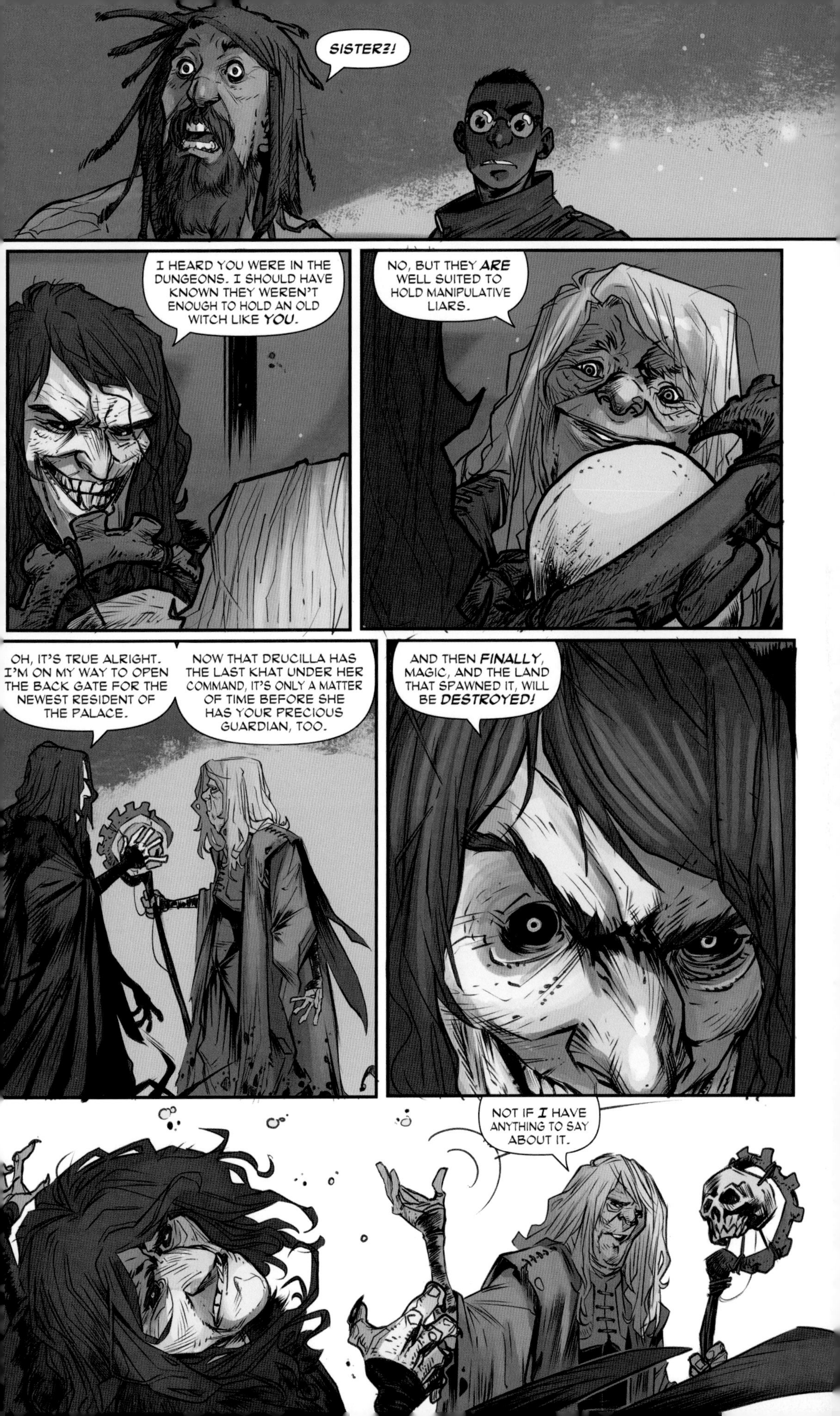
SISTER?!
I HEARD YOU WERE IN THE DUNGEONS. I SHOULD HAVE KNOWN THEY WEREN'T ENOUGH TO HOLD AN OLD WITCH LIKE YOU.
NO, BUT THEY ARE WELL SUITED TO HOLD MANIPULATIVE LIARS.
OH, IT'S TRUE ALRIGHT. I'M ON MY WAY TO OPEN THE BACK GATE FOR THE NEWEST RESIDENT OF THE PALACE.
NOW THAT DRUCILLA HAS THE LAST KHAT UNDER HER COMMAND, IT'S ONLY A MATTER OF TIME BEFORE SHE HAS YOUR PRECIOUS GUARDIAN, TOO.
AND THEN FINALLY, MAGIC, AND THE LAND THAT SPAWNED IT, WILL BE DESTROYED!
NOT IF I HAVE ANYTHING TO SAY ABOUT IT.

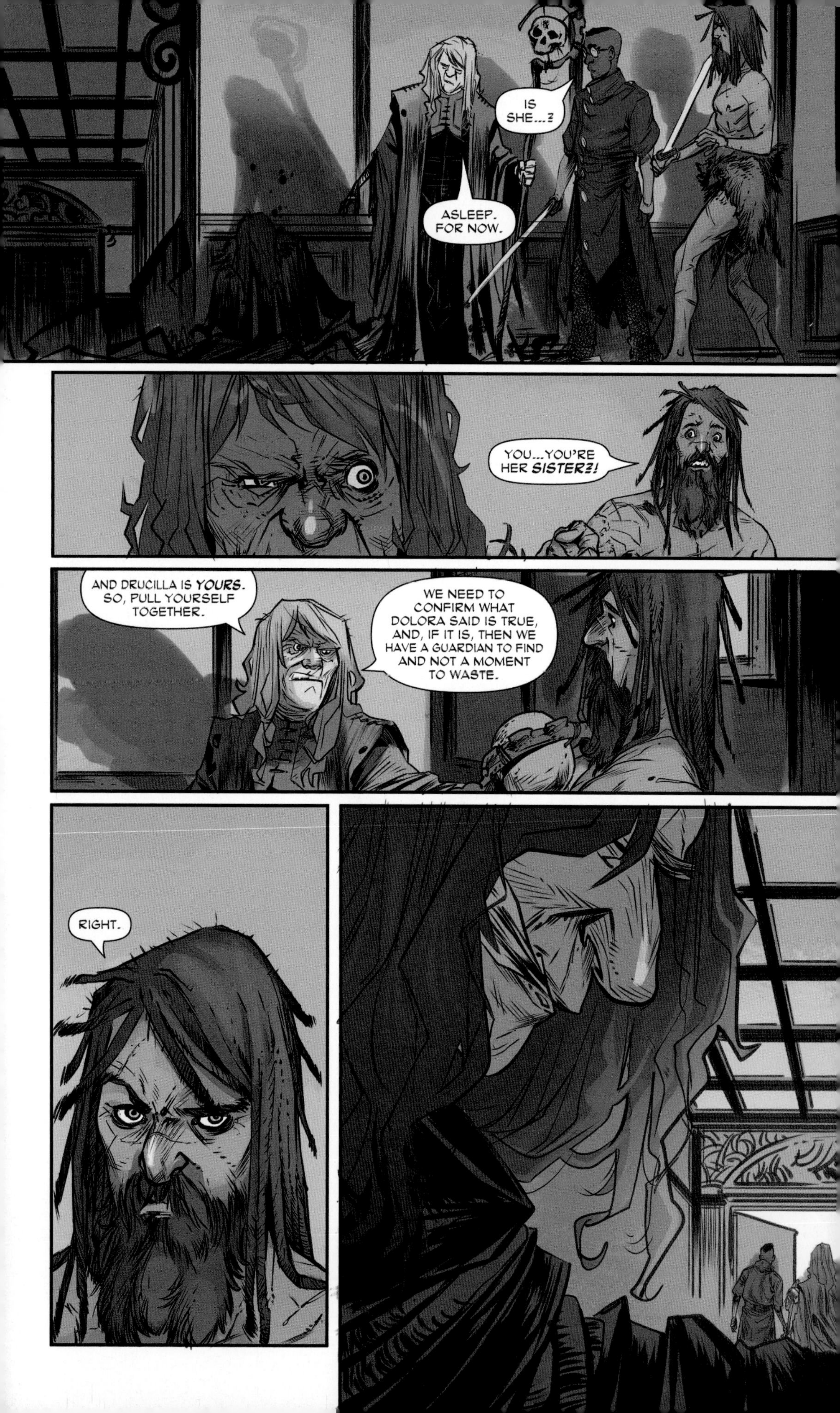
IS SHE...?
ASLEEP. FOR NOW.
YOU...YOU'RE HER *SISTER?!*
AND DRUCILLA IS *YOURS*. SO, PULL YOURSELF TOGETHER.
WE NEED TO CONFIRM WHAT DOLORA SAID IS TRUE, AND, IF IT IS, THEN WE HAVE A GUARDIAN TO FIND AND NOT A MOMENT TO WASTE.
RIGHT.

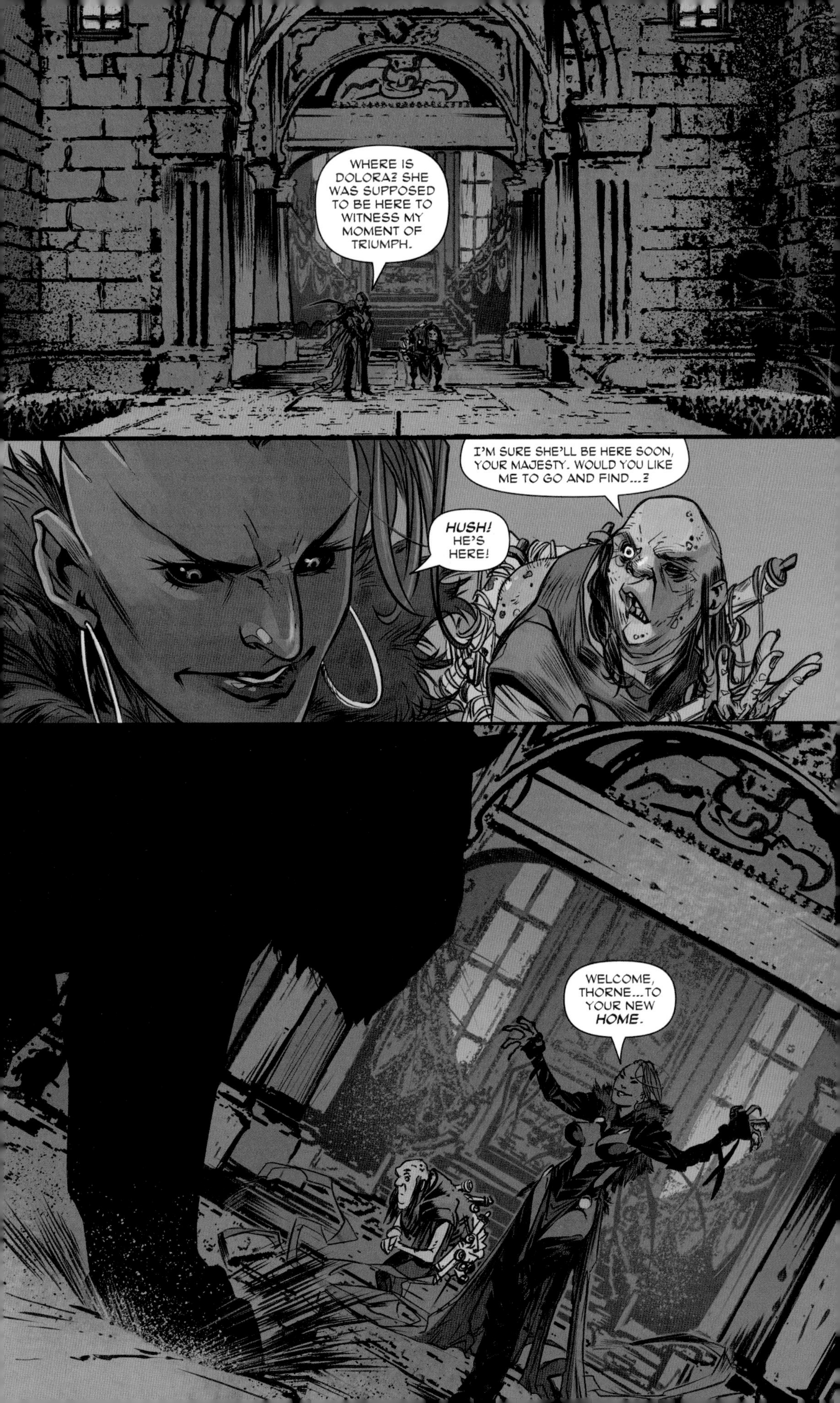
WHERE IS DOLORA? SHE WAS SUPPOSED TO BE HERE TO WITNESS MY MOMENT OF TRIUMPH.
I'M SURE SHE'LL BE HERE SOON, YOUR MAJESTY. WOULD YOU LIKE ME TO GO AND FIND...?
HUSH! HE'S HERE!
WELCOME, THORNE...TO YOUR NEW HOME.

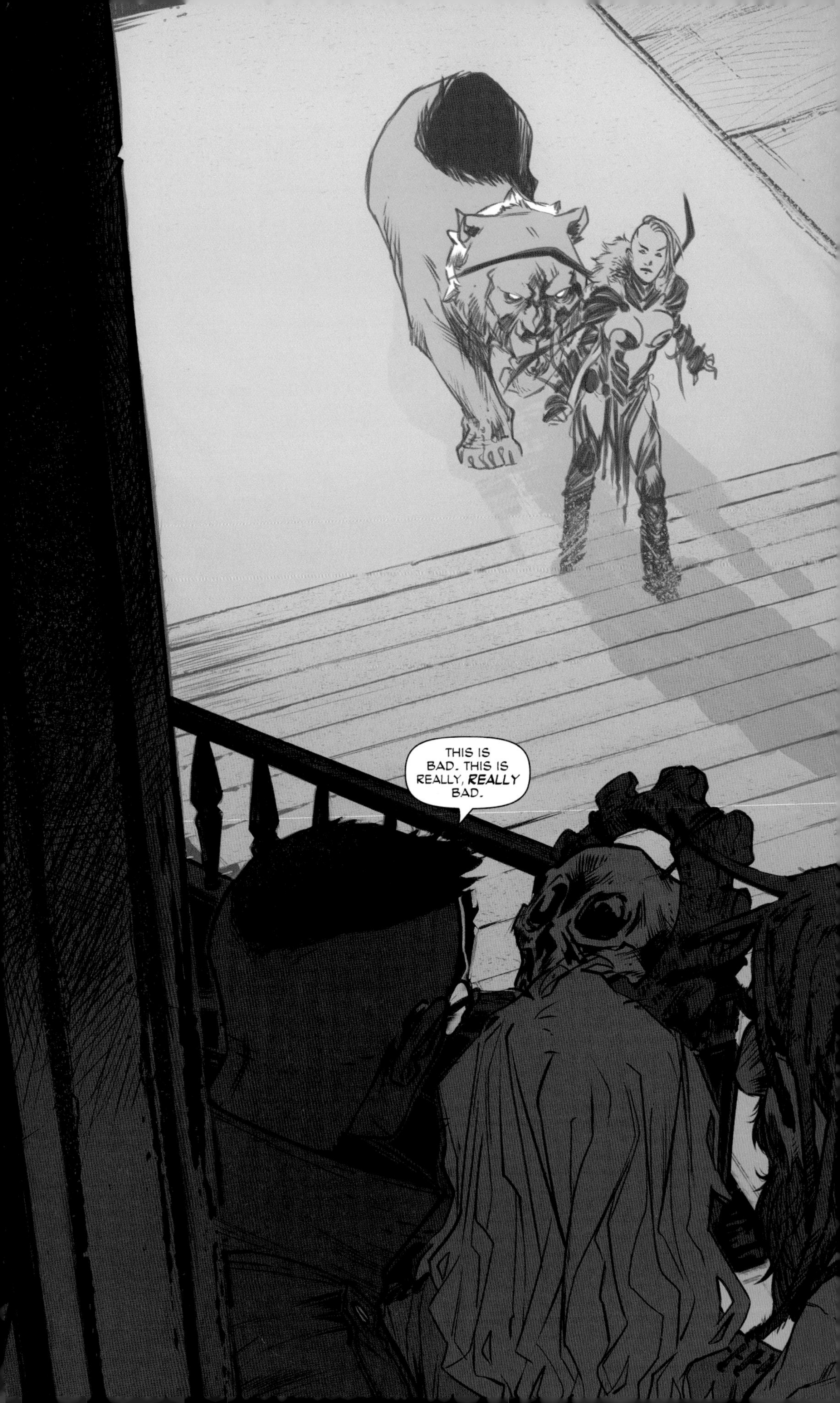
THIS IS BAD. THIS IS REALLY, *REALLY* BAD.

ELEVEN

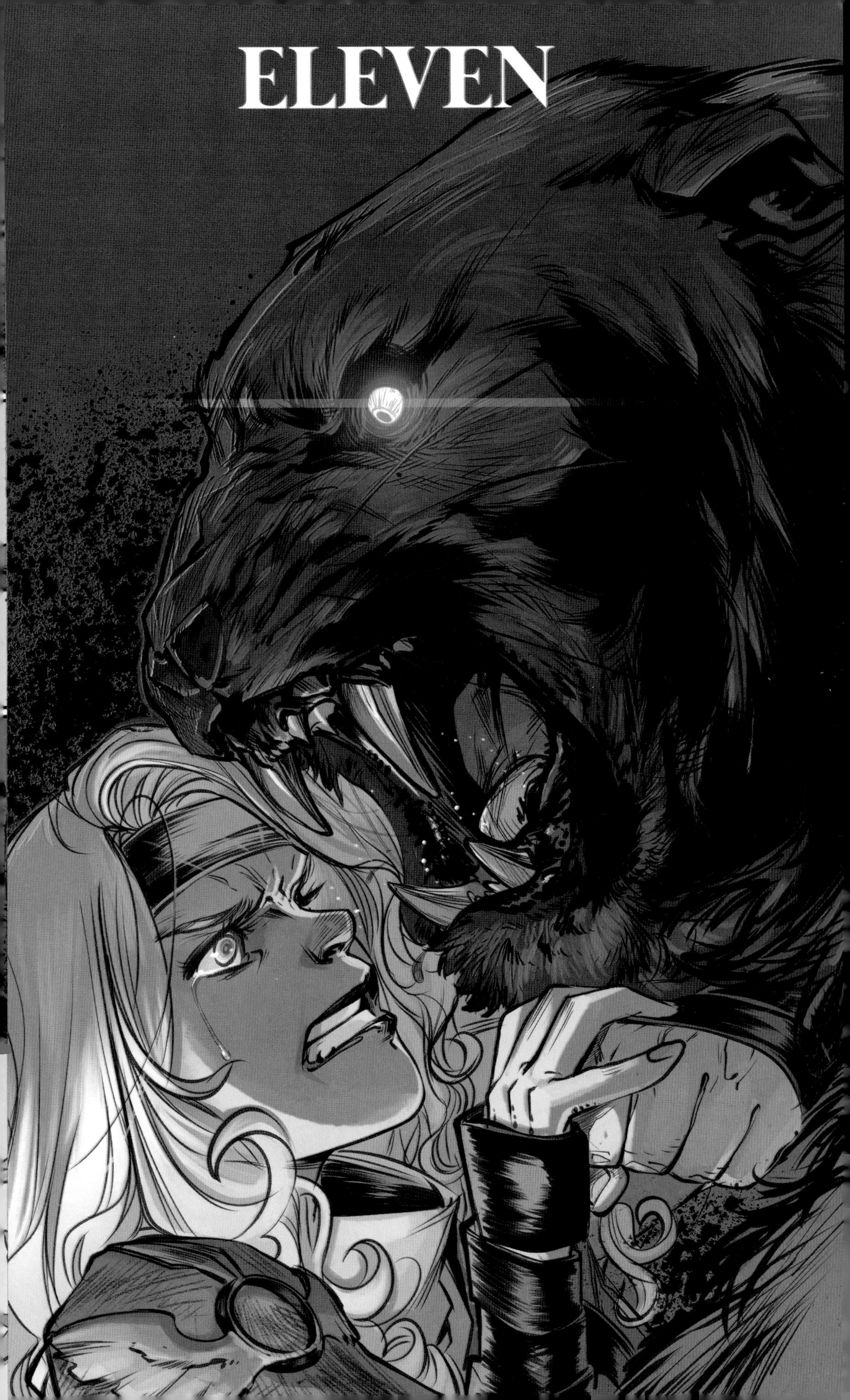

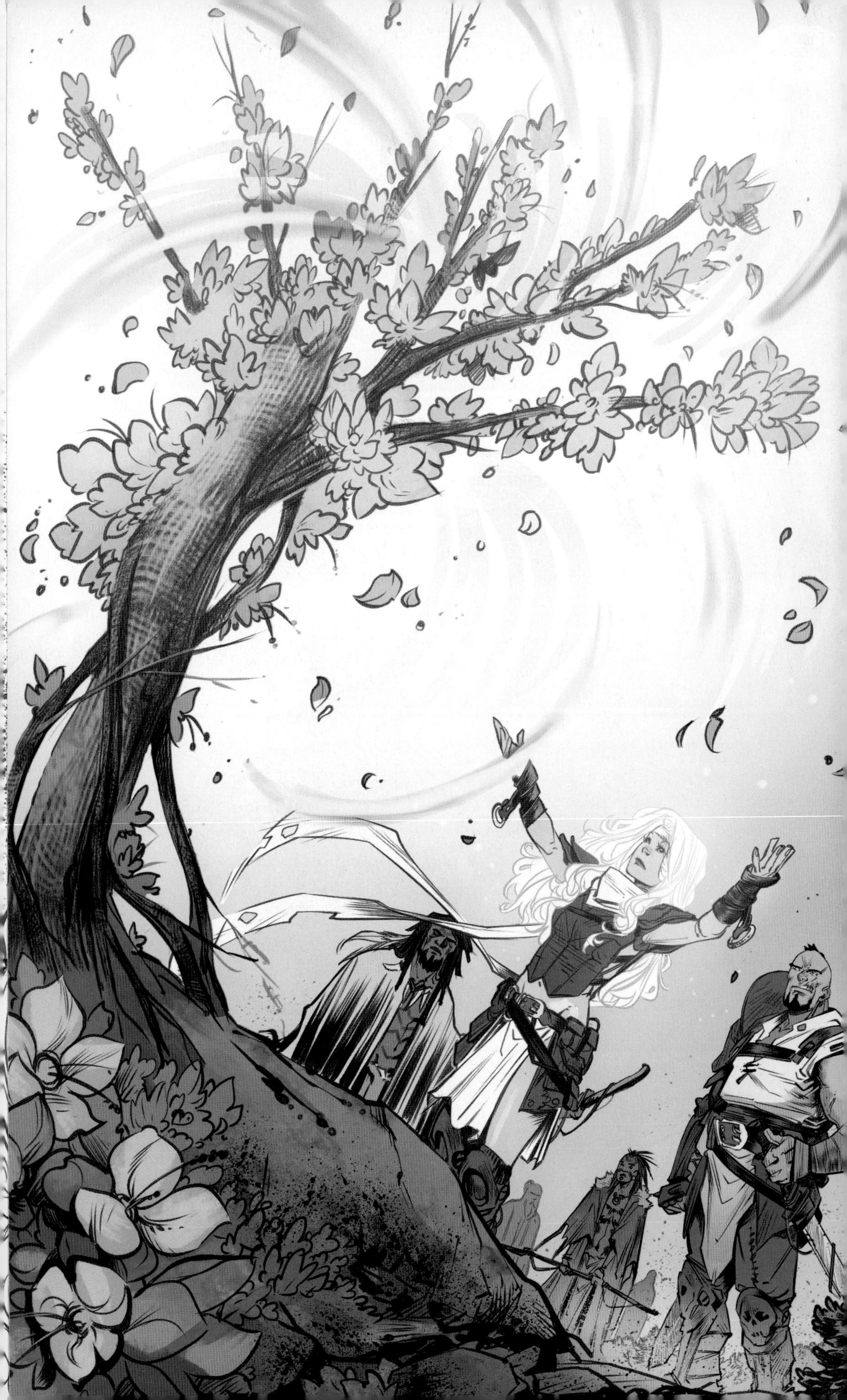

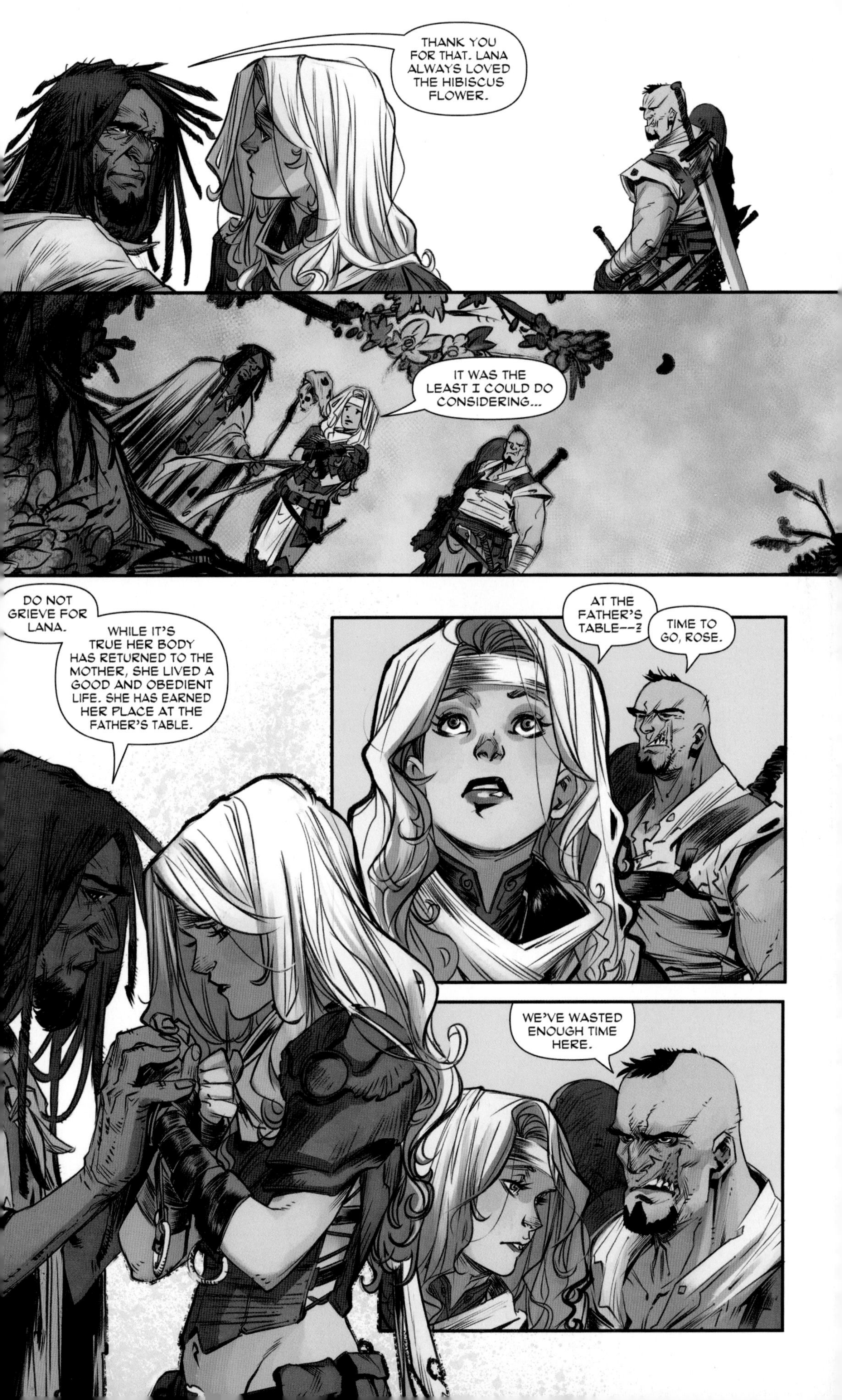
THANK YOU FOR THAT. LANA ALWAYS LOVED THE HIBISCUS FLOWER.
IT WAS THE LEAST I COULD DO CONSIDERING...
DO NOT GRIEVE FOR LANA.
WHILE IT'S TRUE HER BODY HAS RETURNED TO THE MOTHER, SHE LIVED A GOOD AND OBEDIENT LIFE. SHE HAS EARNED HER PLACE AT THE FATHER'S TABLE.
AT THE FATHER'S TABLE--?
TIME TO GO, ROSE.
WE'VE WASTED ENOUGH TIME HERE.

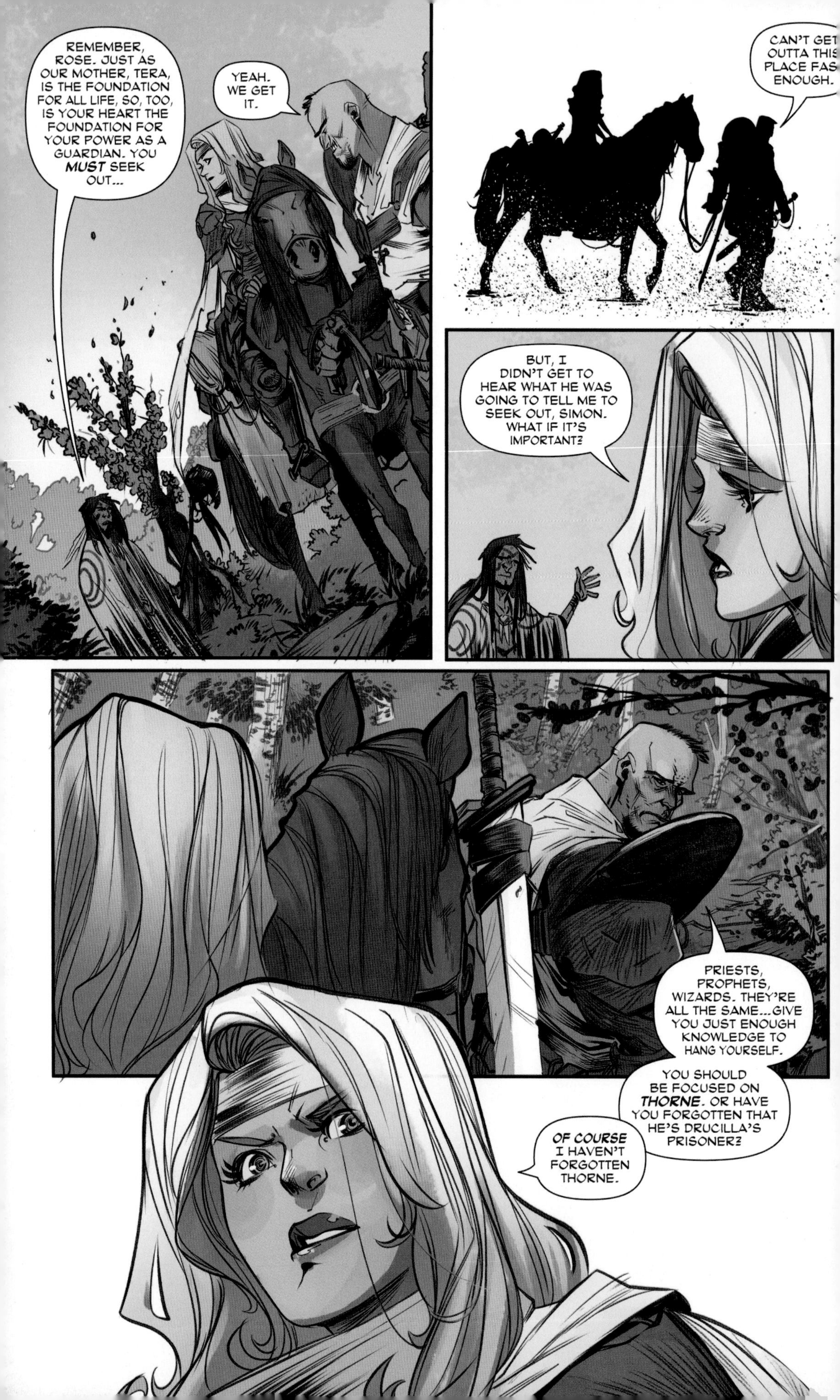
REMEMBER, ROSE. JUST AS OUR MOTHER, TERA, IS THE FOUNDATION FOR ALL LIFE, SO, TOO, IS YOUR HEART THE FOUNDATION FOR YOUR POWER AS A GUARDIAN. YOU MUST SEEK OUT...
YEAH. WE GET IT.
CAN'T GET OUTTA THIS PLACE FAS ENOUGH.
BUT, I DIDN'T GET TO HEAR WHAT HE WAS GOING TO TELL ME TO SEEK OUT, SIMON. WHAT IF IT'S IMPORTANT?
PRIESTS, PROPHETS, WIZARDS. THEY'RE ALL THE SAME...GIVE YOU JUST ENOUGH KNOWLEDGE TO HANG YOURSELF.
YOU SHOULD BE FOCUSED ON THORNE. OR HAVE YOU FORGOTTEN THAT HE'S DRUCILLA'S PRISONER?
OF COURSE I HAVEN'T FORGOTTEN THORNE.

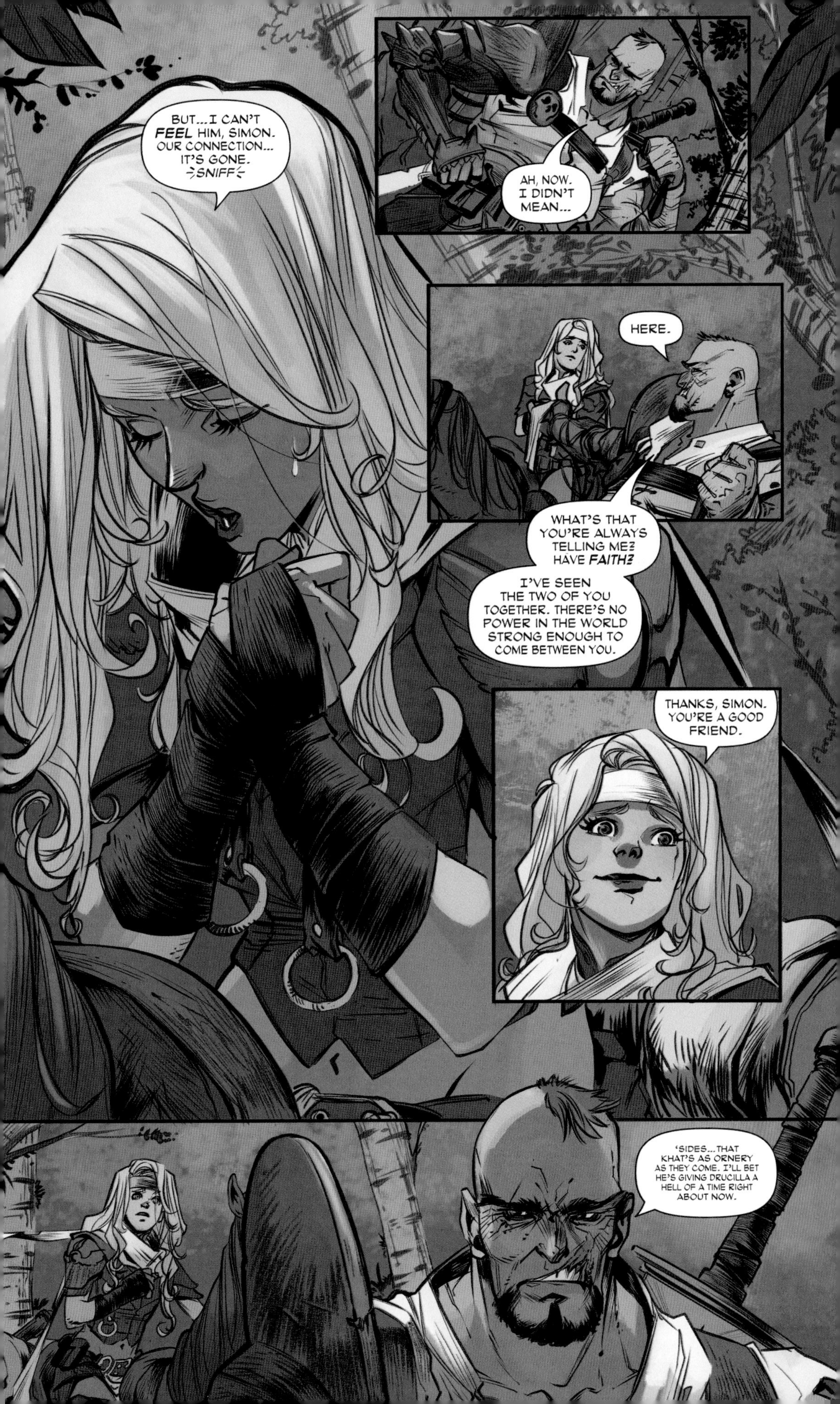
BUT... I CAN'T FEEL HIM, SIMON. OUR CONNECTION... IT'S GONE. *SNIFF*
AH, NOW. I DIDN'T MEAN...
HERE.
WHAT'S THAT YOU'RE ALWAYS TELLING ME? HAVE FAITH?
I'VE SEEN THE TWO OF YOU TOGETHER. THERE'S NO POWER IN THE WORLD STRONG ENOUGH TO COME BETWEEN YOU.
THANKS, SIMON. YOU'RE A GOOD FRIEND.
'SIDES... THAT KHAT'S AS ORNERY AS THEY COME. I'LL BET HE'S GIVING DRUCILLA A HELL OF A TIME RIGHT ABOUT NOW.

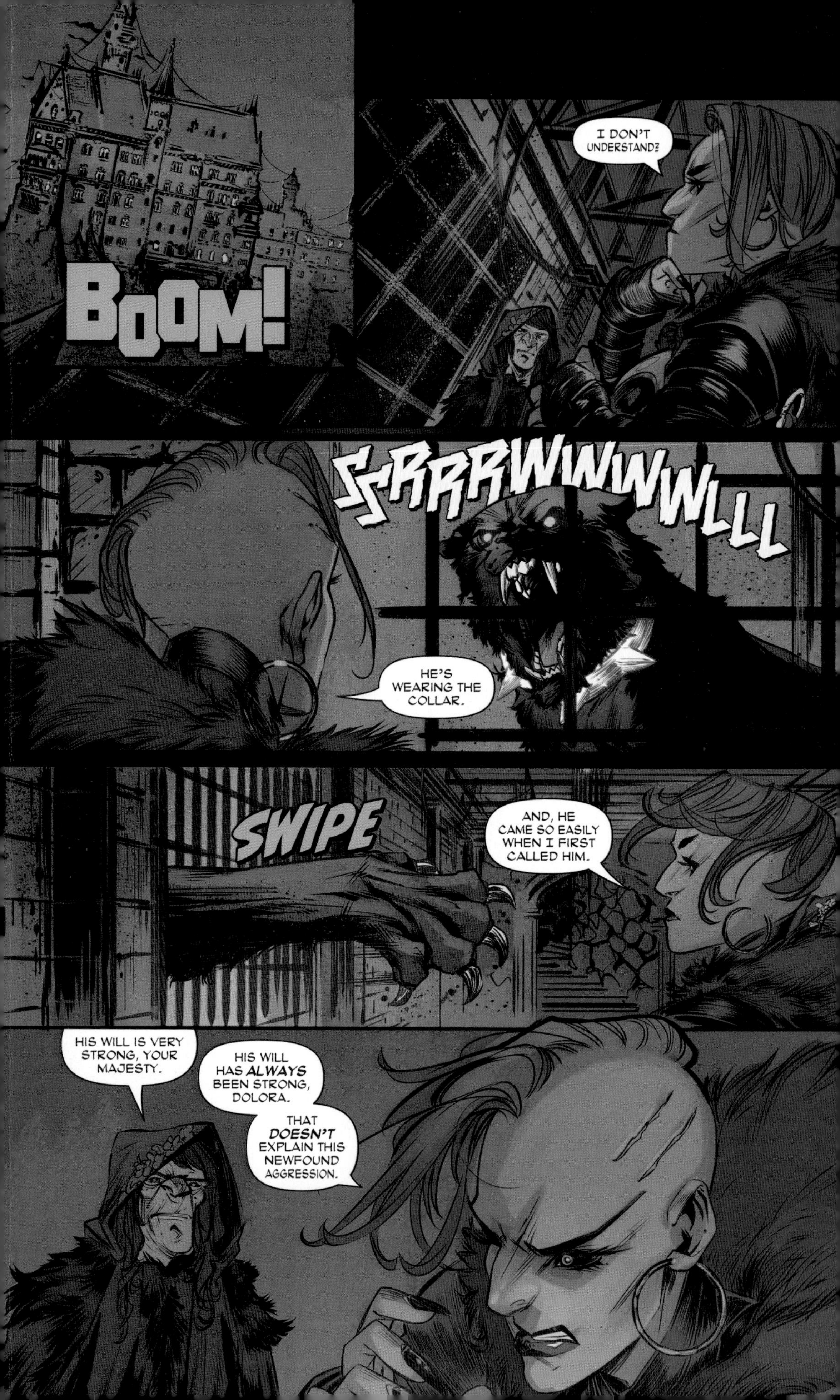
BOOM!
I DON'T UNDERSTAND?
SRRRWWWWLLL
HE'S WEARING THE COLLAR.
SWIPE
AND, HE CAME SO EASILY WHEN I FIRST CALLED HIM.
HIS WILL IS VERY STRONG, YOUR MAJESTY.
HIS WILL HAS ALWAYS BEEN STRONG, DOLORA.
THAT DOESN'T EXPLAIN THIS NEWFOUND AGGRESSION.

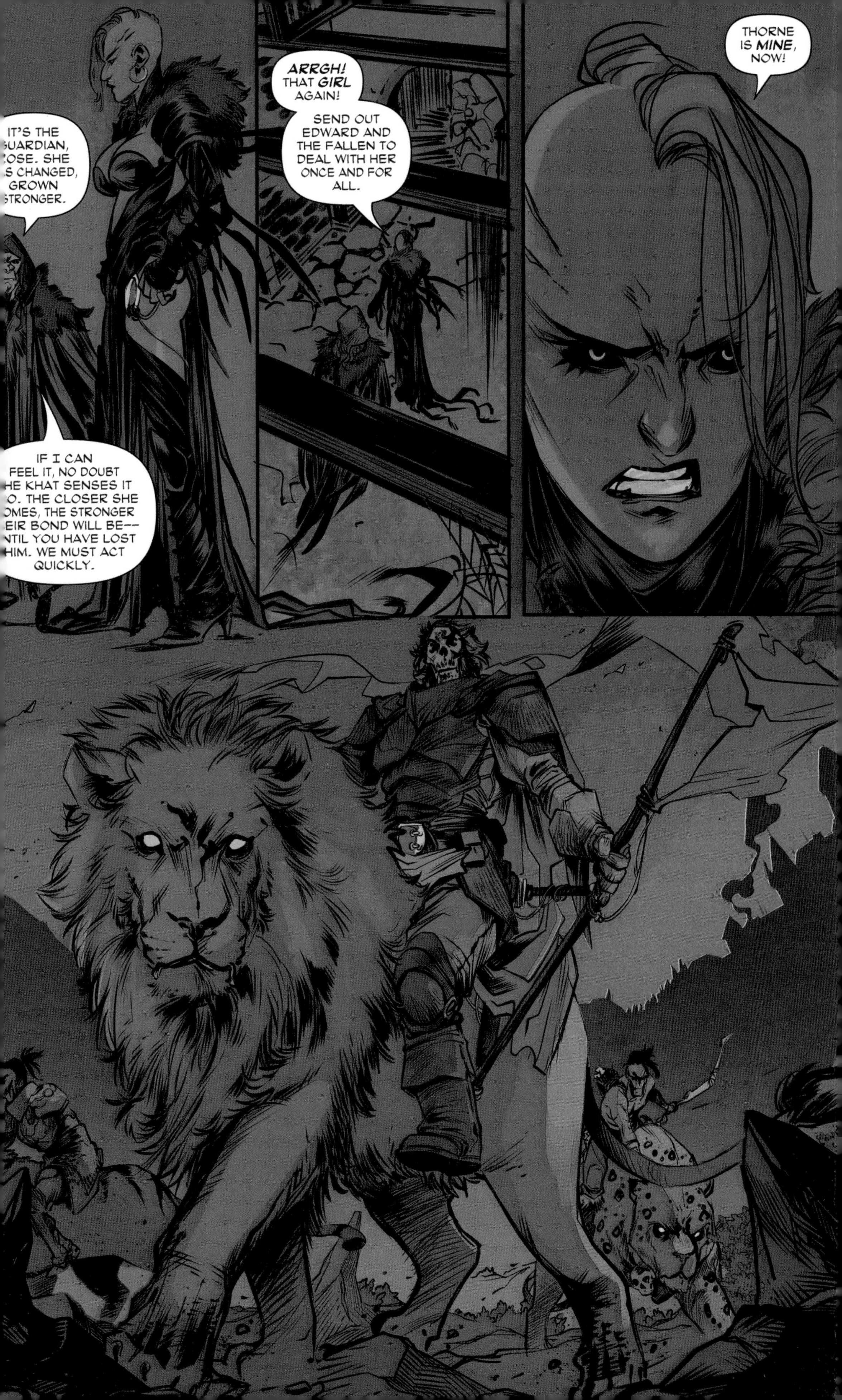
IT'S THE UARDIAN, OSE. SHE S CHANGED, GROWN TRONGER.
IF I CAN FEEL IT, NO DOUBT HE KHAT SENSES IT O. THE CLOSER SHE OMES, THE STRONGER EIR BOND WILL BE-- NTIL YOU HAVE LOST HIM. WE MUST ACT QUICKLY.
ARRGH! THAT GIRL AGAIN!
SEND OUT EDWARD AND THE FALLEN TO DEAL WITH HER ONCE AND FOR ALL.
THORNE IS MINE, NOW!

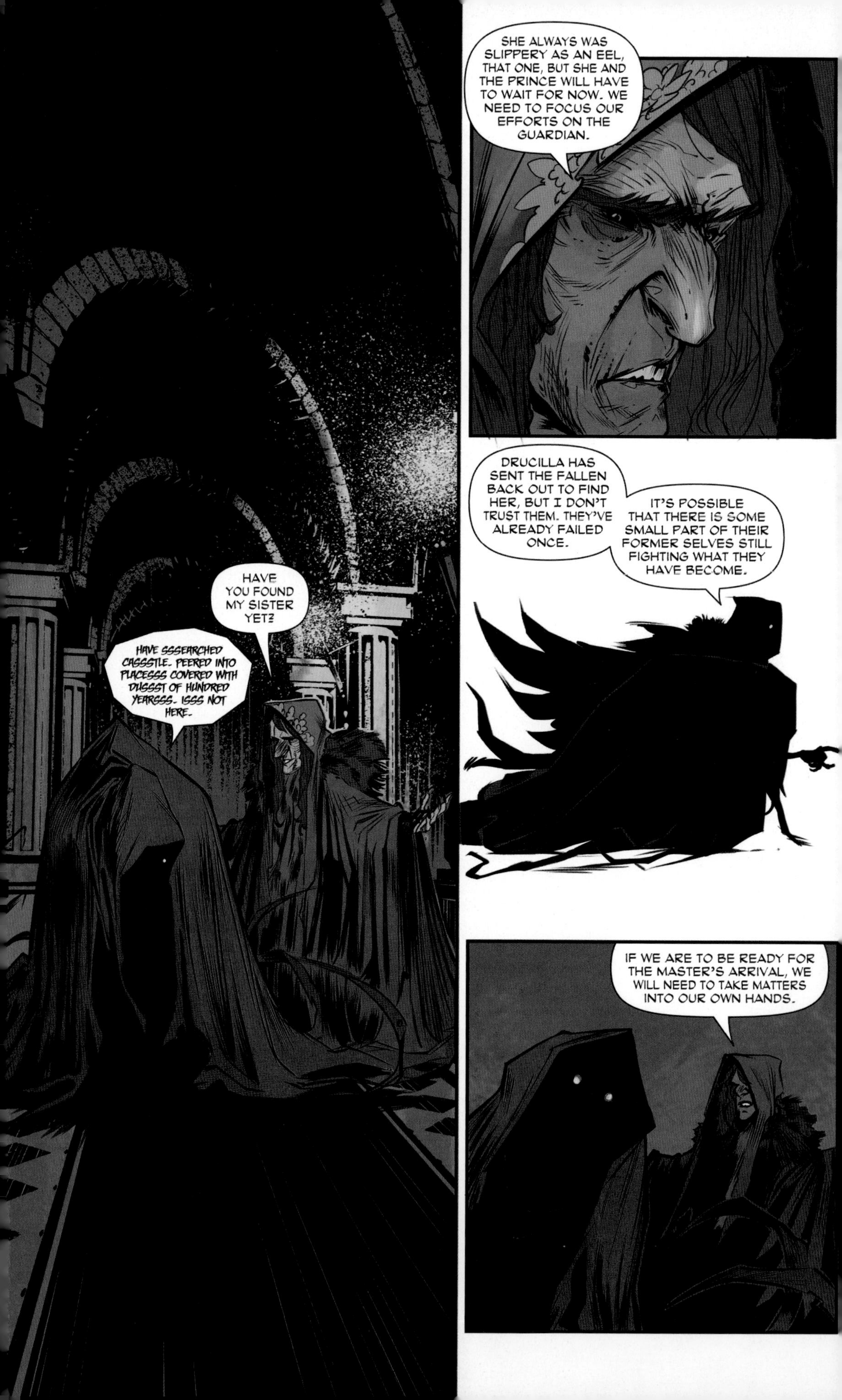
HAVE YOU FOUND MY SISTER YET?
HAVE SSSEARCHED CASSSTLE. PEERED INTO PLACESSS COVERED WITH DUSSST OF HUNDRED YEARSSS. ISSS NOT HERE.
SHE ALWAYS WAS SLIPPERY AS AN EEL, THAT ONE, BUT SHE AND THE PRINCE WILL HAVE TO WAIT FOR NOW. WE NEED TO FOCUS OUR EFFORTS ON THE GUARDIAN.
DRUCILLA HAS SENT THE FALLEN BACK OUT TO FIND HER, BUT I DON'T TRUST THEM. THEY'VE ALREADY FAILED ONCE.
IT'S POSSIBLE THAT THERE IS SOME SMALL PART OF THEIR FORMER SELVES STILL FIGHTING WHAT THEY HAVE BECOME.
IF WE ARE TO BE READY FOR THE MASTER'S ARRIVAL, WE WILL NEED TO TAKE MATTERS INTO OUR OWN HANDS.

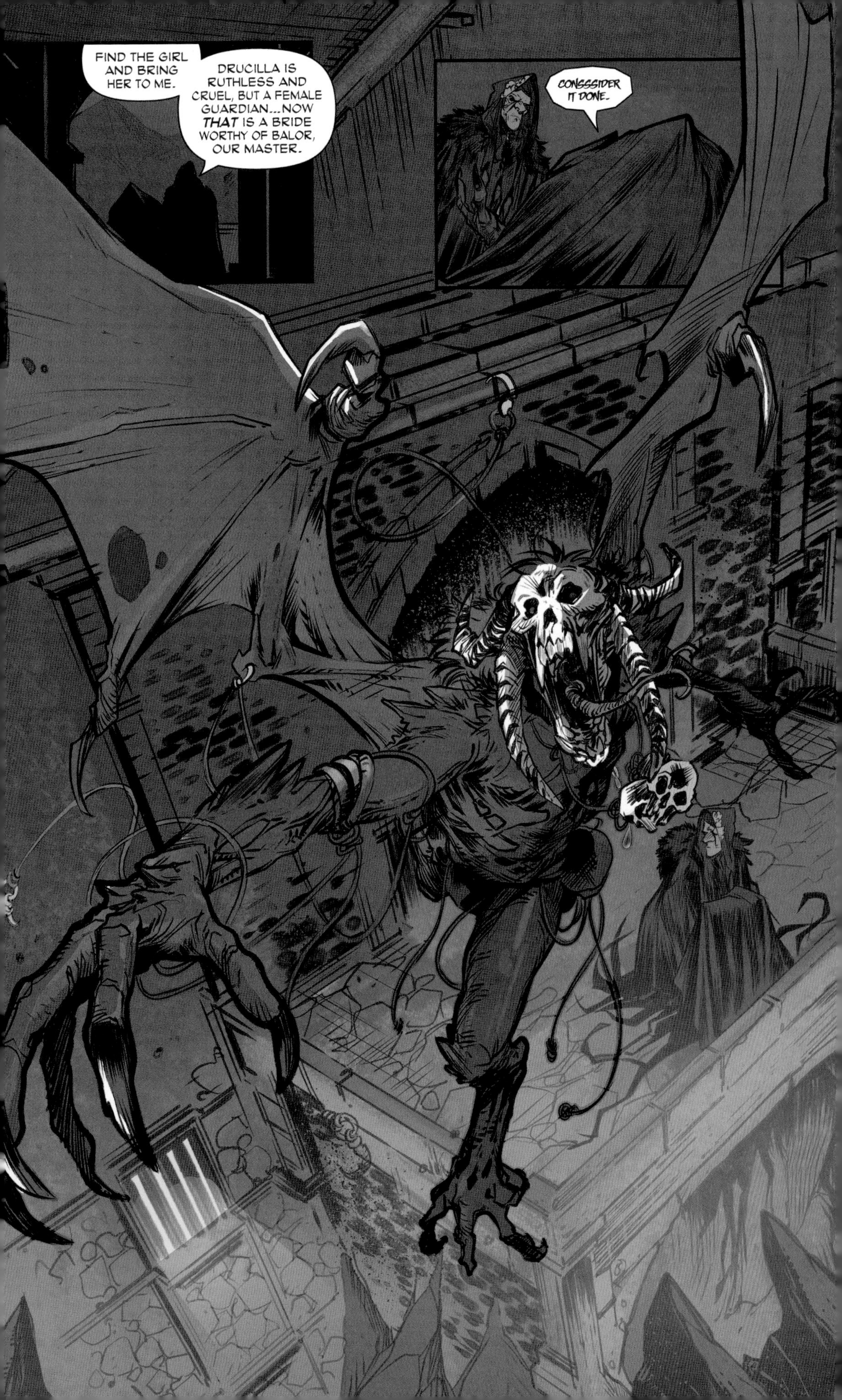
FIND THE GIRL AND BRING HER TO ME.
DRUCILLA IS RUTHLESS AND CRUEL, BUT A FEMALE GUARDIAN...NOW THAT IS A BRIDE WORTHY OF BALOR, OUR MASTER.
CONSSSIDER IT DONE.

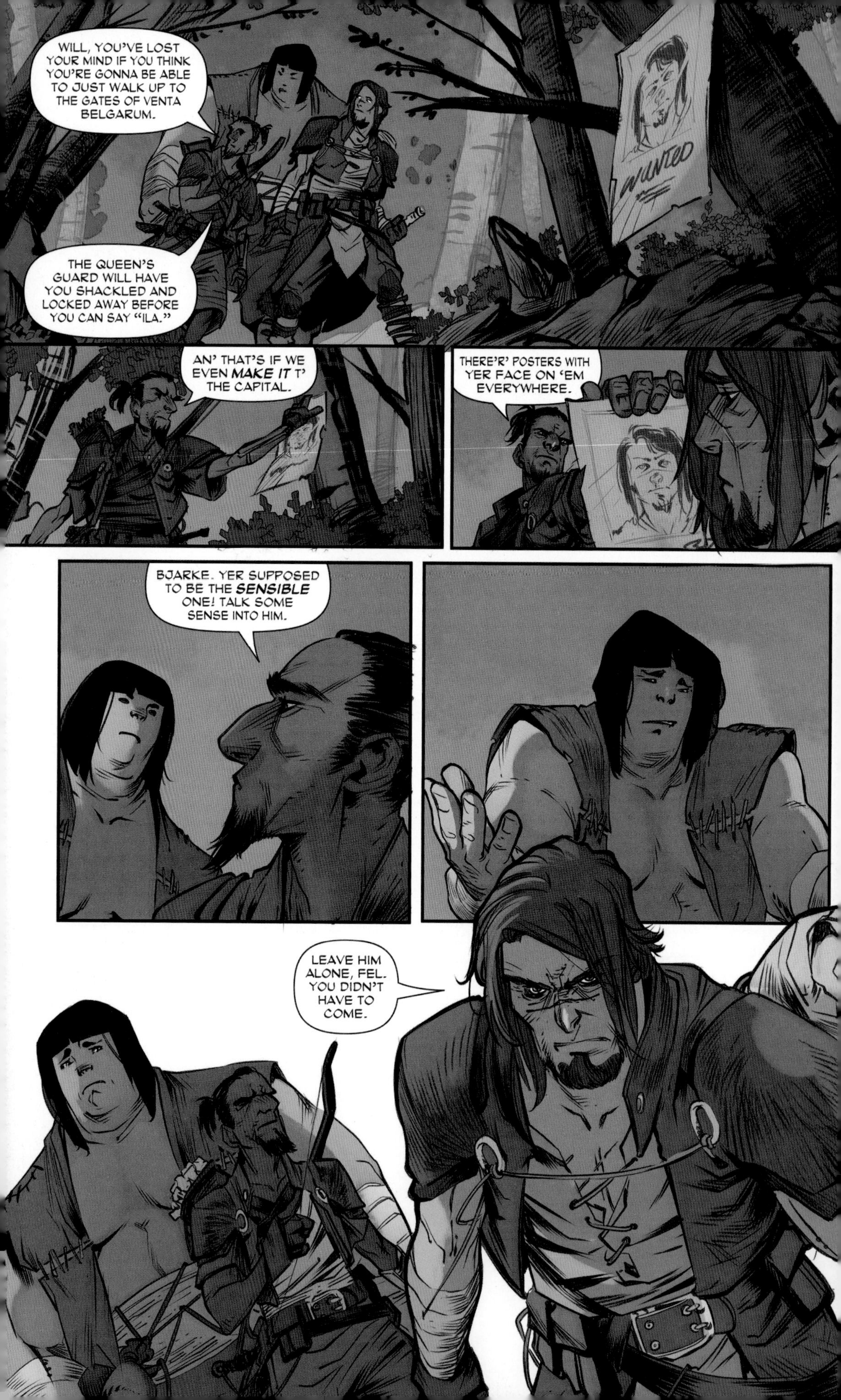

WILL, YOU'VE LOST YOUR MIND IF YOU THINK YOU'RE GONNA BE ABLE TO JUST WALK UP TO THE GATES OF VENTA BELGARUM.
THE QUEEN'S GUARD WILL HAVE YOU SHACKLED AND LOCKED AWAY BEFORE YOU CAN SAY "ILA."
WANTED
AN' THAT'S IF WE EVEN *MAKE IT* T' THE CAPITAL.
THERE'R' POSTERS WITH YER FACE ON 'EM EVERYWHERE.
BJARKE. YER SUPPOSED TO BE THE *SENSIBLE* ONE! TALK SOME SENSE INTO HIM.
LEAVE HIM ALONE, FEL. YOU DIDN'T HAVE TO COME.

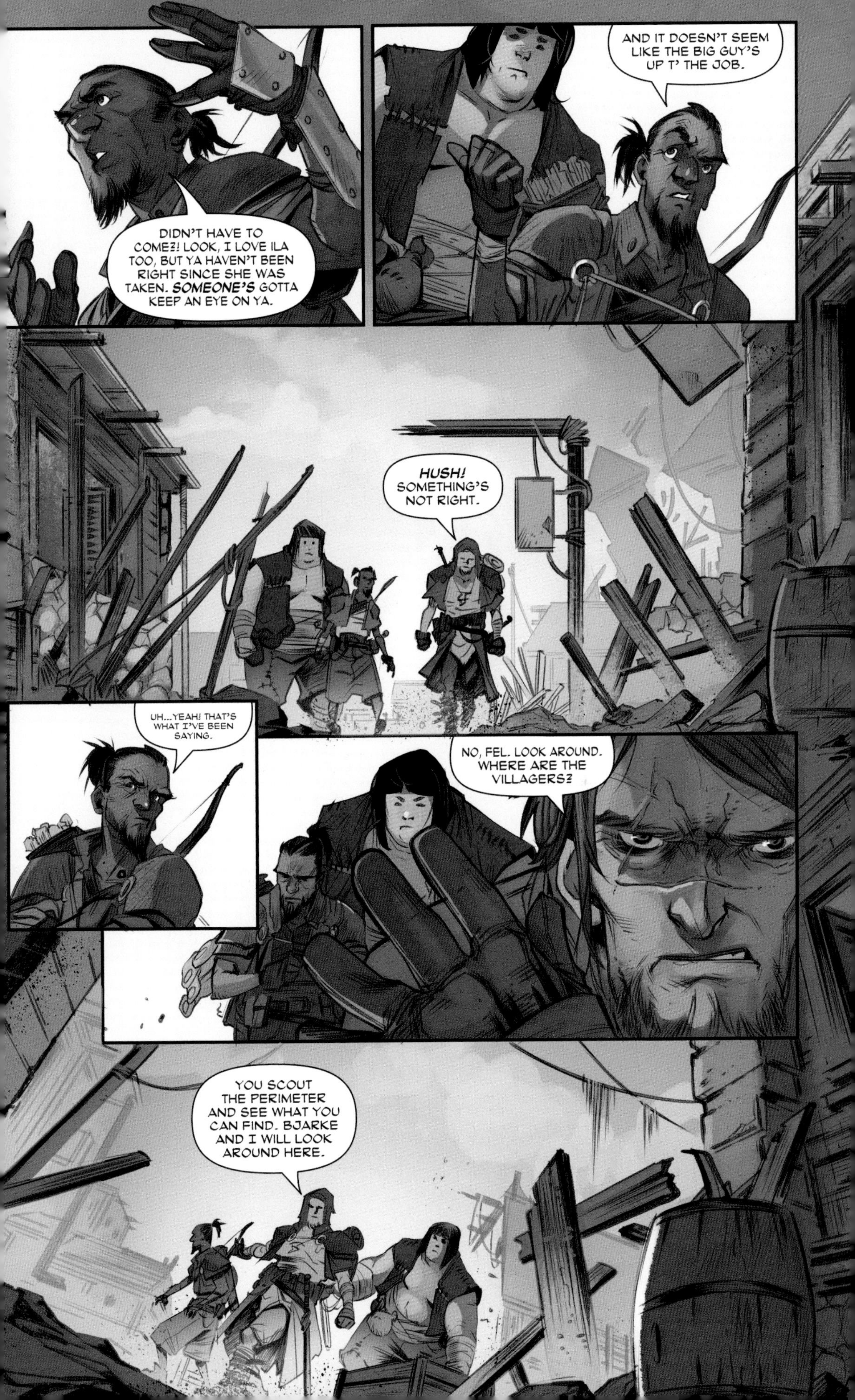
DIDN'T HAVE TO COME?! LOOK, I LOVE ILA TOO, BUT YA HAVEN'T BEEN RIGHT SINCE SHE WAS TAKEN. SOMEONE'S GOTTA KEEP AN EYE ON YA.
AND IT DOESN'T SEEM LIKE THE BIG GUY'S UP T' THE JOB.
HUSH! SOMETHING'S NOT RIGHT.
UH...YEAH! THAT'S WHAT I'VE BEEN SAYING.
NO, FEL. LOOK AROUND. WHERE ARE THE VILLAGERS?
YOU SCOUT THE PERIMETER AND SEE WHAT YOU CAN FIND. BJARKE AND I WILL LOOK AROUND HERE.

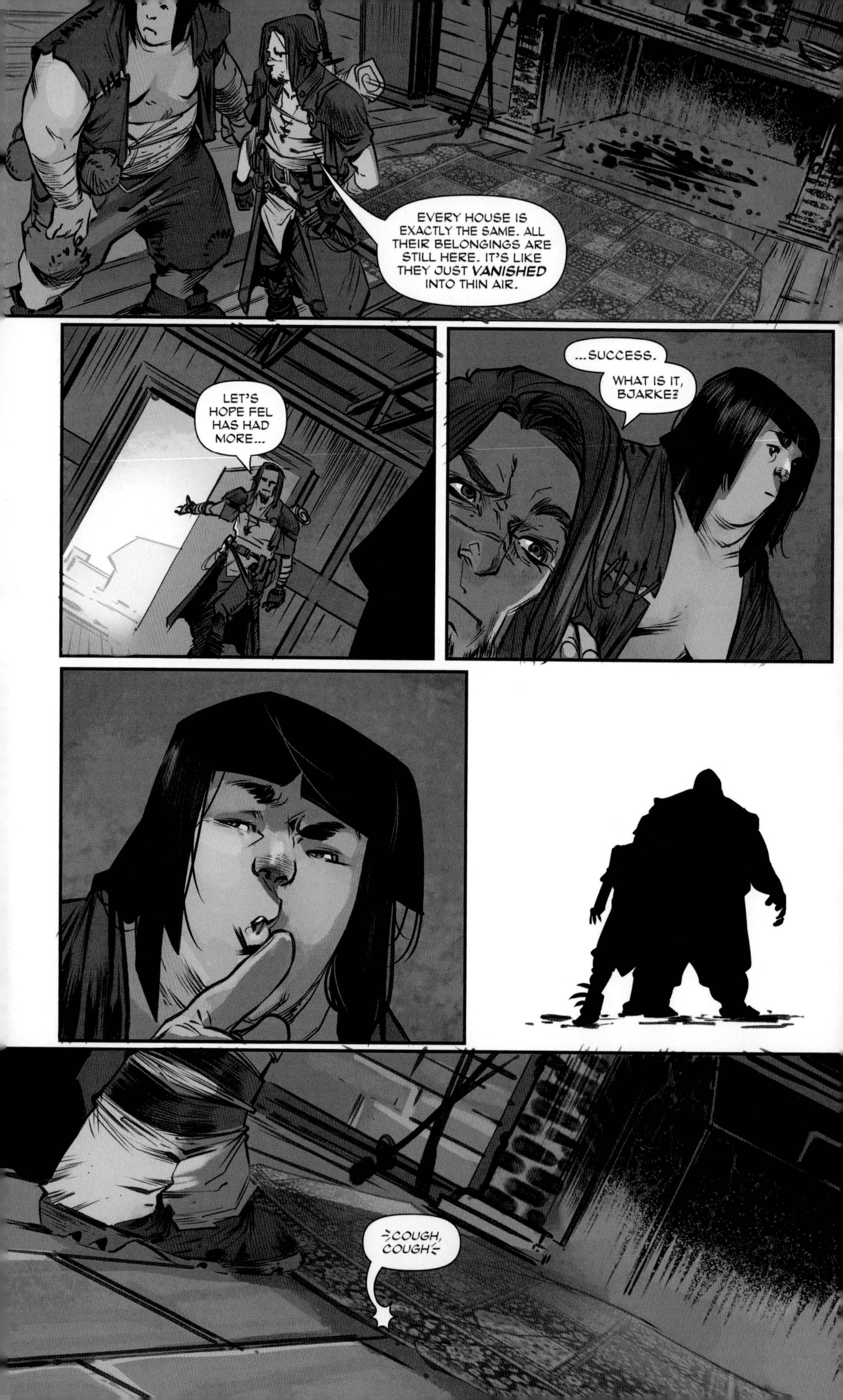
EVERY HOUSE IS EXACTLY THE SAME. ALL THEIR BELONGINGS ARE STILL HERE. IT'S LIKE THEY JUST *VANISHED* INTO THIN AIR.
LET'S HOPE FEL HAS HAD MORE...
...SUCCESS.
WHAT IS IT, BJARKE?
COUGH, COUGH

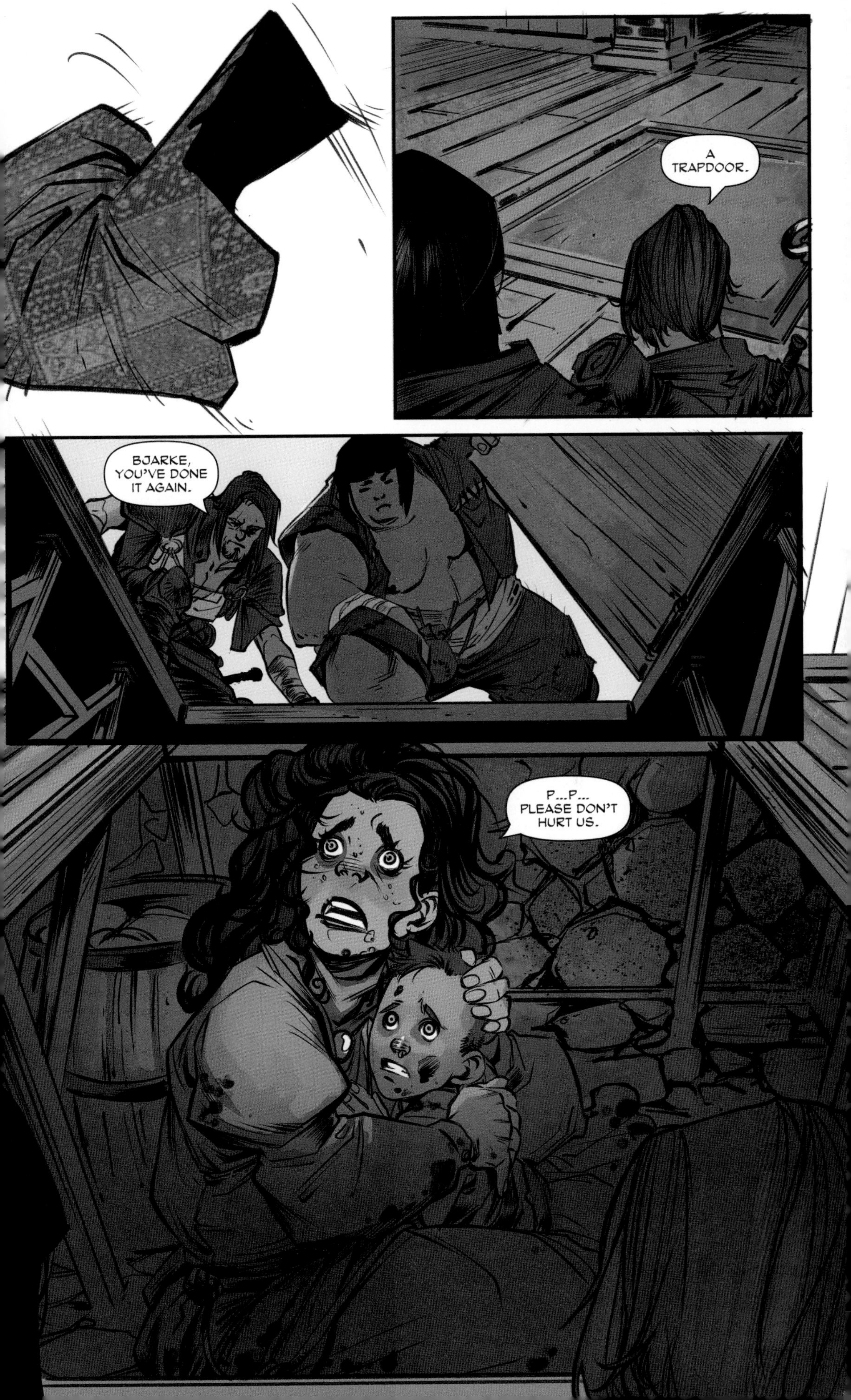
A TRAPDOOR.
BJARKE, YOU'VE DONE IT AGAIN.
P...P... PLEASE DON'T HURT US.

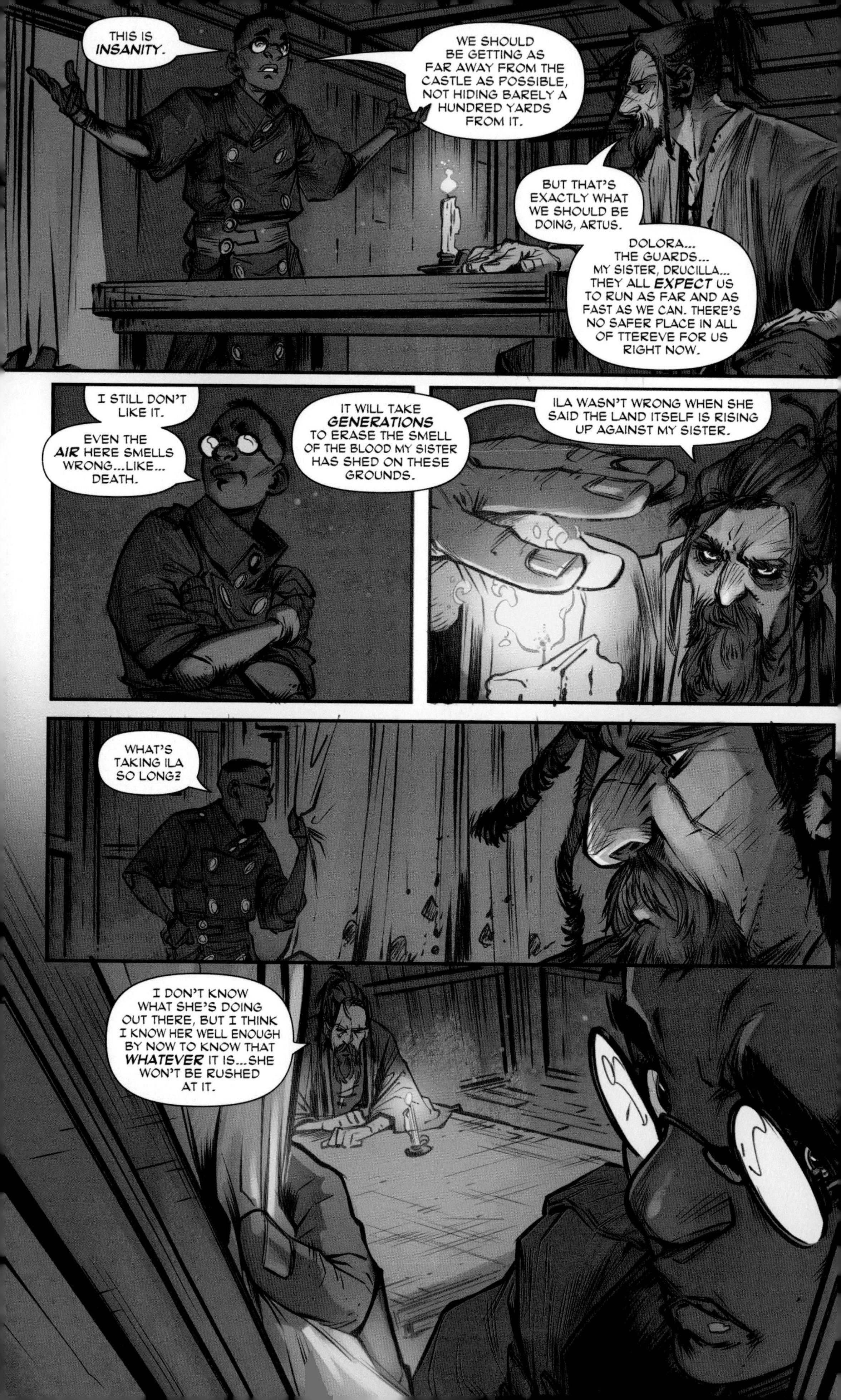
THIS IS INSANITY.
WE SHOULD BE GETTING AS FAR AWAY FROM THE CASTLE AS POSSIBLE, NOT HIDING BARELY A HUNDRED YARDS FROM IT.
BUT THAT'S EXACTLY WHAT WE SHOULD BE DOING, ARTUS.
DOLORA... THE GUARDS... MY SISTER, DRUCILLA... THEY ALL EXPECT US TO RUN AS FAR AND AS FAST AS WE CAN. THERE'S NO SAFER PLACE IN ALL OF TTEREVE FOR US RIGHT NOW.
I STILL DON'T LIKE IT.
EVEN THE AIR HERE SMELLS WRONG...LIKE... DEATH.
IT WILL TAKE GENERATIONS TO ERASE THE SMELL OF THE BLOOD MY SISTER HAS SHED ON THESE GROUNDS.
ILA WASN'T WRONG WHEN SHE SAID THE LAND ITSELF IS RISING UP AGAINST MY SISTER.
WHAT'S TAKING ILA SO LONG?
I DON'T KNOW WHAT SHE'S DOING OUT THERE, BUT I THINK I KNOW HER WELL ENOUGH BY NOW TO KNOW THAT WHATEVER IT IS...SHE WON'T BE RUSHED AT IT.

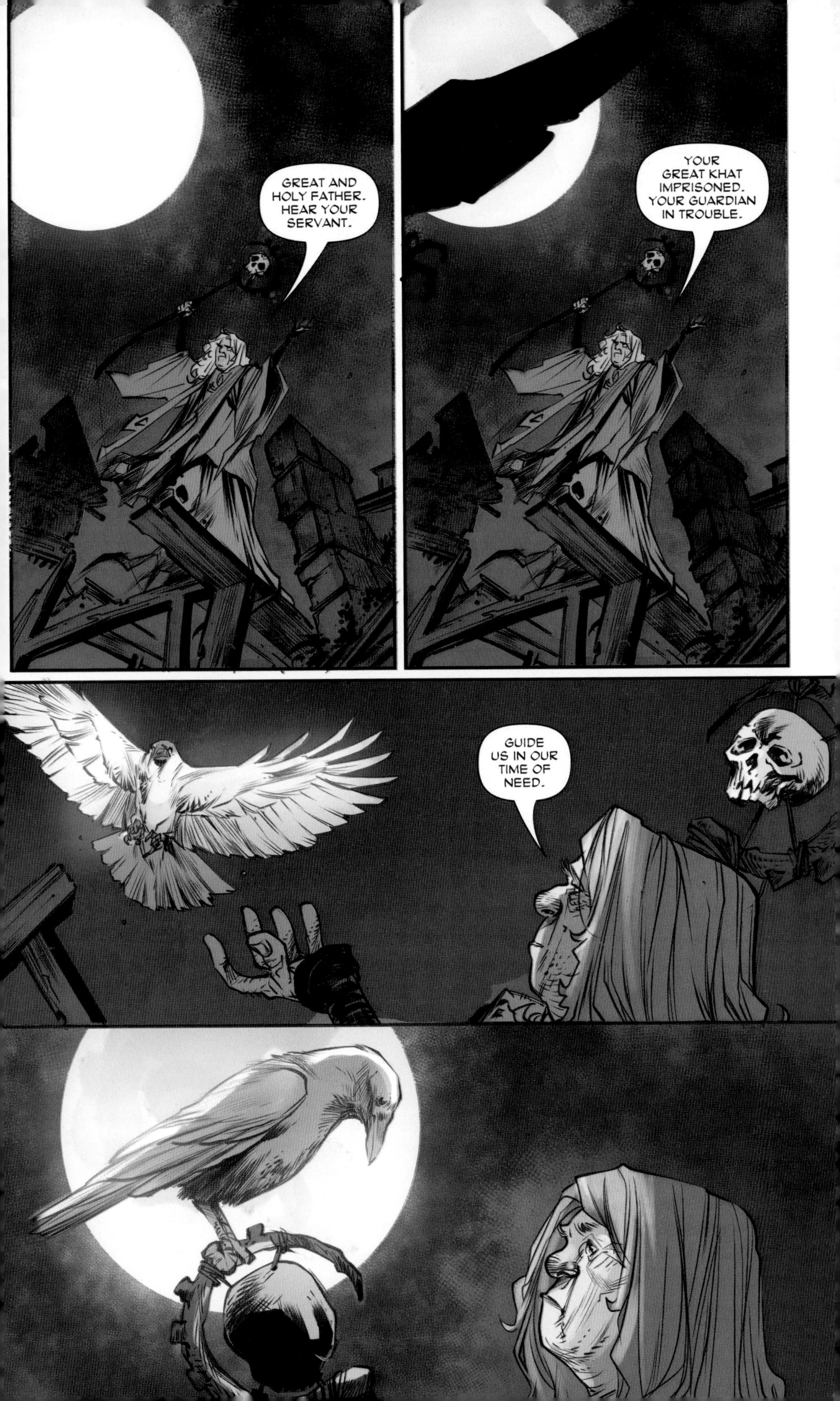
GREAT AND HOLY FATHER. HEAR YOUR SERVANT.
YOUR GREAT KHAT IMPRISONED. YOUR GUARDIAN IN TROUBLE.
GUIDE US IN OUR TIME OF NEED.

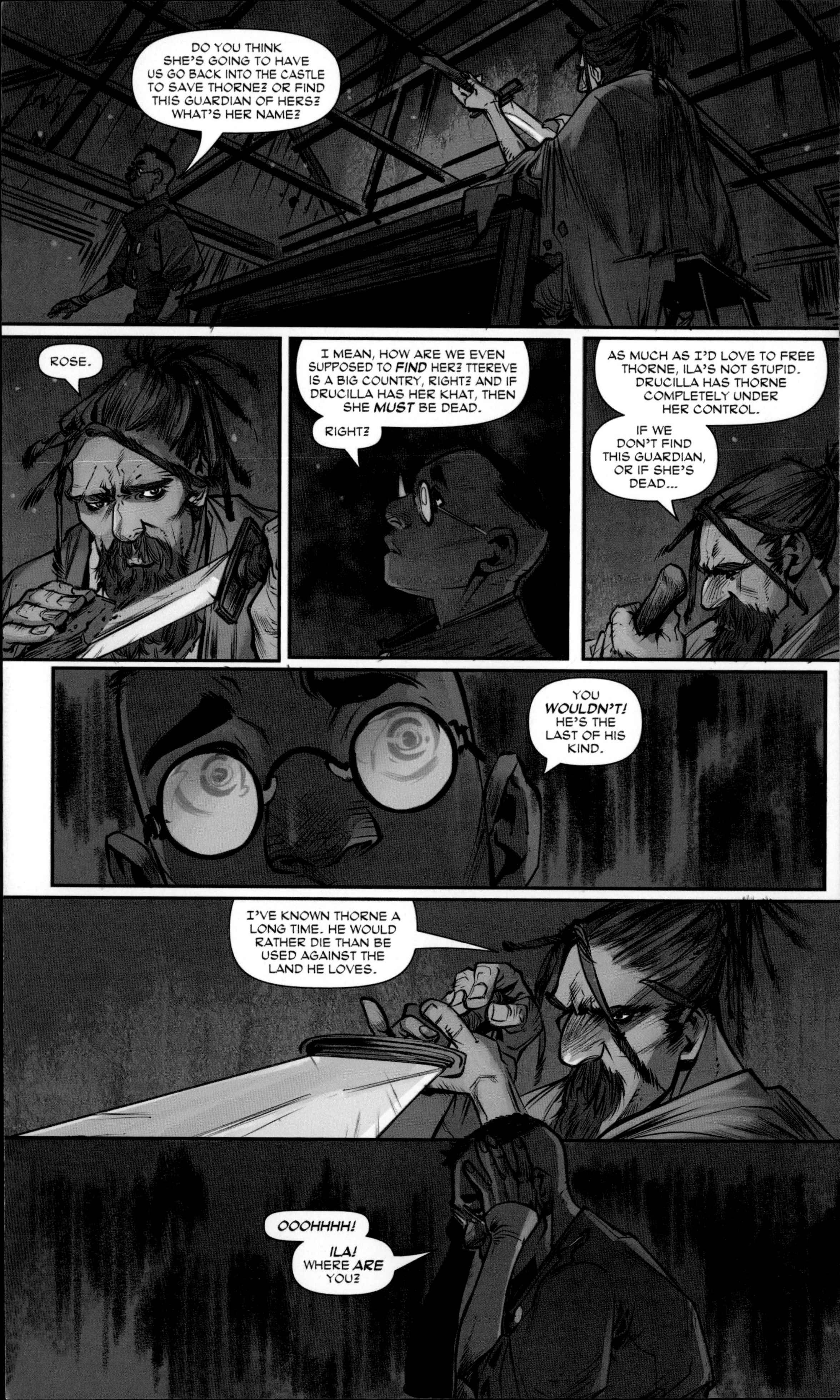
DO YOU THINK SHE'S GOING TO HAVE US GO BACK INTO THE CASTLE TO SAVE THORNE? OR FIND THIS GUARDIAN OF HERS? WHAT'S HER NAME?
ROSE.
I MEAN, HOW ARE WE EVEN SUPPOSED TO *FIND* HER? TTEREVE IS A BIG COUNTRY, RIGHT? AND IF DRUCILLA HAS HER KHAT, THEN SHE *MUST* BE DEAD.
RIGHT?
AS MUCH AS I'D LOVE TO FREE THORNE, ILA'S NOT STUPID. DRUCILLA HAS THORNE COMPLETELY UNDER HER CONTROL.
IF WE DON'T FIND THIS GUARDIAN, OR IF SHE'S DEAD...
YOU *WOULDN'T!* HE'S THE LAST OF HIS KIND.
I'VE KNOWN THORNE A LONG TIME. HE WOULD RATHER DIE THAN BE USED AGAINST THE LAND HE LOVES.
OOOHHHH!
ILA! WHERE *ARE* YOU?

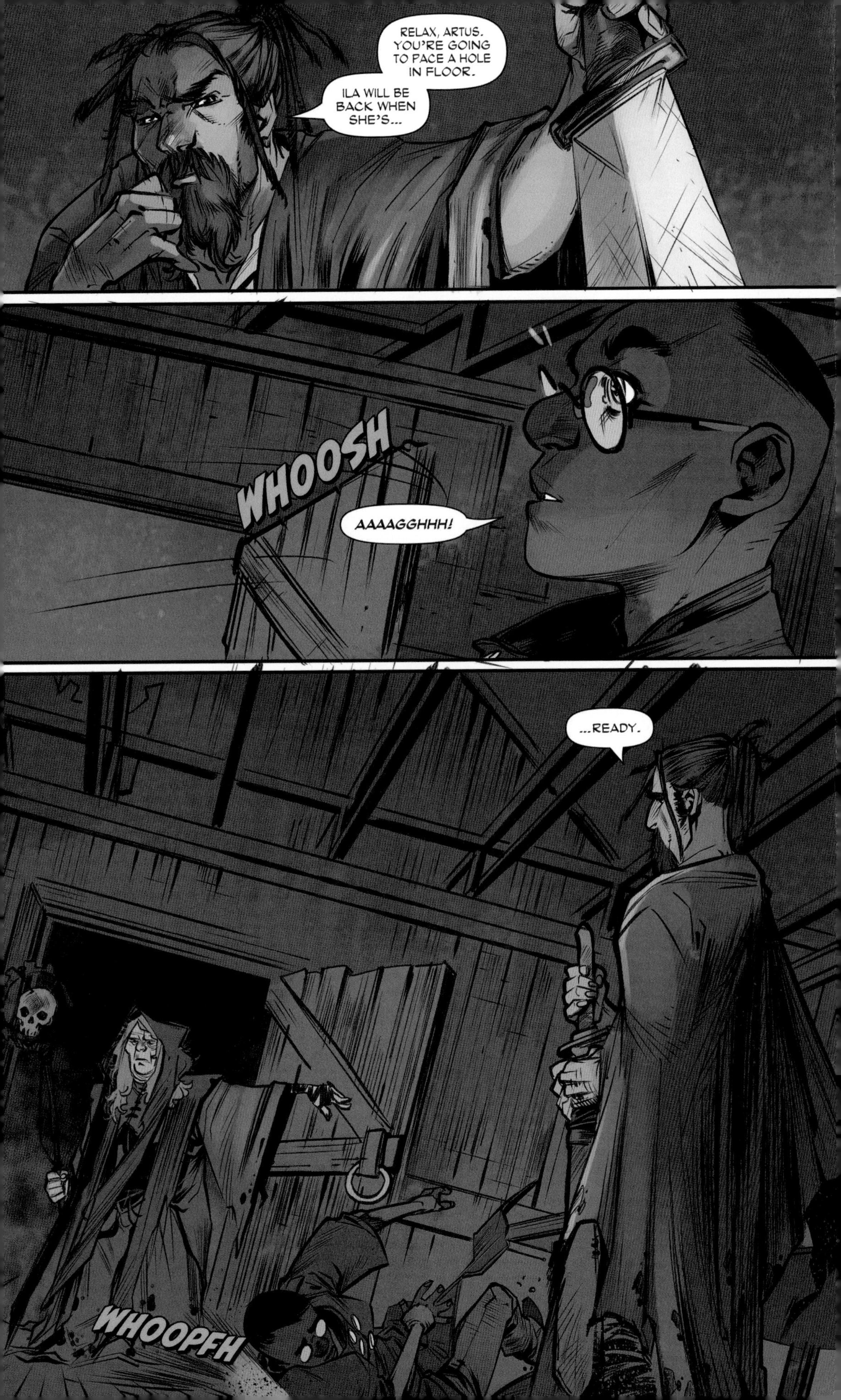
RELAX, ARTUS. YOU'RE GOING TO PACE A HOLE IN FLOOR.
ILA WILL BE BACK WHEN SHE'S...
WHOOSH
AAAAGGHHH!
...READY.
WHOOPFH

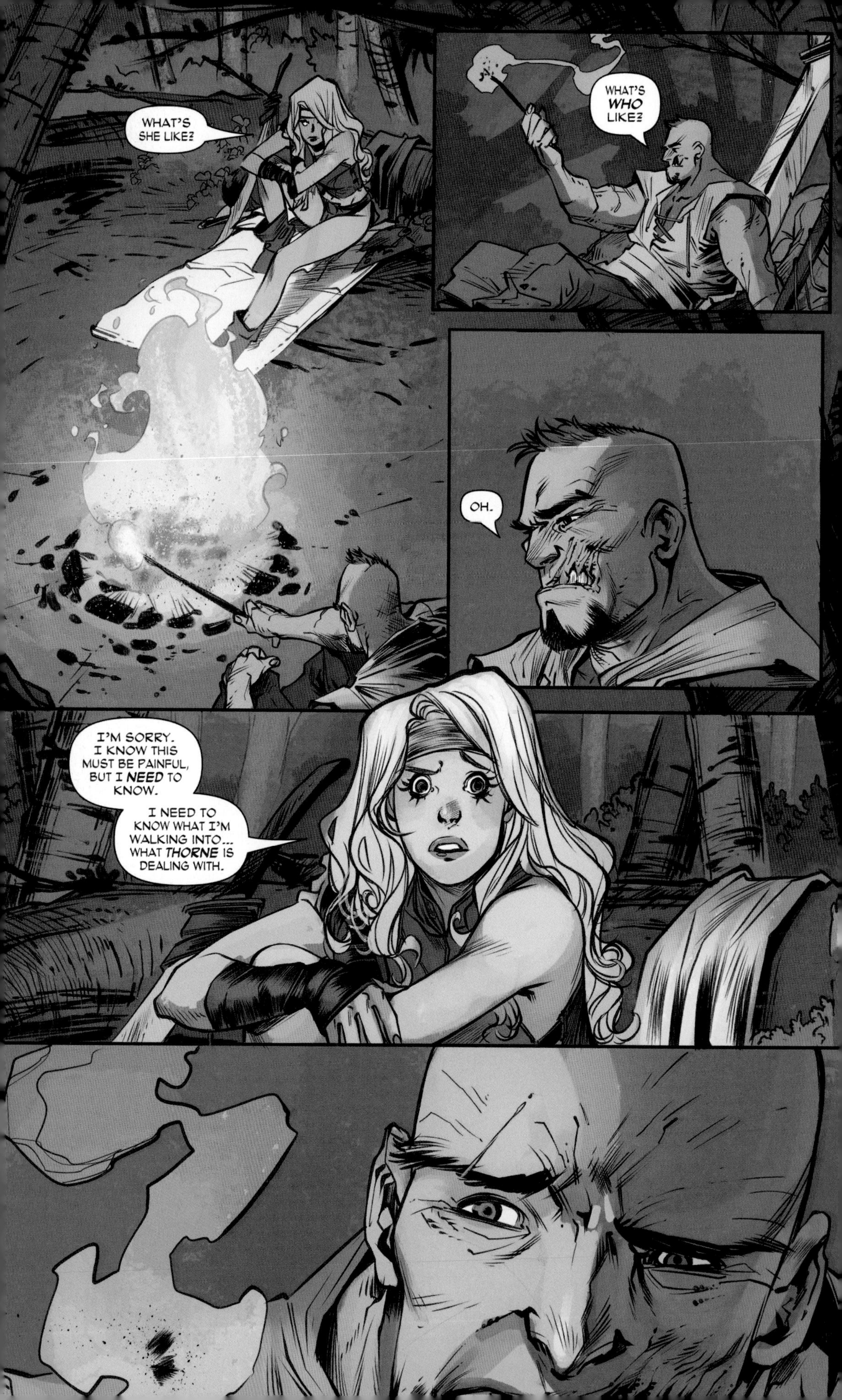
WHAT'S SHE LIKE?
WHAT'S WHO LIKE?
OH.
I'M SORRY. I KNOW THIS MUST BE PAINFUL, BUT I NEED TO KNOW.
I NEED TO KNOW WHAT I'M WALKING INTO... WHAT THORNE IS DEALING WITH.

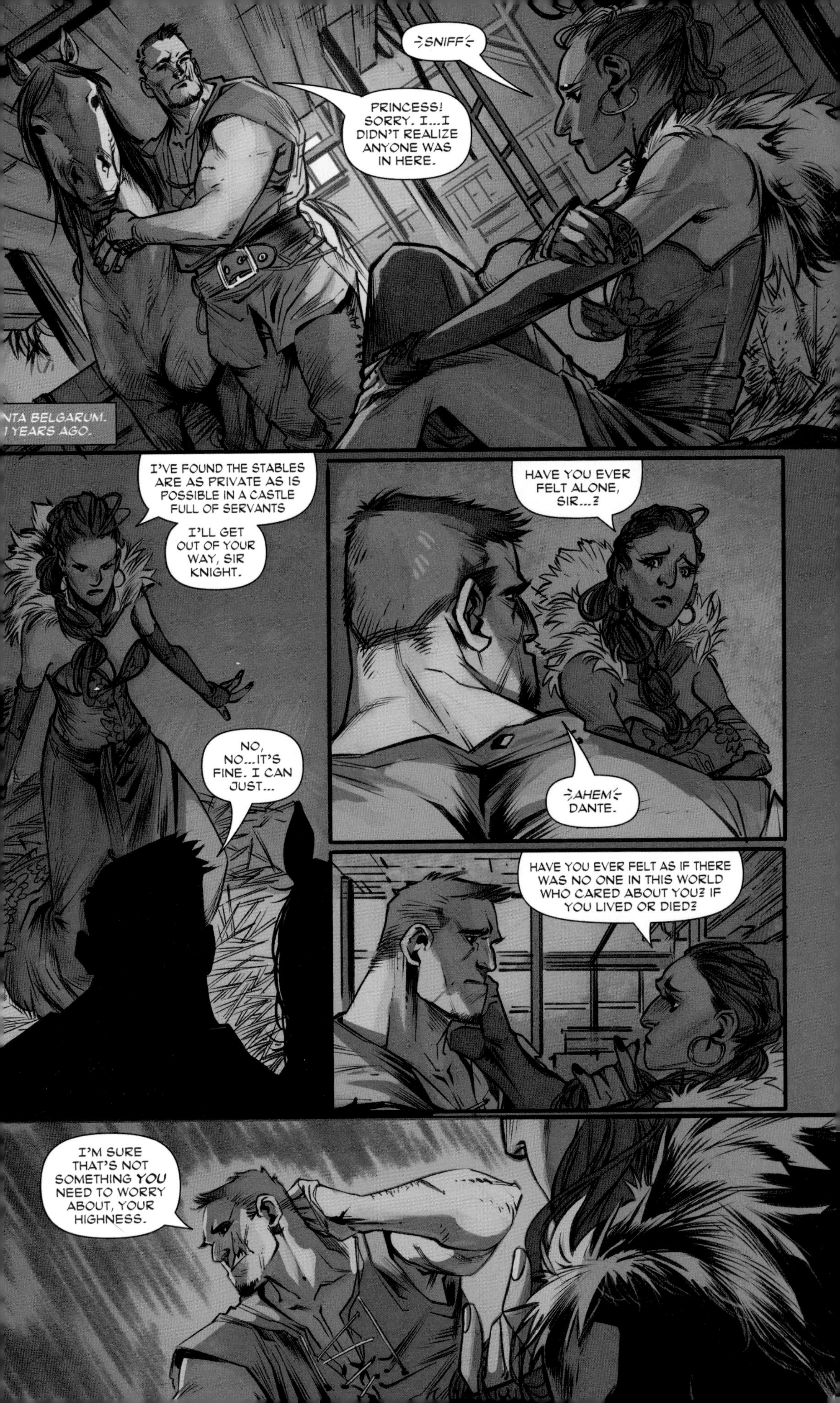
⇢SNIFF⇠
PRINCESS! SORRY. I...I DIDN'T REALIZE ANYONE WAS IN HERE.
NTA BELGARUM. I YEARS AGO.
I'VE FOUND THE STABLES ARE AS PRIVATE AS IS POSSIBLE IN A CASTLE FULL OF SERVANTS
I'LL GET OUT OF YOUR WAY, SIR KNIGHT.
NO, NO...IT'S FINE. I CAN JUST...
HAVE YOU EVER FELT ALONE, SIR...?
⇢AHEM⇠ DANTE.
HAVE YOU EVER FELT AS IF THERE WAS NO ONE IN THIS WORLD WHO CARED ABOUT YOU? IF YOU LIVED OR DIED?
I'M SURE THAT'S NOT SOMETHING YOU NEED TO WORRY ABOUT, YOUR HIGHNESS.

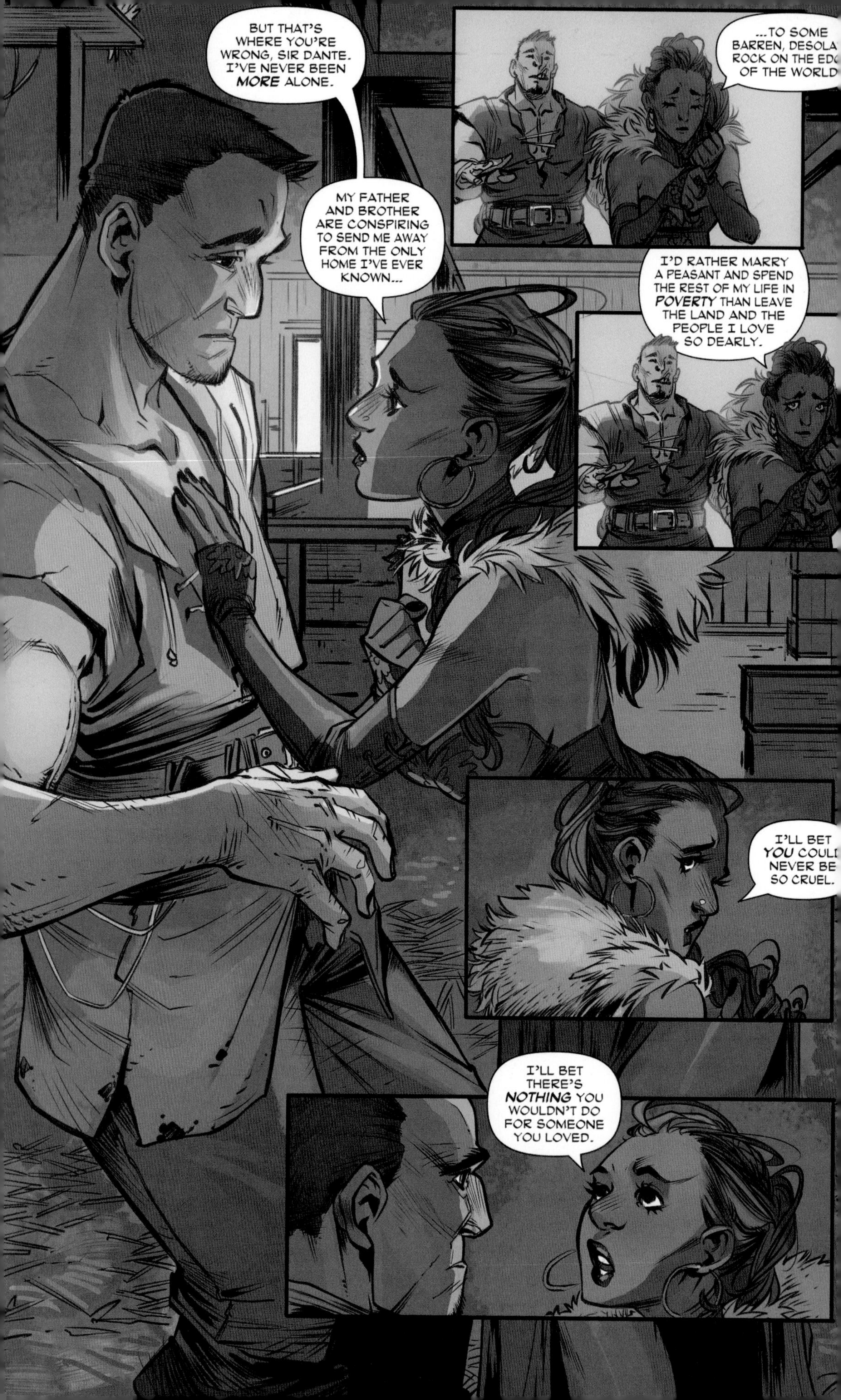

BUT THAT'S WHERE YOU'RE WRONG, SIR DANTE. I'VE NEVER BEEN MORE ALONE.
MY FATHER AND BROTHER ARE CONSPIRING TO SEND ME AWAY FROM THE ONLY HOME I'VE EVER KNOWN...
...TO SOME BARREN, DESOLA ROCK ON THE EDG OF THE WORLD
I'D RATHER MARRY A PEASANT AND SPEND THE REST OF MY LIFE IN POVERTY THAN LEAVE THE LAND AND THE PEOPLE I LOVE SO DEARLY.
I'LL BET YOU COULI NEVER BE SO CRUEL.
I'LL BET THERE'S NOTHING YOU WOULDN'T DO FOR SOMEONE YOU LOVED.

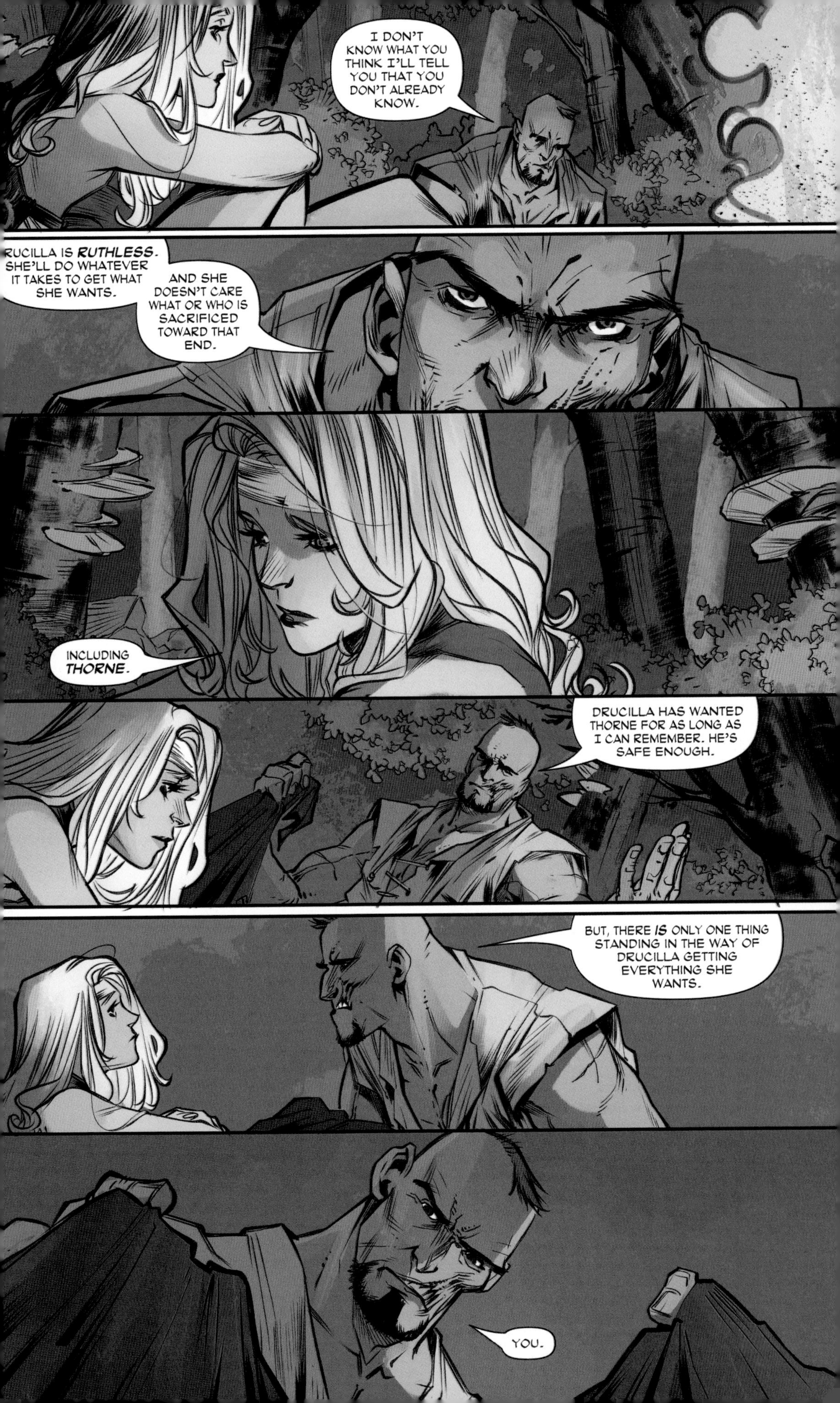
I DON'T KNOW WHAT YOU THINK I'LL TELL YOU THAT YOU DON'T ALREADY KNOW.
RUCILLA IS RUTHLESS. SHE'LL DO WHATEVER IT TAKES TO GET WHAT SHE WANTS.
AND SHE DOESN'T CARE WHAT OR WHO IS SACRIFICED TOWARD THAT END.
INCLUDING THORNE.
DRUCILLA HAS WANTED THORNE FOR AS LONG AS I CAN REMEMBER. HE'S SAFE ENOUGH.
BUT, THERE IS ONLY ONE THING STANDING IN THE WAY OF DRUCILLA GETTING EVERYTHING SHE WANTS.
YOU.

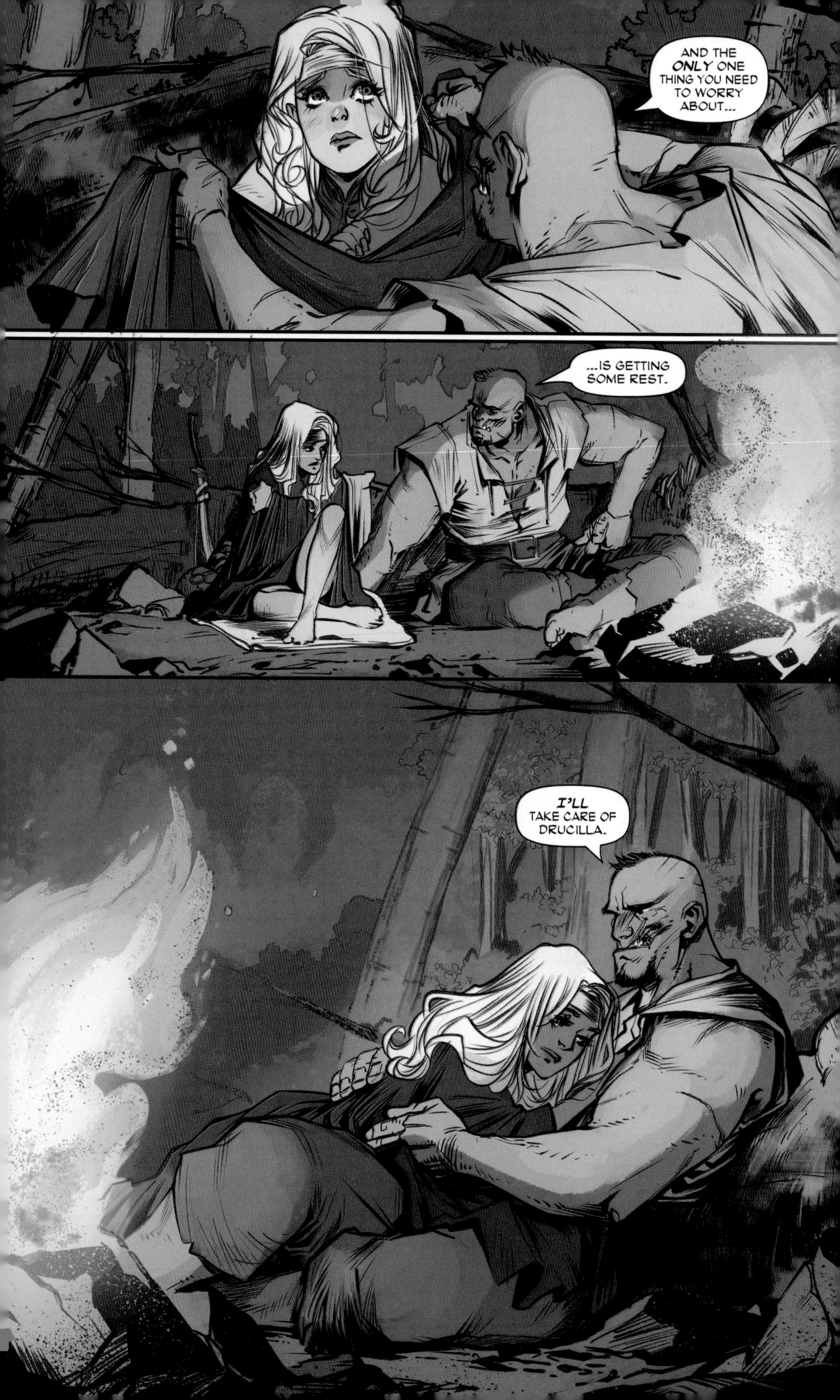
AND THE ONLY ONE THING YOU NEED TO WORRY ABOUT...
...IS GETTING SOME REST.
I'LL TAKE CARE OF DRUCILLA.

TWELVE

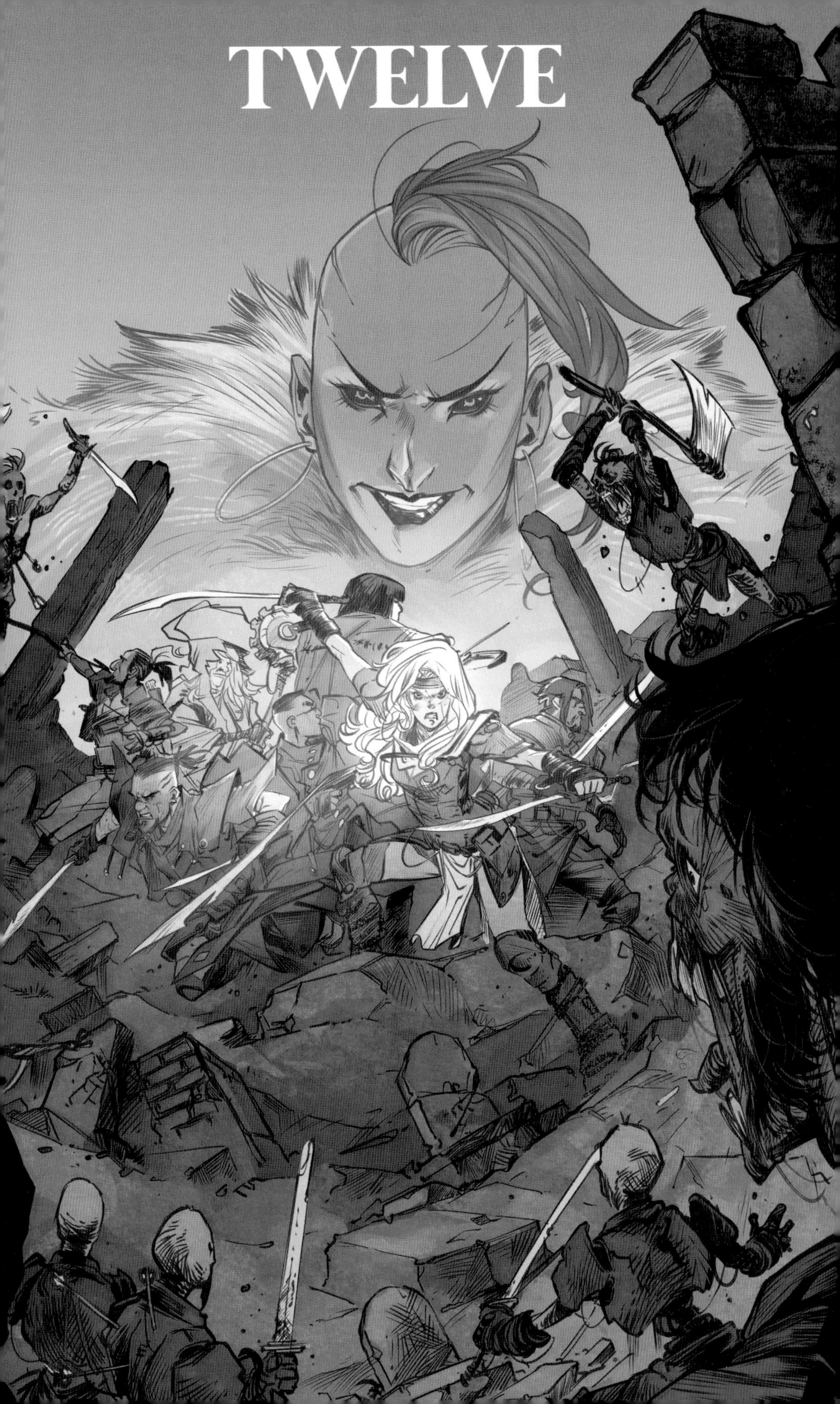

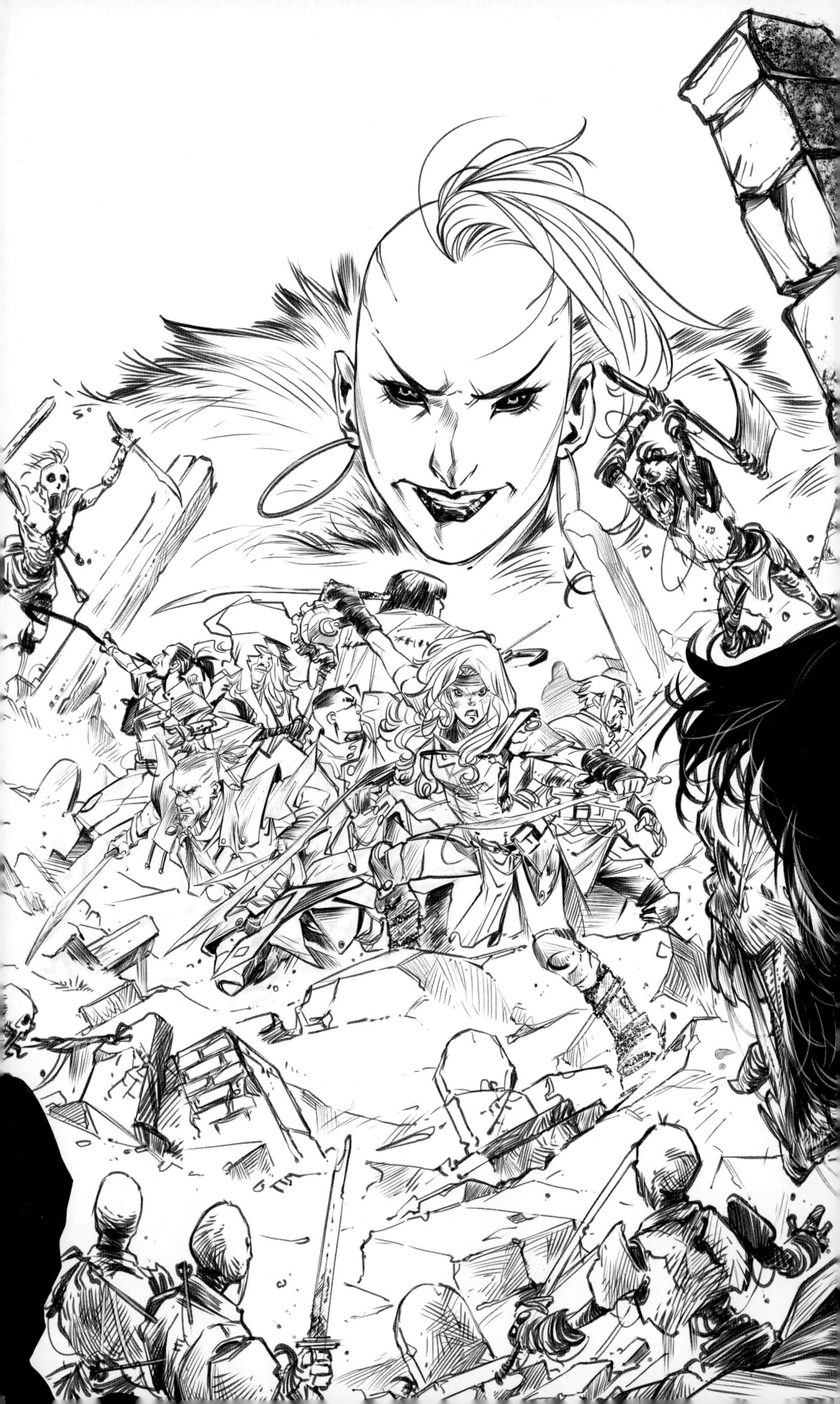

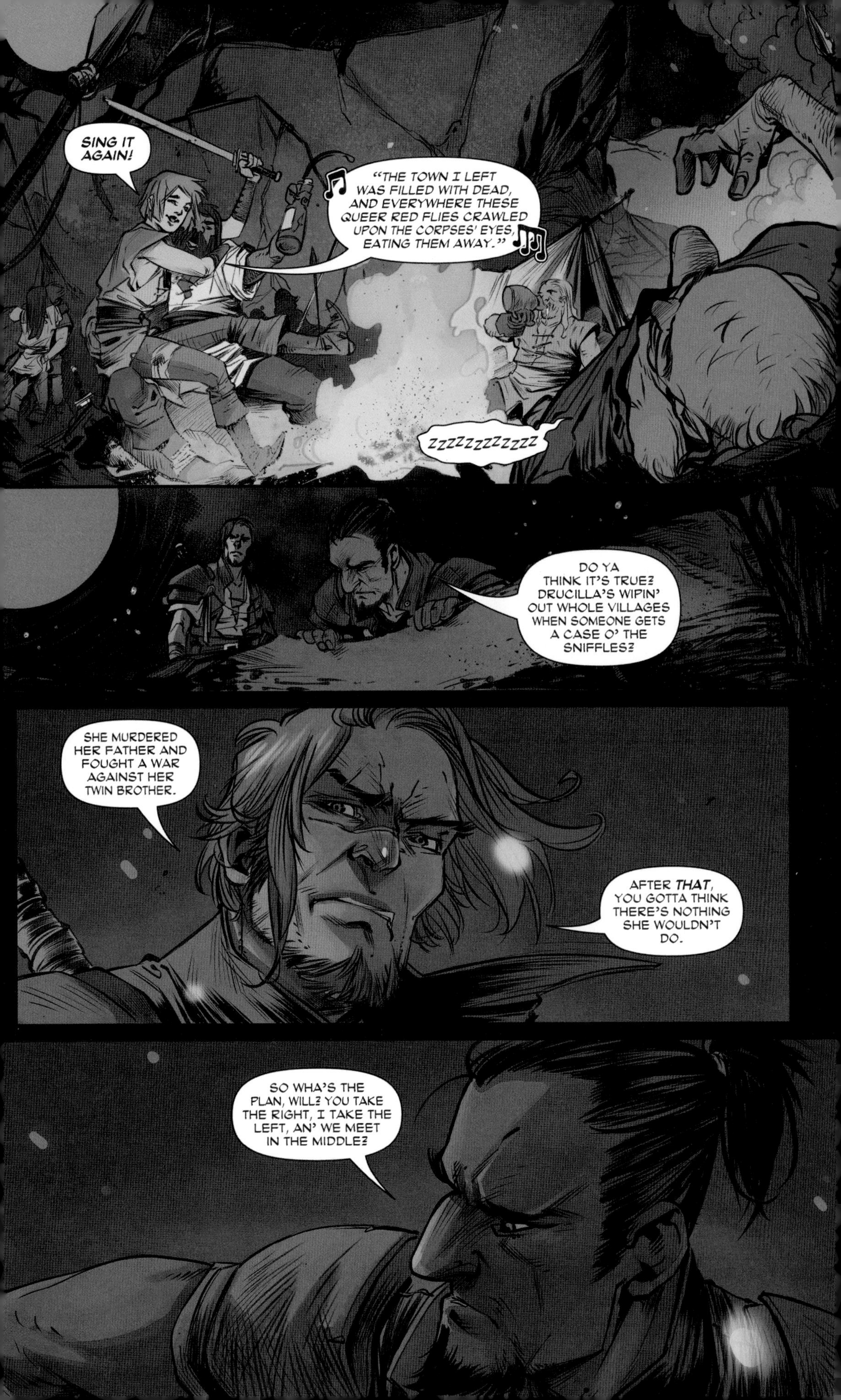
SING IT AGAIN!
"THE TOWN I LEFT WAS FILLED WITH DEAD, AND EVERYWHERE THESE QUEER RED FLIES CRAWLED UPON THE CORPSES' EYES, EATING THEM AWAY."
ZZZZZZZZZZZZ
DO YA THINK IT'S TRUE? DRUCILLA'S WIPIN' OUT WHOLE VILLAGES WHEN SOMEONE GETS A CASE O' THE SNIFFLES?
SHE MURDERED HER FATHER AND FOUGHT A WAR AGAINST HER TWIN BROTHER.
AFTER *THAT*, YOU GOTTA THINK THERE'S NOTHING SHE WOULDN'T DO.
SO WHA'S THE PLAN, WILL? YOU TAKE THE RIGHT, I TAKE THE LEFT, AN' WE MEET IN THE MIDDLE?

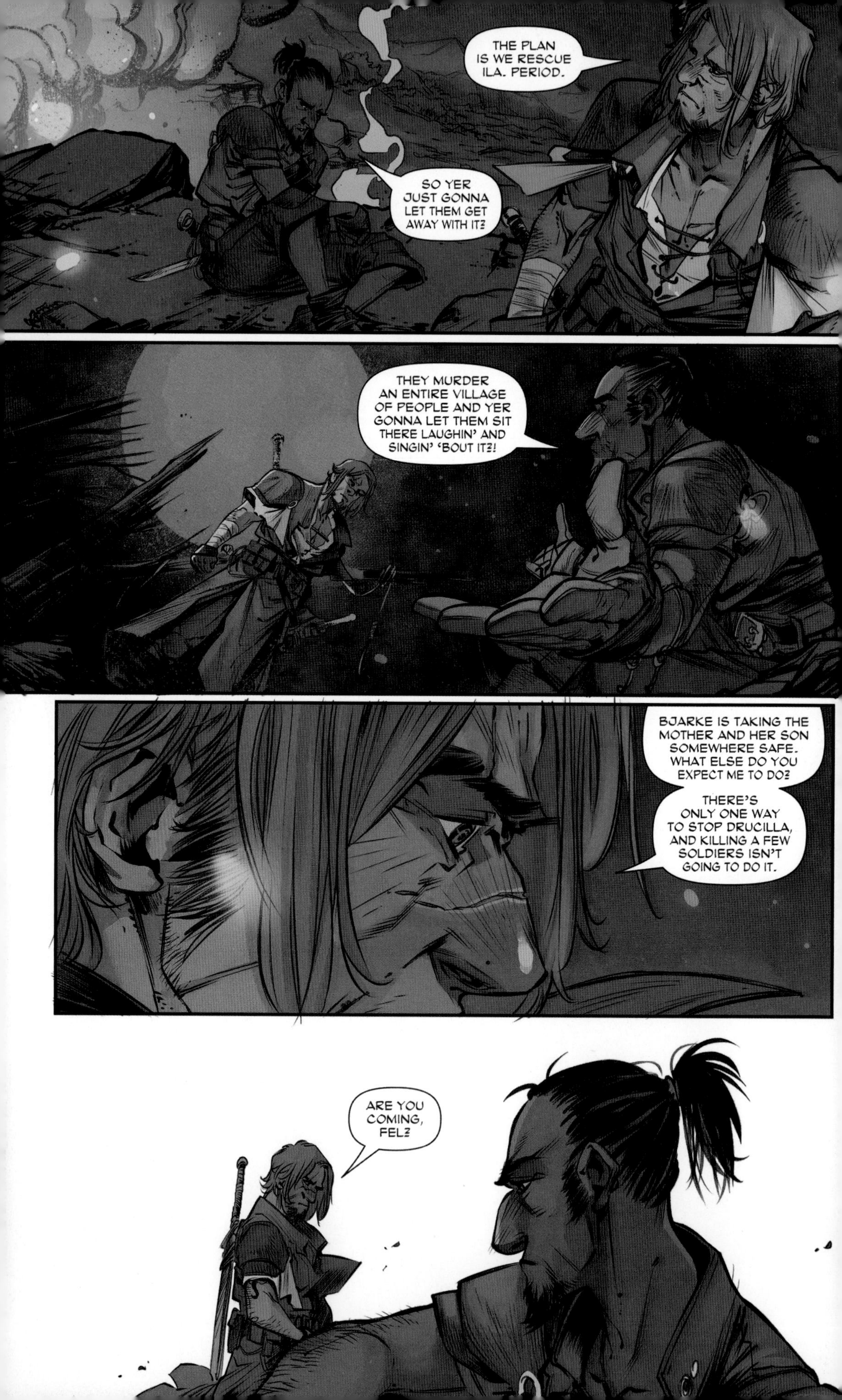
THE PLAN IS WE RESCUE ILA. PERIOD.
SO YER JUST GONNA LET THEM GET AWAY WITH IT?
THEY MURDER AN ENTIRE VILLAGE OF PEOPLE AND YER GONNA LET THEM SIT THERE LAUGHIN' AND SINGIN' 'BOUT IT?!
BJARKE IS TAKING THE MOTHER AND HER SON SOMEWHERE SAFE. WHAT ELSE DO YOU EXPECT ME TO DO?
THERE'S ONLY ONE WAY TO STOP DRUCILLA, AND KILLING A FEW SOLDIERS ISN'T GOING TO DO IT.
ARE YOU COMING, FEL?

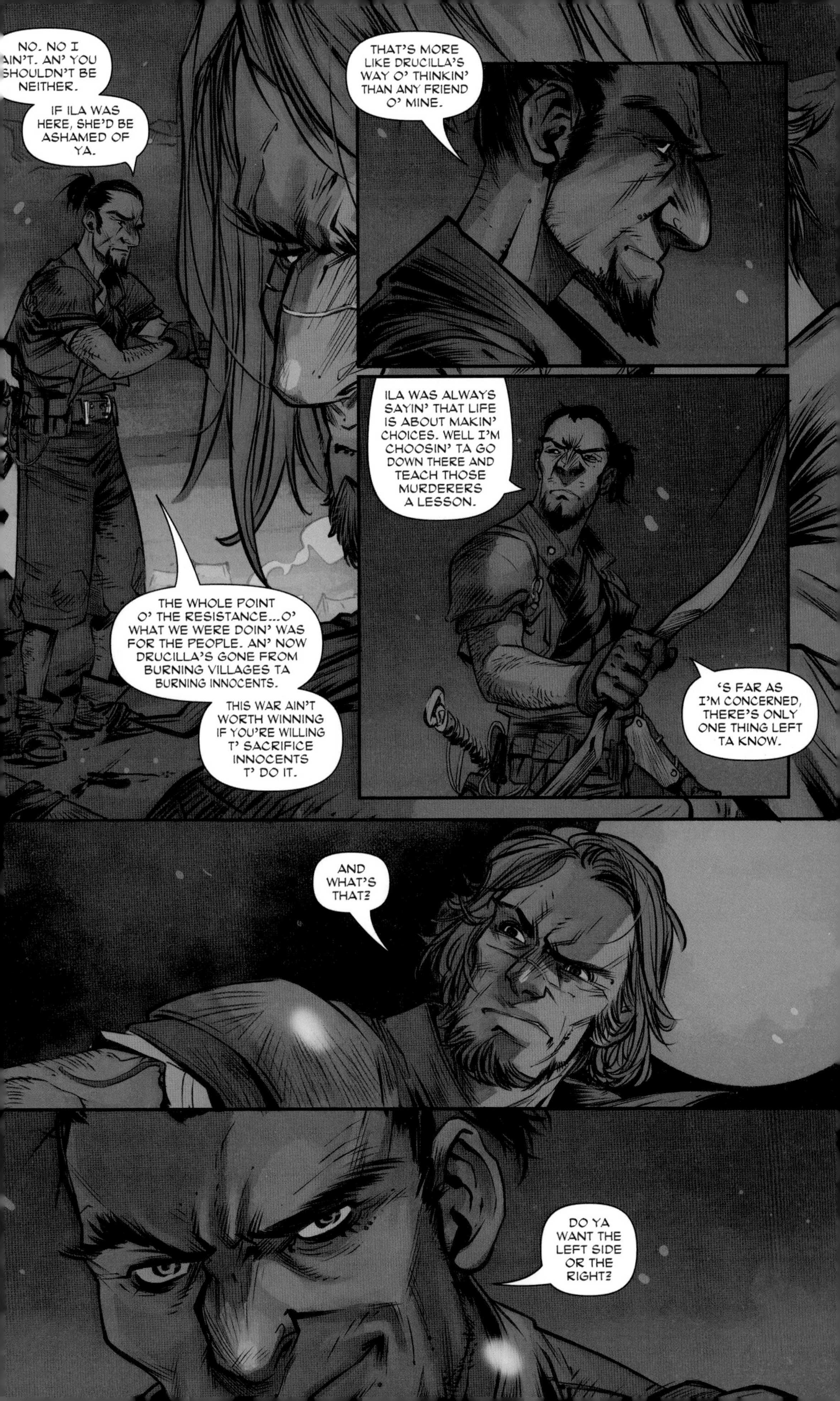

NO. NO I AIN'T. AN' YOU SHOULDN'T BE NEITHER.
IF ILA WAS HERE, SHE'D BE ASHAMED OF YA.
THAT'S MORE LIKE DRUCILLA'S WAY O' THINKIN' THAN ANY FRIEND O' MINE.
THE WHOLE POINT O' THE RESISTANCE...O' WHAT WE WERE DOIN' WAS FOR THE PEOPLE. AN' NOW DRUCILLA'S GONE FROM BURNING VILLAGES TA BURNING INNOCENTS.
THIS WAR AIN'T WORTH WINNING IF YOU'RE WILLING T' SACRIFICE INNOCENTS T' DO IT.
ILA WAS ALWAYS SAYIN' THAT LIFE IS ABOUT MAKIN' CHOICES. WELL I'M CHOOSIN' TA GO DOWN THERE AND TEACH THOSE MURDERERS A LESSON.
'S FAR AS I'M CONCERNED, THERE'S ONLY ONE THING LEFT TA KNOW.
AND WHAT'S THAT?
DO YA WANT THE LEFT SIDE OR THE RIGHT?

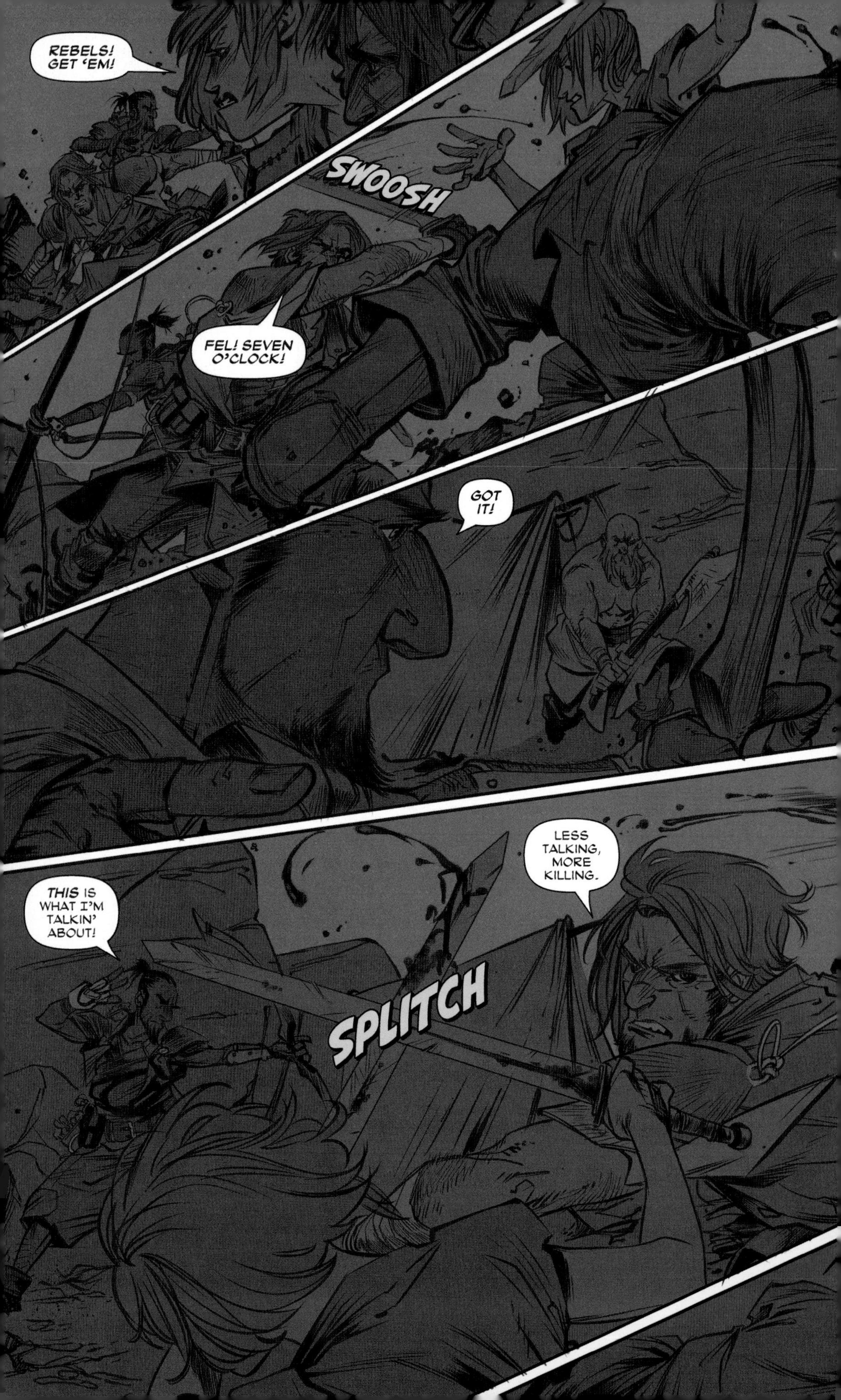
REBELS! GET 'EM!
SWOOSH
FEL! SEVEN O'CLOCK!
GOT IT!
THIS IS WHAT I'M TALKIN' ABOUT!
LESS TALKING, MORE KILLING.
SPLITCH

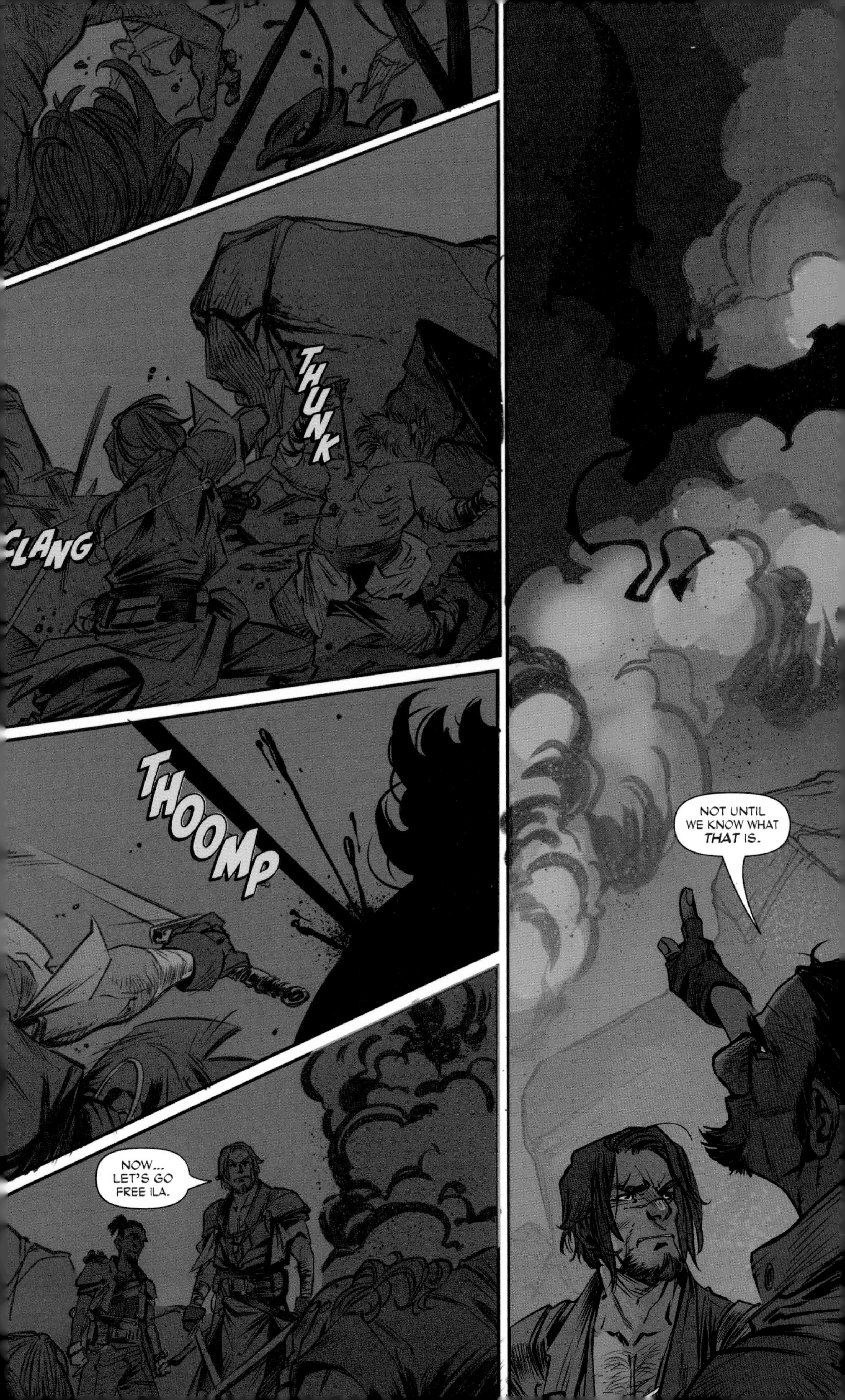
THUNK
CLANG
THOOMP
NOW... LET'S GO FREE ILA.
NOT UNTIL WE KNOW WHAT *THAT* IS.

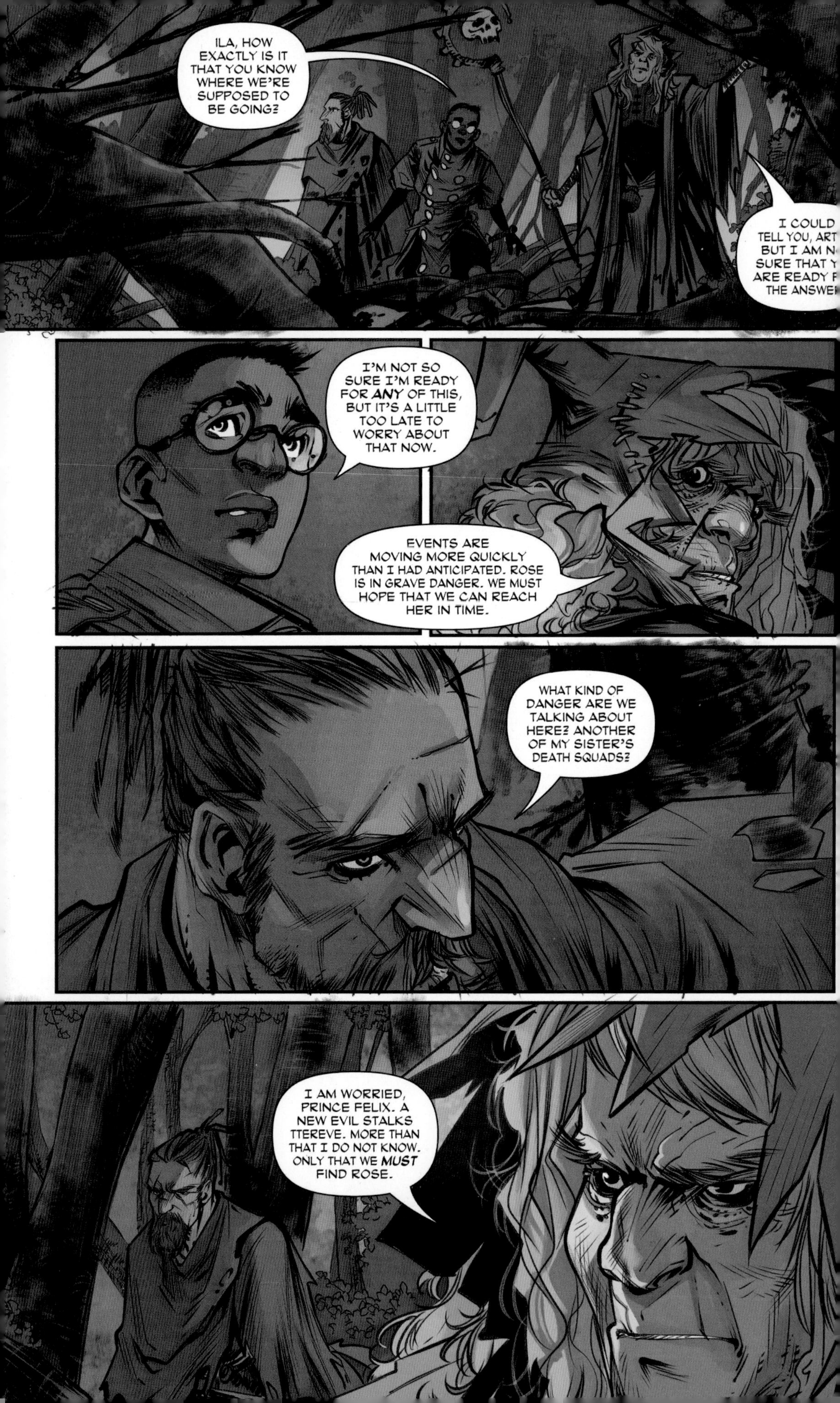
ILA, HOW EXACTLY IS IT THAT YOU KNOW WHERE WE'RE SUPPOSED TO BE GOING?
I COULD TELL YOU, ART BUT I AM N SURE THAT Y ARE READY F THE ANSWE
I'M NOT SO SURE I'M READY FOR ANY OF THIS, BUT IT'S A LITTLE TOO LATE TO WORRY ABOUT THAT NOW.
EVENTS ARE MOVING MORE QUICKLY THAN I HAD ANTICIPATED. ROSE IS IN GRAVE DANGER. WE MUST HOPE THAT WE CAN REACH HER IN TIME.
WHAT KIND OF DANGER ARE WE TALKING ABOUT HERE? ANOTHER OF MY SISTER'S DEATH SQUADS?
I AM WORRIED, PRINCE FELIX. A NEW EVIL STALKS TTEREVE. MORE THAN THAT I DO NOT KNOW. ONLY THAT WE MUST FIND ROSE.

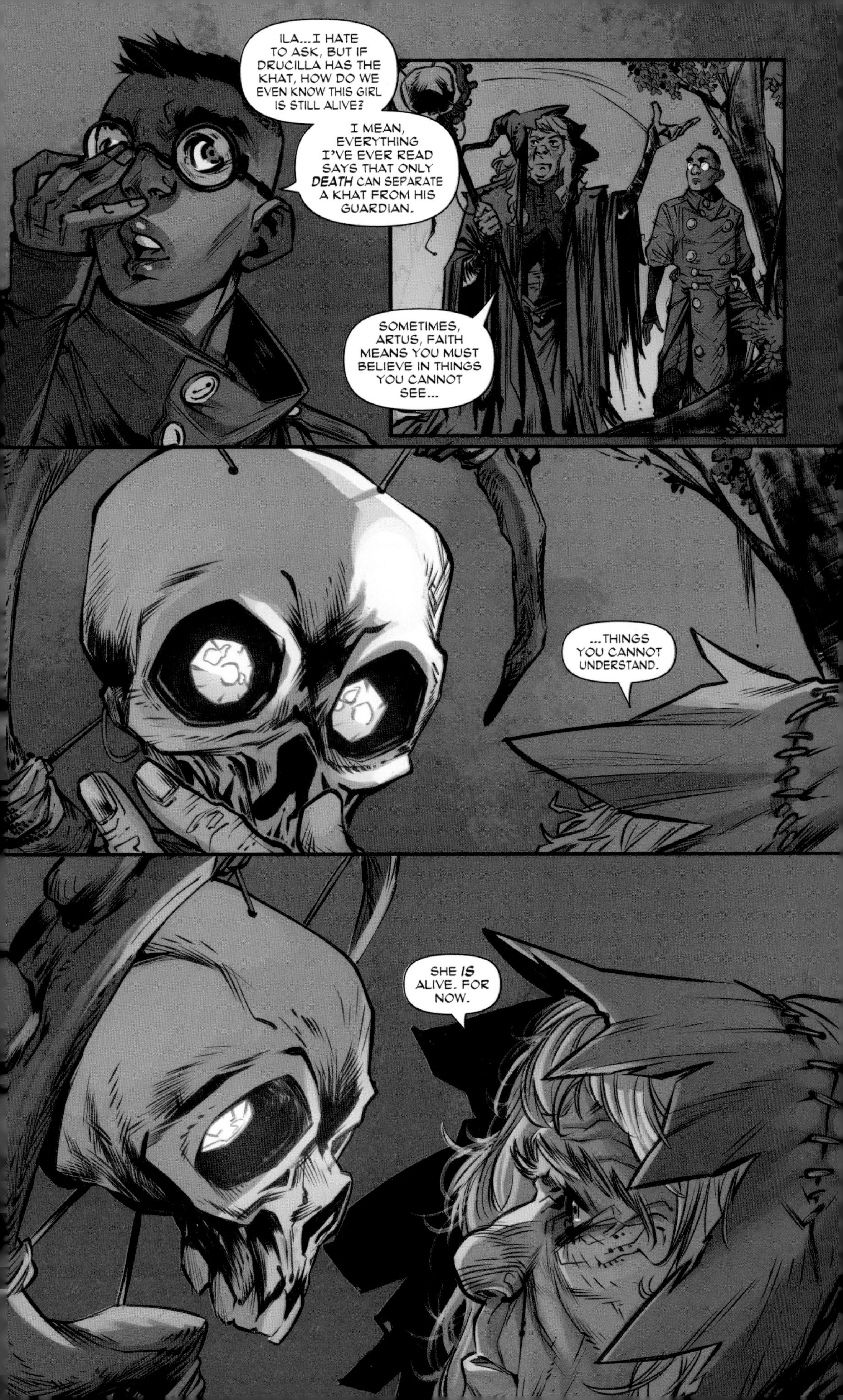
ILA...I HATE TO ASK, BUT IF DRUCILLA HAS THE KHAT, HOW DO WE EVEN KNOW THIS GIRL IS STILL ALIVE?
I MEAN, EVERYTHING I'VE EVER READ SAYS THAT ONLY *DEATH* CAN SEPARATE A KHAT FROM HIS GUARDIAN.
SOMETIMES, ARTUS, FAITH MEANS YOU MUST BELIEVE IN THINGS YOU CANNOT SEE...
...THINGS YOU CANNOT UNDERSTAND.
SHE *IS* ALIVE. FOR NOW.

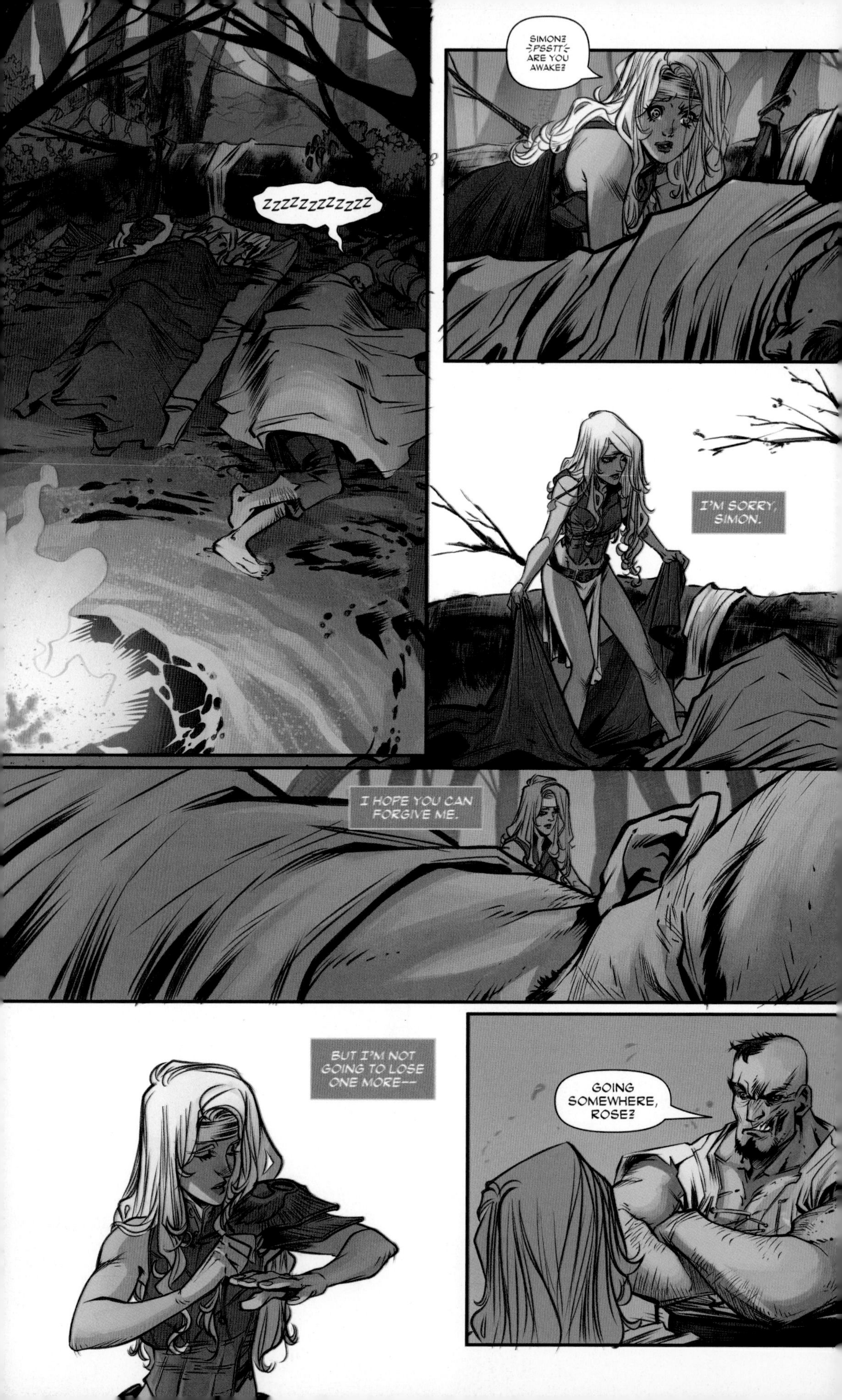
ZZZZZZZZZZZ
SIMON? PSSTT ARE YOU AWAKE?
I'M SORRY, SIMON.
I HOPE YOU CAN FORGIVE ME.
BUT I'M NOT GOING TO LOSE ONE MORE--
GOING SOMEWHERE, ROSE?

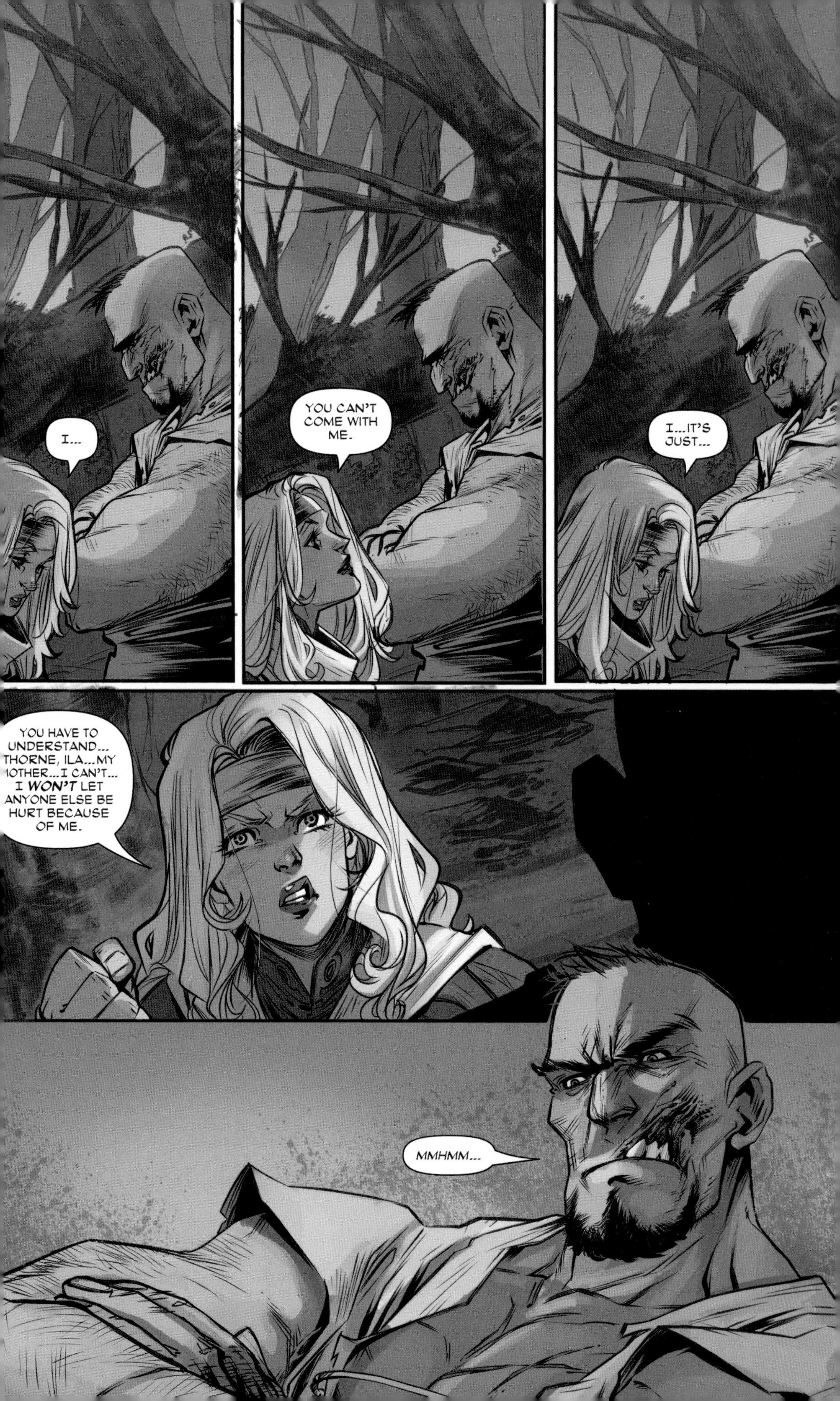
I...
YOU CAN'T COME WITH ME.
I...IT'S JUST...
YOU HAVE TO UNDERSTAND... THORNE, ILA...MY MOTHER...I CAN'T... I **WON'T** LET ANYONE ELSE BE HURT BECAUSE OF ME.
MMHMM...

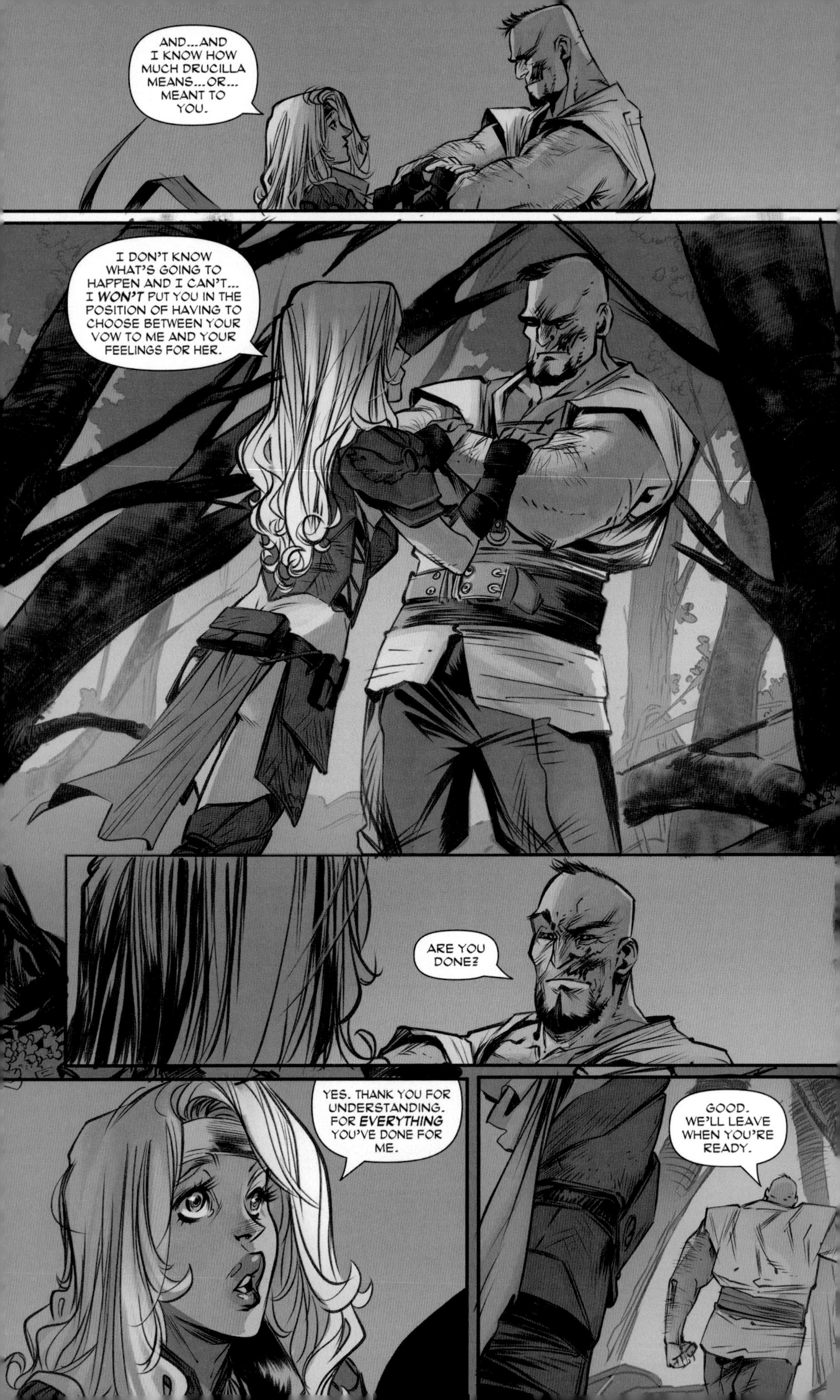
AND...AND I KNOW HOW MUCH DRUCILLA MEANS...OR... MEANT TO YOU.
I DON'T KNOW WHAT'S GOING TO HAPPEN AND I CAN'T... I WON'T PUT YOU IN THE POSITION OF HAVING TO CHOOSE BETWEEN YOUR VOW TO ME AND YOUR FEELINGS FOR HER.
ARE YOU DONE?
YES. THANK YOU FOR UNDERSTANDING. FOR EVERYTHING YOU'VE DONE FOR ME.
GOOD. WE'LL LEAVE WHEN YOU'RE READY.

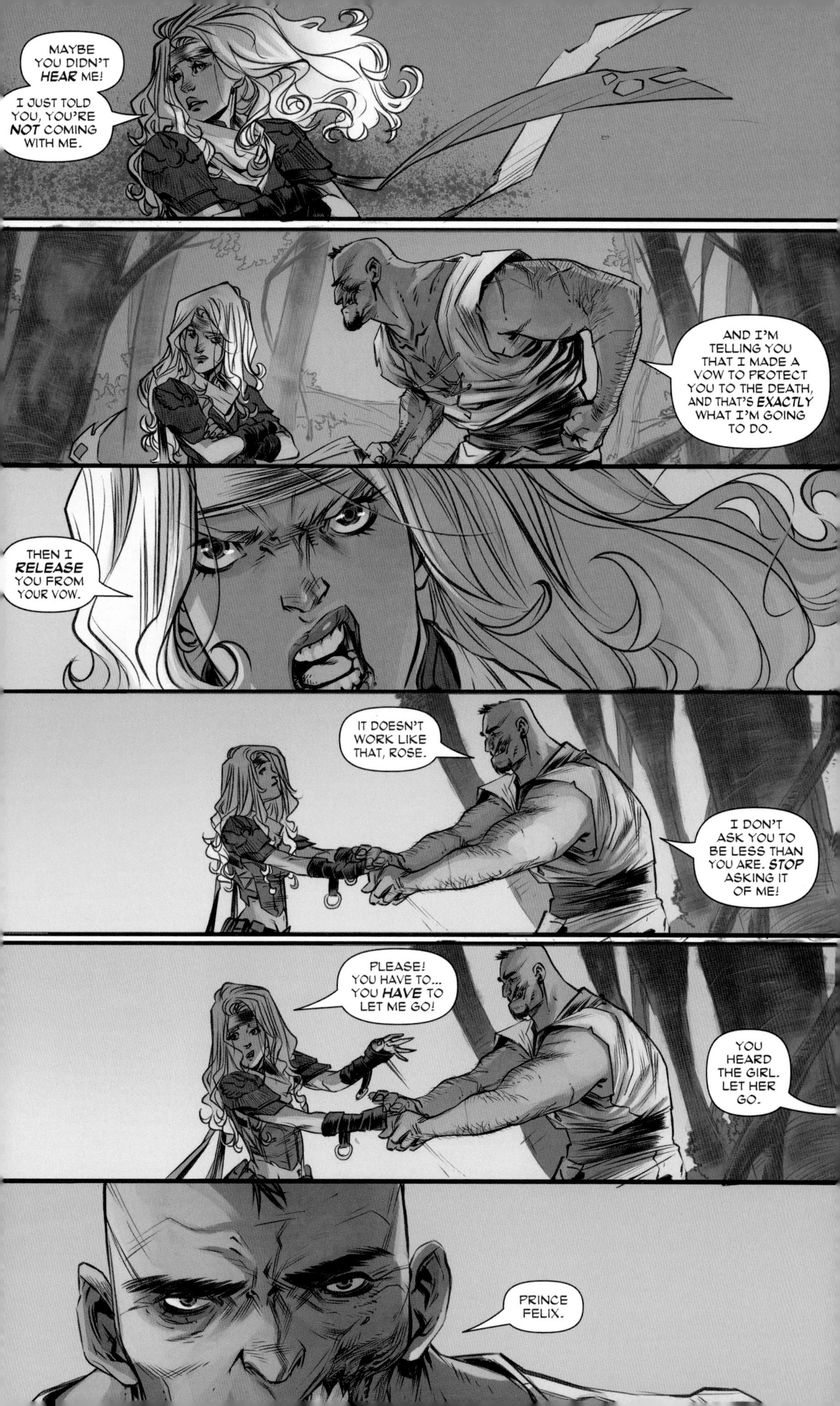
MAYBE YOU DIDN'T *HEAR* ME!
I JUST TOLD YOU, YOU'RE *NOT* COMING WITH ME.
AND I'M TELLING YOU THAT I MADE A VOW TO PROTECT YOU TO THE DEATH, AND THAT'S *EXACTLY* WHAT I'M GOING TO DO.
THEN I *RELEASE* YOU FROM YOUR VOW.
IT DOESN'T WORK LIKE THAT, ROSE.
I DON'T ASK YOU TO BE LESS THAN YOU ARE. *STOP* ASKING IT OF ME!
PLEASE! YOU HAVE TO... YOU *HAVE* TO LET ME GO!
YOU HEARD THE GIRL. LET HER GO.
PRINCE FELIX.

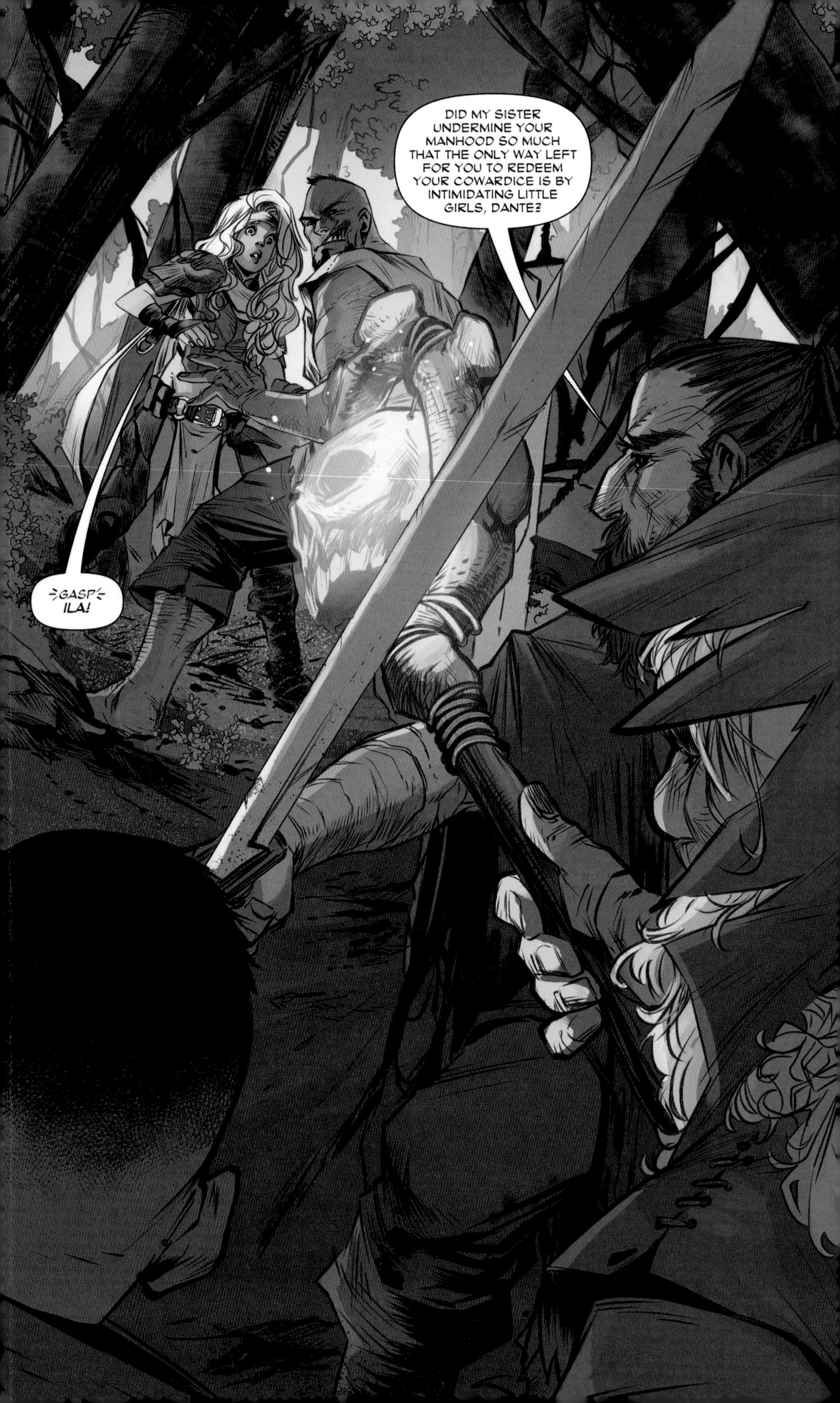
DID MY SISTER UNDERMINE YOUR MANHOOD SO MUCH THAT THE ONLY WAY LEFT FOR YOU TO REDEEM YOUR COWARDICE IS BY INTIMIDATING LITTLE GIRLS, DANTE?
GASP ILA!

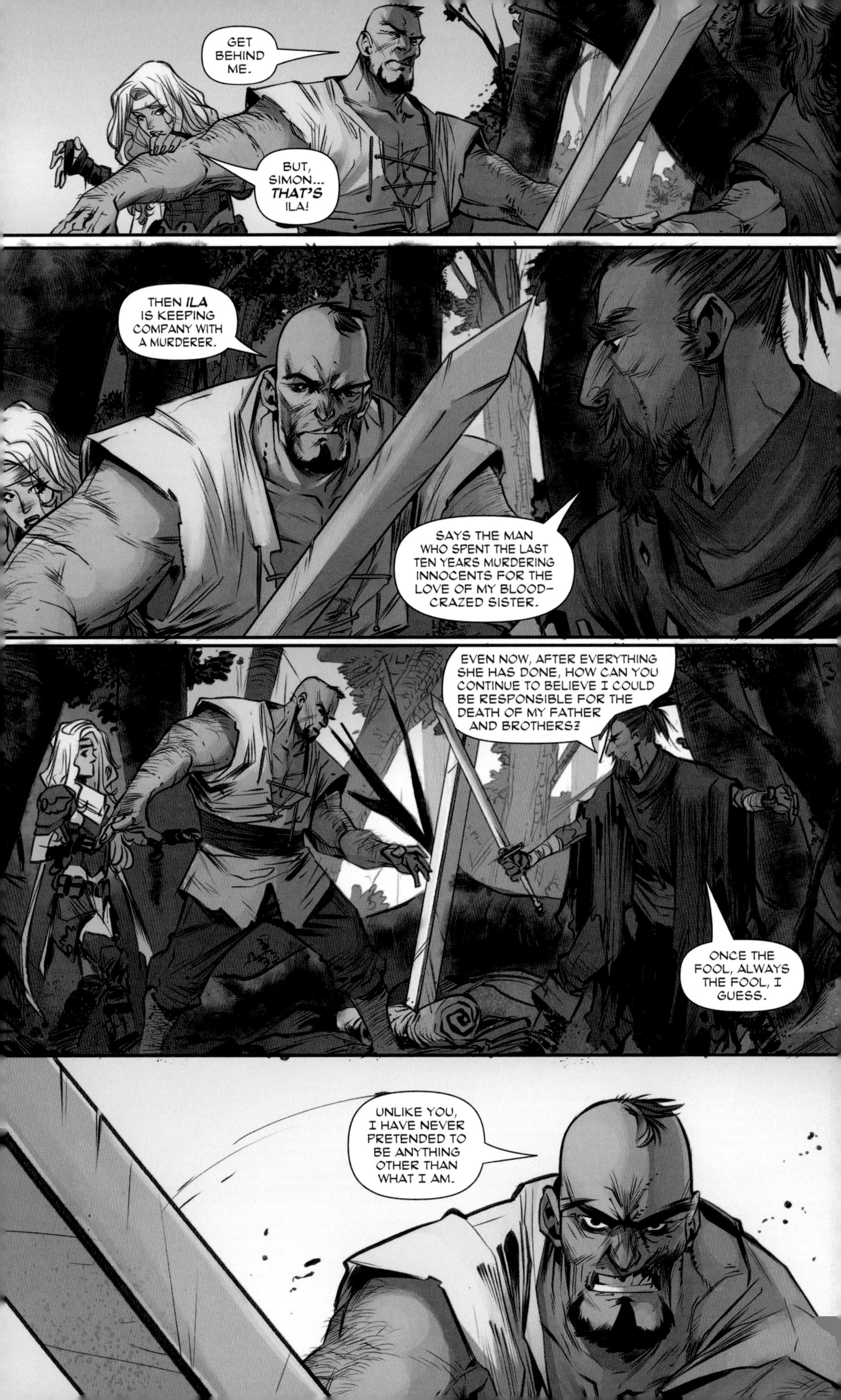
GET BEHIND ME.
BUT, SIMON... *THAT'S* ILA!
THEN *ILA* IS KEEPING COMPANY WITH A MURDERER.
SAYS THE MAN WHO SPENT THE LAST TEN YEARS MURDERING INNOCENTS FOR THE LOVE OF MY BLOOD-CRAZED SISTER.
EVEN NOW, AFTER EVERYTHING SHE HAS DONE, HOW CAN YOU CONTINUE TO BELIEVE I COULD BE RESPONSIBLE FOR THE DEATH OF MY FATHER AND BROTHERS?
ONCE THE FOOL, ALWAYS THE FOOL, I GUESS.
UNLIKE YOU, I HAVE NEVER PRETENDED TO BE ANYTHING OTHER THAN WHAT I AM.

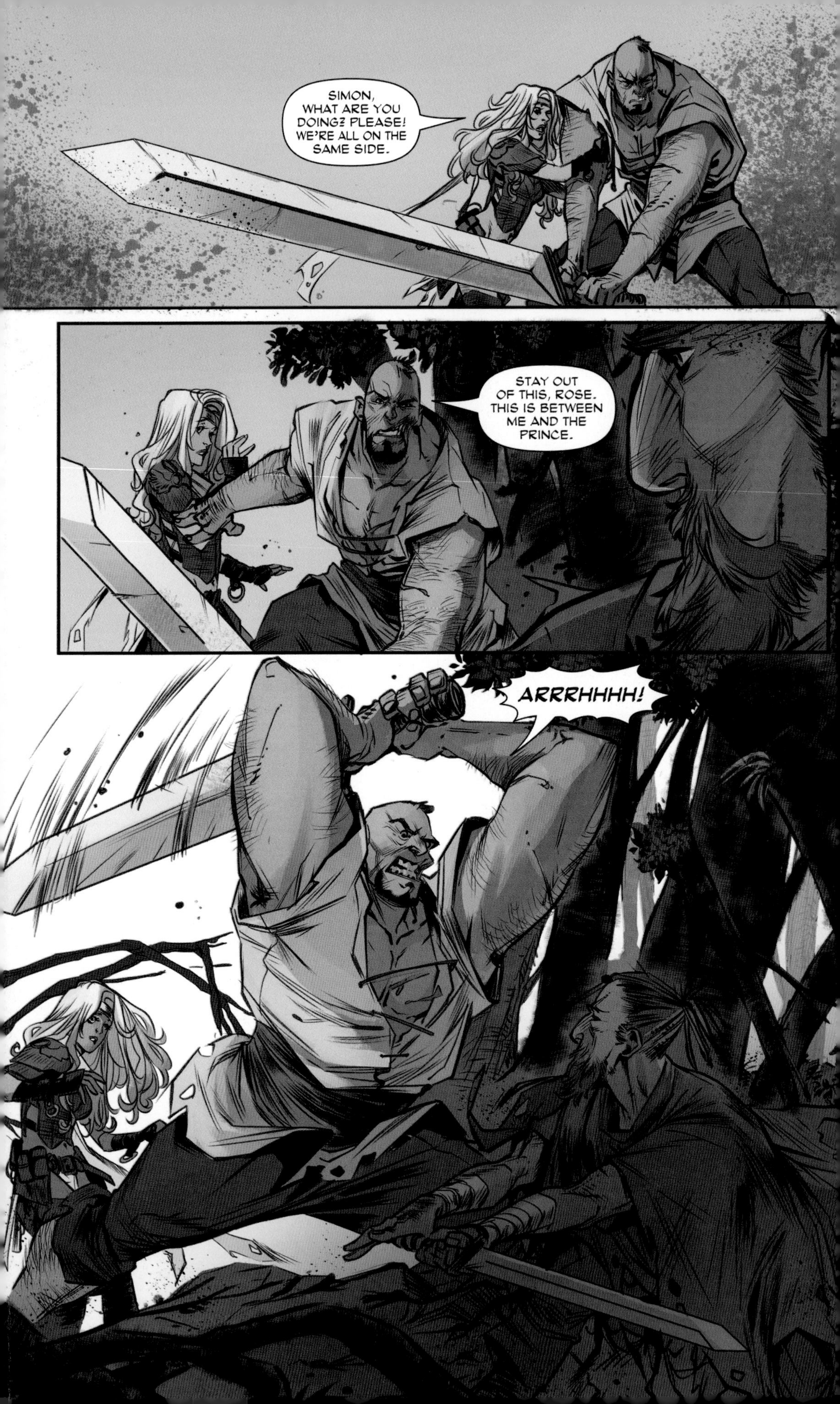
SIMON, WHAT ARE YOU DOING? PLEASE! WE'RE ALL ON THE SAME SIDE.
STAY OUT OF THIS, ROSE. THIS IS BETWEEN ME AND THE PRINCE.
ARRRHHHH!

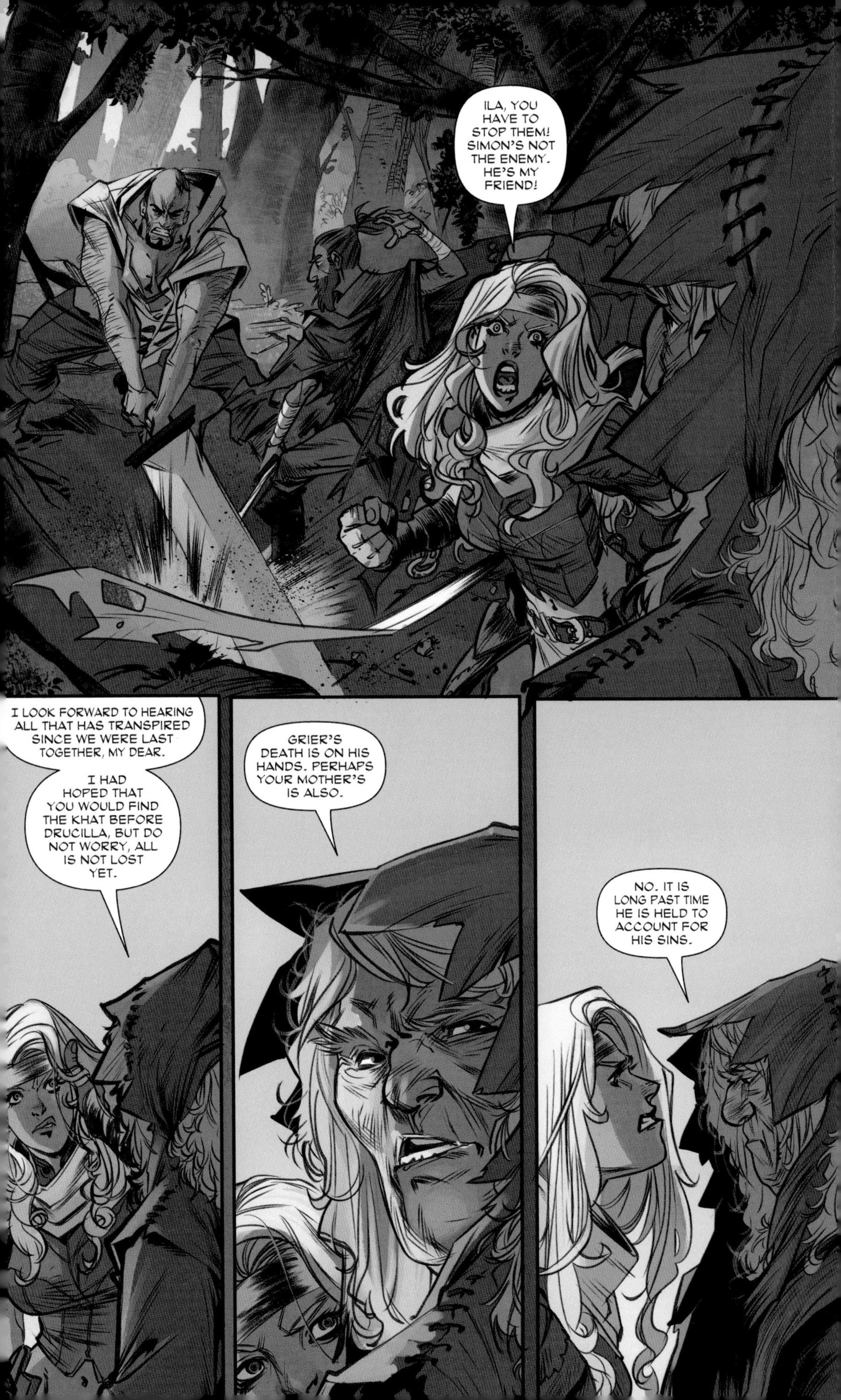
ILA, YOU HAVE TO STOP THEM! SIMON'S NOT THE ENEMY. HE'S MY FRIEND!
I LOOK FORWARD TO HEARING ALL THAT HAS TRANSPIRED SINCE WE WERE LAST TOGETHER, MY DEAR.
I HAD HOPED THAT YOU WOULD FIND THE KHAT BEFORE DRUCILLA, BUT DO NOT WORRY, ALL IS NOT LOST YET.
GRIER'S DEATH IS ON HIS HANDS. PERHAPS YOUR MOTHER'S IS ALSO.
NO. IT IS LONG PAST TIME HE IS HELD TO ACCOUNT FOR HIS SINS.

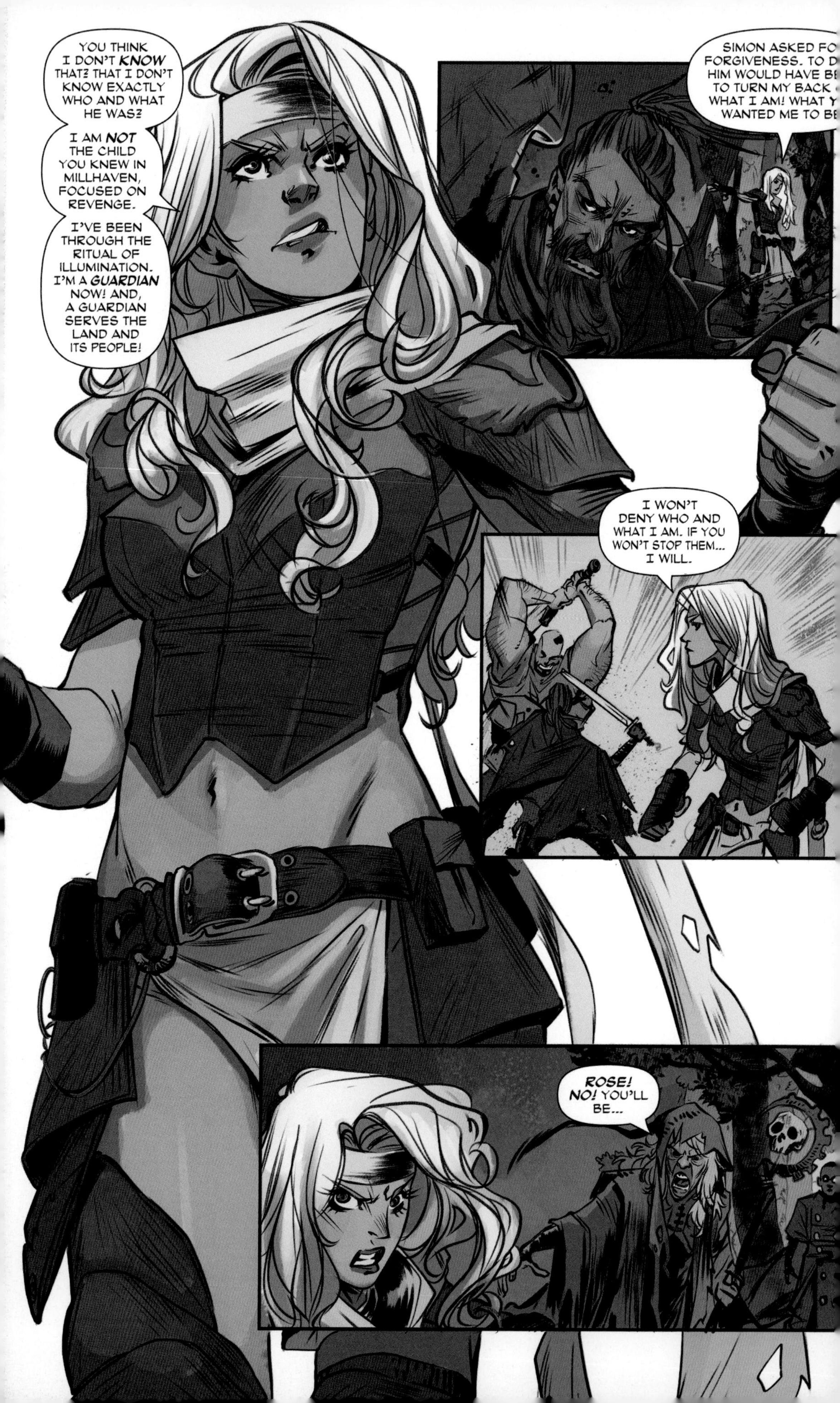
YOU THINK I DON'T KNOW THAT? THAT I DON'T KNOW EXACTLY WHO AND WHAT HE WAS?
I AM NOT THE CHILD YOU KNEW IN MILLHAVEN, FOCUSED ON REVENGE.
I'VE BEEN THROUGH THE RITUAL OF ILLUMINATION. I'M A GUARDIAN NOW! AND, A GUARDIAN SERVES THE LAND AND ITS PEOPLE!
SIMON ASKED FO FORGIVENESS. TO D HIM WOULD HAVE BE TO TURN MY BACK WHAT I AM! WHAT Y WANTED ME TO BE
I WON'T DENY WHO AND WHAT I AM. IF YOU WON'T STOP THEM... I WILL.
ROSE! NO! YOU'LL BE...

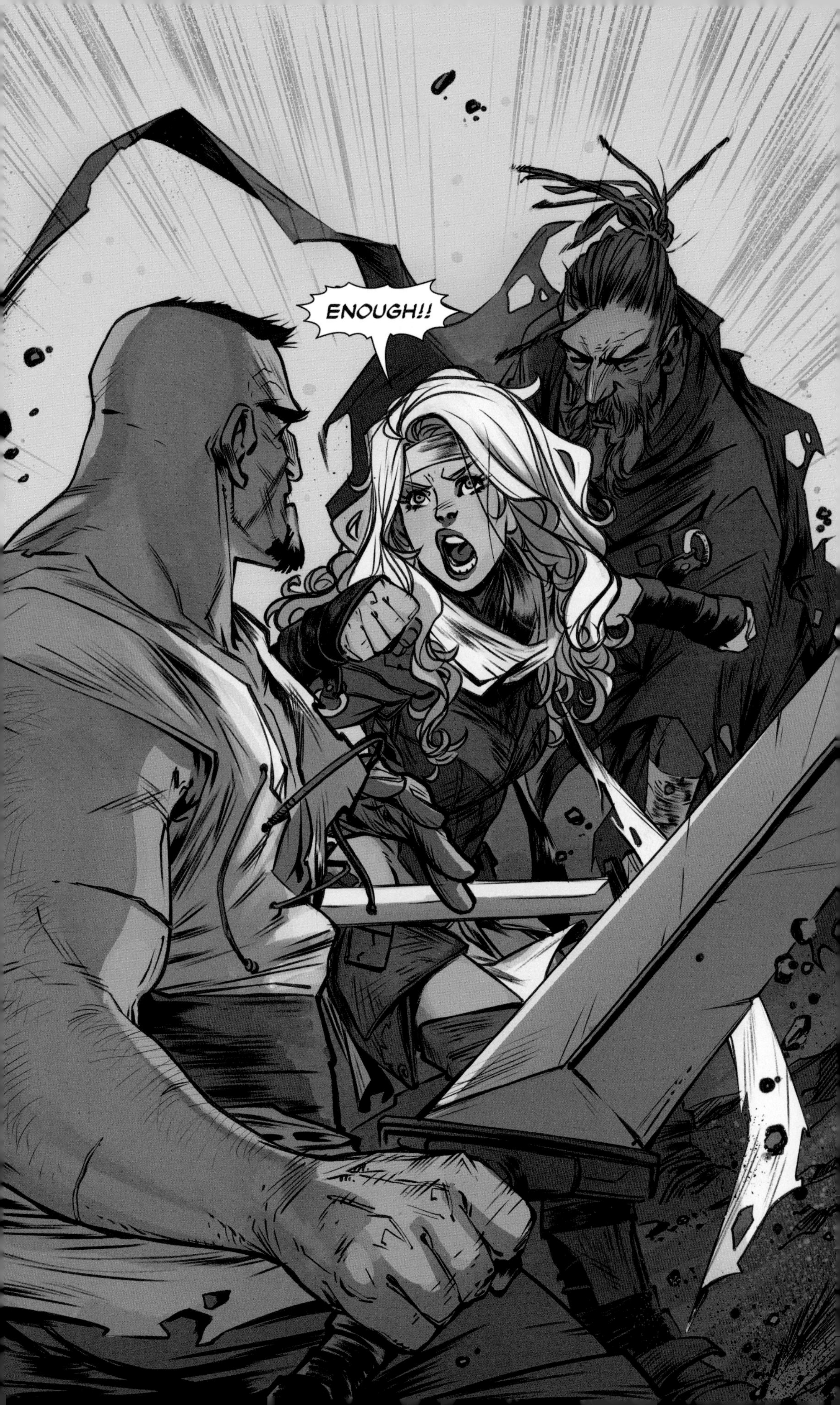
ENOUGH!!

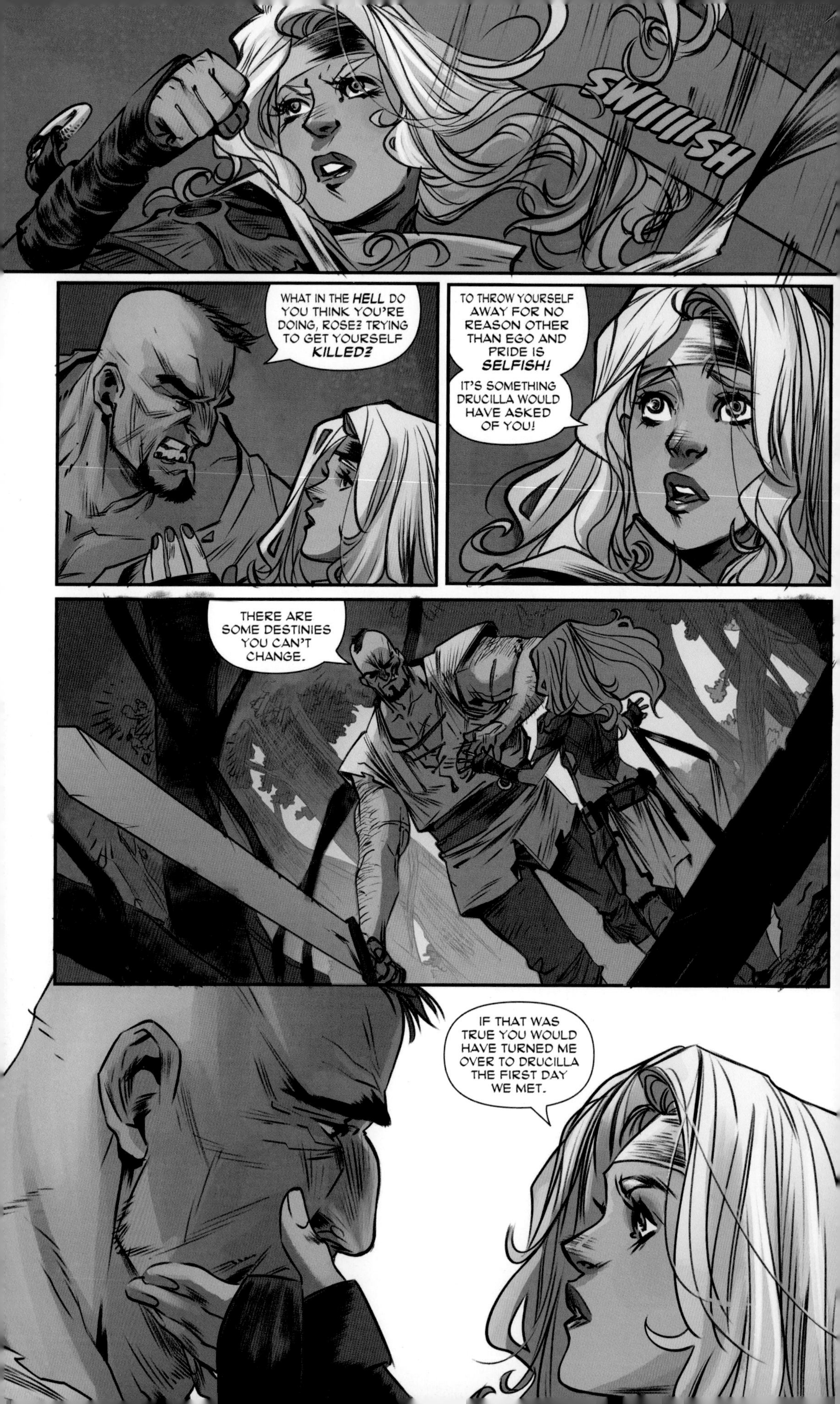

SWIIIISH
WHAT IN THE HELL DO YOU THINK YOU'RE DOING, ROSE? TRYING TO GET YOURSELF KILLED?
TO THROW YOURSELF AWAY FOR NO REASON OTHER THAN EGO AND PRIDE IS SELFISH!
IT'S SOMETHING DRUCILLA WOULD HAVE ASKED OF YOU!
THERE ARE SOME DESTINIES YOU CAN'T CHANGE.
IF THAT WAS TRUE YOU WOULD HAVE TURNED ME OVER TO DRUCILLA THE FIRST DAY WE MET.

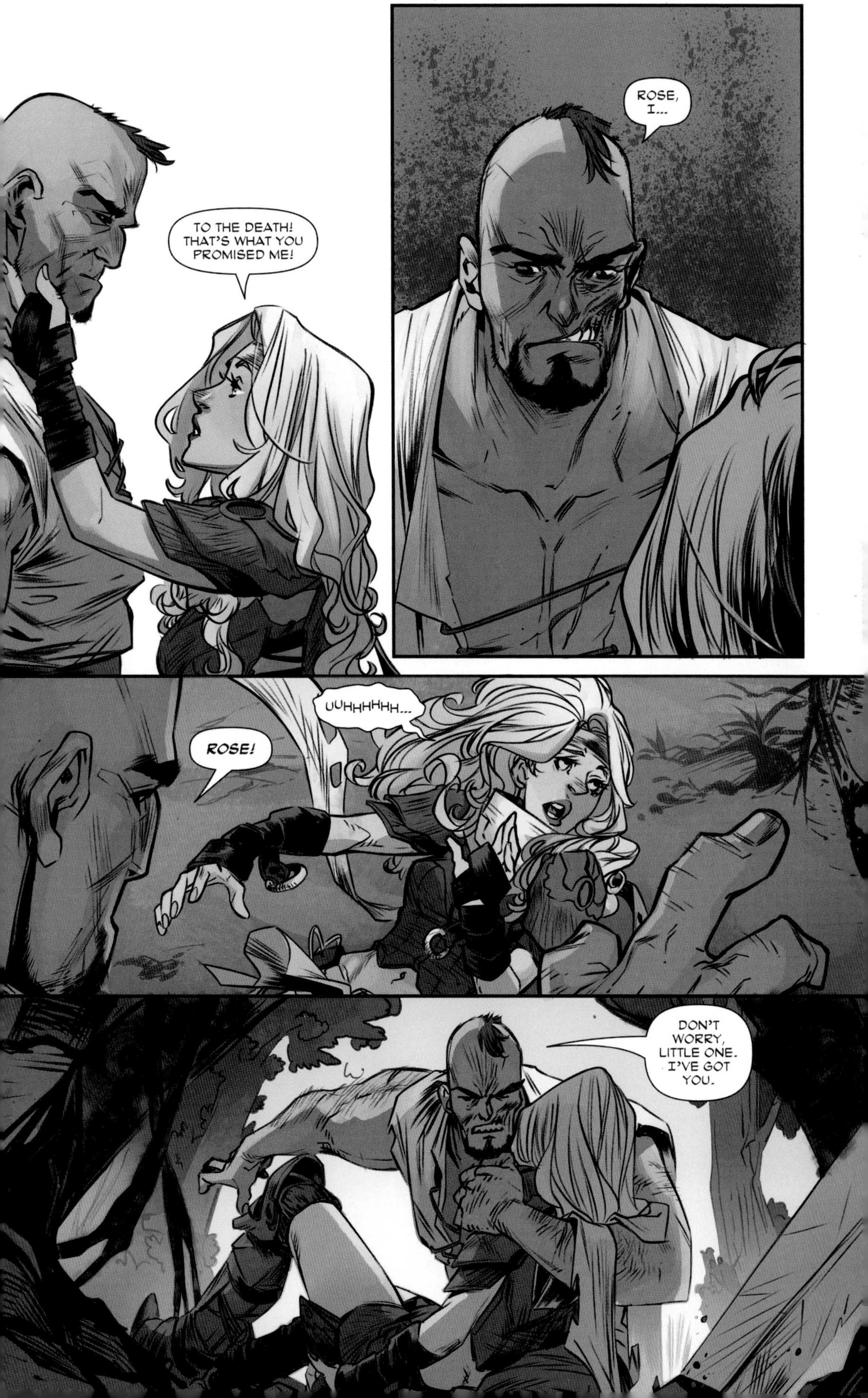
TO THE DEATH! THAT'S WHAT YOU PROMISED ME!
ROSE, I...
UUHHHHHH...
ROSE!
DON'T WORRY, LITTLE ONE. I'VE GOT YOU.

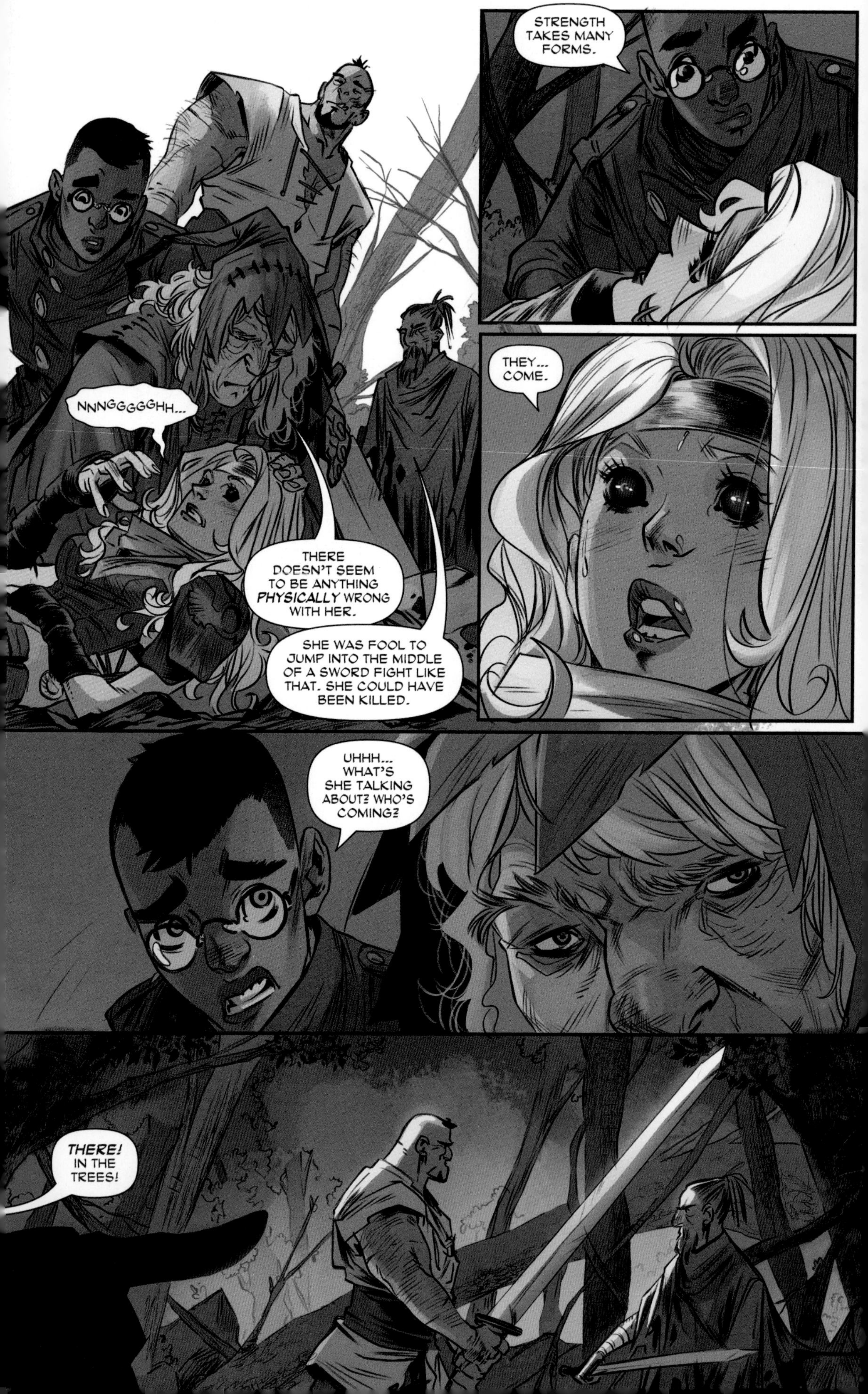
NNNGGGGHH...
THERE DOESN'T SEEM TO BE ANYTHING *PHYSICALLY* WRONG WITH HER.
SHE WAS FOOL TO JUMP INTO THE MIDDLE OF A SWORD FIGHT LIKE THAT. SHE COULD HAVE BEEN KILLED.
STRENGTH TAKES MANY FORMS.
THEY... COME.
UHHH... WHAT'S SHE TALKING ABOUT? WHO'S COMING?
THERE! IN THE TREES!

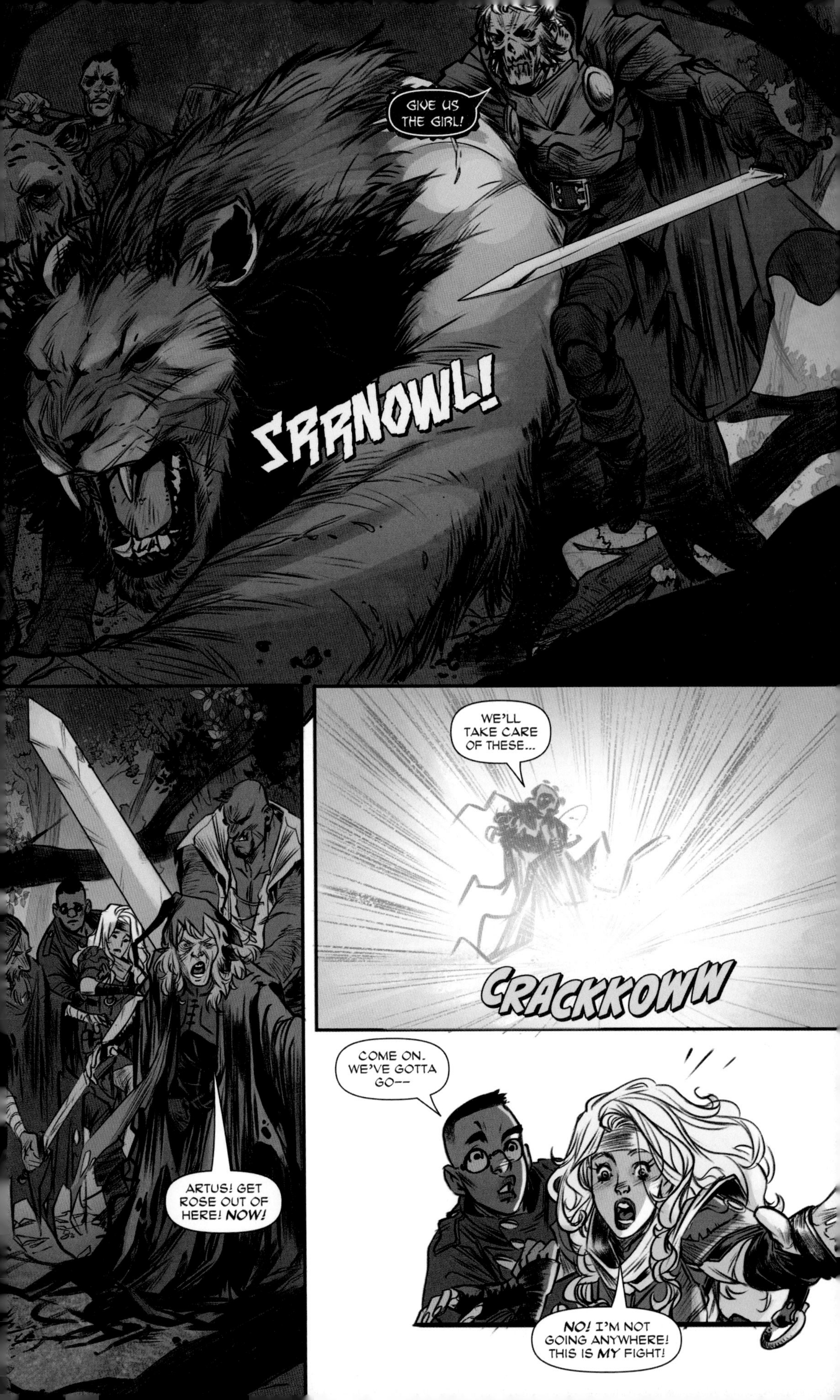
GIVE US THE GIRL!
SRRNOWL!
ARTUS! GET ROSE OUT OF HERE! NOW!
WE'LL TAKE CARE OF THESE...
CRACKKOWW
COME ON. WE'VE GOTTA GO--
NO! I'M NOT GOING ANYWHERE! THIS IS MY FIGHT!

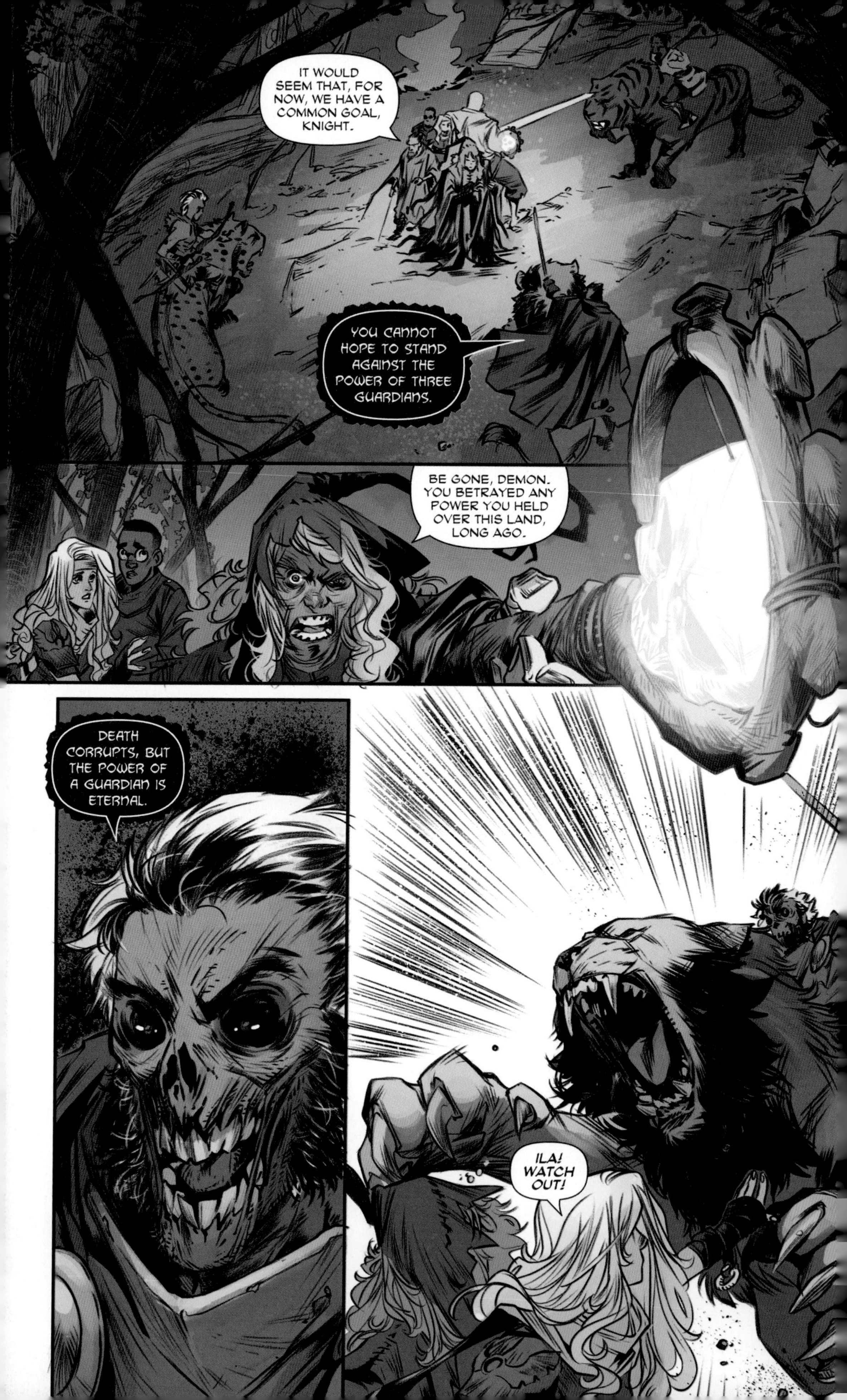
IT WOULD SEEM THAT, FOR NOW, WE HAVE A COMMON GOAL, KNIGHT.
YOU CANNOT HOPE TO STAND AGAINST THE POWER OF THREE GUARDIANS.
BE GONE, DEMON. YOU BETRAYED ANY POWER YOU HELD OVER THIS LAND, LONG AGO.
DEATH CORRUPTS, BUT THE POWER OF A GUARDIAN IS ETERNAL.
ILA! WATCH OUT!

Cover Gallery

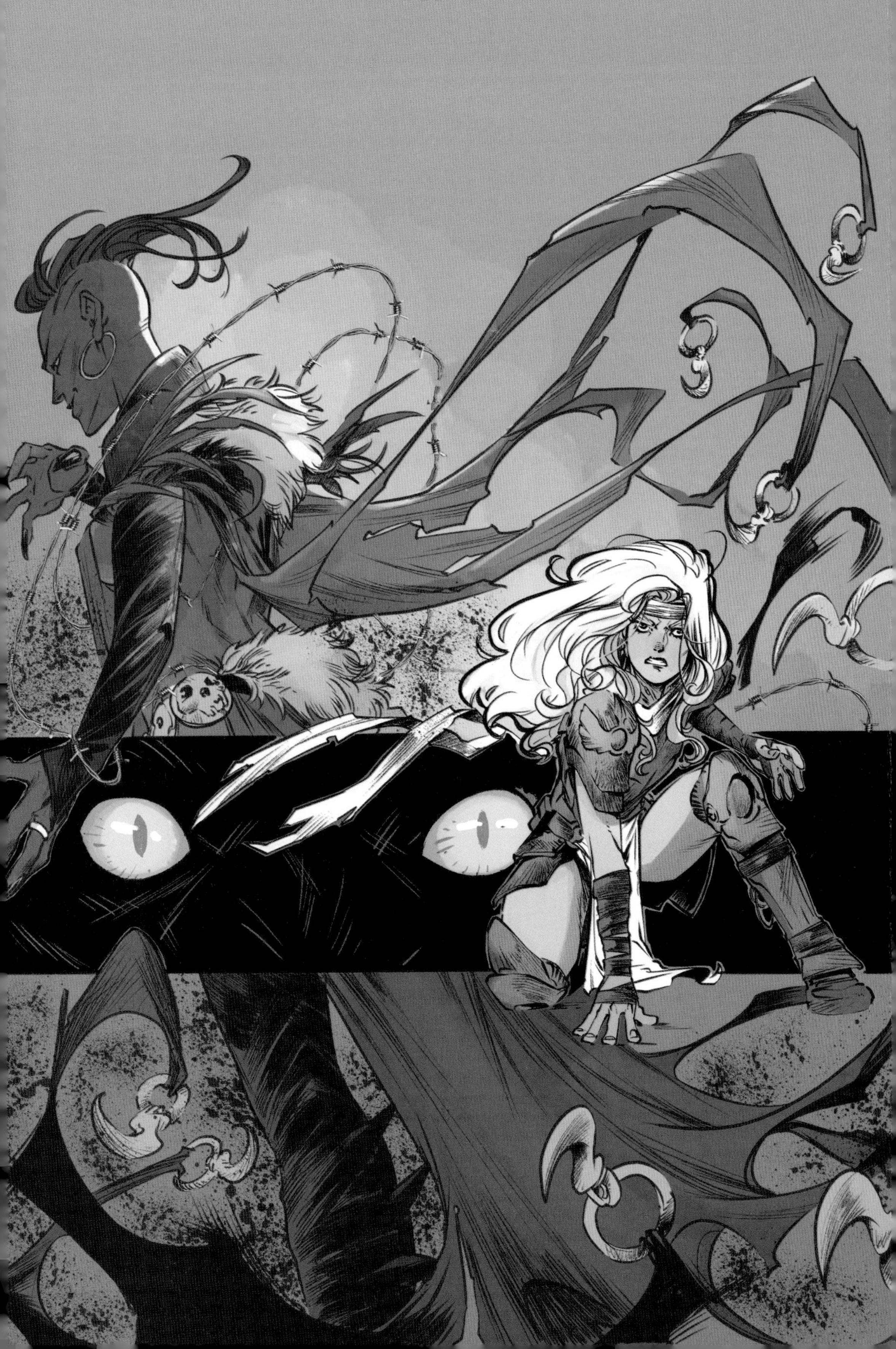

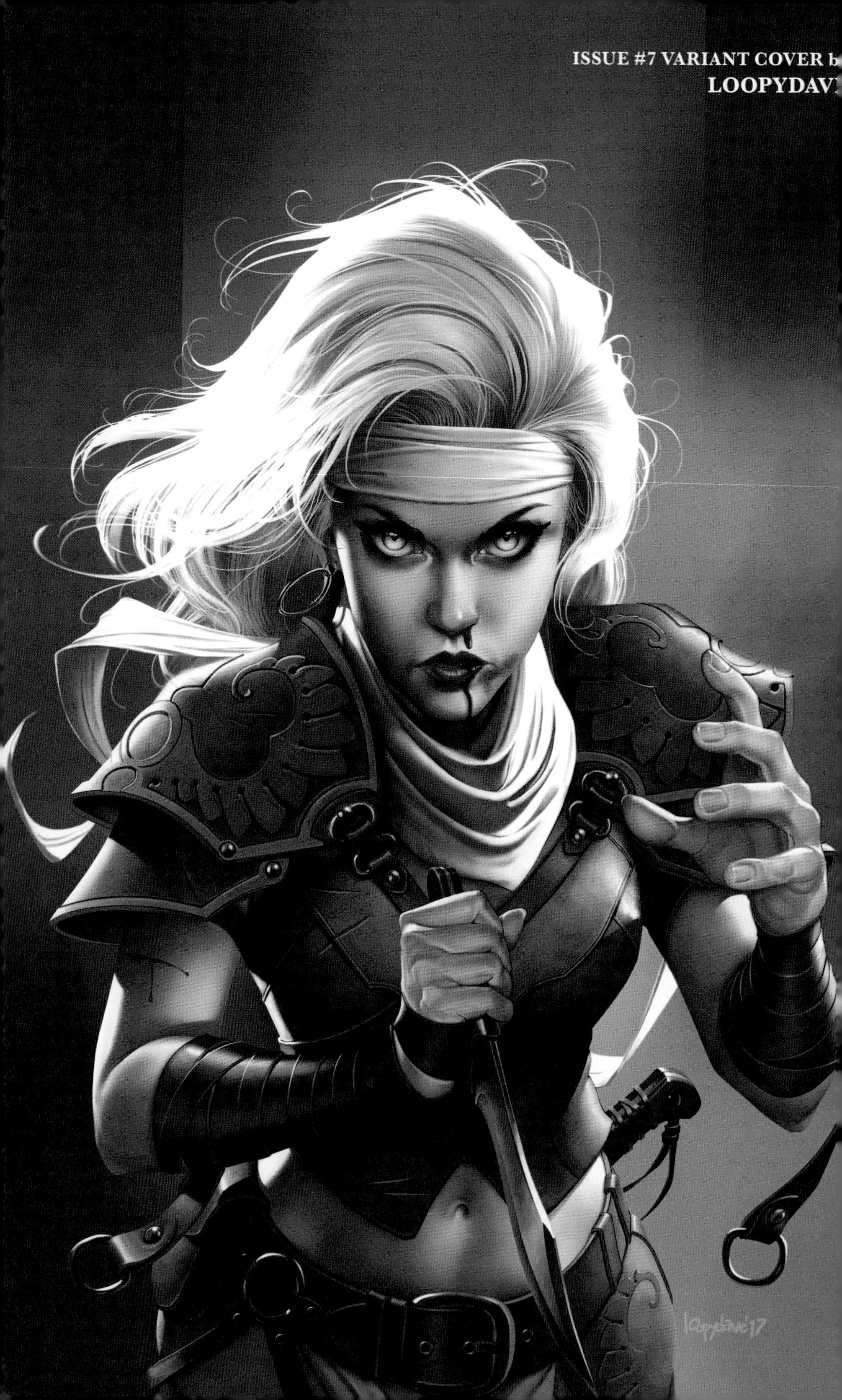

ISSUE #7 VARIANT COVER b
LOOPYDAV

ISSUE #7 VARIANT COVER by
ERIC BASALDUA & SABINE RICH

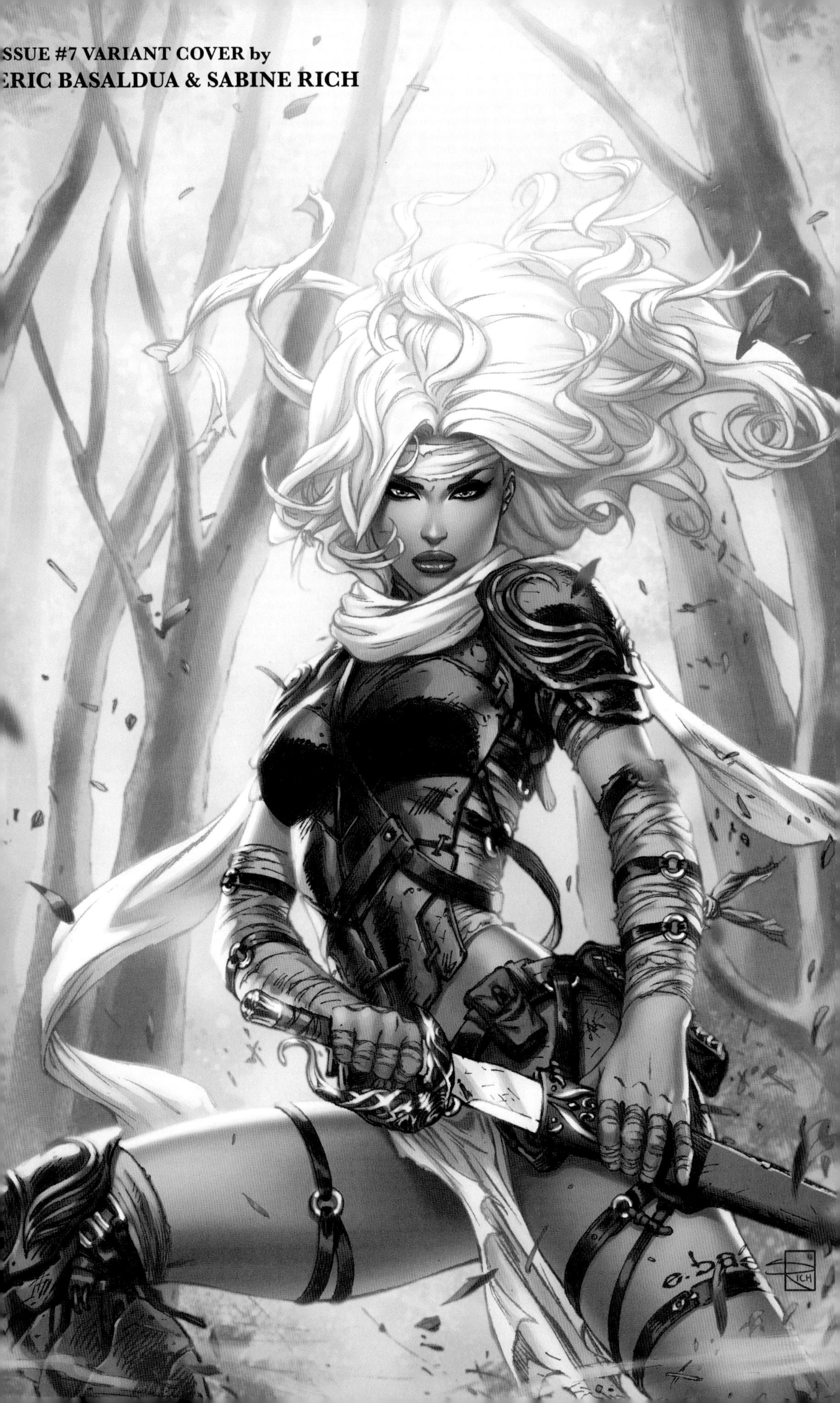

ISSUE #8 VARIANT COVER by
LOOPYDAVE

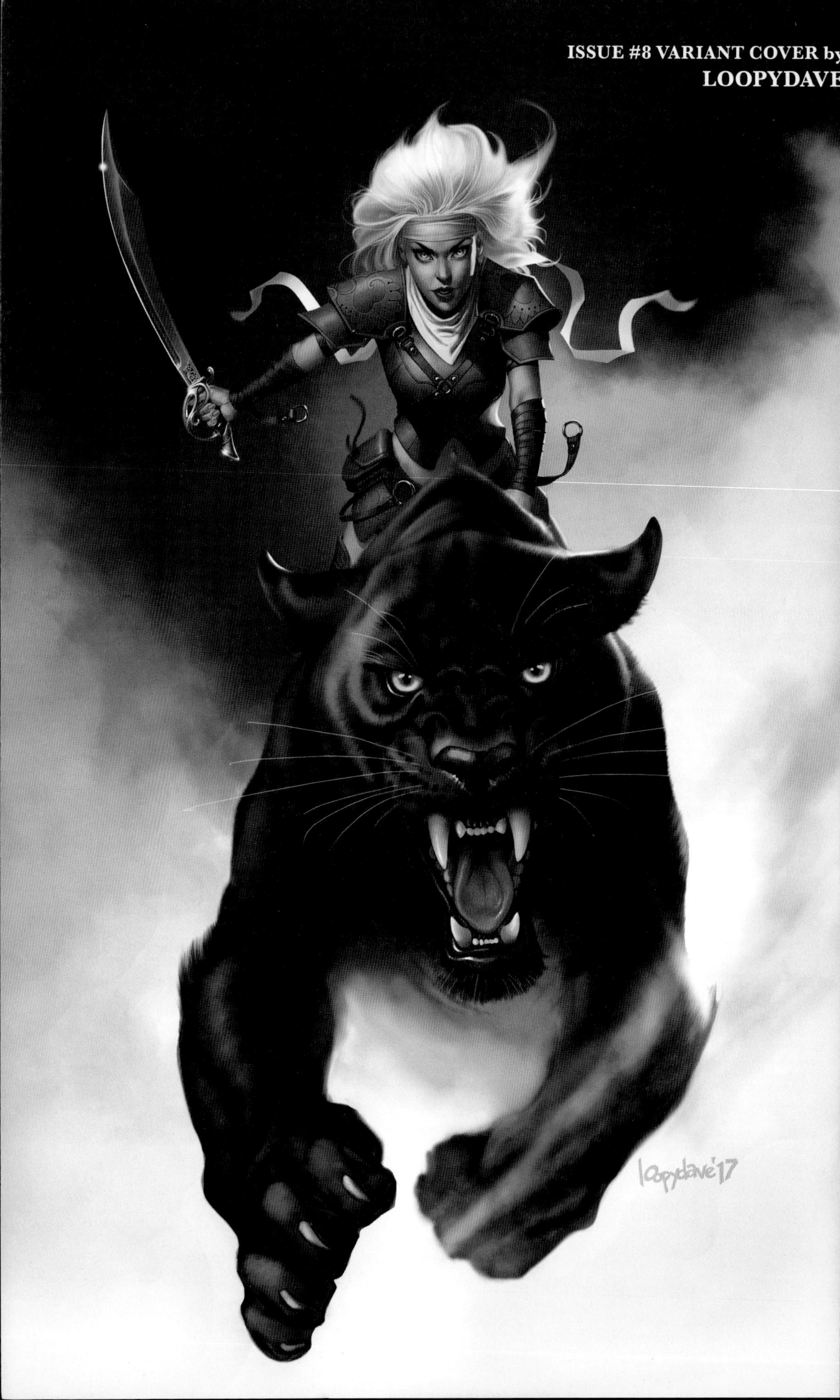
loopydave'17

SUE #8 VARIANT COVER by
G GUARA & TRIONA FARRELL

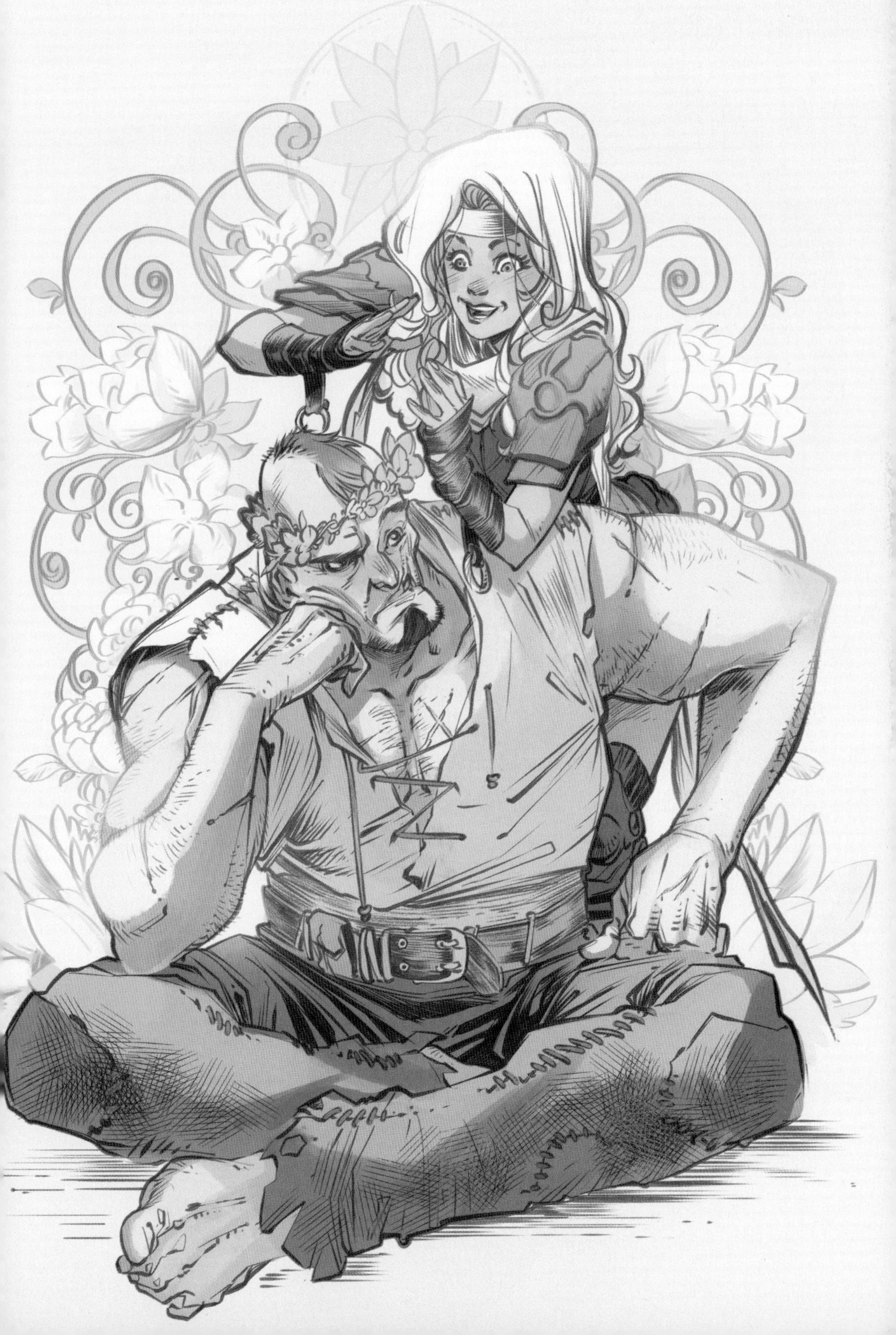

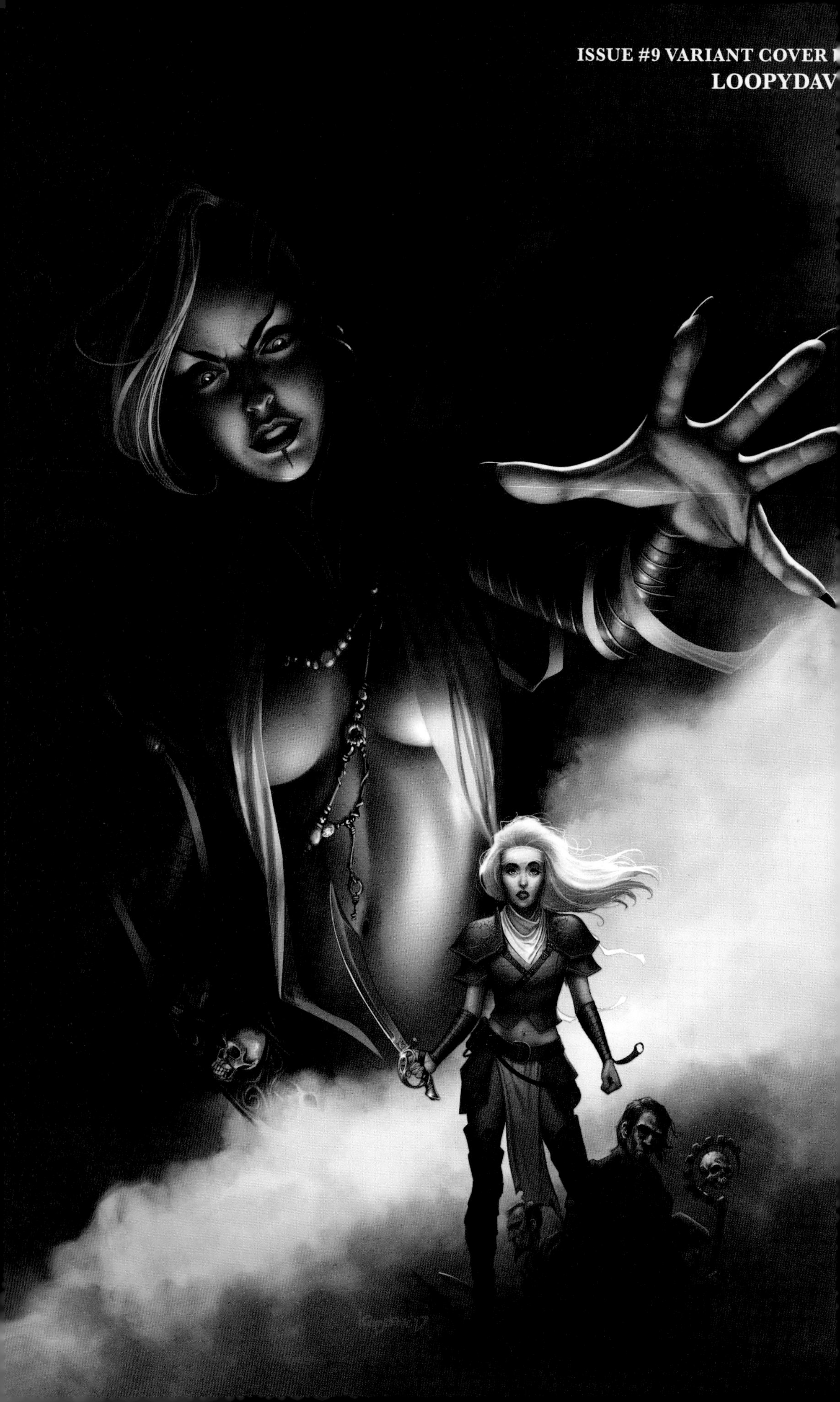

ISSUE #9 VARIANT COVER
LOOPYDAV

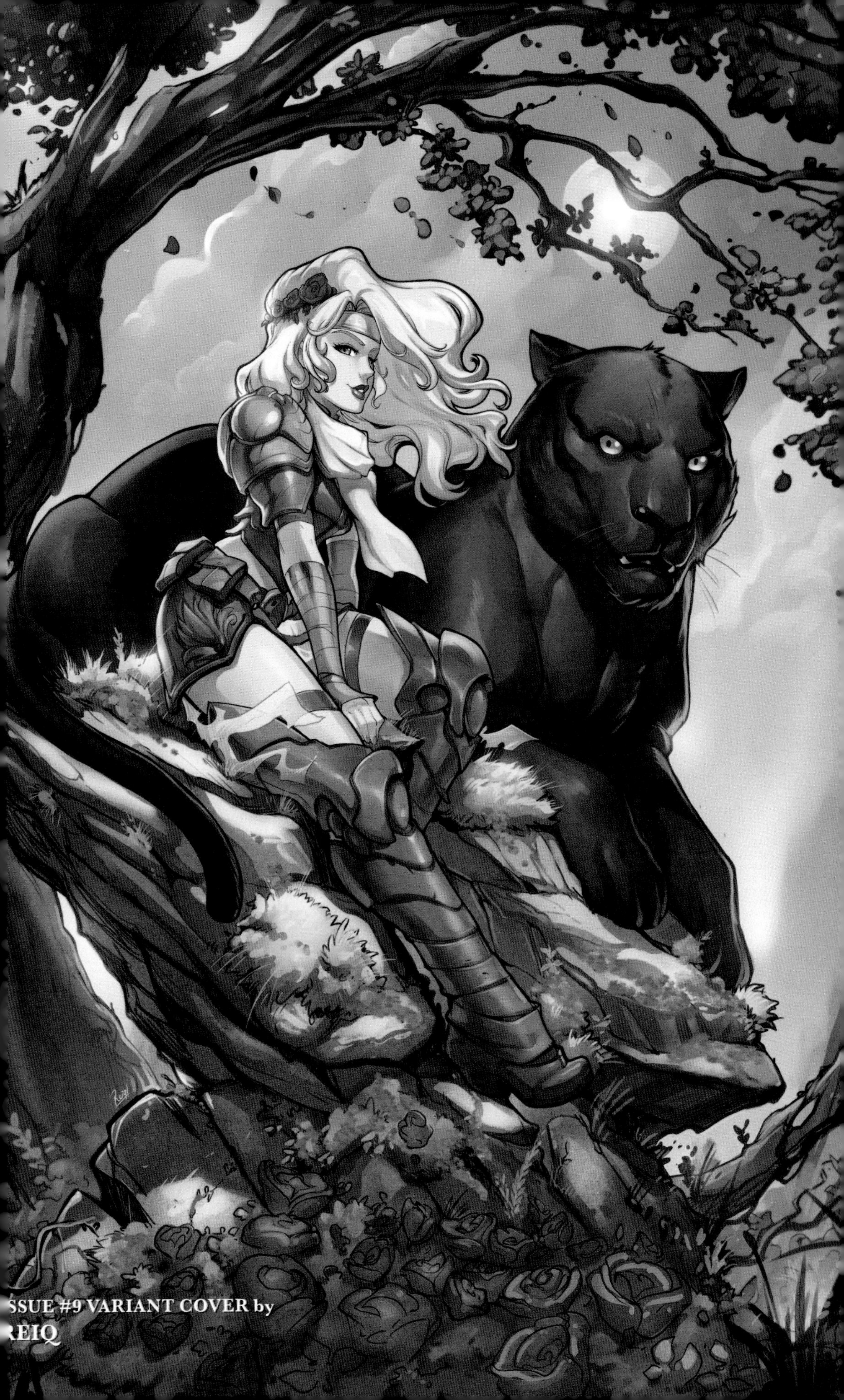

SSUE #9 VARIANT COVER by
REIQ

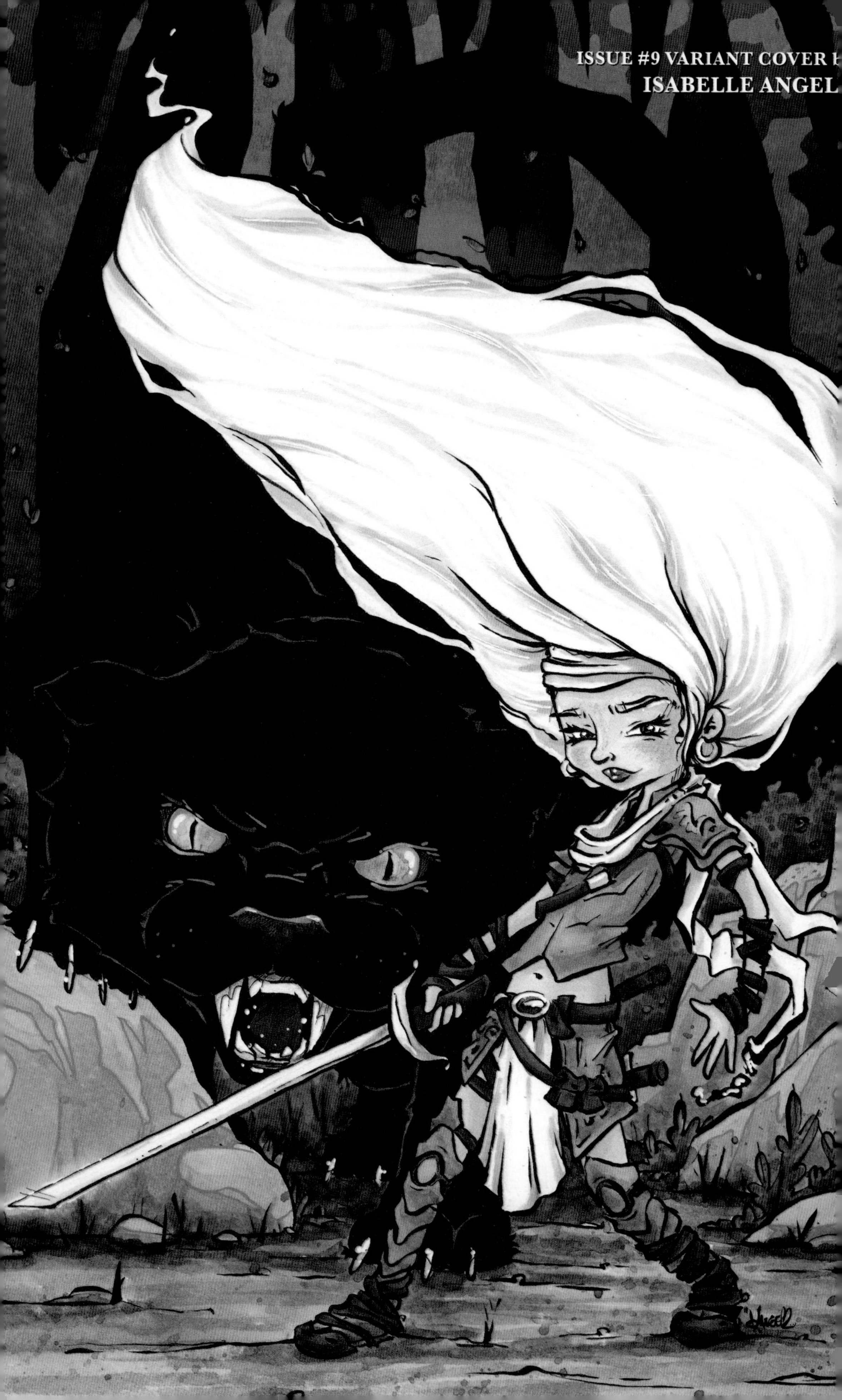

ISSUE #9 VARIANT COVER
ISABELLE ANGEL

ISSUE #9 VARIANT COVER by
LOOPYDAVE

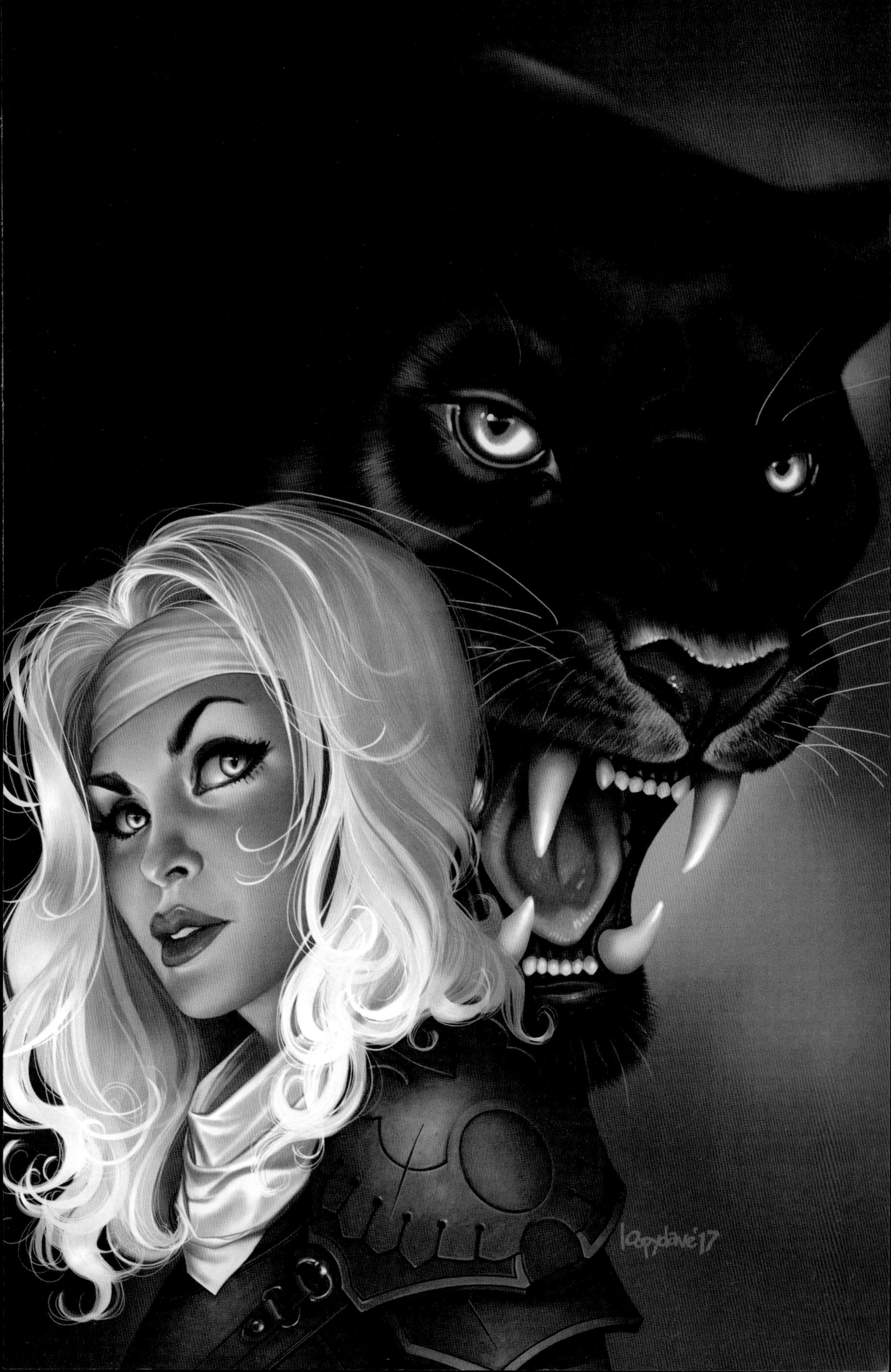
loopydave'17

ISSUE #10 VARIANT COVER b
KEVIN MAGUIRE & TRIONA FARRELL

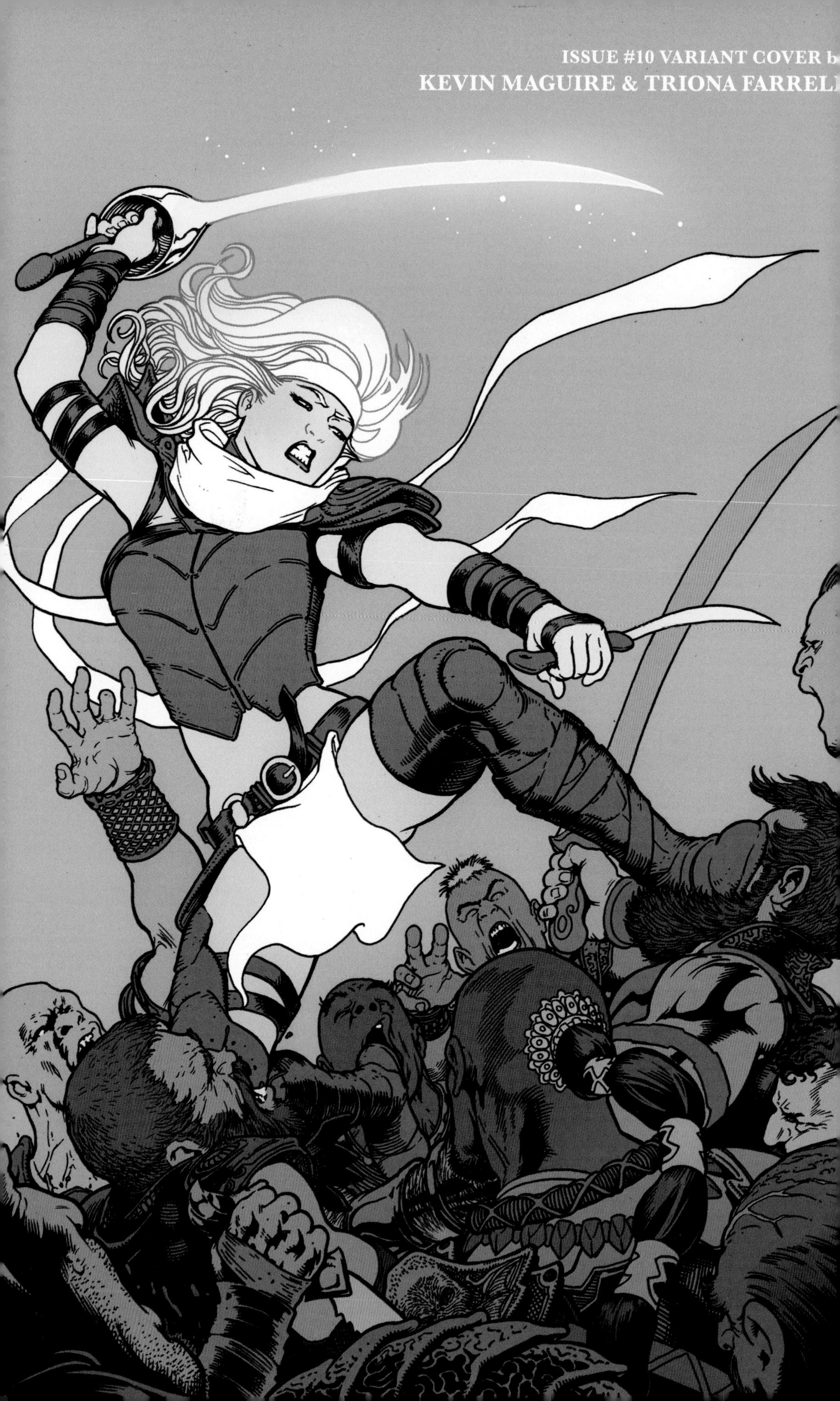

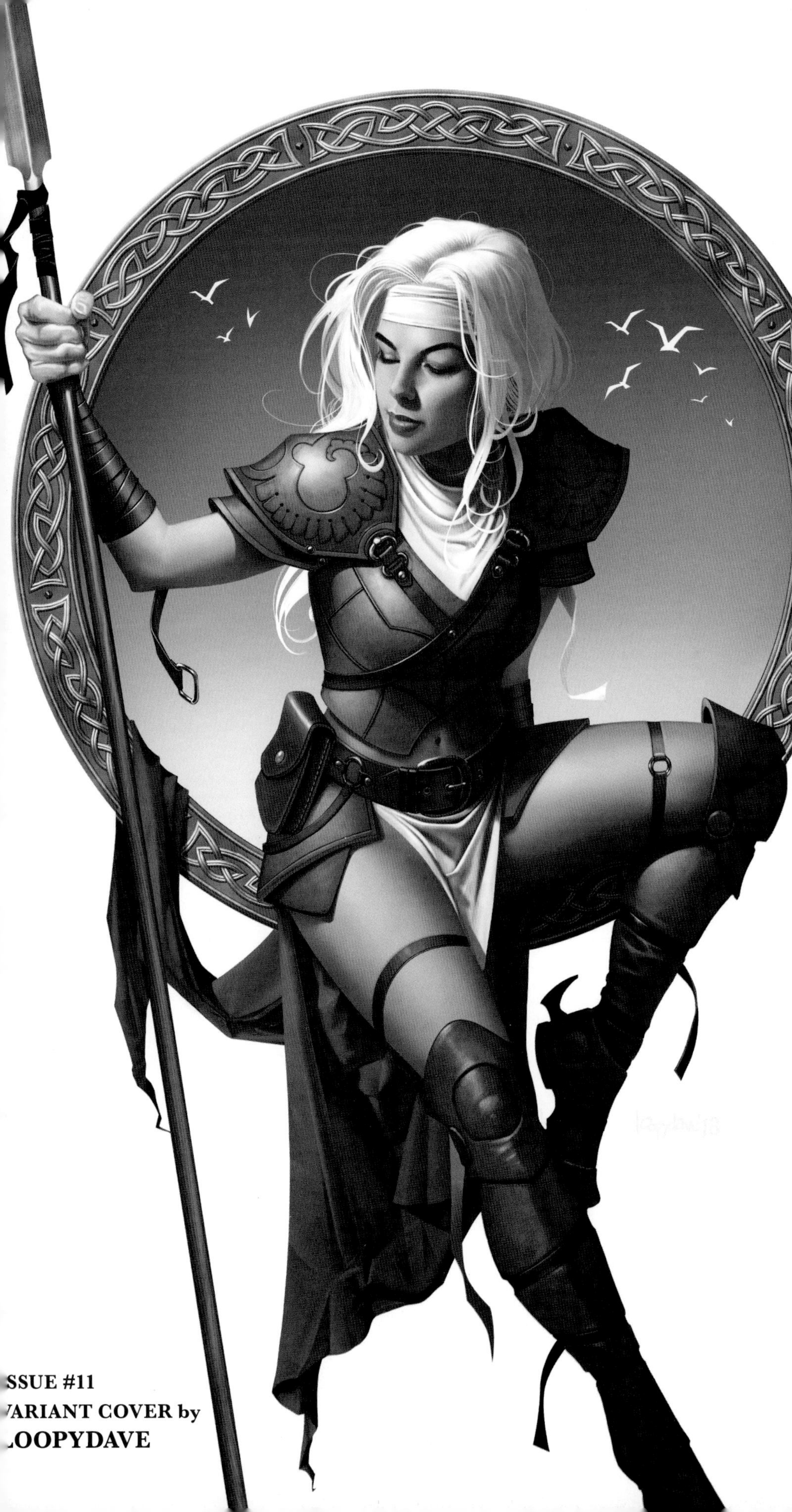

SSUE #11
'ARIANT COVER by
.OOPYDAVE

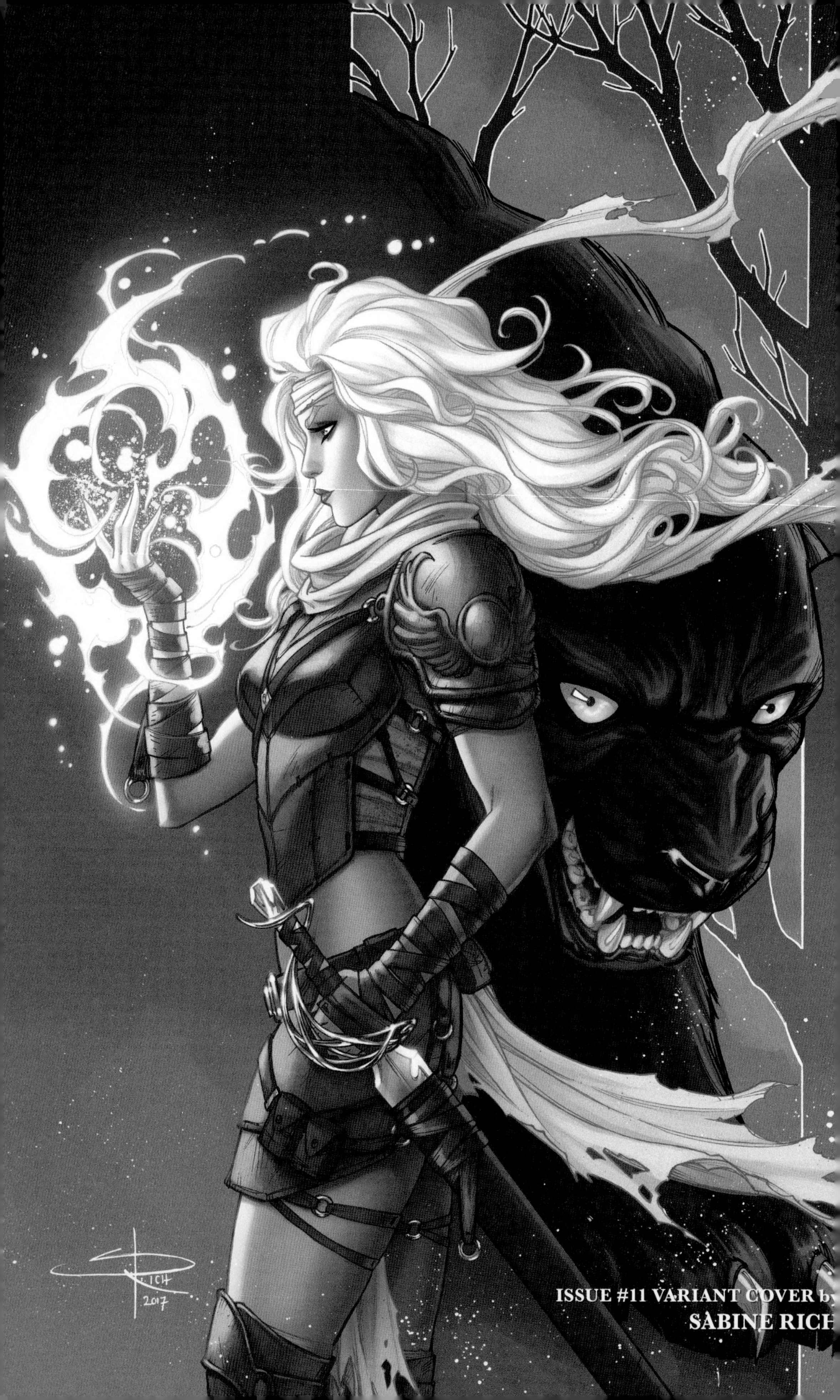
RICH
2017

ISSUE #11 VARIANT COVER b
SABINE RICH

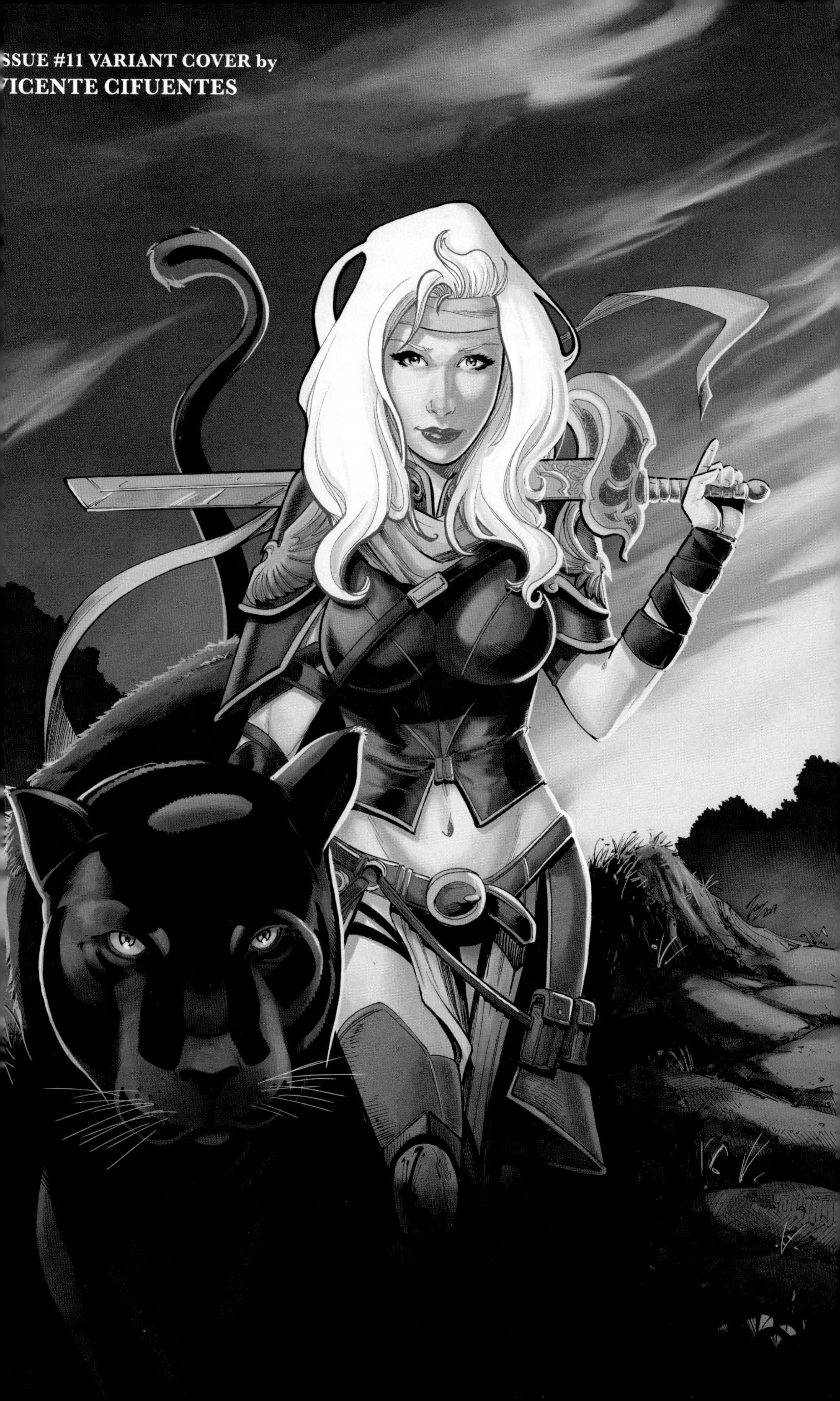

SSUE #11 VARIANT COVER by
VICENTE CIFUENTES

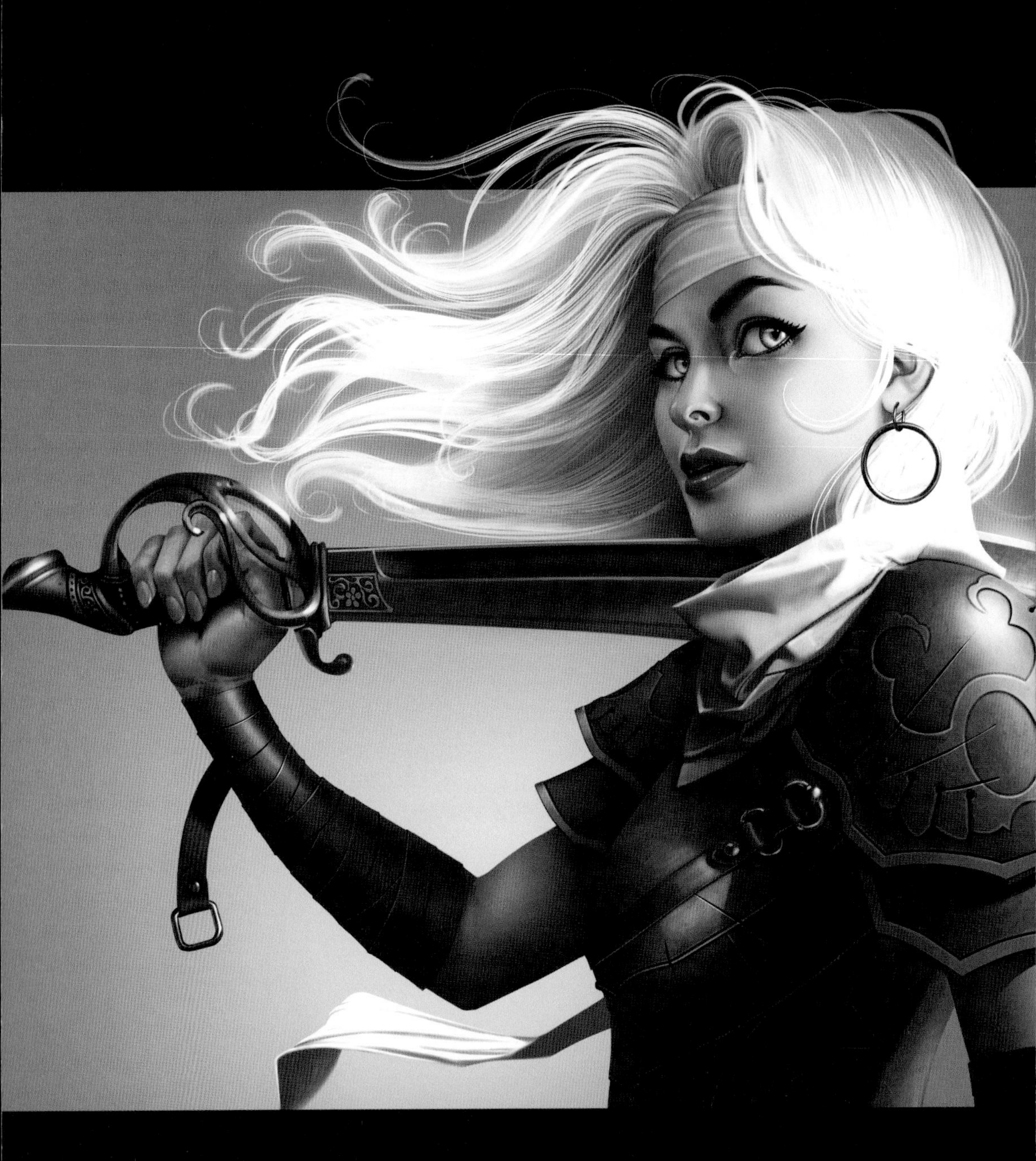

ISSUE #6
VARIANT COVER by
DAWN MCTEIGUE

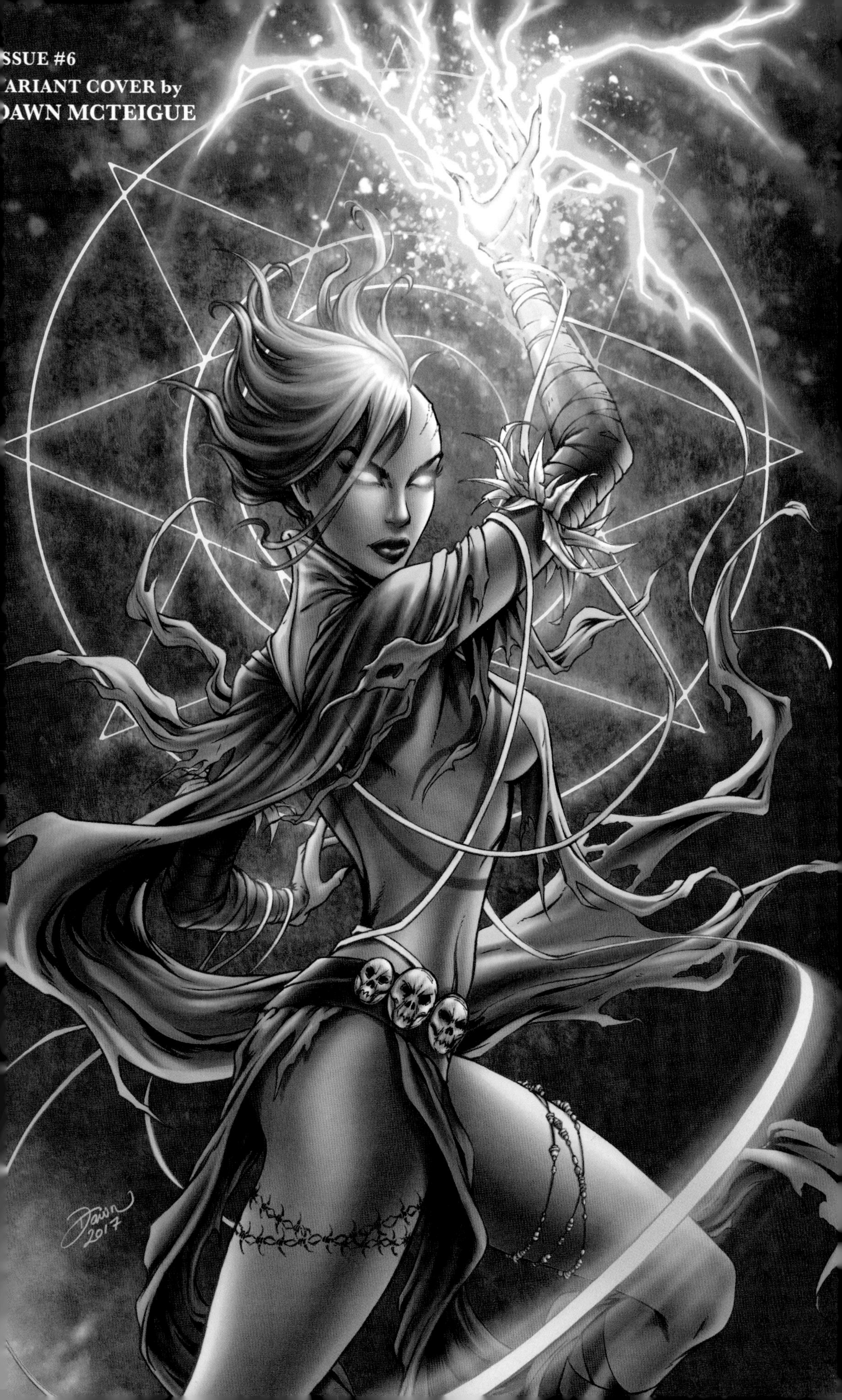
Dawn
2017

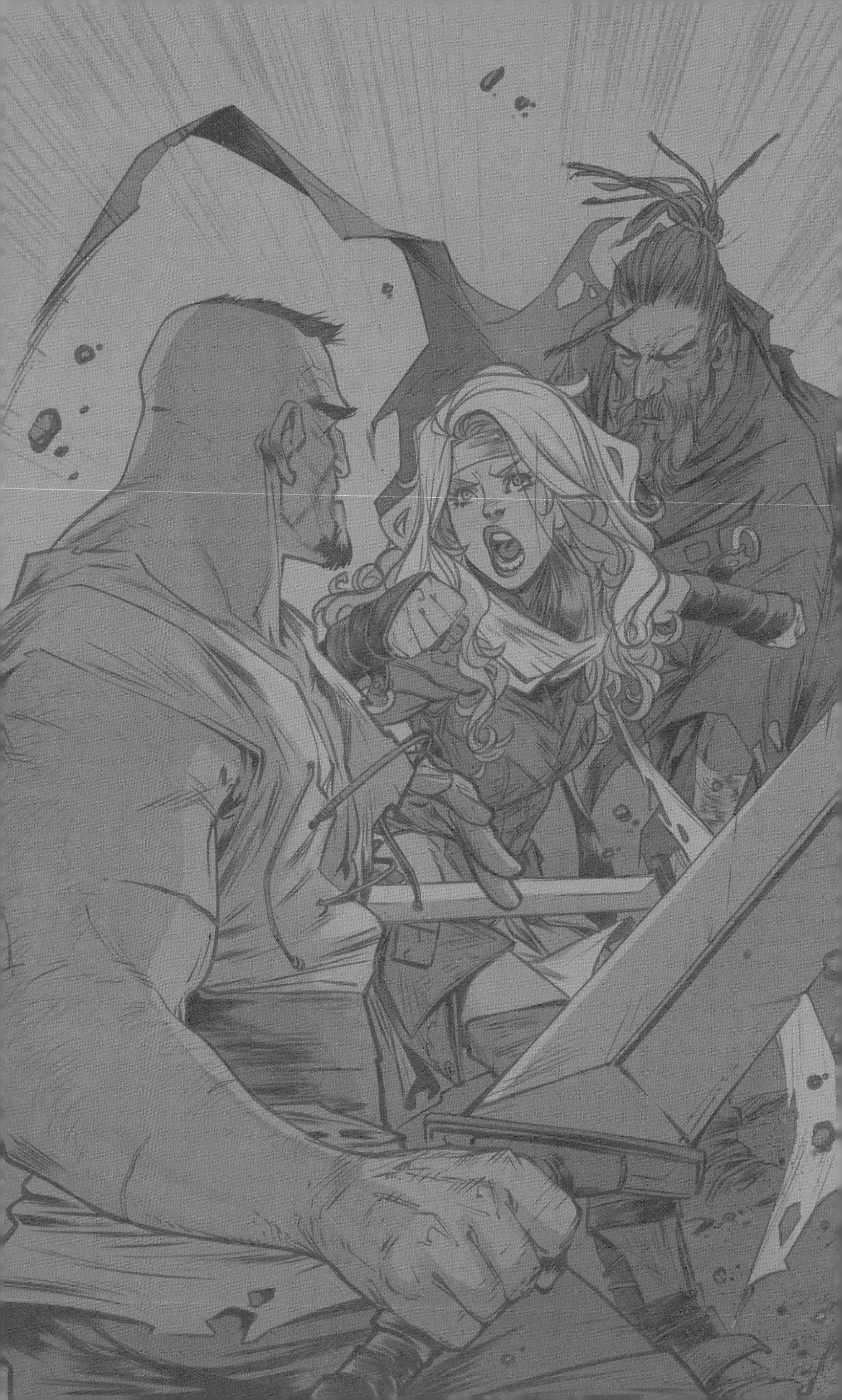

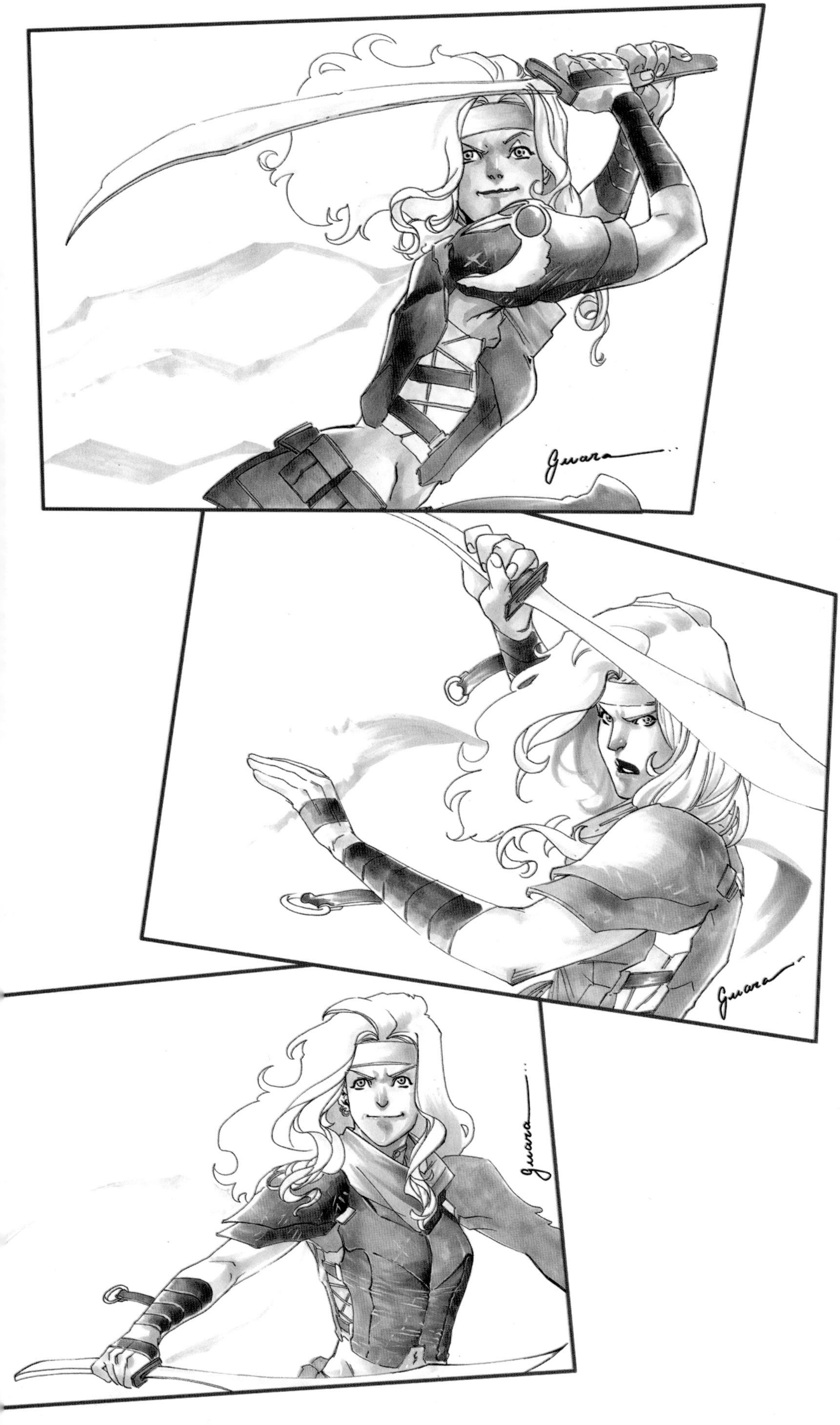
Guara
Guara
Guara

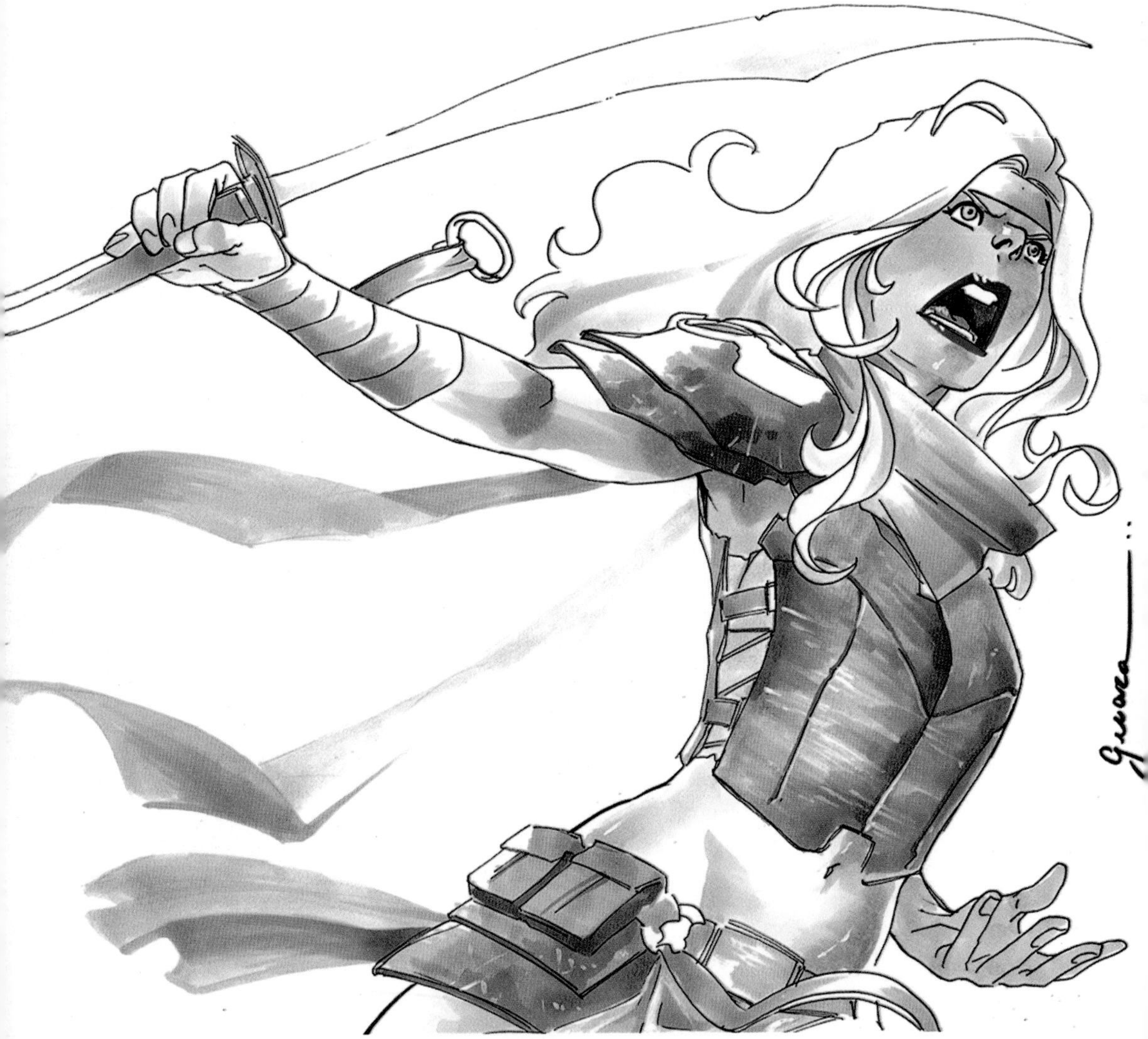

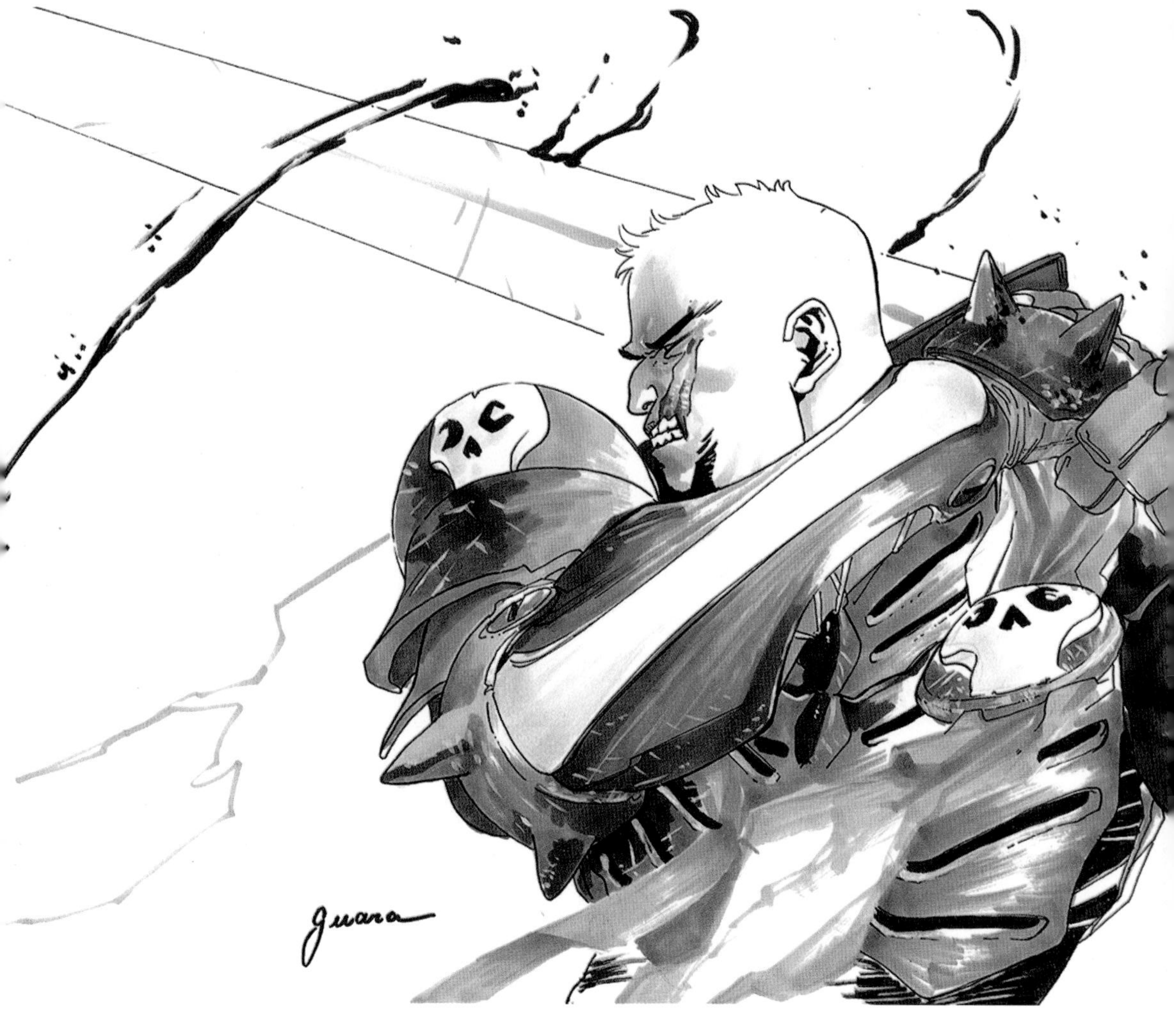

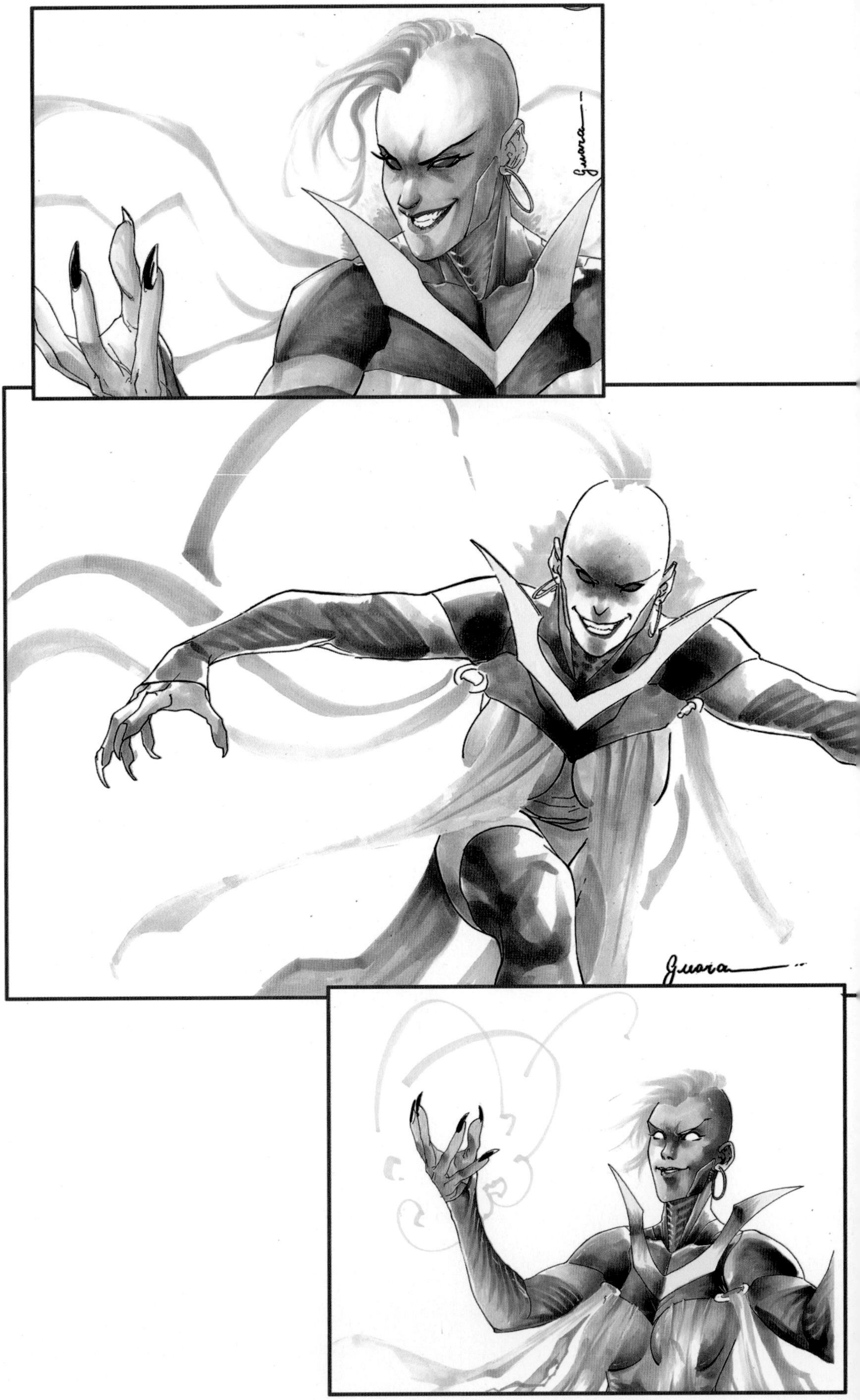